THE LOST APOSTLES

BOOK 2 OF THE STOLEN GOSPELS

THE LOST APOSTLES

Brian Herbert

WordFire Press
Colorado Springs, Colorado

WordFire Press

The STOLEN GOSPELS series was created by Brian Herbert.

Published by
WordFire Press, an imprint of
WordFire Inc
PO Box 1840
Monument CO 80132

ISBN: 978-1-61475-035-2

First Trade Paperback Edition: January 2012
Printed in the USA

www.wordfire.com

DEDICATION

For my talented, special daughters, Julie, Kim, and Margaux. As women, you are the members of a very select group—and you are far more complex and interesting than men.

ACKNOWLEDGEMENTS

Over the years there have been numerous advisers and editors on this project, and the suggestions of Jan Herbert, Kevin J. Anderson, Robert Gottlieb, Matt Bialer, Martin H. Greenberg, John Silbersack, Mary Alice Kier, and Anna Cottle have all been greatly appreciated. I am also grateful to Rebecca Moesta-Anderson, for her work on this novel.

INTRODUCTION

The Lost Apostles, Sequel to *The Stolen Gospels*

This novel is the second half of an epic story that my wife Jan and I originally conceived in the mid-1990s, a tale that became so large in the writing process that it eventually had to be divided into two novels—*The Stolen Gospels* and *The Lost Apostles.*

As I have said in the introduction to *The Stolen Gospels*, this project has a long and checkered history, and the story has never before been published in traditional form. In part, this has to do with the story's radical nature—both from a feminist and religious standpoint—and the fact that most of the submissions my literary agents made involved publishing it as one huge book. In addition, it spanned several literary genres—containing elements of a religious thriller, combined with science fiction and fantasy. Most publishers prefer to stay within one genre or another.

Eventually a publisher did offer me a contract—a contract that was never signed. So, this epic story was never published. Until now.

At long last, sixteen years after Jan and I began brainstorming this far-reaching, heroic story, I am pleased to finally make both novels available in e-book form.

Brian Herbert

September 10, 2011

Brief Summary of Events in *The Stolen Gospels*

Teenager Lori Vale and her mother attend a goddess circle meeting in a Seattle suburb, unaware of a bitter rivalry between the event organizers (United Women of the World) and their archenemies the male-supremacy Bureau of Ideology. During the meeting, the BOI launches a violent commando attack against the group, hoping to kill the UWW's second in command (Dixie Lou Jackson), who is making a guest appearance. In an attempt to save Lori's seriously injured mother, Dixie Lou connects her to a life support system on an escape aircraft, taking Lori along as well. Lori's mother dies. Dixie Lou—sensing that she has known Lori Vale before, and that it is important—takes her into custody and flies her to the UWW headquarters in Greece, effectively kidnapping her.

At the secret headquarters, a heavily guarded fortress in an ancient Greek monastery, a group of radical women is creating an earthshaking religious text, the *Holy Women's Bible*. The new sacred book will include the *Old Testament* and the *New Testament*, edited to alter gospels that are detrimental to the interests of women, such as passages asserting that they should obey their husbands, remain silent in churches, and suffer the burden of Eve's sins.

The teenager learns that a third section of the *Holy Women's Bible* is even more of a bombshell, the *Testament of the She-Apostles*. It asserts that Jesus Christ had 24 apostles, not 12, and that half of them were women called "she-apostles." Eleven she-apostles have been reincarnated in modern times as female children, and are revealing new female-oriented gospels about the life of Jesus, stories that were omitted from the *Bible* by male church authorities who decided what to include in the *Bible* and what to leave out of it, in order to assert the power and dominance of men over women. According to evidence in the hands of the radical women, the ancient gospels of the she-apostles were stolen by such men and relegated to the rubbish heaps of history.

At the monastery, Lori develops a paranormal relationship with one of the reincarnated children (eliciting a valuable scriptural story from the child)—and Lori soon begins to suspect that she may have been connected to the female apostles of Jesus in ancient times, when the Son of God walked the earth and preached to the people of the Holy Land.

While information about Lori's past is unfolding, she finds herself caught in a BOI-UWW war, a violent conflict that has immense historical repercussions. Powerful, brutal men want to suppress the emerging gospels of the she-apostles, men who are hell-bent on destroying United Women of the World and their heretical texts. The women race to get their material completed and published before they are annihilated, but they have another big problem: the twelfth she-apostle—Martha of Galilee—has not been found yet, and the other she-apostles say she holds a dark secret that could do enormous damage to the cause of women, and to the entire planet.

Lori is given some freedom to move around the monastery, but not to leave. She finds herself falling in love with Alex Jackson (the son of Dixie Lou), a young man who dislikes his own mother. Alex brings Lori into a conspiracy to rescue the she-apostles, who are being abused by the UWW in their obsession to extract new gospels from them. The rescue attempt fails, and the two of them (along with their co-conspirators) are imprisoned. Before their capture, Lori and Alex witness a murder committed by Dixie Lou.

Soon afterward, the monastery is attacked by the Bureau of Ideology. Lori, Alex, Dixie Lou, the eleven she-apostles, and a handful of others escape in four small aircraft, and fly north across the Mediterranean Sea. . . .

Other Books by Brian Herbert

The Stolen Gospels (Book 1 of THE STOLEN GOSPELS)

Sidney's Comet
The Garbage Chronicles

Man of Two Worlds (with Frank Herbert)

Sudanna Sudanna

Prisoners of Arionn

The Race for God

Memorymakers (with Marie Landis)
Blood on the Sun (with Marie Landis)

Timeweb (Book 1 of THE TIMEWEB CHRONICLES)
The Web and the Stars (Book 2 of THE TIMEWEB CHRONICLES)
Webdancers (Book 3 of THE TIMEWEB CHRONICLES)

Dreamer of Dune

Forgotten Heroes

Hellhole (with Kevin J. Anderson)

DUNE Series (with Kevin J. Anderson)

House Atreides	*The Butlerian Jihad*
House Harkonnen	*The Machine Crusade*
House Corrino	*The Battle of Corrin*
Hunters of Dune	*Paul of Dune*
Sandworms of Dune	*The Winds of Dune*
The Road to Dune	*Sisterhood of Dune*

Part One

WILDERNESS

Chapter 1

The unknown is a double-edged sword, concealing both the sublime and the terrible.
—Amy Angkor-Billings, before her capture and crucifixion by the Bureau of Ideology

March 2, 2034 . . .

Satellites were of no use in the powerful storm, as thick, raging clouds prevented electronic eyes from observing the battlefield in the mountains of Greece. At his Bureau of Ideology office across the world in Washington state, a large, blond-haired man hung onto hope, but he felt extreme frustration. Styx Tertullian needed to see, needed immediate information—but the communication systems had gone offline, including the Internet, the radio, and phone services. For all he knew, the enemy headquarters at Monte Konos had already been completely destroyed, along with the heretical women and their blasphemous *Holy Women's Bible*. He prayed it was so.

Or his archenemy might have pulled off something startling, turning the tables on his attack forces and annihilating them. The vile United Women of the World were resourceful enough, and God knew they could very well accomplish something like that, especially under the cover of bad weather. They might even show up here at BOI headquarters for a surprise onslaught.

Despite all of the intelligence reports he had received, the Bureau of Ideology leader harbored a nagging worry that the UWW headquarters in Greece was just a decoy, a diabolical facade designed to divert BOI attention and conceal the women's true military intentions. The thought chilled him to the core. His defensive forces were on full alert here, but were they enough?

It was one of the problems he'd experienced with his former boss, Minister Culpepper, a father figure to him, but a man who had been foolishly incapable of grasping the terrible extent of the danger from these women—leaving Styx no option except to stab the old man to death and get him out of the way.

During his tenure, Culpepper had treated the UWW as little more than an annoyance, like insects to be swatted occasionally. He had procrastinated, fumbled, and made bad decisions. Styx, on the other hand, had a better way of dealing with those women, using decisive, deadly force. Pursue them to the ends of the earth; leave them no place to hide, nowhere to breathe. Exterminate them.

My attack squadron should be reporting something to me by now . . . unless there's no one to do it . . . unless they're all dead.

It was a preposterous thought, he tried to convince himself. He was worrying too much. In his position, a leader shouldn't panic; he had to remain composed at all times—not only in the outward face he revealed to others, but internally, in the face he showed God.

The thought of God's presence always comforted Styx Tertullian, calming him immeasurably. He tried to tell himself the Lord Almighty would not allow anything to go wrong now, at this critical point in time. God would not allow heretics to destroy the sacred Bureau.

Agonizing minutes passed, and finally Styx received a phone signal over the secure line. Nervously, he held the receiver in his hand, and heard the deep voice of the unit commander, Major Allion Smithee. "Monte Konos destroyed, sir. We blew the top off the bloody mountain!"

"Fantastic! And the women?"

"They must be dead, sir. Except for those aboard four small aircraft that escaped and disappeared into the storm."

"Escaped, you say? Disappeared?" Styx wanted to strangle the man for his incompetence and stupidity.

Chapter 2

We have unconfirmed reports of military action in the Macedonian mountains of northern Greece. The Greek government denies any knowledge of this, but refuses to allow reporters into the region.
—From an Associated Press news story

Buffeted by strong winds, the helicopter followed three other stealth aircraft through a night storm, with the female pilot remaining as far back as she could without losing contact. Fifteen year old Lori Vale sat behind her in the low illumination of the cockpit, with a handgun on her lap. She wore khaki jeans and a heavy knit sweater.

Tall and auburn-haired, Lori was old beyond her years, having survived a startling series of events in which the female apostles of Jesus had come back to life in the form of children, and had dictated the new gospels of a sacred book, the *Holy Women's Bible*. Now the caretakers of the young she-apostles, the United Women of the World, were fleeing a brutal military attack on their headquarters by the ultra-conservative Bureau of Ideology, who wanted to murder the children and prevent their gospels from being released. Lori and the other passengers aboard the squadron of aircraft had barely escaped with their lives.

The window at her side was rain-streaked and foggy, and in the surface she saw her own shadowed reflection. She wiped the glass, but the rainy darkness outside prevented her from seeing where they were going, or their companion craft. The pilot, Rea Janeg, could be heard transmitting code words over the radio, gibberish that made Lori think of ancient Aramaic—the language of Jesus that was spoken by the she-apostle babies and toddlers.

On a round screen, Lori watched the progress of the escaping aircraft as they crossed the Mediterranean Sea in the middle of the night, heading southwest. A stocky brunette, the pilot answered questions about the equipment, and the answers seemed to make sense to Lori. Even though these were all covert aircraft, the pilots in the squadron sent encrypted transponder signals to each other, and data appeared on their navigation screens, showing the formation.

"If we stop sending signals, they can't see us anymore in this weather," the pilot said.

Lori found the comment interesting. "Why are you telling me so much?" she asked.

"Because I admire you. A lot of the women do. I've heard them talking." She was referring to Lori's attempt to free the young apostles from the captivity imposed on them by the United Women of the World and its ambitious, brutal leader, Dixie Lou Jackson.

"Thank you." For the moment, Lori didn't let her guard down, but knew she would have to trust someone, sometime. Barring that, she would never be able to sleep. She couldn't go off on her own, and felt honor-bound to remain with the four toddler she-apostles on this helicopter, to make certain they were protected. She had Mary Magdalene, Veronica, and two of the other children, along with a couple of members of the UWW council—Fujiko Harui and Wendy Zepeda. Lori had to take a chance and trust someone, but whom? Alex Jackson, Dixie Lou's rebellious son, had been her most trusted confidante, but he'd gotten into trouble, along with Lori, for trying to free all of the children. Now he was aboard one of the other aircraft, under guard.

As she considered this, she peered through the windshield while the stealth vessel flew toward the northern coast of Africa. In the darkness she could not see any sign of land yet, only glints of white on the cold vault of the sea, as whitecaps rolled beneath them. To the naked eye, her helicopter seemed to be alone out here. Overhead, storm clouds blocked the stars, but in the distance a patch of sky came into view just above the horizon, where she saw a few faint stars and a flash of lightning.

"Could our helicopter stop sending transponder signals and still pick up theirs?" Lori asked.

"Absolutely," Rea Janeg responded. She glanced back, showing curiosity in her expression.

"Interesting," Lori said. "Shut it off, and don't reply if they radio us."

The pilot changed settings on the instrument panel.

Over the ensuing minutes, the radio made intermittent static sounds, and voices crackled over the air. "Number three, do you read me?" a voice asked.

Following Lori's orders, her pilot did not respond.

Then Lori changed her mind, and said, "Tell them we're fine, and we're tracking their signals."

The pilot nodded, sent the message.

"Roger," came the response. Then: "Say, shouldn't we use a woman's name instead of Roger?"

"How about Rogerette?" another pilot suggested.

Women's laughter, followed by static. Then one of them said, "Hold on. The wind is increasing."

Lori's aircraft jerked and pitched as her pilot fought to maintain control.

And over the radio, the pilot in the command helicopter said, "It's hard to stay in the air. We'd better touch down at the first landfall."

Moments later, hearing a commotion inside the passenger compartment, Lori opened the door and peered out, warily. She saw the two councilwomen wrestling in the aisle, screaming at one another and pulling hair as the helicopter pitched around in the storm. Wendy Zepeda was much larger than Fujiko Harui, but the smaller woman was holding her own.

"Stop it!" Lori shouted, waving her gun at them. She had to hold onto the door jamb.

"Wendy has a knife in her purse!" Fujiko yelled, as the two councilwomen separated. "She reached for it when we were arguing, and I stopped her."

"She's telling the truth," said a bespectacled woman with red, braided hair. Michelle Renee was the on-board translator of the Aramaic spoken by the she-apostles.

Lori scowled. "Where is the knife?"

"Under that seat," Fujiko said, pointing.

Lori saw it.

"Use your foot and slide it out into the aisle," Lori said to Fujiko. "Then kick it toward me."

Fujiko did this, and Lori picked up the weapon, a hunting knife.

"Now tie Zepeda up and put her with the guards," Lori ordered.

"With pleasure," Fujiko said. "Then I must talk with you."

Five minutes later, Fujiko sat with Lori in the passenger compartment, while the helicopter continued its bumpy ride across the sea. Still not trusting the councilwoman, even though she seemed to be cooperative, Lori kept her hand on her gun.

"There's something you need to know," the Japanese woman said. "Back at Monte Konos, one of the she-apostles said something important." Nervously, Fujiko secured her shoulder harness as the aircraft was buffeted by winds, and then she continued. "Lydia said that Dixie Lou Jackson developed false gospels with a fake Martha of Galilee. Lydia says that the real Martha remains missing."

"I thought there was something strange about that Martha," Lori said, remembering that she'd felt an extrasensory sensation when touching the skin of the Apostle Veronica, but had felt nothing like that when making contact with the twelfth female apostle, the latest arrival. And beyond that, Lori had been troubled about Martha, sensing something about her that she could not quite identify.

"That's not all, either," Fujiko said. "According to Lydia, the real Martha of Galilee, wherever she is, has testimony about a She-Judas, a female apostle who conspired with Judas Iscariot to betray the Savior."

Lori caught her breath. "Did Lydia say anything else?"

"Not that I know." Fujiko looked back at the translator. "Michelle, anything more?"

The woman was wiping off her eyeglasses. "That's the essence of it," she said. "Lydia did not provide much in the way of details, just the broad statements you recounted."

Deep in thought, Lori returned to the cockpit. Just as she was locking the door, the helicopter jerked, and a cabinet by her popped open, disgorging bundles of large denomination American bills. As she stuffed them back into the cabinet, she saw the pilot glance back.

"Guess they forgot to lock that," the pilot said. "Dixie Lou likes to keep spending money all over the place."

"How much is here?" Lori asked.

"I don't know. Maybe five million, hidden all over this 'copter, and the same on the other aircraft. I heard a couple of councilwomen talking."

Lori stared at the closed cabinet door, then looked away. It amazed her that the women were handling such large sums so loosely, but at the moment, money was the last thing on her mind.

An hour later, the pilot said, "We're off the coast of Libya, and our friends are in holding patterns, circling the sand."

"Go to complete radio and transponder silence," Lori said.

She then ordered the pilot to veer wide around the other three aircraft, and to steer out over the desert.

* * *

An urgent voice brought Dixie Lou out of a light slumber. Straightening in her seat, the black woman didn't know how long she'd been asleep, having lost her wristwatch somewhere in the wild confusion of the escape from Monte Konos. She had been dreaming about what she thought she saw during the BOI attack, when the she-apostle Candace vanished before bullets could hit her, and then reappeared after the deadly projectiles passed. Dixie Lou remembered exchanging gazes with Lori Vale after the incident. The teenager had seen the same thing. Curiously, no one else in Dixie Lou's entourage had mentioned it to her. Had only the two of them seen it?

She had mixed feelings about the entire phenomenon of the reincarnated she-apostles, the gospels they brought with them, and the spectrum of paranormal events surrounding them. On one level, she was highly skeptical, not believing any of it was possible. But on another, the part of her that didn't think—and instead sensed things—she knew otherwise. A very large unknown was opening around her; she found it fascinating and frightening at the same time.

"One 'copter dropped back," the pilot said. "We've lost track of it."

"Which one?" Dixie Lou demanded.

The answer told her it was the one with Lori Vale, two councilwomen, and four she-apostles aboard. Then she remembered that Vale had been the one to suggest that they split the she-apostles into several aircraft. Had it been the girl's premonition of danger, or her trick? Uncertain of whether she should be angry or worried, Dixie Lou rubbed her chin thoughtfully.

She focused on a flight map on the gray screen of her laptop computer, and heard two matrons down the aisle expressing their concern over BOI satellite surveillance. While the escaping UWW aircraft had stealth capabilities, and they were in a storm, the women were worried about the Bureau having even more sophisticated technology that could still detect them. They mentioned the previous incident in which one of the UWW's high-tech stealth planes had been shot down over the Mediterranean. Dixie Lou wondered about the security leaks that gave mere matrons such information, and felt irritated by this. But she had other priorities right now.

Overhead, the rotors of the helicopter pulsed and vibrated. Dixie Lou felt it in the seats and armrests, and in the floorboard. She blinked her eyes from a nearby flash of lightning, then saw another flash farther away over land, a jagged orange line scribed across the indigo night sky. Thunder boomed, and the helicopter jerked.

"Still no sign of the missing aircraft," the pilot announced, her voice agitated as she watched her instruments. "Hopefully we can find it after the storm clears. But in this weather, especially with blowing sand that can cause havoc with the engines, I'd recommend that we set down, *immediately*."

The Chairwoman had to make a quick decision. With Council-woman Deborah Marvel looking on, she voice-activated her computer to bring up a detailed, secure schematic of the ground. They were over a desert region on the eastern coast of Libya, in North Africa. Once a pariah nation to much of the civilized world for sponsoring terrorism, they had changed regimes, but still had a despotic ruler and a violent secret police. Not the best place to land, but the weather was dicey.

According to the schematic, two villages were nearby. The escaping vessels had crossed the Mediterranean Sea, going in a southerly direction from Monte Konos. The big storm had worsened along the course they'd flown, giving them a rough, jolting ride and forcing them off course, away from the coast of Tunisia where they had intended to land. The weather had apparently, however, provided them with cloud cover, concealing their location from the ever-present, prying eyes of enemy patrols and satellites.

In these extended range aircraft, the Chairwoman had not expected to have to land here, but she gave the order for all of them to set down. They had ground camouflage gear on board for the aircraft, and would need to move quickly to set it up, thus making them difficult to detect on the ground through visual or other sensors.

* * *

As sand swirled around Lori's helicopter, the craft flew over the lights of a small desert settlement. In poor visibility the pilot complained about cross winds and sand interfering with the operation of the engines, preventing her from getting full power out of them. They sputtered, and she shouted, "We need to land, quick!"

"Do it!" Lori yelled.

Still in her seat behind the pilot, she held onto a safety strap while the helicopter dove and spun, with powerful winds slamming into the hull and driving it one way and another. Metal plates around her stretched and creaked, and seemed ready to come apart. She didn't like the feeling of helplessness as a passenger, would much rather be at the controls herself, making her own life and death decisions.

Suddenly a hard "kwummmph!" sounded, and she felt the jolt of hard contact as they landed. The helicopter tilted hard to the left, then righted itself. The rotors coughed and came to a whining, grinding stop. Lori was shaken up, but not injured.

Back in the passenger cabin, people groaned, and the children cried. Lori's first thoughts were for the welfare of the she-apostles. She rushed to check on them, and found they were upset but unharmed. Odd sensations flashed in the teenager's brain as she looked at the children, and especially when she drew close to each one. Unable to identify her feelings, she restrained from touching the children, even though two of them reached their hands out to her.

One thing seemed certain. She wanted to spend time with them alone, away from the prying eyes . . . and ears . . . of anyone.

Through portholes, Lori saw the sky beginning to clear. As sand settled from the air she made out details of the landscape, with the milieu illuminated by starlight and a sliver of moon low over the horizon. Faintly, the regular pattern of desert dunes could be seen, and jagged escarpments topped by wizards' caps of stone.

The pilot activated stabilizers, which whooshed into place beneath the craft. She emerged from the cockpit. "In addition to the engine problem, our ground camouflage system is out of commission," she said. "We can be seen here."

Lori glowered, heard the wind howling outside.

"We'll spend the night here," she said. "We don't have any choice."

"I'll see if I can get the engines and camouflage going at first light," the pilot said.

Lori nodded.

Hearing a foreign language spoken, she saw the translator Michelle Renee speaking to the children, presumably in ancient Aramaic. Lori did not understand the words, but they brought to mind a strange word that Veronica had mouthed to her one day in the Scriptorium.

Iktol.

It had not been Aramaic. Instead, it was from a secret language unknown to the translators. And, inexplicably, Lori had understood it.

Iktol . . . Murder.

Chapter 3

There can be tremendous beauty in a powerful storm, and a drab, predictable ugliness in serenity. Look at the woman who survives an immense force of nature, how she draws strength from it, absorbing the raw elemental power of our female deity and converting it to her own use.
—Amy Angkor Billings

After ordering the pilot into the passenger compartment, Lori locked herself inside the cockpit and tried to get some sleep. It was not easy. For more than an hour, she just sat on the deep-cushion of the pilot's seat, with it tilted back as far as possible. Too many thoughts whirled through her mind. Countless troubles, dangerous possibilities. Across the expanse of desert, she saw the cloud cover opening up more, and a silver-sprinkling of stars against the deep indigo of the sky.

It occurred to her that the women in the back might take the four she-apostles and run off with them, might even go out in the night looking for Dixie Lou Jackson and the others. But she discounted the possibility. She had landed at least ten kilometers from Dixie Lou's camp, and anyone on foot could get lost out there. At the minimum, she had until dawn to get a few hours of rest.

Through the windshield, she watched flashes of lightning illuminating desert escarpments for brief moments before flickering out like wicks, and saw the sliver of moon slipping below the horizon. She heard the wind picking up around the helicopter and the solid pelting of tiny, granular pieces of silica against the outside of the aircraft, as the break in the weather proved short-lived.

The fresh memory of automatic weapons fire returned, and of the tiny she-apostle Candace seeming to shift time around her . . . and avoiding certain death. Lori had so many questions about the she-apostles, and no answers.

She dozed off, and when she awoke the storm had subsided. Lori opened a small side window to allow fresh air into the cockpit, and then drifted off to sleep again. Several times, she awoke, and then slipped back into slumber.

In a dream, Lori saw flickering lights approaching on the desert, and soon realized they were lanterns, carried by people in dark robes. A woman called out from their midst, but in a language Lori didn't understand, a tongue that rolled and flowed, like water streaming across the sands.

Lori counted six robed shapes, each with a lantern. As they drew close she saw dark skin and mysterious, glinting eyes beneath overhanging hoods. All appeared to be women. They continued to approach. In their unknown tribal language they spoke rapidly. Were they Arabs, or perhaps Berbers?

In the foreground, a toddler stood on the sand, looking at them.

With a start, Lori realized it was not a dream and she had been peering through the windshield of the helicopter. People really were standing out there, a group of women talking to one of the she-apostles, who stood by herself, with no attendant. Lori heard the women through the open side window, chattering rapidly in their language. She saw additional lanterns behind them, and the hulking shadows of camels.

Which child was it? In the low light of the lanterns, Lori saw red hair. *Mary Magdalene.* The toddler did not appear to be saying anything, and was just staring up at the hooded faces around her.

As Lori straightened in her seat, the women looked up at her and pointed. She also heard activity in the back of the helicopter, and voices back there.

Concerned for the safety of Mary Magdalene, Lori opened the cockpit emergency door, and was about to climb down onto the sand when she remembered the guns she had. After hesitating for a moment, she climbed down without the weapons.

"This is your child?" one of the women asked, in heavily accented English. She was quite large, the size of a big man. Her face was half in shadows, half in lantern light.

"I'm responsible for her," Lori said, as she stepped onto the soft sand. Reaching down, she clasped one of the she-apostle's hands, and felt a slight dizziness, which passed quickly.

"You are English?" the woman asked. She and her companions wore veils as well as hoods, but her veil was pulled to one side so that her face could be seen when the lights shifted. Lori heard the camels making noises in the background.

Lori nodded, thinking that they would not know the difference between the British and the Americans. After decades of terrorism, it was not always wise to admit that you were an American. "We had trouble in the storm and were forced to set down here."

An odd sensation passed through the teenager, running from her hand holding little Mary up her arm. It made Lori feel a little light-headed, and something more that she could not quite identify.

"Your friends are setting up camp over there," the woman said, pointing across the dark desert. "All of you seem to have experienced problems in the storm."

Lori hesitated, then said, "They *aren't* my friends." This was not completely accurate since she did have at least one friend in their midst, Alex, and she cared about the welfare of the eight she-apostles in the group.

"They are your enemies?"

"Some of them are, very much so. It's a very complicated story."

"Life is like that, isn't it?" the woman said, in her accented English. She held her lantern close to Lori's face, looked into her eyes, and commented, "You carry truth in your face."

"And you in yours," Lori said, with a gentle smile. The woman appeared to be around thirty-five, with dark, sun-baked skin and glinting black eyes. Her face had a strength and hardness to it. Glancing around, Lori saw what she thought were the bulges of weapons beneath the robes of the group. She took a deep breath.

"I am a desert princess and these are my attendants," the woman announced. She then said something to her companions in what Lori presumed to be Arabic, and they all laughed, which made Lori doubt if she really was a princess.

"Your life sounds very interesting," Lori said.

She looked up at the portholes of the large helicopter, where dim lights were on inside and faces were pressed against the glass, peering out. She heard children crying. As Lori held little Mary's hand a warm feeling ran through her and she felt comforted, that somehow the she-apostle was communicating with her.

"I'm sure your own story is much more interesting," the Arab woman said, "but I will not ask you to talk about it if you don't want to. We only wish to be of assistance to you in your time of need."

"Thank you," Lori said, "but I don't know what you could possibly do. Our pilot is going to work on the engines when it is daylight, and as for my enemies, I'm afraid that is my problem."

The woman narrowed her eyes. "There might be something I could do, if we are friends. I am called Malia Ali Khan."

Lori considered not providing her own real name, but a small interior voice told her to take a chance—and she gave it to her, including her surname.

"Very nice to meet you." Malia smiled broadly, revealing dark gaps in her teeth. She looked down. "And your young companion. What is your name, little one?"

When the child did not answer, Lori said, "Mary."

"And you are not old enough to be her mother."

"You're right. She is not my child."

"Jesus Christ's mother was named Mary," Malia said, a somewhat surprising comment. "I know something of your religion, because in

Islam we respect your holy teachings." She paused. "You are a Christian?"

"Not a very good one, I'm afraid."

The robed woman leaned down to touch Mary's face, then straightened and said to Lori, "Now that we are friends, I shall attack your enemies and kill them. We have many weapons, even machine guns."

"They have more firepower than you do in those helicopters." She nodded toward the aircraft. "Like this one. Besides, they have eight small children with them, and I don't want them hurt."

Malia nodded. "Very well, but I can still create a diversion for you, to give you time to get away. Would you like that?"

"Maybe. What do you have in mind?"

"We will offer them the hospitality of our village, and a very long meal. Perhaps in that time, you can get your repairs completed and leave."

"Be very careful with the one called Dixie Lou Jackson. She is extremely dangerous."

"But Allah is with us. And with you, too, as our special friend. There is only so much we can do in the form of a diversion, however. Perhaps only a few hours of keeping them busy, so you must hurry and get away from here."

"Thank you. That will be a big help."

Though she didn't say so because she didn't want to offend the woman, Lori wished she could fly as far away from here as she could get, with the four toddler she-apostles that she had in her care, Mary Magdalene, Veronica, Priscilla, and Sarah. It was dangerous to remain here, where Dixie Lou might find her. The other three aircraft had set down only a few kilometers away. But she couldn't leave, not until the pilot fixed the engines, if that was even possible.

In addition, Lori had a peculiar feeling that she should remain, that she should not abandon the other eight she-apostles. The sensation confounded her, and she had difficulty imagining how to rescue them. She would have to sneak into Dixie Lou's camp, find the children and get them out—basically by herself.

She did have a potential ally in Fujiko Harui, but she wasn't certain she could rely on her yet. Especially not for something so critically important. Dixie Lou still had leverage on Fujiko, since she held her daughter Siana as captive, in punishment for the young woman's participation in the attempted rescue of the she apostles. But that could go both ways, could cause Fujiko to seek vengeance against the Chairwoman.

"Please, let us pay you for your help," Lori said. "You are going to a lot of trouble for us."

"We do not accept payment from honored friends—such as yourself. No, there will be no charge."

Malia means well, Lori thought, as the Arabs departed into the night with lanterns bobbing in the darkness, and boarded their camels. *But she will have her hands full trying to deceive Dixie Lou.*

Lori climbed back up to the cockpit, taking the silent, mysterious toddler with her.

Chapter 4

The sins within her skirts are many; her garments are the murk of twilight, her adornments are tainted with corruption.

—Manuscript from the fourth cave, Dead Sea Scrolls

Shortly before dawn, after only a few hours of fitful rest while waiting for the storm to pass, Dixie Lou activated a hatch door. It opened with a whir and a squeal, and she left the cramped quarters, descending a metal stairway to the sand. The wind blew the back of her braided hair behind her. She wore a dun-colored robe.

Following her instructions, everyone in the party met with her between the aircraft, which had been protected after they landed with chameleon camouflage, an electronic "fabric" that the pilots said utilized pulse-signals to match the nearby landscape. The ships on the ground were now invisible from the air, they said.

In the illumination of portable lamps, she met the gaze of her son Alex, who stood with matrons, translators, and councilwomen, some of whom held the eight she-apostles who remained with her. She corrected herself. In reality, it was only seven, since Martha was secretly a fake. "After we set up camp," Dixie Lou said, "I'm sending out search parties, to see if we can find the missing helicopter."

It irked her that four of the real she-apostles were missing, along with Lori Vale, Fujiko Harui, and Wendy Zepeda. She didn't care that much about the teenager or the little Japanese woman—the latter of whom reminded her too much of the late UWW leader Amy Angkor-Billings—but Wendy was one of her most staunch allies. Dixie Lou hoped that she and the she-apostles were safe. The lives of the children only mattered to her for what they could do for the UWW, and especially for her as Chairwoman. They were more useful alive than dead, but if they were dead, she would make the appropriate arrangements. It meant that she would have to come up with four more fake she-apostles. Things would be more complicated, but she had learned with the bogus Martha that it could be done.

From compartments in the hulls, the pilots brought out survival packs, containing tents and other articles. "Press these buttons," one of the pilots said. This was done, and the habitats snapped together quickly in a space between the camouflaged aircraft, with alloy rods extending and clipping into frames, and sheets of weathercloth fitting and sealing over them. Dixie Lou watched as the other women put the she-apostles inside one tent. Some of the children fussed and cried, and were tended to by their handlers.

The tents were tied into the electronic camouflage system, and within moments she saw the fabric shifting in color, taking on the hues and subtle tones of the desert. It was only when close to them that she could make out the outlines of the enclosures. . . .

* * *

While helping make camp, Alex Jackson saw the approach of flickering lights . . . lanterns, he decided. He made out the shapes of robed figures on camels. At Dixie Lou's command, her youthful guards pointed semiautomatic rifles at them. Safeties clicked off.

"Stay away from us!" Dixie Lou shouted.

A woman shouted back, in what could be Arabic.

"We don't understand," Dixie Lou said, impatiently. "Don't any of you speak English? Get out of here!" She pulled a handgun from her robe, and fired a shot in the air.

They started backing the camels up.

Apparently it wasn't quickly enough, because Dixie Lou fired a clip full of wild shots in their direction.

The camels galloped away with their riders, disappearing into the night. Someone dropped a lantern, which Alex retrieved. It was still burning.

"You didn't need to shoot," Deborah Marvel said. They weren't threatening us."

"How do we know?" Dixie Lou shrilled. "They probably speak English, and understood everything I was saying. Maybe more of them were waiting in the darkness, where we couldn't see them."

"We can't suspect everybody," Deborah insisted. "They're just poor Arabs—probably wanted to help us."

"They can help by staying the hell out of our way," Dixie Lou snarled. She reloaded the gun, replaced it in her pocket.

Suddenly a heavily accented female voice broke the darkness of the night, speaking English: "You aren't a very good shot."

"I wasn't trying to hit you," Dixie Lou countered. She looked around warily, reached into her pocket but didn't bring out the weapon. "Who are you?"

"We have guns, too," the voice said, "and we outnumber you." A volley of shots rang out, and Alex dove for cover along with everyone else. The camp lights were turned off, and people found cover. Children cried.

"Hiding will do no good," the voice said. "We see in the dark."

"Then why are your people carrying lanterns?" Dixie Lou shouted back.

The voice laughed, and to Alex it seemed to come from a different direction this time. He heard Deborah Marvel and one of the pilots talking about the possibility of getting into one of the helicopters, in order to gain access to its .50 caliber machine guns and floodlights.

"That is a good question," the thickly accented voice shouted. "You have a quick wit."

"Perhaps we made a mistake," Dixie Lou said. "We didn't understand that you only want to be friendly. That is true, isn't it?"

"We desire only to offer assistance to you, in case any of you might be injured. We saw your aircraft having trouble as you came down. It is difficult to fly in a storm."

"I'm sorry for the misunderstanding."

"Some of your people wear strange robes," the voice said. "Very unsuitable for the desert, even at this time of year. Too heavy."

"Why don't you come out where we can see you?" Dixie Lou demanded. Alex heard her crawling along the sand.

"Why do you come here wearing strange robes?" the voice asked. "What tribe are you?"

"No tribe, and we didn't intend to land here. The storm forced us down."

"But the storm is past, and it would be safe to fly away now. Your behavior is most peculiar."

"We're not quite ready to go." Dixie Lou looked around, trying to find the speaker's location.

"Problems with your sophisticated equipment?"

"Just need to check the flight systems for safety."

"And the reason you have camouflaged everything, making you invisible from a distance? We watched you land, and saw you vanish a short time afterward—until we approached to within a few meters, close enough to see that you were still there. Are you hiding from someone?"

"Of course not. Camouflage is just a secondary feature of the electronic veiling system we activated around the aircraft, to protect them from bad weather, because windblown sand can cause a lot of damage. As for the camouflaged tents, they are tied into the system, too."

"I see," the woman said, but Alex wasn't certain if she believed his mother, whose lie about weather protection seemed obvious. But only to a westerner, perhaps, he told himself. This Arab might not be able to tell.

Alex approached the she-apostles' tent, wanting to comfort the children inside, who were fussing and crying. Through the open doorway he saw the shadowy outlines of small shapes lying and sitting in air-cribs. Suddenly a guard stepped forward, and forced him away. Alex moved off to one side, but the guard didn't leave.

"You have many children here," the Arab voice said, out in the darkness. "We do not wish to harm them."

"Come out where I can see you," Dixie Lou said. "We'll talk."

Alex heard a flurry of movement behind Dixie Lou, and a muffled voice said, "We're right behind you." A lantern went on, and Alex saw three intruders behind his mother.

Dixie Lou whirled, but before she could get to her weapon, a robed woman put her in a headlock and jammed a knife against her throat. A veil covered the lower portion of the woman's face, revealing only her eyes. Two smaller, hooded shapes stood with her. They lit another lantern, which showed that they were boys holding carbines.

"Permit me to introduce myself," the woman said. "I am Malia Ali Khan. And you?"

Dixie Lou didn't respond.

"Tell your guards to toss their weapons on the ground," Malia said, in her heavily accented English. She was much taller than Dixie Lou.

"Do it!" the Chairwoman shouted. In the dim light, Alex saw rage and indignation on her face.

Guns and rifles thudded onto the sand.

"And the one in your pocket," the tall woman demanded.

Dixie Lou added it to the others, and the knife was withdrawn from her throat.

"My English is not so good," Malia said. "But I suspect it is better than your Arabic. We are Bedouin, from a village just over there." She pointed across the sand.

Alex saw Dixie Lou staring at the weapons on the sand, and guessed she was trying to estimate how many more people were hiding in the shadows, behind waves in the sand. The boys had an air of deadly maturity about them, as if they knew how to handle the rifles they held.

"Do any of you have injuries?" the Arab woman asked.

"A few bumps and bruises," Dixie Lou snapped, glaring at her. "We've administered first aid."

Malia looked up at the pre-dawn sky. Then, lifting a finger to feel a slight breeze, she said, "By the grace of Allah, the storm is passed. You are safe now."

Dixie Lou didn't respond.

"We would like to offer you the hospitality of our village," Malia said.

Studying her armed visitor, Dixie Lou responded, "Your generosity is much appreciated, but we really don't have time." But Alex heard something in his mother's tone, a forced politeness and formality.

"You must make the time. Hospitality is the way of our people."

"How large is your village?" Dixie Lou asked.

"We'll take you there by camel, and you can see for yourself." She pointed. "It is that way, a few kilometers."

"By *camel?* We don't know how to ride camels, and we have small children with us."

"These are not problems. We have the means to accommodate passengers of all ages. Or, the children can remain here while we show you around the village and give you a fine Bedouin meal."

"Do you have computers or videophones in the village?" Dixie Lou asked.

"You need them for some purpose?"

"To make an Internet connection."

"You westerners are very amusing to us." She stood there smiling, then said something in Arabic to her young companions. The pair nodded.

"We will be back this afternoon," Malia said.

"You have Internet?" Dixie Lou pressed.

"Perhaps. We shall discuss it this afternoon."

"All right."

"It is late now, and you will want to sleep in, as you say." She slid her veil aside and smiled, revealing black gaps where teeth were missing. "An English woman used to live in our camp, and she taught me many of your phrases."

With a smooth motion, Malia whirled and flowed off into the cool shadows, followed by her youthful armed escort. The lanterns went out, and in the minimal light of approaching dawn, Alex saw the movement of many human shapes, boarding camels and riding away.

* * *

"Seven ball in the side pocket," Zack Markwether announced, confidently. In his brother's private game room at the White House, they were spending the evening together, after a long day. Zack leaned over the green felt table, lining up his shot with the cue stick. His officer's coat and white gloves were draped over a chair, and a pair of aviator sunglasses sat open on a ledge. The walls were lined with photographs and paintings of foreign dignitaries who had visited the White House in years past—kings, queens, princes and princesses, prime ministers, premiers, presidents, shahs, dictators, ambassadors. . . .

"You don't need to call your shots," the President groused. "Just shoot the stupid ball, OK?"

With a self-satisfied smile, Zack snicked the purple seven ball into the designated pocket.

Chalking his own stick, the President said, "Incidentally, you need to stay away from the White House interns, Brother. I'm getting complaints."

Calmly, Zack walked over to a side table, took a sip from a bottle of imported German beer. "You're just trying to break my concentration. Actually, I'm only dating one of the interns, and she's not even one of the youngsters I'm rumored to be with. She's almost thirty."

"Just be careful not to do anything to embarrass yourself, or me. I recall some stories about you in high school, back when I was a sophomore and you were a senior. Cheer leaders, weren't they?"

With a broad grin, Zack said, "The old stories about me were all true. Nowadays, though, you shouldn't believe everything you hear."

"You gonna marry this one?"

He shook his head. "Not my style. Never has been." He took another sip of beer. "Say, what about my letter to the Pope on Vatican security? Have you looked it over yet?"

"I'll get around to it."

Lowering his brow in displeasure, Zack said, "I didn't do all that work for nothing, you know. Took me over a week in the Library of Congress and CIA Archives—researching old records that were never scanned for the Internet, either because they were quite old, or classified. In the Library of Congress I found information about an underground tunnel that connected Vatican City to the Castel Sant'Angelo, an impregnable fortress in Rome where popes took refuge during military attacks. Even the existence of that tunnel was a secret for centuries, though information on it eventually got out."

He took a deep breath and continued. "But at the CIA I found more, descriptions of an even more secret, alternate tunnel system that also led from the holy city to the castle, developed because information about the main tunnel route had gotten into the wrong hands. The second route is more circuitous and longer, but the distance is still not that great, and it is a quick way to get from one place to the other undetected."

"Interesting."

"Obviously you didn't read the research documents I provided to you."

"I've been busy."

"All right," Zack said, "but those subterranean passageways worry me. "Maybe I should just send the letter to him directly, to make sure any tunnels are permanently blocked off, and can't be reopened."

"You could do that, but he might never see it. Some lower level functionary could just round file it. A letter from my office, on the other hand, would not be thrown in the trash."

"OK, but get around to it, all right?"

"A President has many responsibilities."

"If I miss the next shot, will you look at it this afternoon?"

President Markwether laughed, a boisterous cachinnation. "I'll bet they have security you can't begin to imagine, big brother. The Vatican has to be one of the top terrorist targets in the world."

"Still, I suspect our Catholic friends may have grown complacent, overconfident. I get gut feelings about these things based upon a few observations—the chatting guards, the emphasis on ceremony over substance, the perimeter defensive gaps—and it makes me wonder about the rest of the operation. Are people manning the security cameras, watching every screen every second, or are there lapses? What are the backup systems? Some of my comments have to do with morale, with esprit de corps. I've been right about these things before, and you know it. The security program I developed for our federal buildings has saved hundreds, maybe thousands of lives. My concept for a—"

"I know, and we all appreciate that. Your White House suggestions were excellent, too, except for the flack from some of my staff who resent your presence." He sighed. "So much politics to wade through, on all levels. All right, I'll move your letter up on my priority list."

Setting his beer aside, Zack bent over the pool table to line up his next shot. He hesitated, looked peripherally at his brother and asked, "Say, your delay wouldn't have anything to do with the fact that you aren't Catholic, would it?"

The President responded in his most statesmanlike voice, "My non-adherence to the faith and your embrace of it has nothing—I repeat, *nothing*—to do with my actions."

"Have you even looked at my letter?"

"Of course."

"Then what does it say about St. Peter's Basilica, the Sistine Chapel, and—"

"Do not interrogate me! I am the President of the United States!"

Irritated, Zack shanked his shot, making a shuddering sound with his cue stick as it glanced off the white cue ball. In disgust, he threw the stick down on the table and left.

* * *

Following the departure of the Arabs, the female pilots finished setting up Dixie Lou's camp, using the extensive survival gear that had been kept in these aircraft for contingencies, by order of Amy Angkor-Billings. Seven tents were arranged between the camouflaged aircraft, and electric lanterns were set up to provide yellowish illumination, along with separate units to zap insects, causing little fizzes and pops. The lanterns would not be needed for much longer; daylight was creeping across the sands from the east.

During this work, Dixie Lou sat off to one side, speaking to Alex energetically, moving her hands for emphasis. She brought the handgun out of her robe pocket, fiddled with it in a way that made him nervous.

"Did you have anything to do with Lori getting away?" she demanded.

"Of course not. I just hope she's safe, that her helicopter didn't crash."

Looking at him skeptically, she said, "I wish I could trust my own son."

Alex didn't hold gazes with her as forcefully as he would have liked, because the expression on her face was crazier than usual, with her dark gaze darting around wildly. He wanted to kick himself for not handling the whole situation better, and getting Lori in trouble. His mother was crafty, deadly clever, and the teenager was always in her cross hairs. For all he knew, Dixie Lou had arranged for her to be killed, maybe even with everyone else aboard the missing aircraft.

She waved the gun at him. "I'd better not find out you've been lying to me."

"Or you'll kill your baby boy?" Alex said, his tone almost taunting. He'd always done better in his relationship with his mother whenever he showed strength, not cowering to her.

But Dixie Lou said, "Worse than that." Without warning, she swung the gun and hit him on the side of the neck with the barrel. Recoiling, Alex glared back at her. Pain devils burned his neck.

She didn't show any concern, and instead went on to describe in detail what horrendous tortures she would inflict upon him if he dared to defy her. "Your death will not be quick or painless," she warned.

After his mother went inside her tent and closed the flap, Alex crossed the campsite and stared out into the awakening desert, worrying more about Lori than about himself. His neck throbbed, and he cursed his misfortune for being born of a monster like Dixie Lou Jackson. He no longer considered her his mother, would rather have no mother at all than her.

A bug fizzled into the zapper near him. He heard his mother bumping around inside her tent, making angry grunts. She was not in a good mood.

He noticed two guards a distance away, watching him. Rookies like most of the other guards in this party, they had been in training just before the attack on Monte Konos, and were all his mother could salvage. If the women were attacked again—maybe even by those Arabs—the guards were not going to be much protection for anyone.

But if Alex saw an opportunity to get away, they might fit the bill nicely, with their inexperience. Perhaps he could slip by them when his mother was away in the village, and escape.

He needed to find Lori and make certain she was safe. He prayed that her helicopter had not crashed in the storm.

* * *

Alone in her tent, and in her thoughts, Dixie Lou cursed and slammed things around: her bedding, a pair of binoculars, clothing. Daylight seeped into the tent. She still felt agitation at having a knife held to her throat, and was troubled by the missing helicopter, and by her inability thus far to get the *Holy Women's Bible* published on the Internet.

The Chairwoman had one more big concern. She had convinced herself that one day, probably soon, Lori would give birth to the missing twelfth she-apostle, the one the others called Martha of Galilee. She sensed this very strongly, even though the teenager wasn't even pregnant yet. Or was she? Lori had associated with undesirables in Seattle, street people. Maybe one of them had gotten to her. Maybe the missing she-apostle wasn't from Mexico, after all.

Dixie Lou sensed something extraordinary about the real twelfth child, something more than the other eleven had shown so far, and even more than Candace had done against bullets. Her vanishing act.

The best had been saved for last. And the most dangerous. The She-Judas? What did that mean? So many unknown elements were encircling Dixie Lou, and closing in on her.

Later this morning, despite the risk of detection by satellites, she would send out a search helicopter, to see if Lori and the rest of her party could be located. Dixie Lou's pilots were checking one of the 'copters now, to make certain its stealth features were fully operational, and had not been damaged in the storm.

But first, she had some questions to ask of the she-apostles, and she did not intend to be pleasant about it.

*   *   *

Acting Minister Styx Tertullian watched a high-resolution wall screen that showed recorded images of the attack. The top of Monte Konos was erupting like a volcano, and he saw the complete destruction of all buildings in the ancient monastery.

"Praise God!" he shouted.

His eyes were open wide, his mouth agape, as he absorbed everything. In fact, the destruction was so beautiful against the night sky that he decided to have the Bureau lab prepare a still photograph for him, to be displayed in his office.

He remained deeply troubled, though, by the four aircraft that had escaped.

Chapter 5

There are two basic world views, one male and the other female. They are diametrically opposed to one another, and always will be.
—Ancient Saying

Golden sunlight passed through the windshield of the helicopter, filling the cockpit with warmth and hazy illumination. Lori had been awake for a few minutes, heard the cries of birds outside. Having moved to an air mattress that she'd set up inside the cockpit, she pushed aside a thin insul-blanket that bore the green-and-orange sword-cross emblem of the UWW.

She heard other sounds, and opening the side window more to look outside, she saw Rea Janeg working alongside the fuselage, at an open panel box that contained the controls for the electronic camouflage system. The pilot had been up since dawn working on it, cleaning dust out of everything. Lori had offered to help when she'd first heard her out there, but the woman had declined, saying she could do it faster on her own.

Looking up at Lori now, the pilot grinned. "Got the camouflage system operational," she said. "Just needed to clean a few parts." She closed the panel cover. "First things first, to conceal where we are. The twin engines are next."

"That's great," Lori said. Then, pulling her head back inside, she looked at her watch, which had automatically set itself to Libyan time:

7:45 AM. She would have liked to have slept longer, recalled lying awake at dawn as the pilot was just beginning her work.

Now her thoughts drifted to Alex, and she hoped he was safe.

Having been sleeping in her underclothes, Lori swung out of bed, put on a light green blouse, khaki jeans, and sport shoes. Through the open side window she felt a slight breeze. And, able to see out through the camouflage (like one-way glass, the pilot had explained), she saw a flock of birds winging over the desert, heading out toward the blue waters of the Mediterranean Sea, which stretched to the horizon. Some of the birds were white, others black, and of varying sizes. It seemed odd to her that they were all together, in one formation.

Hearing the unmistakable throb of a helicopter, her heart skipped a beat. She didn't see the aircraft yet, but shouted out the window, and then into the passenger compartment: "Under cover, everyone! Under cover!" Energy from the camouflage system crackled around her.

Lori had ordered everyone not to venture out of the camouflaged area, and to wear robes or dark scarves in case they made the mistake of going further. Within seconds, she saw and heard scurrying, and low voices. They had a .50 caliber machine gun on the helicopter and Lori had the access code, but she had no thought of firing at any approaching aircraft, because other she-apostles could be aboard. Her only sensible strategy was to be defensive, and try to hide.

The noise became very loud, but still she saw nothing, leading her to believe the aircraft was in a visual stealth mode, but for some reason its sounds were not being dampened as much as usual—maybe something wrong with it. For several agonizing moments the 'copter seemed to hover directly overhead, and she thought she saw a disturbance in the air, slight and barely perceptible. Then, gradually, the throb of rotors faded away, and the anomaly in the air disappeared with it.

* * *

A few kilometers away, Alex's thoughts were on Lori, just as hers had been on him. In every waking moment, and even in dreams when he caught snatches of sleep, the young black man could not get her out of his mind. She was only fifteen, and technically too young for him, but he cared deeply about her in a very pure way, and perhaps one day—if they made it through these dangers—they could be together in the manner he would like.

As he walked around the encampment in the morning sun, feeling dismal, he wanted desperately to hear the melodic tones of Lori's voice and to gaze into her gentle lavender eyes. But he had no idea where she was or if she was still alive.

He saw his friends Liz Torrence and Siana Harui standing by a tent, with a guard talking to them sternly. Since leaving Monte Konos, Alex had not been able to speak to the two young women who'd been involved with him in trying to free the she-apostles, because they were being kept away from him by that tyrannical guard. The guard, a short redhead, seemed angry about something, and raised her voice. He couldn't make out the words.

* * *

Fearing detection by BOI satellites, the effort to find the missing helicopter had been confined to half an hour. The pilot brought her report to Dixie Lou while she was questioning the she-apostles in front of her own tent through a translator, asking them about Candace's ability to vanish, and about the missing twelfth she-apostle, Martha of Galilee. The children were not being cooperative, and Dixie Lou had slapped two of them, causing them to cry.

"I'm sorry to interrupt you," the pilot said, "but I thought you would want to know that there is no sign of the missing aircraft. It probably went down in the Mediterranean."

"A logical conclusion," Dixie Lou said, "but they have the same stealth and ground camouflage systems we do, don't they?"

With a perplexed expression, the pilot nodded. "But why would they hide from us?"

"I'll ask the questions around here."

Dixie Lou didn't put it past the troublesome, defiant Lori Vale to take over the helicopter and direct it to her own destination. When it came to that annoying teenager, nothing was simple or straightforward.

All of the possibilities, when added to Dixie Lou's other concerns, had been putting her in an edgy mood today. . . .

* * *

That afternoon, Dixie Lou saw a robed rider on a camel coming over the top of a rise of sand, moving briskly toward the camp. More people appeared afterward, on camels. She counted eight women, all dressed in long robes and veils, with a train of riderless camels behind them. They must be the Bedouin. A tall woman sat astride the animal in the front, using a whip to urge it on—Malia Ali Khan, she realized.

Dixie Lou sent the children away, with their matrons and translators.

"Still wearing those unsuitable robes, I see," Malia said, as she jumped down onto the said. Her companions remained behind her, on their mounts.

Peering over the top of her veil, the Arab woman showed her continuing disapproval of the coarse gray garments worn by these western women. The Arab women on the camels wore burnooses and veils. The two boys rode up behind them, but Dixie Lou noticed that they were unarmed this time.

"I rather like my robe," Dixie Lou said. "The air is cool this morning."

"At this time of year, you might get by," Malia agreed, "because it is not so terribly hot. But since we are a traveling people most of us pack no more than one robe apiece, and these hooded cloaks. If it is cool we wear more underneath."

"Layering," one of the councilwomen said, "a backpacking trick." It was Tamara Himmel, whose soft form did not look as if it had seen much physical exertion, of the outdoor variety or otherwise.

"You are traveling people, too?" Malia inquired, looking closely at Dixie Lou.

"For the moment."

The Arab's eyes narrowed. "I think you are fleeing something."

Dixie Lou's features hardened. "I told you we're not hiding from anyone."

"Words are of little significance. My people are adept at reading what is not said. This is a necessary skill in the desert, where anyone you meet can be a friend, or a deadly foe."

"You don't appear to be armed this time. Apparently you've decided we aren't a threat to you."

"Our burnooses conceal much." Malia extended a welcoming hand. "Come to our village, and dine with us, as our guests." Malia adjusted her veil, which had slipped down a little, revealing a thin scar on her upper lip.

Dixie Lou had been having second thoughts about going with the Arabs. But based upon the determination exhibited by Malia—the firm tone and fire in her eyes—Dixie Lou didn't think that she or her people would appreciate being rejected, and would certainly take it as a sign of disrespect. So she nodded.

"Some of the children haven't been feeling well," Councilwoman Deborah Marvel said. "Perhaps one of us should remain behind with them, along with the guards?"

"Yes," Dixie Lou agreed. "You stay here, Deborah." She looked at Malia. "We also have prisoners, and they must be guarded." She pointed at her own son. "That's one of them."

"Ah!" Malia said. "You are as interesting as I suspected. What has he done wrong?"

"He violated our law. So did one who is aboard a missing helicopter. Have you seen another craft anywhere, or western people like us, with small children?"

"None of that. If they have broken your law, that is a very serious matter, because the law is very important. We, too, must abide by our own, the Law of Allah."

* * *

Leaving Alex and others behind, Dixie Lou and seven of her councilwomen accompanied the Arabs. The camels provided for them had fine saddles with places all around to hold onto, and no need to guide the animals, because they followed the others. In the brightness of the sun the Arabs and their guests rode toward the Mediterranean Sea, and then traversed a well-tramped dune crest, where Malia halted.

Pointing at a rock escarpment to the west, she said, "There is a story that Prophet Mohammed, blessings be upon him, once stood on that rock, and received a message from Allah."

"Very interesting," Dixie Lou said.

"Prophet's Rock is holy ground," Malia said, "guarded by our people. We would consider it a sacrilege if you or any other—" She smiled as she paused. "—infidel—were to go anywhere near it. Please take no offense at the word. All non-Muslims are considered infidels."

"I understand." Dixie Lou took a long, hard look at the rock as her camel followed Malia along the dune crest, and she saw people moving around near the base, presumably the Muslim guards. Presently, as the trail wound down the dune, she lost sight of the rock.

They made their way to a community just inland, at the base of the largest dune she had ever seen. The village was more than she had expected, more than she had noticed in the nighttime storm. Black goats'-hair tents flapped in the wind, and there were many women, children, and animals. There were even a number of small, portable buildings, and weathered trucks. It was a sizable encampment.

As they reached the desert settlement, dozens of children ran out to greet them, chattering excitedly in Arabic. The arriving party passed more camels tethered at a watering hole and continued on to a large tent, which was of a finer design and construction than the others, but which still bore evidence of weathering and wear. Like the discarded abode of a Persian King, it had ragged tassels, with faded purple and gold fabrics and braided gold stitching around the doors and windows.

After everyone was off the camels, Malia said, "Come inside, please." She moved off to one side of the main entrance, gestured with one arm.

Dixie Lou smelled a flinty dustiness as she stepped onto a ragged carpet inside, placed directly on the sand. She and her companions were directed to sit on the floor of a spacious main room that had two side enclosures, separated by hanging beads and tassels. Islamic designs and artwork adorned the walls.

They sat cross-legged around a cleared central area. Presently a teenage boy entered, carrying a large fire-blackened pan of meat, which he placed in the middle of the group. A dark-haired girl of around the same age—wearing a red dress and veil—brought a spotted metal pitcher, and a tray of stained ceramic cups.

Malia asked for a moment of silence, and uttered an Islamic blessing over the meal they were about to enjoy.

Afterward, Dixie Lou waited as the girl poured steaming hot coffee into her cup. There were no plates or eating utensils.

"I haven't seen any men here," Dixie Lou said. "Only women and young people."

"Oh we have many men," Malia said, as she waited for her own coffee. "They are away on—business. Some of the older men and women are here; around this time they like to break into groups and drink coffee."

"What sort of business are your men away on?" Dixie Lou inquired. Her nose curled from the unappetizing odor of the coffee. She tried not to think of it and sipped, taking care not to burn her lips. The brackish brew was strong, but tasted better than expected.

Malia and her companions adjusted their long cloaks so that their arms were more free, and removed their veils, so that they could eat and drink. A wry smile formed on Malia's mouth. "Our men are selling computers," she said. "They have many camels, all fully loaded. A very long caravan of computers."

Dixie Lou smiled herself, since she didn't believe a word of it. This foreign woman was just toying with her, and had an irritating demeanor. Was it some sort of a plot to rob them . . . or worse? Were they actually Arab terrorists, or agents of the despotic Libyan government? Were their men attacking Dixie Lou's camp at that very moment?

It occurred to her that perhaps she should have flown off the night before—following the visit by the Bedouin. But that might have been worse, as it could have been noticed by satellite surveillance or other means they employed, thus bringing the pesky Bureau down on them. These desert people, although potentially dangerous, could not possibly be associated with the BOI. Or could they? She looked into the dark eyes of Malia, and of two women who sat beside her, but their eyes were indecipherable.

On Dixie Lou's left, the narrow-faced Councilwoman Nancy Winters giggled, and for this infraction she received a piercing glare from her superior.

"I'm sorry," Nancy said, "but the image of computers on camels—" Her voice trailed off.

"We are not primitives," Malia insisted, in a huffy voice. From the central pot she took a handful of dark meat with her bare hands, and stuffed it in her mouth. Brown sauce dribbled down her chin, which she wiped on her bare arm. "Do you think we know nothing of modern technology?"

"No, of course not," Dixie Lou said. "It is obvious from your words that you have some familiarity with western ways."

"Western ways." Malia spat on the carpet, lifted her chin proudly and said, "Centuries ago. Arab people possessed the most advanced knowledge of mathematics, science, and literature, far ahead of the Europeans. It was our period of enlightenment, during the western dark ages."

Dixie Lou took her own handful of meat, chewed and swallowed. "This is really quite good." Actually she fought to keep from showing revulsion at the gamy, almost rotten flavor. She had no idea what it was, didn't think she wanted to ask.

Noticing that Tamara Himmel wasn't eating, Dixie Lou nudged her in the ribs, hard.

With a deep sigh, Tamara took a small morsel and nibbled on it.

In a short time the pan of meat was nearly empty, with most of it having been consumed by the Arabs, who were licking their fingers.

"Our men will return soon," one of the Arab women said, in a barely noticeable accent. She had lighter skin than the others.

"We are a trading people," Malia said, "as our people have always been." She snapped her fingers.

Two women entered from one of the side rooms. Dixie Lou did a double-take. They were carrying computer equipment.

"See," Malia said, proudly. " The latest technology. You would be surprised at what we have. Even a high-powered modem."

"But how do you charge the batteries—for the computers, the support system?"

"We have generators, of course. We are very advanced here, and have access to low-cost gasoline for the generators. Now, what is it you wish to transmit over the Internet?"

"You can make a satellite link?"

"Of course. For our business, we must remain on—how do you say it?—the cutting edge."

Dixie Lou could hardly wait to finish her meal, but was disappointed when another large pan of meat was brought in.

Chapter 6

It is not possible to do business with the devil.
                    —Old Christian Saying

During the long meal, Dixie Lou learned more about the Bedouin tribe. A very talkative woman, Malia claimed to be the granddaughter of a legendary Arab chieftain, though not through legitimate hereditary channels. Instead she had been born to a sheik's harem girl and cast out at a young age, left to wander aimlessly, picking up whatever menial employment she could obtain along the way in order to earn food, shelter and clothing.

"I've never worked as a prostitute," she announced proudly, "though at times that might have been the easiest course for me to take."

Dixie Lou's eyes narrowed, because years ago she had toiled in that ignominious profession herself, in Baltimore. But she said nothing, and instead glanced furtively at Malia's laptop computer, which had been folded open to reveal the screen and keyboard. She couldn't tell much about the machine from looking at it, but noted it was an American brand like her own, with a voice-activation system and a backup keyboard, all similar to her own. In a secure pocket of her robe, Dixie Lou carried a microcylinder containing a copy of the *Holy Women's Bible*, and which she would keep with her until it could be transmitted.

"You took the admirable course," Dixie Lou said.

With a smile Malia continued. "At the age of nineteen I found myself working in Alexandria, on the northern coast of Egypt. I was a cleaning girl for a wealthy carpet merchant, Aga Dali. What an elegant and magnificent home he had, with indoor fountains and exotic furnishings from all over the world! One day he entertained a Bedouin caravan master of some renown, Rashid Ali Khan. The two men were bargaining over the price of fine Persian carpets, and Mr. Khan was not pleased with the price my employer was demanding.

"In a dramatic gesture Mr. Khan rose and bowed, as if to leave. Then, spying me as I performed my chores, he said, 'Aga, you drive a ferocious bargain and make it difficult for me to remain in business. I'll tell you what, though. Throw in that tall servant girl and we have a deal.'

"Thus it was done. I was sold and became the third wife of a caravan leader. Two years later his first and second wives were killed when bandits raided our camp, and I became Rashid's favorite. Now I am his first wife, and two other women must bow to me and do my bidding."

She nodded to her right and left, at the women with her, whose eyes were downturned.

The meal went painfully slowly, because Dixie Lou was so anxious to find out more about the computer capabilities of these people. After the meat course, a bowl containing figs and dates was placed in front of each diner, and more coffee was poured.

"I don't know much about computers myself," Dixie Lou admitted, trying to get away from the endless anecdotes Malia had been telling. "But yours looks promising." She nibbled on a date, found the sweetness and flavor pleasing.

With a smile Malia said, "I have noted your interest in it, and if I am correct in my guess, you have a microcylinder or two in a pocket of your robe? Is that a tiny bulge I see there?"

The comment irritated Dixie Lou, for she didn't like having a stranger examine her so closely and read her so well, perhaps even her body movements, the expressions on her face, the tone of her voice, and more. . . She found it irritating, and unnerving.

"Thank you for eating our food with such grace," Malia said. "It must be difficult for you."

"Oh no—" Dixie Lou cut herself short, remembering the observational abilities of this woman. She reached in her bowl and selected a fig.

"I have tried to eat western foods, and I must confess that I would not have been nearly as gracious. To me your food cannot be swallowed. My throat constricts and won't accept it."

"What did you attempt to eat?" Nancy Winters asked. She took a sip of coffee.

"A very large hamburger and extremely greasy little fried potatoes."

Dixie Lou and her councilwomen laughed.

"Rashid had heard so much about the American fast food restaurants that he took all of his wives out to dinner in Cairo one evening. We had intended to visit three American fast food restaurants, sampling the fare of each. After the first stop, though, none of us could go on. The food was so alien to us that we were sick for hours. I feel queasy even to this day, just thinking about it."

As I will feel remembering this meal, Dixie Lou thought, staring at the blackened, empty meat pot in the center of the circle. No vegetables had been served with the meal.

"Shall we see what's in your pocket?" Malia inquired, looking at Dixie Lou.

The Chairwoman brought out the microcylinder and held it in the palm of her hand. She felt her pulse quicken, but tried to conceal her anxiety.

* * *

Not far away, Lori wore a robe that she had found in one of the helicopter's storage lockers, and she had the hood pulled up over her head. She stood in filtered light beneath an electronic camouflage cover, watching as the female pilot leaned into the engine compartment, working on it. Not certain who, if anyone, she could trust, Lori kept a handgun at the ready, in a pocket of her robe.

A short distance away, also beneath the camouflage, Fujiko sat on the sand with the four she-apostles in their custody, rolling a small ball back and forth, a toy that the translator had brought for them. The toddlers, all of whom wore dark scarves over their heads, participated, but looked as if they were only tolerating the game, as if they were the adults and Fujiko was the child who needed entertaining.

To Lori they seemed like "old souls," the phrase that Dixie Lou had used about her when they met at the goddess circle, and when she later described the she-apostle Veronica. Of all the things that the loathsome Chairwoman had said to her, Lori had to admit to herself that this one actually made some sense, though she was not exactly sure why.

"Hey, let me out of here!" Wendy Zepeda shouted in a voice muted by the passenger compartment of the helicopter, where Fujiko had handcuffed her to a seat back. No one answered her, but every few hours Fujiko had been escorting her to the restroom, and brought food to her at mealtimes.

The two youthful guards were seated near Zepeda, also under restraint and attended to by Fujiko. These were the three that Lori felt certain she could not trust. There were also a pair of middle-aged matrons and the scholarly translator Michelle Renee, all of whom Lori had decided not to lock up, and who had the primary responsibility of taking care of the children.

Still four months shy of her sixteenth birthday, Lori felt much older than that. In Seattle, she had felt twenty, from the emotional development she had undergone with her friends. Now she felt twice her actual age, and she had shown enough force of personality to take control of this helicopter. Even Councilwoman Fujiko Harui seemed to accept that. At least, Lori was willing to give her the opportunity to prove her loyalty. The diminutive woman had displayed remarkable courage, and obviously felt deep sadness over not being with her daughter.

"I have to start the tandem engines to test them," the pilot said, climbing up into the cockpit by the separate hatch. "Even if I engage the rotors, we can leave the electronic camouflage on."

Not entirely trusting her, Lori followed her into the cockpit, carrying the handgun.

Moments later, with the two of them sitting side by side, the engines whined on, then grew louder as the pilot moved a lever.

"They don't rev to full power," the pilot said, making a face of disapproval as she accelerated and decelerated the linked engines. "I'll have to take the fuel system apart, to see if sand got into it."

"How long will that take?"

"A day if it's only the fuel system and maybe the air filters, longer if it's more than that." She tried the engines again, shook her head in disgust, and shut them down. "Lucky for you, I'm the best aviation mechanic at Monte Konos."

When the pilot resumed working on the engines, Lori remained close, where she could see what was going on, and could prevent the pilot from taking the aircraft and flying off with it.

Within a half hour, engine parts were spread out on a plastic tarp that had been laid on the sand. The air was motionless, not blowing gritty particles, but the pilot said she was prepared to cover the parts quickly if necessary, and she would wipe all of them off before reinstalling them. Now Lori felt confident enough to venture a short distance away, where Fujiko was still trying to play with the children. She had a tunecube out now, with popular music blaring from it. Kneeling by the little girls, Fujiko passed the small device around to them. Each examined it with only a little curiosity, sometimes fiddling with the dials and changing the settings and tunes.

As Lori approached, she noticed that Fujiko began to cry, and then looked away when the teenager approached, as if embarrassed. "What's wrong?" Lori asked.

"I'm sorry. One of the songs on the tunecube reminded me of my daughter. I wish we could go over to Dixie Lou's camp and break Siana out, but that could get her killed. I don't even know if she's still alive, but can only hope. I feel like a coward, like I should do something more."

"You're doing everything you possibly can," Lori said, kneeling and putting her arm around Fujiko's shoulders.

"Thank you." The Asian woman wiped her tears away.

Lori noticed the four toddlers looking at her simultaneously, eight eyes gazing in unison, as if from a single entity. Momentarily, she focused on each of the little people. Their eyes were filled with wisdom, experience, and compassion, but tinged with an eternal sadness. They were not the eyes of children, and hardly the faces of children, either, when she studied them closely . . . just small in size. She felt as if she knew them, as if she understood why they didn't play enthusiastically with Fujiko. They had more important things on their minds. But she only sensed this, without specifics.

And the specifics were driving her crazy. Lori felt as if she had the weight of the world lowering on her moment by moment, that she was taking on more and more responsibility with each passing second. She saw this in the way the children looked at her, with deference, respect, and even love. They were becoming dependent on her.

Slowly, as if in a dream, Lori felt herself pulling away from Fujiko and seeming to float closer to the children, but knew she couldn't really be moving in that manner. She must be walking toward them. Within moments, she knelt with them, and they gathered around her. One of the children—Veronica—turned down the tunecube, then shut it off and handed it to Lori.

"*Olto Karida*, " Veronica said to Lori, with a wise little smile. "*Olto Karida.*"

Viscerally, Lori knew what the words meant, and they comforted her. But intellectually she could not make the connection and translate into English.

Off to one side, she saw the bespectacled redhead, Michelle Renee. "What did she say to you?" the translator asked. "That wasn't ancient Aramaic."

"I don't know," Lori said. And this was the truth.

* * *

The tall, black-haired man stood calmly in the doorway, while Styx considered the irritating personality of this functionary. It was shortly after 5:00 AM in Bureau headquarters, and the staff had been up all night. A bleary eyed Kylee Branson, the Vice Minister of Doctrine & Faith, had just delivered a monotone report on the status of the search for the four missing UWW aircraft: No new information.

It wasn't that Branson couldn't perform his job; on the contrary, he was quite good at it, and fiercely loyal to the privately funded bureaucracy. But he had a condescending manner about him, a way of making Styx feel inferior to him, no matter their respective ranks. Of course Branson behaved that way out of custom and breeding, but at times he seemed to play up his business and familial connections, oblivious to the potential danger this placed him in. The Acting Minister, while he couldn't fire this entrenched employee easily, had other, even more decisive, ways of dealing with people.

As far as Styx was concerned, Branson's unquestioned loyalty to the Bureau was his only redeeming feature. Styx appreciated this, no matter the different paths the two men had taken to get here. It annoyed him, though, that Branson was loyal to the Bureau first and only secondarily to Styx Tertullian.

Styx lifted his coffee cup and took a long sip. He'd been pouring it non-stop all night. He reminded himself (as he had several times before) that the relationship the two of them had was an imperfect one in an imperfect world. So be it. He would work with what he had. Worse men could be in Branson's position.

"This is the point where I should yell at someone for not finding the aircraft," Styx said, with more resignation in his voice than dissatisfaction. "As our Vice Minister of Doctrine & Faith, some of the failure would seem to fall on your shoulders, wouldn't you agree? I mean, dealing with the UWW is a religious matter, isn't it?"

Branson scrunched his brow, and in the haughtiness of his expression it appeared to Styx that he accepted no blame whatsoever. He had, after all, passed on to Styx what he called "the concerns of other Bureau officers" prior to the attack on Monte Konos, and while the man had professed to support the attack, he had done so only grudgingly. Branson was undoubtedly thinking now that Styx had made the military decision on his own, and any failure stemming from such a risky, foolhardy expedition was the responsibility of him alone.

"Well, answer my question!"

"Uh, Minister Culpepper assigned it to Minority Affairs, and uh–"

"I was Vice Minister of Minority Affairs at the time. Do you mean to say that I was responsible for the failure?"

"No, sir."

"In any event, Culpepper isn't around anymore, so whatever I say goes. And I want Doctrine & Faith to handle the UWW from now on. Is that understood?"

"Yes, sir." Some of the haughtiness was melting, from the application of heat.

"Do you think anyone important escaped?" Styx asked. He looked sidelong at a newly placed photograph on the wall, showing the destruction of Monte Konos in full color, with the top of the mountain afire like a volcano. It was a spectacular scene.

"Hard to say," Branson responded. "Hopefully, it was just some low-level people who took the aircraft in the heat of battle, saving their own skins."

"That might have happened, and in such an eventuality we'd have little to worry about, wouldn't you agree? Guards–or other "low-levels" as you say–would probably ditch the aircraft at the first opportunity and be happy to escape with their lives."

"That would seem likely."

"Such people would not be likely to reorganize the UWW, would they?"

"No."

"So, do you think the UWW is dead, a flopping, useless body without a head?"

"One would hope so."

"But what do you *think*?"

"There aren't enough facts at this point, sir. I can't make an intelligent call."

"But what do you feel in your guts? What instincts do you have?"

"I only operate on facts, sir."

"And that's why you'll never sit in my chair, Kylee."

Branson looked shocked. He straightened himself. "Will that be all, sir?"

"That's all." His tone became saccharine. "Now, if it isn't too much trouble, Kylee, I'd appreciate it if you would get the—" He bit his lower lip to keep from swearing. "Just get out of my sight, OK?"

Chapter 7

You are our shelter, and we are yours.
　　　　　　　　　—From the Gospel of Veronica

"What's that noise?" Dixie Lou asked, as they stepped out of the tent. "Sounds like an engine."

"Seems to be coming from over there," Tamara Himmel said, pointing across the roofs and black tent tops of the village.

"Just one of our generators," Malia said, lying, "at the caretaker's residence, by Prophet's Rock."

"Sounds bigger than that," Dixie Lou said. "An airplane, maybe, or a helicopter?" She looked at the cerulean blue sky, saw nothing but thin, drifting clouds.

"No, it's just our fancy new generator. I told you, we have the latest technology around here. Come, I will show you our advanced computer center."

As Dixie Lou and her companions followed Malia past dusty tents and simple structures, worries floated through the Chairwoman's mind, as they often did. She wondered if this was just a delaying trick, while Arab men—BOI agents?—were taking over her own camp at that very moment, murdering Alex, the she-apostles, and everyone there. She also worried about the whereabouts and fate of Lori Vale.

Dixie Lou heaved a deep sigh. The child of Lori . . . would it really be the missing twelfth she-apostle? She hated this situation, which was so much out of her control. Her thoughts shifted to another priority. Too many of them.

The Holy Women's Bible.

Malia led the way into the most substantial structure in the town, a one-story, modular building that was at least twice as big as the tent in which they had all dined. They went through one doorway and then another, with doors closing behind them as they entered. Dixie Lou heard fans whirring, and the drone of a generator as it kicked on.

They entered a central room, and for a moment Dixie Lou caught her breath. Banks of computers and related equipment lined the walls and the center of the room. Arab women and young men busied themselves operating the machines.

"And now," Malia said, as she paused at one of the terminals, "if you would hand me the microcylinder, I would be most happy to transmit it, as you specify."

"I prefer to do it myself," Dixie Lou said, trying not to reveal too much concern or emotion.

"As you wish. I will prepare the machine."

As Malia got the computer going, Nancy Winters leaned close to Dixie Lou and whispered, "I don't think we should do this. Not enough security."

The stocky black woman shook her head. Moving away from the Arabs for privacy, she said, "Our options are limited. We need to make every effort to publish the *Holy Women's Bible*, improving our odds. Any delay is dangerous, and foolhardy."

"This course of action is foolhardy," Winters said.

"You dare speak to me that way?"

"These are trying times."

With fervor, Dixie Lou responded, her voice an angry whisper. "Remember the way it was for the she-apostles in ancient times. Their gospels had to be concealed from those who would destroy them, but the precious written words were found and destroyed anyway, except for the copies that were hidden by brave women. It's like that now. We're hiding copies of the sacred gospels until they can be widely disseminated, and our copies are in danger of discovery and destruction. Women have been given a second chance now, and there might not be another."

"But the transmission could be intercepted, cut off without our knowledge. We might be attacked. BOI forces are everywhere, maybe only minutes away." She paused, looked around. "Maybe in this very room."

At the moment, Dixie Lou didn't like her options. But she had to take any opportunity to transmit, no matter the risk. If the new holy book succeeded, she would ride the wave of popularity with it; but if the reverse happened, if it was ridiculed and debunked, she would go down with it.

Glaring sidelong at the councilwoman, Dixie Lou said, "Amy would agree with me, and you know it."

The slender woman bristled, and her large eyes opened wide. "I don't know that at all! If we risk an unsafe transmission, the she-apostles could be killed! Think about *that*, Madame Chairwoman!"

Taking notice of the argument, Malia stared at them, a quizzical expression on her face. She was beyond earshot. Her computer beeped, and she looked back at it.

Dixie Lou whispered, "Don't argue with me about this, Nancy. We publish the book *now*, and that's it!"

Dixie Lou's fingers tightened around the microcylinder. The *Holy Women's Bible*—flawed though it was by the fake Gospel of Martha— could solve one of the outstanding problems. Perhaps its publication would draw the missing she-apostle out.

But that could have potentially dangerous ramifications, she realized. Uncertainty threatened to paralyze her. For some time now the Chairwoman had tried to envision the various scenarios in detail, and had realized that certain decisions she made were not entirely logical. Instead, they were based upon visceral feelings, or upon some internal driving force . . . neither of which could be explained to the logical side of her brain . . . or to any other person.

Her decision to falsify one of the gospels and rush publication might still be reversed. Even if Malia's computer could connect to the Internet,

Dixie Lou didn't have to transmit. She could suppress what she had, and perhaps correct the text of the holy book later if the authentic last she-apostle ever showed up.

She wondered if the troublesome Katherine Pangalos might have been right after all . . . her assertion that the falsified Gospel of Martha could bring the entire *Holy Women's Bible* into question. One lie, as all good interrogators knew, suggested a string of them. Should Dixie Lou edit the material before transmitting it, making changes to the introduction and deleting every reference to Martha? Go with eleven gospels, not twelve? But something—the visceral feeling or an internal driving force—told her *not* to do this, that she should transmit as is, *if she could*. Too many things might go wrong if she delayed. The material might be discovered by enemies of the UWW and destroyed.

"It's ready," Malia announced, a few seconds after the computer beeped loudly. "We're online." She sat cross-legged on a carpet, with the computer and modem in front of her. The screen was amber, and had a pulsing, bright red section in the upper right hand corner.

Over-anxious, Dixie Lou hurried over to her. Through bleary eyes she looked down at the computer, and only peripherally saw Malia move aside.

The Chairwoman sat down, inserted the microcylinder. The machine clicked and whirred as the dataload locked into place.

"Do you know how to operate this model?" Malia inquired.

Dixie Lou nodded, and asked for privacy. The woman stepped away.

Dixie Lou studied the screen, noted that Malia had made an Internet connection with her own codes. Activating a box to enter the word processing program, Dixie Lou brought up the *Holy Women's Bible* microcylinder and downloaded it. Then, with trembling hands, she used her own codes to activate a deep-access keyboard. She typed in the UWW broadcast codes, then touched the transmitting button at the top of the screen. As the information was transmitted, sand dropped through an hourglass on the screen. In a few seconds, when this was complete, she repeated the procedure, just to play it safe.

It all seemed to be going through, but Dixie Lou had her concerns. Was this a real satellite connection, or was Malia tricking her? Dixie Lou couldn't see any reason for such a ruse, since Malia might have killed her and taken the microcylinder—or destroyed it—if she'd had a mind to do so. Besides, Dixie Lou had been able to use her deep-access keyboard, linking to the UWW's own Internet system. Even so, she didn't trust anyone, and certainly not a stranger . . . especially not one from a different culture and religion. She erased the path she'd taken, to prevent anyone from retracing her steps—or at least to make it more difficult.

But on impulse, before deleting the downloaded *Holy Women's Bible* from Malia's computer, Dixie Lou did a quick scan of the contents, checking again to see if the formatting looked all right. On the very last page, right after the final words of the new UWW publication, she noticed a row of tiny hieroglyphics.

Calling Malia over, Dixie Lou asked about them.

"Oh, just a minor flaw in my computer," Malia said, kneeling down and pointing at the strange symbols. "It's difficult to get repair personnel out here. Nothing to worry about, though. I see that your files have been transmitted." She pointed to a bar on the top of the screen, "See, it says 'message sent.'"

Scowling, Dixie Lou deleted her file quickly, before the woman could read much of the ending of the holy book. As the UWW leader did this, Malia said nothing.

An irony occurred to Dixie Lou. If this was an authentic Internet hookup, dependent upon satellites, she was turning the tables on the Bureau—because the BOI had used satellites to spy on the UWW, and attack them. With the e-book publication of the *Holy Women's Bible*—and she hoped it was successful!—the UWW was placing the Bureau's anti-female religious beliefs into question, one of the most sacred foundations of their male-oriented organization.

And she thought of another irony. Under any interpretation, the new bible was a Christian book, but Islamic women were helping to disseminate it at a critical time. They might not be happy to learn that.

Asking for privacy again, Dixie Lou entered a complex series of codes to contact the UWW military base in Tunisia, where she wanted to set up her new headquarters. In view of the aggressiveness of the BOI, she needed to make certain that there were no problems in her path. She double-checked the codes, then wrote and transmitted a brief e-mail letter, including copies to other UWW military bases. Again, she saw the "message sent" confirmation.

Under the protocol she had established, she was supposed to receive an immediate response from Tunisia—but that did not come, not in the two minutes she waited. And, looking at her e-mail again, she saw the odd hieroglyphics there, too, at the end of her message. She hoped Malia was right and truthful, that this was just a minor glitch.

Most troubling was the lack of an immediate response from Tunisia, but she tried to convince herself that it was nothing, that someone had just stepped away from their terminal at the wrong time. She shut down the system, retrieved her microcylinder and slipped it into her pocket.

"Don't worry," Malia said, as Dixie Lou rose to her feet. "I see that you are concerned, so the messages you transmitted must be very important. I'm confident that they have gone through perfectly!"

"Yes, I'm sure you're right," Dixie Lou said. Bowing slightly, she said, "Thank you for your gracious hospitality, and for your assistance."

As Dixie Lou returned to her encampment, she considered the momentous occasion in which she was involved. If the e-book transmission went through, it meant that the most startling publication in history had just been dumped on the worldwide web, for instant access everywhere.

Chapter 8

Any person can be compelled to do anything.
> —Dixie Lou Jackson, private comment

That evening, Dixie Lou continued her intense questioning of the she-apostles, a session that had been interrupted by the arrival of the Arab women. She wished she could only do this without witnesses, but she needed translators, and needed help to handle seven rebellious children, to keep them under control while she administered punishment. It was one of the responsibilities of leadership, something she had to do.

The she-apostles stood or sat on the sand, while Dixie Lou strutted back and forth in front of them, studying each defiant little face. Behind the children, translators, matrons, and councilwomen held the babies and kept the toddlers standing in place, no matter how much the children fussed and objected, though none of them cried. Dixie Lou found this interesting, the way they were not acting so much like tiny children right now. Maybe it had something to do with the harrowing escape from Monte Konos, and the challenges of battle and survival had matured them. Off to one side, she saw her son Alex watching her, his face reflecting his now-familiar attitude of disapproval.

Coming to a stop, Dixie Lou knelt in front of the flaxen-haired she-apostle, Candace. The two-year old squinted at her in the bright light, and tried unsuccessfully to free herself from the translator who held her hand tightly.

"You know what I want, don't you?" the Chairwoman asked. In the moments before the translator repeated her words in ancient Aramaic, Dixie Lou thought she saw a flicker of understanding in Candace's eyes, suggesting that she was faking, that she and her tricky little companions understood English.

Dixie Lou wondered, as she had since landing here, if their supposedly authentic gospels were reflective of true events at the time of Jesus Christ, or if these strange children had made everything up . . . or concealed information of tremendous importance. It was the second time she had questioned them on this matter, and this time she would get what she wanted out of them.

Candace stopped struggling, and stared back at her peevishly.

"All of you are concealing important things from me, information I need to know. I demand to know what it is."

Dixie Lou glanced around, at the matrons, translators, and councilwomen. That morning, she had asked each of them if they saw what Candace did, vanishing when a bullet was headed toward her, and then reappearing a moment later. None of them admitted seeing it, but Dixie Lou remained convinced that it *had* happened. The solution to that particular puzzle was a critical part of the enigma of the she-apostles.

The children, even the tiniest, just stared at her blankly, emotionlessly. Obviously, they didn't care one whit about Dixie Lou Jackson or what troubled her. The Chairwoman had a bleak, dismal feeling. She didn't want to push the issue, didn't want to interrogate these special children or even know what more they had to say. But she had to know it nonetheless, in order to do her job, and in order to survive.

In only a short period of time, since leaving Monte Konos, it was becoming a compulsion with her.

Taking a deep breath, because the biggest question filled her with fear, Dixie Lou said, "Tell me about the twelfth she-apostle." Why should such a question terrify her so? Nonetheless, it did, inexplicably. She had to know why.

None of the children spoke. She found their expressions irritating, condescending.

"I'll keep you awake all night if necessary," Dixie Lou snapped, "as long as it takes. No sleep, no food, no water. We'll see how long you last out here in the desert." Again, her words were translated, but Dixie Lou thought she heard a tone of disapproval in the woman's voice, a thin brunette with pageboy hair.

"Are you translating me word for word?" Dixie Lou asked her.

"Of course, Chairwoman."

"Well, I hear something in your tone that I don't like."

"I'm sorry, I didn't mean to do that."

"These little ones are smart. They pick up vocal inflections, facial expressions, even hand movements. If you show any objection to what I'm saying, it makes them more difficult for all of us to handle. Do you understand that?"

"Yes, ma'am. I didn't mean to—I'm sorry if I sounded that way."

Raising her voice so that all of the handlers could hear her clearly, Dixie Lou said, "Don't think for one moment that these are only children. They're little demons, more advanced than any of you can imagine. They deserve whatever I do to them, and more."

"*Demons*, ma'am?" Deborah Marvel said. "But they recited holy gospels."

"Call them tricksters instead of demons, if you wish," Dixie Lou said. "It was only a figure of speech."

Privately, though, the more Dixie Lou saw of these children, the more she was beginning to doubt their gospels, feeling that the children were lying for some reason. Her personal doubts were not anything she wanted to admit to anyone, or she would have to kill them afterward. The gospels of these children, and of the four who had gone with Lori, had taken on a life of their own. They had become the bedrock supporting the future of United Women of the World.

"I'll deal with this one," Dixie Lou said. Putting her face only inches from the Candace's, she raised her voice. "Are you going to answer me?"

Her words were translated.

Candace remained immobile, said nothing.

On impulse, Dixie Lou swung an open hand, intending to slap the child very hard for disobedience.

Though she had been able to slap two other children earlier, this time her hand seemed to go into slow motion. The child, and all the she-apostles with her, vanished. Dixie Lou's hand struck nothing, and as she went around in slow motion it threw her off balance, causing her to tumble onto the sand.

A moment later, the she-apostles reappeared, and time sped up again.

"Did you see that?" Dixie Lou asked, sitting up and looking at Deborah Marvel.

"Don't try to hit these children again," Deborah said, angrily.

"Are you threatening me?"

"Just don't do it. I'm glad you missed. It's wrong to strike them, no matter how uncooperative they seem to be."

"*Missed?* They vanished into thin air, then reappeared!"

"What do you mean?" Deborah asked.

"You didn't see it?"

"They didn't vanish. They've been here all the time."

"Did anyone see what I saw?" Dixie Lou demanded, looking at the women, settling for a moment on each face.

They all shook their heads, muttered in low tones. Dixie Lou could not understand why they didn't see it, when she had, quite clearly. It was like the incident with the bullets. That time, only she and Lori seemed to have seen it, as if they had special eyes that could peer into an alternate realm.

The Chairwoman shuddered.

"Remember, these are unusual children," Deborah said. "Maybe they don't understand what you want to know."

"My words were translated."

"The children may still have trouble understanding." Deborah paused, and added, with emphasis, "They *are* only children."

After glaring daggers at the suddenly argumentative councilwoman, Dixie Lou took a deep, fitful breath and looked up at the heavens, with only a few stars visible because of a haze in the sky caused by the crescent moon being concealed behind clouds. The children *had* disappeared, an event that apparently took only a fraction of a second.

I saw it, and I will not forget!

For the moment, Dixie Lou backed off. But she intended to resume interrogations the following morning inside her command helicopter, conducting a one-on-one, intensive session with each child.

But she was not destined to get the opportunity. In a matter of hours, all seven of the authentic she-apostles would be gone . . . this time for good. Only the counterfeit Martha would remain behind.

Chapter 9

The She-God is not a fully developed ethereal power. She is presumed to be benevolent, but there are elements of cruelty and vengeance in her holy soul. The She-God carries within her the simmering power of all women who have been wronged throughout history, who have been raped, murdered, enslaved, and otherwise downtrodden. She is, indeed, a vast repository of angry souls, all seeking redress. The She-God is forming; the She-God is coming. And when this most powerful of all female entities is manifest, all humankind will tremble before her.

–Notes of Amy Angkor-Billings, 7th Chairwoman,
United Women of the World

That evening Lori Vale found herself unable to sleep, and lay awake in the darkness. She had considered a number of alternatives for her sleeping arrangements, and had finally settled on this one, waiting until the others were asleep and then sneaking out of the helicopter cockpit, locking it behind her.

The supply tent at one side of the camouflaged encampment seemed preferable, where she lay now on the fabric floor, with a window flap open to allow in a fresh night breeze. The sand beneath the tent was comfortable, better than the air mattress in the helicopter. She kept a gun handy, just in case.

In a very short period of time, Lori had exerted control over a small group of women and children who had escaped with her from Monte Konos. The she-apostles were in the care of the two matrons, the translator, and Fujiko Harui, and Lori was giving the adults orders that they followed without argument, orders that involved the physical well-being of the children.

As she had noticed before, the little people didn't really seem like children to her, and she didn't know how much control she actually exerted over them. They were more like adults—very *old* and independent adults—in young bodies. As Lori made such observations, it seemed to her that any modicum of control she exerted over the children was only physical . . . but the she-apostles were *not* primarily physical beings. Since they truly were reincarnated, by definition this meant that they moved from one physical form to another, that they inhabited another, more spiritual realm.

As these thoughts kept her awake, Lori wondered if her parochial mental processes could really comprehend such astounding concepts, if she had the intelligence, experience, and other requisite abilities to grasp the subject. She also asked herself if her own mind was in the physical or spiritual realm . . . or if it could possibly occupy both simultaneously.

Sometimes the she-apostles reminded her of little angels, and thinking of their cherubic faces now, she smiled into the darkness beneath the eaves of the tent.

Through the open window flap she saw glittering stars encrusting a black canopy of sky over the desert. Though it had been hazy only a short while earlier, she now found it amazing how many distant suns were visible, and felt reassured by their presence. They were more than balls of flaming energy and light; somehow they imparted spiritual strength to her, a sense that they were watching over her, protecting her.

At long last she dozed off, and when she awoke only one bright star remained visible. The celestial light was brilliant and large and quickly grew . . . and seemed to draw closer. She thought it was accelerating toward her.

Inside a nearby tent, someone slept soundly, making buzz-saw noises. But she hardly noticed it. Like a fawn caught in a blinding spotlight, Lori Vale was transfixed by the light.

Abruptly she became aware of an Otherness, a black halo around the brightening illumination. A stygian companion traveling at the same speed as the light. It chilled her blood.

The dark halo grew larger and swallowed the light in front of it. An inky black sphere now, it drew close to Lori and she felt magnetized by it, pulled toward a great, yawning abyss, like a black hole. She screamed and almost tumbled in helplessly, when suddenly the light returned, from where she could not determine, and the blackness faded, faded, faded . . . until it could no longer be seen.

Now the light became brighter, a miniature sun, but somehow it did not burn her eyes.

"My Lord?" she whispered, without knowing why.

"*Hama oro ibil*," a soothing female voice said . . . and she understood it: *Do not be afraid.*

Then a powerful epiphany struck Lori, and in that instant she realized that the words were in the secret tongue of the she-apostles of Jesus Christ, and that it was one of the lost languages of earth.

A chill ran down her spine.

Floating off to one side, in a golden glow, Lori saw the childish, angelic countenance of Mary Magdalene, with her lips moving as she uttered the arcane words. "*Ilya dusil jerxi aba enge, naba ilya.*" . . . *You draw strength from us, and we from you.*

Illumination streamed through the window into the tent, bathing Lori Vale in warmth, and for an instant she was transported to an ethereal realm of light in all forms and textures, so that she gasped from the astonishing beauty of it. Then, before she was ready, she felt herself transported back—in the blink of an eye—to the shadowy temporal tent where she dangled between consciousness and dreams.

A distant light receded in the sky, became a star, and finally disappeared entirely. The heavens became completely dark, as if all the solar lamps in God's empyrean universe had been switched off.

Within the teenager's slumbering, barely conscious mind, she floated on a limitless, sparkling sea, on a tiny cosmic life raft. She became convinced that she had been saved from something terrible.

From the black sphere.

What had it been, and what had rescued her from it?

As moments passed, Lori decided she had only been dreaming, but this thought tumbled away over a precipice, and she lost it.

"My Lord," she whispered in her sleep. And the same in the ancient, secret language of the she-apostles. "*Jelana Ve . . .* "

* * *

It seemed more like a night for witches than for angels. Through her open window flap, Lori saw bloodlike streaks on the crescent moon, and icy clouds drifting across it, borne on a high wind over the Mediterranean.

An hour ago, as she emerged from the strange dream, she had called out the name of the Lord. In two languages—or so it seemed to her at the time. But a secret language of the apostles? Where did she get such information? Directly from God?

With her mind fatigued and overburdened, she wanted to put on the brakes, and tried to convince herself that her thoughts were no more than the products of a wild teenage imagination, perhaps the residue of past drug abuses. She began to play devil's advocate with herself. Dreams could be deceptive, imparting authenticity to bizarre scenarios. She might only be imagining that the apostles had their own secret language. A dream was only a dream. It didn't merge into the real world, no matter how lifelike it seemed.

But what was "real," and what was not? Did a teenager even have the capacity to decide on this important question, based upon the filter of her limited personal experience? The world . . . and the universe . . . were much larger than her infinitesimally small brain.

She wondered if she might solve the conundrum from different angles. Just as she was considering this, Lori heard something outside her tent. Like the wind, or the rustling of fabric.

Poking her head out through the door flap, she saw people standing some distance away, their stocky, robed shapes profiled against the starlit sky and crescent moon. The people were not moving.

Lori squinted, counted eleven of them, and then they all moved, in unison. She caught her breath. They were coming toward her, walking in a herky jerk fashion, large heads bobbing.

For a moment, she lost perspective and felt dizzy, until she realized that they were all very small, and they were right in front of her, not nearly as far away as she had thought.

The she-apostles? But she only had four in her camp, not eleven. Arab children, then?

Whoever they were, they tossed the hoods of their robes back, revealing their youthful faces in the moonlight. She recognized them all as she-apostle toddlers and babies. Anxiously, she counted them again, and noted that Martha of Galilee was not among them. Lori recalled that one of the she-apostles—Lydia—had said this Martha was a fake, and that the real twelfth she-apostle remained missing.

Eleven.

Another trick of the mind? A dream? Curiously, even the babies, some of them less than six months old were walking. How could that be possible, and how had seven small children walked so far from Dixie Lou's camp?

"I don't understand. I—" Lori's words faltered. There had only been four in her helicopter. How had the rest of them gotten here?

A small voice said something, from the group. *"Olto Karida. "*

Lori identified the speaker. Veronica, saying the same thing she had said the day before, when Lori sat in a circle with Fujiko and four of the children. This time, though, Lori knew what it meant: *Beloved Mother.*

But I'm not her mother. What does Veronica mean by that?

She looked from face to face, identified each of the silent visitors. Only Martha was missing.

"Olto Karida," the children said, in unison. *Beloved mother.* They moved close to her, clutching her robe and her hands.

* * *

Seated on a fiber mat with a computer on his lap, Rashid Ali Khan perused the web as he did early each morning. Dressed in a white desert cloak of with a turban, he was outside his dirty beige canvas tent, in front of the doorway. The sun had not risen yet, but to the east, on the Mediterranean horizon, the sky began to brighten. Soon he would kneel here to pray. He considered himself a good Muslim, and performed the traditional prayers five times a day, from dawn to sunset. Nestled in the sand beside him was a metal laving bowl, with ablution water in it.

His missing leg ached from the coolness of the air, as it often did, and he reached around the computer to scratch the nub of the stump, just below the knee. As a boy in the Sinai he'd lost the limb, after stepping on a long-forgotten land mine. For years he'd cursed his fate, but after the blessing of his marriage to Malia and the two sons produced by their union, he'd felt differently—more gratitude than misery. Unhappiness was a relative state, he'd come to realize, and a matter of perspective. Any person could lament his lot, but Rashid never liked that course, didn't like the way it made him feel. He much preferred to be upbeat, even when the ferocious winds of life blew proverbial sand into his eyes and stung his skin.

The image of Malia came to mind, and he felt a longing in his heart and in his loins for her. He didn't like to split his caravan as it was now, leaving the women, children, and old people behind. But the demands of business had required that he and the other men travel light and fast, so that they could deliver their goods—clothing and household products—to a wealthy merchant in time for the opening of a large store. Rashid traded in a wide variety of merchandise and kept it all organized with a computerized inventory and order system. That's what he usually took care of each morning, sending e-mails on business matters.

He sneezed loudly, the force causing his stuffy head to throb. For more than a day he'd been feeling nasal congestion, perhaps a strain of flu that had been going around the caravan.

The others weren't awake yet, and no one even seemed disturbed by the sound he'd made. He heard the fitful snoring of his brother Meshdi, coming from a nearby tent. The rumbling stopped, and in the ensuing silence Rashid thought of how much he loved the serenity of the desert.

This morning, in the dry, still air not an animal, bird, or insect stirred. He took a deep breath, and his fingers danced over the keyboard. He preferred this somewhat antiquated method of using a computer, instead of voice activation, mental links, or other high-tech methods. He was an active person, liked to move around. For him, the life of a Bedouin was ingrained in his soul. He could not stand the thought of being sedentary.

The tapping of the keys grew louder and faster, and he brought up the Global News Network website, highlighting events of the day. No matter how far he was from the busy centers of world commerce, he liked to stay in touch with what was going on; he prided himself on his knowledge of current events. Each day he checked the news before taking care of business.

What's this? he thought, as he scrolled through the articles.

Half of the current stories were about a new publication, The *Holy Women's Bible*. It had been released the day before, authored by the United Women of the World . . . a pig-swill story about the reincarnated female apostles of Jesus.

He laughed. Just another Christian fringe organization. There were so many of them. Though there were some sensible Christians in the mainstream—he'd done business with a number of them—the large number of "born-againers" and other radicals on the right wing were incapable of carrying on a rational conversation without quoting scripture, and distorting it to serve their own purposes. He was thankful that the vast majority of Muslims were not like that. Truly, Allah had blessed his people with infinite wisdom!

He tapped the keys again, closed and opened computer windows to return to his personal mailbox. His in-box contained no new e-mail. Most peculiar. His number-one wife Malia usually transmitted a message to him every day. He scratched his bald pate, under the carefully wrapped turban, and was about to send a note to her when he noticed a tangerine orange sun half-visible on the eastern horizon. Averting his eyes from the orb's brilliance, he shut down his computer, and with water from the laving bowl he ritualistically washed his hands, arms, feet, head, and face. Then, with his head covered, he rolled out his fiber mat and knelt in prayer, with his body turned toward the holy city of Mecca in Saudi Arabia.

Outside each tent the others were up now, bearded men in burnooses and turbans, kneeling on their prayer mats.

"*Allahu akbar*," Rashid intoned, with the others. *God is greatest.* He went on to murmur a prayer from the sacred *Qur'an*: "Praise be to God, the Lord of the worlds! The compassionate, the merciful! King of the day of judgment!—"

When the holy words were complete, the pious men put away their prayer mats and laving bowls. They were only a few kilometers from the desert town of Awen, where their goods would be delivered. It would be a busy day, and Rashid was not feeling that well. He would write to Malia tomorrow, or perhaps the next day.

* * *

Dixie Lou Jackson, a black female who grew up in poverty and became a prostitute and a murderess, could become the most important woman in the world, if the *Holy Women's Bible* was successfully received around the world. Though she'd seen a "message sent" confirmation that the entire book had been transmitted over the Internet, she still worried. Had her incredibly important publication actually gone through?

Another serious problem. After transmitting the holy book, she had sent an emergency e-mail message to the UWW base in Tunisia, where she intended to set up a new headquarters. Under the protocol she had established, there should have been an immediate response, but there had been none. This gave her an uneasy feeling, a sense of being alone. What if the Bureau had gotten to that base and destroyed it? Or, what if they had laid a trap there, and were waiting to spring it on her when she arrived?

Odd hieroglyphics had appeared on the last page of the *Holy Women's Bible* computer file, and on her e-mail message to Tunisia. The purported glitch with Malia's computer, but what if it was something else?

And she had other big concerns. Since leaving Monte Konos, the seven she-apostles still in her custody were behaving more and more strangely. They didn't seem interested in playing with toys, didn't even seem to care when their favorite foods were withheld from them. Even though the gospels of these seven were purportedly complete, Dixie Lou had been using the translators to try to get the children to talk more about ancient times, to reveal information she was sure they were withholding. It was something the Chairwoman had been sensing in recent days, that they knew something very important, even essential, but were keeping it to themselves.

Considering how to deal with them, she sat alone in her tent. Through a mesh window she saw the sun rising over Libya's northern desert, splashing the sky with tints of red, orange and gold. Sunrises and sunsets never ceased to delight her, filled as they were with subtle colors that changed from moment to moment.

This was a Muslim country, and as a black woman Dixie Lou knew something of the faith from childhood friends and members of her family, who had converted to it. She knew Islam had a code of honor and high moral standards, but it was one of the male-dominated religions that would require the most attention from United Women of the World, in order to improve the position of women. In the Muslim faith women did not lead; typically they wore veils and followed the commands of their husbands, fathers, and brothers. Under such circumstances the radical male government of Libya would not be pleased to learn of the existence of a rebel contingent of women on their soil.

For a lot of reasons, she hoped no one would think to look for her here.

Hearing a noise behind her, she turned.

Deborah Marvel poked her blonde head in through the open flap of the doorway. "Some of the councilwomen are troubled that only your political opponents were left behind on Monte Konos, presumably to die there."

"Who's asking?" Dixie Lou snapped.

"Sorry, I should have said *all* of them are asking."

"Including you?"

She shook her head. "I've always been your friend, Dixie Lou. I'm only relaying the message."

"Tell them it was a coincidence. Katherine must have been meeting with her friends when the BOI struck us, and they just got unlucky."

"I'm sure you're right." Deborah said. She bowed and left.

As far as she knew, the council had ten members now instead of sixteen (assuming Wendy Zepeda and Fujiko Harui were still alive), and all would vote as Dixie Lou wished. Anyone who didn't would be eliminated.

Chapter 10

My hosannas have been forged in a crucible of doubt.
 —Fyodor Mikhailovich Dostoyevsky

The air pad on which Alex lay was uncomfortable, and he had not slept well. Awake for only a few moments, he heard the low voices of women as the encampment began to awaken.

He sat up, and through a mesh window he saw a large black bird fly by, flapping its wings laboriously. Fatigue saturated his bones and muscles, and the side of his neck ached where his mother had hit him with the gun barrel. How he loathed that woman!

He heard the ever-present guards talking outside his tent, saying Dixie Lou Jackson had published the *Holy Women's Bible* on the Internet two days ago.

He poked his head out, saw Deborah Marvel jog into camp and head for her own tent. Deborah always tried to stay in shape. She seemed like an interesting woman to Alex, and quite unlike his own mother. Still, she was supportive of Dixie Lou on the council, to the point where his mother considered her a close friend. Alex wondered about Deborah's motives, though, and suspected she was doing it for her own career advancement. Or survival.

Seeing two rosy faced guards by his tent, he asked, "It's published? The new gospels of the she-apostles? I didn't know the book was ready."

"Neither did we," the shorter of the pair, a redhead, said.

"Your mother is up early this morning and in a good mood," the other said, a tall brunette who had been flirtatious to Alex. "She received confirmation of the transmission, and feedback from people who've seen the e-book version on the worldwide web—a lot more positive response than she ever expected."

Alex smiled, but with a hard edge to it. His eyes narrowed to slits. "My mother is in a good mood, actually cheerful? I don't know if I can get used to that."

"It does sound unusual," the redheaded guard said.

"I'll tell you this," Alex said. "Even when she's in a good mood, she's dangerous. I once saw her shoot a guard in the back of the head. Had a uniform on just like yours."

"Don't kid with us," the taller guard said, grinning. She stared at him with large blue eyes.

But the other guard wasn't smiling. She backed up, nudged her companion. They went a distance away, spoke in low tones while looking over at Alex.

He didn't care what they were saying, wasn't afraid of his mother.

Suddenly a big commotion broke loose in the camp, as matrons and translators ran around, screaming that the she-apostles were gone—all except for Martha of Galilee.

At first, Alex worried about the children. Then he smiled to himself, and thought, *Lori must have saved them. I don't know how, but she saved them!*

The guards and other women searched carefully, scouring the camp and aircraft, running out into the desert and looking for tracks. They found no sign of them, and this pleased Alex immensely. It only left one child in the custody of his demented mother.

* * *

"This wasn't supposed to happen," Acting Minister Tertullian said as he stared through wire-rimmed eyeglasses at a computer screen. His hair was uncombed. A dark stubble of beard covered his narrow face. Beside him stood Vice Minister Kylee Branson. They were in the reception area outside Tertullian's office, where Branson had been summoned in the middle of the night.

Tertullian had briefly scanned the contents before Branson's arrival. Now the Acting Minister made a voice command, and the dedication page of the *Holy Women's Bible* appeared, a tribute to Amy Angkor-Billings, whom he had personally dispatched to the realms of hell. Below that were the words, "The ancients speak." His heart was racing.

The ensuing pages were an introduction, and as Tertullian read them he felt his face heat up. *Gospels of the reincarnated she-apostles of Jesus? Blasphemy! The She-God?* He recalled the single sheet of paper he'd seen, a purported "gospel" of the Apostle Mary Magdalene. Using a search command he found it again:

> Glory be to She-God Almighty, Creator and Destroyer.
>
> Her power shall last forever.

Turning to another heretical "gospel," he placed a fingertip against a touch-box on the screen. A baby appeared, dressed in a tiny black robe, with a golden sword-cross dangling from her neck—the reviled symbol of the UWW. A caption identified the child as a "she-apostle," and she spoke gibberish that was supposedly ancient Aramaic. A translator explained her words:

> Jesus said to the women who were his close companions,
>
> "Go now and spread the holy word. Tell women everywhere
>
> they are no longer to be treated as inferior, that they are equal
>
> to men in all respects and shall lead great nations."

Tertullian felt like smashing the computer screen. Slowly his gaze turned to meet the fearful eyes of Branson.

"This is all your fault, you know," Tertullian said. "As Vice Minister of Doctrine & Faith, you should have been on top of this situation. You should have prevented the release of this book!"

"I uh—I don't think that's fair to—" Branson's voice cracked, and in the face of criticism he couldn't form a sentence.

Hot blood pumped through Tertullian's veins. Angry sweat poured down his brow, stinging his eyes and fogging his wire-rimmed glasses.

Blinking, he wiped the glasses, then fumbled with the computer, searching pages for publication information, for the location from which they had transmitted this. Nothing was obvious; the devious UWW women were still in hiding, making trouble from one of their devil-holes. Still, he would put his computer experts to work on it, to see if the blasphemers had overlooked something—a tiny detail that would betray their location.

"We are faced with a great challenge," Branson said, solemnly.

Tertullian sneered at the remark. He directed a number of insults in response, then said, "Find out what that kid was really saying, assuming it's really the Aramaic spoken in biblical times. I want the translation checked."

"Yes, Acting Minister."

"This is a UWW trick. I know it. I just don't know how they're pulling it off, how they're getting babies to do that. A computer animation trick?"

"We'll find out sir."

"Get on the fraud angle right away."

"Yes, sir."

"You'd better do it fast," Styx said. "A lot of damage is being done."

Branson bowed and departed. As Tertullian hurried into his office, he feared that the damage was irreversible.

Chapter 11

There is no word for the ability to think without words.
—Martha of Galilee

On the morning of her third day in the desert, Lori wore a heavy coat when she went outside, zipped all the way up. It was early, the first daylight, when it was safest to do the work, without the worry of lights that might be detected at night. Nearby, the stocky pilot, in a leather jacket, stood on a platform, still working on the engine. The day before Rea Janeg had taken the fuel system and air filtration units apart and cleaned them, and she'd said there were other supposedly minor mechanical problems. Today she was putting things back together, clanking tools inside the engine compartment. She had a bandage on her forehead where she had bumped it the day before, and her knuckles were red and nicked from the work.

Just before going outside, Lori had been in the passenger compartment of the helicopter, which had now become a brig for Wendy Zepeda and the two guards, all three of whom remained under confinement. The tough little Fujiko Harui had the primary responsibility of watching the handcuffed prisoners, including feeding them and allowing them bathroom privileges. Lori had decided to trust her completely.

Inside, Lori had spoken to the prisoners one by one, probing their thoughts in an effort to determine their loyalties. Preferring not to keep them locked up, she had hoped to be able to release one or all of them. But after intensive questions she'd decided to leave them there, convinced that they could not be trusted. It was a responsibility of command that had fallen on her shoulders, and she didn't particularly like it. But she saw no reasonable alternatives. For their own safety out here in the desert she couldn't let them go, and for the safety of the rest of her group she couldn't let them go, either. And she certainly couldn't kill them.

She had noticed something curious during the individual sessions with the prisoners. It was as if the process caused her to assume a personality she didn't know she had, as if she had become a skilled military or police interrogator asking probative questions. As she spoke with each of the captives, the incisiveness of her own questions had surprised her, the way she was looking through windows into individual personalities and motivations. At one point she even found herself examining the whole process while it was occurring, like watching herself and the prisoner Wendy Zepeda through a high-powered magnification glass.

"I've decided to help you," Wendy had said. "I never liked Dixie Lou Jackson anyway."

"Why don't you like her?" Lori had asked. A simple enough question, not particularly incisive in and of itself.

"A lot of us on the council don't. We're just afraid to oppose her."

That had made some sense, but for a moment, Lori had found herself trying to listen for subtleties in Zepeda's tone of voice and inflection, for hesitations, for stammering. The things a professional interrogator might notice, techniques she had read about and seen in movies. She'd even looked for a flickering of the eyes, for moisture on the upper lip and brow, and muscular twitches. All might be indicators of deception.

But after only a few moments she'd discarded these methods, replacing them with another. Her visceral reaction. An almost innate sense in the pit of her stomach about what was right and what was wrong.

This councilwoman was not to be trusted, no matter what she said or how she said it. And neither were the two young guards. . . .

Now, gazing out on the desert, it looked to Lori as if it should be warmer than expected today, or at least her eyes relayed this information to her brain. But the exposed skin on her hands and face tingled with cold. And out on the desert, she saw sand carried laterally by the wind, but she felt nothing where she stood. In all, it was as if her eyes and skin were in separate realms, or separate locations.

She wished she was back in Seattle, and that none of the terrible events since the goddess circle had transpired. But she knew it was impossible to turn back the empyrean mechanism of time. Like the universe itself, it was a relentless perpetual motion machine, unstoppable in its progress.

With a deep, agitated sigh, Lori tried to accept what had happened and to tell herself that she had been given an important destiny by a higher power, that she had been placed on this path for a reason.

She recalled the strange experience she'd had two nights ago, an event so vivid that it seemed real, of a bright light with the brilliance of a miniature sun bathing her in warmth and seeming to transport her—ever so briefly—to an ethereal realm. So odd, so vivid and strangely sensual. It reminded her in some ways of the earlier vision she seemed to have shared with Dixie Lou Jackson, in which a bright amorphous shape had hovered over Lori . . . a vision that ended with her holding a female child and Jackson backing away in terror and confusion.

Hearing a noise, the teenager turned and saw the children, all eleven of them, emerging from a pair of tents simultaneously, camouflaged habitats that worked in synchronicity with the electronic camouflage over the helicopter and the work area. Wearing robes or coats, the she-apostles walked on their short legs, following Mary Magdalene toward the pilot. It still amazed her to see the babies walking, even though they were not at all proficient. Sometimes they stumbled and fell on the soft sand, but quickly got back up.

Momentarily, the children stood and watched the pilot as she worked, and seemed transfixed on her. Glancing sidelong at them as she used a spanner, Rea Janeg at first made a perplexed face, then resumed her attention to the job. Every once in awhile, she glanced back at the children, but did not seem particularly upset by their presence. If she had been, Lori would have taken steps to remove them, since it was so important to get the helicopter running.

All the while the children watched intently, as if they wanted to understand what was going on mechanically, or as if they already knew, which seemed unlikely. They even examined tools and parts that were laid out on a tarpaulin, but didn't touch them or say much of anything, just occasional words and what seemed to be sentence fragments, in their private language.

Iviapa . . . tiofi . . . obruku . . . aphem . . .

Curiously, Lori understood what she heard, but could not form her own thoughts or words in that language. It was as if she could only listen to them, and that she was mute, without a tongue of her own to speak.

Just as peculiar, the utterances didn't seem to connect with the surroundings. The children were talking excitedly about flowers and trees and birds and animals, but in this desert there was little of that. Lori had seen a few withered flower petals, borne to their campsite by the winds, and flocks of birds heading south. It seemed peculiar to see them flying over the desert in their migration, but they undoubtedly knew where the oases were along the way, like rest stops for travelers.

Those words. So familiar and yet so elusive.

Kneeling by Abigail, one of the babies, Lori held her hands, and looking into her cerulean blue eyes, said softly in English, "I want to speak with you in the secret tongue, but the words will not come to me. Why is it that I understand what you are saying, but I cannot form the words myself in that language?"

"Language is but an imperfect incarnation of thought," the child said, in the ancient parlance. "You think you understand my words, but you are only picking up semblances of meaning. It is this way with all languages, and especially with ours. We she-apostles have an exclusive verbal lexicon, but to fully communicate with us you must learn to think without words, keeping in mind this important caveat: the very act of speaking the thoughts diminishes them, alters their original, pure meaning. Any vocabulary is inherently limited."

"But *iktol*—the word means 'murder' in English. I understood it when Veronica mouthed it to me. It means an unwarranted killing. What subtleties are there to understand about such a word?"

"The very question reflects a lack of understanding."

"But when will I understand?"

"When you are ready. This is how it has always been, and always will be. Compare this phenomenon of language with the questions you asked of the three prisoners, how you determined that they were lying."

"How do you know about that?"

With her tiny hands, Abigail squeezed Lori's fingers. "Maybe it's because we are small and move quietly," Abigail said. "We are able to eavesdrop much more easily than large people." The child smiled, and her face showed an infinite intelligence, far beyond her years.

"You're reading my mind, aren't you?" Lori said, looking down at their linked hands. "When we touch, you can see into my thoughts!"

"Yes, I am peering into your mind now, but my ability is not perfect. I still face large gaps, blocked pathways and regions, although I am improving, growing stronger. When you questioned the prisoners, you considered using familiar lie detection techniques, but discarded them in favor of your gut feelings. That was an excellent decision on your part. You also want to know more about the She-Judas, but we must wait for the testimony of the real Martha of Galilee, not the fake one Dixie Lou brought in. As she-apostles we know some of the details, but it is Martha's story to tell, her holy gospel."

Lori didn't know whether to pull away or continue holding the child's hands. She felt herself shaking with fear. In large part, she realized, it was a fear of the unknown. With a jerk of realization, she now understood why she had analyzed the prisoners in a visceral way, instead of trying to put labels on things or attach words to them. It was like the linguistic comments Abigail had made moments ago about the inadequacy of any lexicon to express true meanings.

"I was able to think beyond words," Lori said. "That's how I knew the three women were lying."

"You are beginning to understand," Abigail said. "We call it wordless purity. And earlier, you sensed something about the twelfth she-apostle that Dixie Lou brought in, before you knew she was a fake. What did you sense?"

"That something was strange about the baby, something that troubled me deeply."

"And you could not put into words what you were feeling."

Lori nodded, but as she looked at Abigail, she realized with a start that the other children were moving in synchronization with her, making the same facial expressions and even mouthing the same words with her—despite what she had said about wordless thought. Apparently oral speech was a subset of their main communication method, which Lori didn't feel close to comprehending yet. Did they communicate through facial expressions, through subtleties in the eyes, or in some other visual fashion? Did they read each other's minds when they touched hands, achieving wordless purity? If so, perhaps it worked better for the she-apostles to communicate with one another in this manner than it did for them to make physical contact with an outsider, such as Lori. She felt as if she were peering into a realm of infinite possibilities.

A shudder coursed Lori's body. Looking up at the pilot, she saw that she still had her head in the engine compartment. The sounds of her tools seemed distant, as if coming from an entirely different dimension.

Letting go of Abigail, the perplexed teenager rose to her feet. She shook her head, and it seemed to clear. All the while, as if she were a laboratory specimen, the children watched her, their eyes bright. . . .

After testing the tandem engines another time, while Lori stayed with her, shadowing the process, the pilot climbed back down from the cockpit to the sand, muttering in displeasure. Her face was red, perspiring. Despite the chill in the air, she removed her jacket and tossed it aside.

"Engines are overheating now," she said.

"Can you fix the problem?" Lori asked as she stepped onto the soft gray sand herself. She was growing increasingly concerned, beginning to lose her patience with the helicopter pilot.

"I'll figure it out." Rea's voice had an edge as she stared at the helicopter.

Lori wondered if the pilot had the necessary knowledge, or if she might be delaying intentionally . . . preventing them from leaving. If that was the case, she was in league with Dixie Lou Jackson after all. The teenager felt her mind working in two ways as she thought about this. On the one hand, she still had access to her old way of thinking, and from an intellectual standpoint she suspected the pilot. Circumstantial evidence pointed to the possibility of deception. But on the other hand, utilizing her nascent visceral ability to discern another level, she didn't suspect Rea at all, and believed in her.

Just then, the children gathered around the pilot's jacket, where it lay on the sand. At first the pilot didn't notice them, but Lori did, and wondered what intrigued them so much about the garment.

Dressed in a black shirt and trousers, Fujiko came out of her own tent. Rubbing her eyes, she looked at the she-apostles and the visibly upset pilot, then came over to see close up. "What's going on?" she asked of Lori.

"Things aren't going well." She described the mechanical problem. "Do you think she's faking it?" Lori asked, keeping her voice low.

"No." The little Japanese woman shook her head, looked at the children. Lori followed her gaze.

Veronica was reaching into the pilot's jacket pocket, and what she brought out caused Lori's pulse to quicken. A small handgun.

The pilot saw this, and said, "Be careful with that!" She started toward the child.

Lori pushed by her, grabbed the weapon first. It appeared to be made of composites, and weighed only a few ounces. "What are you doing with this?" she demanded.

"We live in dangerous times," Rea said, with a shrug.

"Whose side are you on?"

"Ours," Fujiko interjected. "I knew Rea had the gun, saw her pick it up from a fallen guard when we were escaping from Monte Konos." She paused. "I also have a gun. It's in my tent."

"So the two of you are in this together?" Lori asked.

"I didn't know she had anything," Rea said. "But she's right. If I wasn't on your side, Lori, I would have used the gun on you."

"But I searched carefully for weapons," Lori said.

"My coat was in a storage compartment on the 'copter when you checked me," the pilot said, "and that small, lightweight pistol was zipped into an inner lining, not easy to notice."

"You needed people to help you search," Fujiko said, without revealing exactly how she had concealed hers.

"How do I know you didn't intend to use this against me?" Lori asked, looking at Rea and holding the gun up. All the while, her thoughts churned, as she tried to sort them out, separating the intellectual from the emotional.

"I forgot it was in the coat. Doesn't that tell you something? I was upset about the engines running hot. You may have thought I was faking the mechanical work, stalling, but if I was doing that, I wouldn't have forgotten about my ace in the hole, would I?" She nodded toward the weapon in Lori's hand.

"I've been wanting to trust someone," Lori said. "Maybe it's time." She looked hard at the pilot and at Fujiko, and detected no animosity in either of their faces. Only fatigue, from the hardships all of them had endured. Her suspicion faded.

"What do you have?" Lori asked, of Fujiko.

The Japanese woman smiled. "More firepower than the two of you combined. A .45 rapomatic."

Handing the weapon back to the pilot, Lori said, "I want to believe in you, Rea."

Checking the clip and safety, and then slipping the gun into a front pocket in her jeans, the pilot said, "Listen, I hate Dixie Lou as much as you do. I only went to work for the UWW because of Amy Angkor-Billings, since I believed in her. After she died, Dixie Lou got crazier than ever. She seemed happy about Amy dying, maybe even had something to do with it. I wasn't the only one to notice that. Mistrust isn't evidence, but I've watched her, and something doesn't seem right.

She's secretive and unpredictable, has temper tantrums that she tries to hide from important people. I guess I'm considered too insignificant for her to notice, but I have seen some of her bad side."

"So have I," Lori said. "Alex and I saw her murder a guard."

"Really?" The stocky brunette scowled.

"We saw her do it. She tried to blame us for it, but we know what really happened."

Looking at the two women, Lori said, "I guess we're in this together now. I need both of you to help me keep an eye on the others."

"We already have been," Fujiko said. "The matrons and the translator can be trusted, but not the ones we have locked up. Everything is perfect."

"Yeah, just *perfect*," Lori said, shaking her head.

"It'd be nice to know what Dixie Lou is up to," Rea said, stepping back onto the platform to look inside the engine compartment. "She'll want the children back, so we need to get this crate going."

She hardly had the words out of her mouth when an alarm sounded, then went off. All around them, camouflage energy crackled.

"I think we should release the machine gun," Rea said. "I know how to use it." She was referring to a control panel in the cockpit that only Lori now had access to, having ordered the pilot to enable Lori to lock it up with her own access code.

All of the authentic she-apostles were with her now, and Lori felt a need to protect them, without concern that any of them might be aboard an approaching aircraft. She didn't want to harm the fake Martha, because she was an innocent child, but Lori's priorities were different now. She knew that the eleven children with her were authentic, and she felt a deep responsibility to ensure their safety.

Hurrying into the cockpit, Lori activated the codes to unlock the .50 caliber machine gun. She heard what sounded like an aircraft, getting closer. As she did this, the pilot ran aft through the passenger compartment, to a ceiling hatch. Throwing it open, she climbed up into a bubble chamber that extended to both sides, on top of the helicopter.

From the cockpit Lori watched a monitor, and saw the same view as Rea, as the pilot swung the gun around toward the approaching craft. Through an electronic viewer that penetrated the protective camouflage cloth, Lori and Rea saw a slight abnormality in the air, approaching them fast.

"It's coming in on stealth," Rea said, across the intercom system. "But they're having problems with it, just like the earlier fly-over."

"Do you see the slight disturbance in the air?" Lori asked.

"Yeah, but we're not supposed to. I've got it in my sights."

Moments later the monitor showed the anomaly in the air veering off. The sound of engines faded away.

Chapter 12

If Jesus Christ came back from the dead, why not his female and male apostles, to foreshadow his second coming?
—Amy Angkor-Billings, private journals

The sun splashed pools of sunlight around the interior of the dining tent, which had mesh windows on the ends and sides. Dixie Lou Jackson had sent for her son, and he was being brought to her. She sat on the bench of an inflatable table.

It irritated her that she had found no sign of the missing helicopter, or of the she-apostles that seemed to have disappeared into thin air. The difficult teenager Lori Vale had something to do with both problems; she was certain of it. But every search party had come up with nothing.

She had one clue, though, albeit a thin one. The day before, she had gone into the village and questioned Malia at length, trying to see if she knew anything. Though the Arab woman had denied all knowledge, her behavior had been suspicious and her answers too brief, as if she wanted to conclude the discussion quickly and move onto another subject. Having grown up on the mean streets of Baltimore, Dixie Lou had some experience with human nature, and with liars. In any culture, they were the same. She saw things in the behavior of people, in the edginess of their words, the nervous movements, the moist, glistening brows and quivering upper lips.

And Dixie Lou suspected that her son might have something to do with it as well. In her position, she had to suspect everyone, and he had never proven himself above reproach. . . .

Feeling dismal, Alex entered the tent and sat on a bench at the other side of the table. His mother stared at him in an unnerving way, and he wondered what she was thinking . . . and why she had sent for him.

"I thought you might like to see what we've been doing," Dixie Lou said, smiling suddenly. But her dark eyes remained hard. On the table she had a laptop computer, which she always kept charged inside the command helicopter.

Not saying anything, Alex scowled, causing his thick eyebrows to lower over his pewter eyes. His curly black hair was tousled.

"I can't go on-line with this computer yet," she said, "not until we get to civilization and have it repaired. But back at Monte Konos, one of our computer whizzes set up an on-line Concordance of the *Holy Women's Bible*. With it, we can search for any passage. There's one about our enemies, but I don't recall exactly where it is—" From memory, she voiced key words, and the computer searched, then brought up a passage in ornate script, which she turned toward Alex so that he could read it, too:

Our enemies deserve what they

have shown us—no mercy.

"You seem disinterested," Dixie Lou said, looking at him. She shut down the computer and folded its cover shut. "Is there something you wish to say to me?"

"Only that I hate you," Alex said.

"I know you think you do, but that's only because you don't understand the big picture, the challenges I must deal with, the difficult goals we seek. You have no idea what I go through."

"Why can't I talk to Liz Torrence and Siana Harui? They're my friends, but that guards keep me away from them."

"I make the rules around here. That means I don't have to explain them."

Shaking his head, Alex stared at the ceiling of the tent. "And why are you bothering to show me your Unholy Women's Bible?"

"Don't get smart with me, young man."

"Or you'll have me beaten?"

The enigmatic woman showed no emotion in her caliginous features. "I'm trying to decide whether or not to kill you."

"Gosh, Mom, couldn't you just withhold my allowance or ground me?"

"I've never been much of a mother to you," Dixie Lou admitted. "But you've never tried to be a son to me, either."

"Are you trying to bond with me now? Isn't it a little late for that?"

"Maybe so. I don't know what I was thinking." Her eyes narrowed. "I know you had something to do with the disappearance of the children. And so did your little girlfriend. The only think I haven't figured out is why are you still here?"

"Did it ever occur to you that I had nothing to do with it?"

"Where's Lori?"

"I wish I knew. I only hope she's safe."

"Get out of my sight!" Dixie Lou thundered. She shook a fist at him.

"That's more like it," he said, as he stood to leave. "For a moment there, I almost thought you were human."

* * *

A camel caravan snaked along the crest of a dune, forming a long profile against the sunset. High in the saddle of the lead animal, Rashid Ali Khan grimaced; his aching, stuffy head was shaken every time the animal jostled him. He had pushed himself too hard. All day long, he'd been suffering from what felt like a severe bout of the flu. It had begun early in the morning, and had gotten worse with each passing moment. Now he really needed to rest.

Rashid raised an arm and called out to the men: it was time to make camp. He led the way down the face of the dune to a flat section of sand and hardpan where caravans often camped. At other times of the year, when the sun turned the desert into a furnace, Rashid traveled by night and made camp during the day. Now it was cool enough to travel by day and sleep at night, which he preferred. Maybe he would feel better in the morning after a good night's rest.

As he dismounted from the camel, his younger brother Meshdi helped him keep his balance on the loose sand and rock under his feet. Meshdi was smaller than Rashid, with a square jaw and small, narrow-set eyes.

"Lie down for awhile," his brother said, as he spread a fiber mat on a section of soft sand. "I will bring you something to eat and drink."

Despite his pride, Rashid didn't argue. It felt good to stop, to free himself from the rolling, sickening motions of the animal.

On this trip, the men in the caravan had delivered their goods to a wealthy merchant. Following a fine meal at the man's home they had set out for home, along a route so familiar to them that they might have accomplished it blindfolded. That had been four long days ago, and Rashid was ready for this trip to be over.

Late the next evening he would see Malia again, and she would nurse him back to health. She was a nurturing person; he always grew strong in her presence, and withered when away from her. It was worse than usual on this trip, because his feelings of longing for Malia were exacerbated by this sickness. He wasn't the type to complain; never had been and never would be.

I'll just lay my head down for a few moments, he thought, as he stretched out on the thin mat. Beneath his body the sand shifted, adjusting itself as he pressed his form onto it. To the west, the sun looked larger than normal and more orange, from the dust of the desert. He saw turbaned men removing bundles from the camels and opening them in order to set up the tents.

* * *

Across the world, in Washington state . . .

"Well, what do you have?" Styx Tertullian demanded. He stood in front of Kylee Branson's desk, glaring down at him.

"But you just asked for it this morning," the Vice Minister protested. "We're working on the biblical fraud angle, just as you said."

"Just as I *said?*" With a swipe of his hand, Tertullian knocked a picture frame off the desk, onto the carpet. When the glass didn't break, he stomped on it in order to develop the cracking and popping noises that he wanted for effect.

Branson's eyes opened wide in terror.

"I didn't just *say* it," the Acting Minister roared. "It wasn't a *request*. I didn't just mention it in polite conversation, or *propose* it. I *commanded* it, and I expect immediate results!"

"But sir, I already have a translator working on what that baby said on the computer screen, the she-apostle."

"And if the UWW translation was accurate?"

Branson squirmed in his chair. His gaze darted around, as if looking for a means by which he might escape. "You just told me to check it."

"Are you paid enough to think?" Tertullian came around beside Branson, glared menacingly at him.

"Well, yes sir, of–of course." The man scooted his chair back a little, then had second thoughts and returned it to its original place. For him, there was no escape.

"Then what is your contingency plan?"

"Contingency–in case the translation was accurate? Oh, you mean have one of our disinformation labs make the *Holy Women's Bible* look phony anyway?" He scratched his head, forced a smile. "We can come up with something convincing. Our proof could be set up using computer enhancement. We can use the Internet, just like they did."

"Smart boy," Tertullian said, with a condescending slap on Branson's smooth face.

* * *

Pacific Coast of Mexico . . .

Through the partially open bedroom door, Gilberto Inez watched the sleeping woman, with her long, dark hair fanned over her forehead and eyes. For the better part of three days, Consuela Santos had worked extremely hard in the house and yard, completing the work of three men. She was taking a well-deserved afternoon *siesta* now, at the insistence of the Inez brothers. She stirred, turned the other way.

From outside, Gilberto heard hammering, as his younger brother José repaired a window shutter. It was almost 4:00 in the afternoon, and their parents were due at any moment. Earlier in the day, Gilberto had even painted some of the stucco and trim where it had weathered. All was in readiness now for the impending arrival of their parents, except for the matter of the young woman and her tiny daughter, who had been living in the house without permission.

Gilberto held little Marta on his lap, keeping in place a glass baby bottle he'd purchased himself. The child was fussing with the rubber nipple, but sucking occasionally and swallowing formula.

The hammering stopped, and he heard the familiar, smooth pitch of a car engine. He'd know that Alfa Romeo sound anywhere. His parents had driven the mountain roads from Mexico City. He considered rising, but didn't want to disturb the baby, who was finally settling down. Her eyelids were heavy as she slipped into peaceful slumber. Her lips quivered a little, and white formula ran out of one corner of her mouth. Gently, Gilberto used a hand towel to wipe her chin.

The front door of the house burst open, and a grinning José entered, carrying expensive leather luggage. Their mother and father were right behind. Tall and lean, Arsinio Inez had a silvery mustache, heavy black eyebrows, and a square face with a dimpled chin. He carried himself in the dignified manner of a business owner, the operator of a successful export company in Mexico City. His blonde wife Raffaela, nearly his height, was quite a bit heavier and looked older (though they were the same age), with deep creases around her mouth and eyes. A tenured professor at one of the most prestigious medical schools in the country, she carried a sheathe of medical journals. She was constantly reading, keeping up with the latest developments.

"House looks fabulous, boys," Arsinio boomed. "How'd you—" Suddenly he stopped in his tracks, mouth agape, as he noticed the baby in Gilberto's arms.

Marta screamed and wrenched.

"You woke her up," Gilberto complained, trying to get her to accept the nipple again. Then, realizing what his parents must be thinking, he pointed toward the bedroom door and said, "The mother's asleep in there. She's real tired. Uh, it's a long story, Father. And this is *not* your surprise granddaughter, if that's what you're wondering."

"They were here when we arrived," José added, as he dropped the luggage onto the floor with a thump. He went on to tell what he and his brother knew about Consuela and her baby.

Raffaela took the unhappy child from Gilberto and cradled her in her arms, speaking soothingly to her.

Marta stopped crying, and with alert brown eyes she looked up at the large woman. And began to babble, making a series of fragmented word-sounds.

"She does that all the time," Gilberto said. "I think she's trying to talk."

Looking to his left, he saw Consuela standing in the bedroom doorway, looking disheveled in a striped blue and white blouse and dark skirt he'd purchased for her. Nervously, she tucked in her blouse and folded her arms across her chest, never taking her eyes off her daughter.

"Unusual child," Raffaela said. "It's almost like she's speaking to me, though I don't understand a word she's saying. Of course children this age aren't able to talk yet." Seeing Consuela, Raffaela took the baby to her and in a kindly voice asked, "Are you feeling better now?"

The peasant woman nodded. Her expression was grateful as she accepted her daughter, but her eyes were filled with concern. She listened and nodded politely as José made the introductions. Then she said, "I have been staying here without your permission or knowledge, and I am deeply sorry for that, but I was desperate and needed someplace where I could take care of little Marta. I kept detailed records of the food we ate, and all of it will be repaid."

"She doesn't actually owe us anything," Gilberto said. "You should see all the things she fixed and cleaned around here. José and I hardly had to do anything."

With cautious admiration, Arsinio and his wife looked around, nodding their heads.

"Your child makes such unusual sounds," Raffaela said. "In my graduate studies I did some research on the communication of babies, but I don't think I ever heard anything like that." Studying the worried expression on the uneducated Méxicana's face, she added quickly, "I am a professor, but a doctor by training."

Looking alarmed, Consuela said, "I am so sorry to have troubled you. I will pack my things and leave immediately."

Raffaela approached her, but the young woman, obviously terrified, backed up against the wall, clutching her child tightly to her breast. "Please don't hurt my baby," she pleaded.

"We would never do that." Raffaela placed an arm on Consuela's shoulder, in an effort to calm her, but the woman was shaking and shivering. "Why are you so afraid?"

"You are a doctor."

Raffaela laughed, then caught herself. "A lot of people are afraid of doctors, but not terrified of them as you are. *Why*, child?"

Consuela just looked at her with saucer-eyes. She didn't answer.

"I think she needs more rest," Gilberto said. He pointed toward the bedroom. "Do you want Marta with you now?"

Consuela nodded, retreated into the bedroom with sputtering apologies, and closed the door. . . .

An hour later, frantic to find safety for her child—anyplace, she didn't know where—Consuela climbed out the window into the garden and hurried down the road, with Marta bundled securely in a *rebozo*. Before leaving she'd listened at the bedroom door, and heard the Inez men in the living room, talking about her and the baby. They were asking questions, wondering why Consuela was so afraid of doctors. They didn't act as if they knew the frightening secret about her child, but before long word would get out.

When Consuela neared the bottom of the driveway, however, she saw Raffaela striding toward her, carrying a basket of flowers. Apparently she'd been picking them along the road. Consuela tried to walk past her, said, "I'm sorry, *Señora*, but we are too much trouble for you here."

The large woman set her basket down, smiled gently. "Nonsense. I was just picking these flowers for you, to cheer you up. We really want to help you—and your beautiful baby."

Consuela started to cry, and through blurred vision she saw kindness in Raffaela's face. "You won't hurt us no matter what I tell you?" Consuela asked.

"Of course not."

"I don't know everything," Consuela began. "But bad doctors are after Marta. You're not one of them. I trust you." She explained what little she knew, including the woman in white who attacked her in the church, firing a gun as Consuela fled with her child.

With a troubled but kindly expression, Raffaela put a pink wildflower in the young woman's hair. "That looks very nice on you," she said.

"You think so?" Consuela smiled, because she felt better than she had in a long time . . . and safer. These good people would help her and little Marta. She was sure of it.

Chapter 13

These she-apostles are old souls in new flesh. I am haunted by them.
—Dixie Lou Jackson, note in a computer file

Dressed in a camel-colored burnoose given to her by Malia, Dixie Lou stood on the crest of an immense sand dune. It occurred to her that she probably looked like any other Arab traveler from a distance. This was the hottest part of the afternoon, warmer than expected according to the village Arabs, and the North African heat baked into her black skin. The dry heat felt good to her, and she imagined that her ancient grandmothers must have felt this as well, for they had once lived in this part of the world, and on much hotter days than this.

That morning Malia had also given her the hard copy of an encrypted e-mail, along with a microcylinder copy. The message had been sent through her because of the coded e-mails that Dixie Lou had dispatched to various UWW bases from the village. Dixie Lou didn't like the fact that someone else was receiving her replies, and she would need to straighten that out right away.

The message, decoded by Deborah Marvel, had been bad news, but not a total surprise. The UWW base in Tunisia, which had been Dixie Lou's destination when she escaped from Monte Konos—and which had not responded to her messages—had been destroyed in another BOI attack.

It meant that she and her companions were stranded in the desert for the time being, but she had just thought of a way to turn the situation to her advantage.

Following the publication of the *Holy Women's Bible* over the Internet, she had become incredibly famous . . . literally, overnight. Suddenly the worldwide web was full of stories about her, most of them outright conjecture. No one seemed to know where she was, or much about her. Though public opinion tilted eighty percent against her she was pleased that millions of people at least knew who she was, and she felt certain that the tide would shift in her favor as more people actually read the new holy book.

In the bright sunlight it became clear to her what she needed to do next. When her brain should have been overheated, when she should have been crawling for the cool shelter of shade, she surprised herself by thinking very clearly now, and coming up with a marvelous new plan.

Her time in the desert would become the stuff of legend, she told herself; comparisons would be drawn between her and the forty days Jesus spent in the wilderness.

She just required a little more help from modern technology to get the message out. . . .

* * *

Unseen by his mother, Alex Jackson eluded the guards and followed her out on the hot sands. Concealing himself behind a dune where he could watch her, he tightened his fingers around a combat knife, stolen when one of the young guards had left a weapons cabinet unlocked on the VTOL plane.

It would be so easy to kill her. He imagined what it would be like to do that, and envisioned her bleeding to death on the sand. The thought of matricide disturbed him and gave him great pause, but he could not set it aside. She was as close to pure evil as he could imagine.

Sunlight glinted off the blade. His fingers tightened on the handle. He wanted to leap at her and stab her to death, but could not bring himself to do it.

* * *

That evening . . .

Dixie Lou heard a rush of wind-blasted sand ripple the fabric of the dining tent in which she stood. For the moment, the structure held together. She thought back to another windy night, long ago, when she'd gotten a small amount of vengeance against her drunken, incestuous father and uncle by smashing their expensive watches while they slept through a storm—watches they had stolen in a burglary.

In a blind rage, she'd also splashed acid on the clothing in their closets, ruining them. In all, it was not nearly equivalent to what they'd done to her, and they had no idea how lucky they were that she didn't murder them in their sleep or disfigure them. The only reason she hadn't done more was because she would have been the prime suspect; too many people knew how much she loathed them, and why. She had run away from home shortly afterward, taking all the money in her father's wallet, and had never seen her family again.

While Dixie Lou was engrossed in these memories, Deborah Marvel entered the dining tent and re-secured the door flaps. In the light of the lanterns, her blonde hair was wild from the wind, and she said, "We haven't had a good talk for awhile, not the way we used to."

"I'm juggling a lot, too much to discuss. This isn't a good time."

"Maybe if you tried to share your troubles. I just thought you might like my advice, or—"

"Go!" Dixie Lou waved her hand dismissively.

"As you wish." Deborah's blue eyes were open wide in a combination of emotions. Fear, to be certain, but some anger and resentment as well, barely suppressed. She hurried away, leaving Dixie Lou to her own ruminations. Since the release of the *Holy Women's Bible*, the Chairwoman was beginning to feel increasingly confident and untouchable. Already people were speaking of her in the same breath with Amy Angkor-Billings, and soon Amy would be no more than an afterthought, or a footnote. History would credit Dixie Lou Jackson with leading the women of the world out of the wilderness imposed upon them by men.

Half an hour later, Dixie Lou walked out on the moonlit desert. The cool air had grown suddenly still, and the silvery moon was like a cold, low-powered light bulb illuminating the sandscape, imparting a dim, pallid glow. She shivered.

Dixie Lou Jackson had a great deal of optimism about her future, but she still had numerous concerns as well, layers of worry that continued to weigh her down. She harbored secrets that could destroy her if the wrong people learned about them and used them against her.

In her most private thoughts she had worked out details of how to explain the killing of the Monte Konos guard, should Alex or Lori ever tell anyone about it. Dixie Lou would say she'd received a tip that the guard, Linda Cutler, was a BOI agent—and when she confronted her the response had been violent. Dixie Lou had been forced to kill her in self-defense, though she would have preferred to keep her alive to find out what she knew. Yes, she told herself, with a little effort she could make it all sound plausible, asserting that the two young witnesses had arrived too late to see the guard's aggressive behavior.

Reaching a rock outcropping, Dixie Lou scrambled to a higher level, where she stood and gazed down on the flickering nighttime glow of the Arab village. She heard voices drifting in the still air, and then made out the hulking shapes of camels approaching the settlement, and the shouts of men. The caravan was returning.

From the cimmerian recesses of her mind, a troublesome matter bobbed to the surface: how to control the leakage of information about the fake twelfth she-apostle. She counted the number of people who actually knew the truth about the make-believe Martha of Galilee. All were council members, numbering ten because of the six left on Monte Konos to die. Of the remaining councilwomen, any one of them could have told someone else, despite the oaths of confidentiality taken when they accepted their positions.

The moon illuminated the desert, casting the craggy, lifelike shadows of rock escarpments across the dunes. A night wind picked up, and she shivered.

If too many people know a secret, she thought, *it is no longer a secret.*

She bent over and scooped up some sand, which she let drain from her hand slowly, like time falling in an hourglass. Seconds ticked by, and presently another perspective became apparent to her. The remaining council members were in on this with her, because they had authorized the creation of the last she-apostle, to complete the holy book before powerful men got wind of it and suppressed it. Dixie Lou had *not* made the decision alone.

She had been trying to convince herself that the missing helicopter must have crashed, killing everyone aboard including the pesky teenager, four of the she-apostles, and the councilwomen Wendy Zepeda and Fujiko Harui. In addition, it made sense to her that the seven other missing she-apostles must have simply walked off into the desert, where they had died as well.

Taking inventory of the events surrounding her, Dixie Lou placed herself in a historical context. In the early years following the crucifixion of Jesus Christ, devout Christians and Jews had been chased into hiding by Romans, Sadducee priests, and other enemies. In addition, Christians argued with each other—with those claiming to be orthodox accusing others (such as the Gnostics) of being heretics.

In order to protect their precious but forbidden manuscripts, the Gnostics and other beleaguered men and women created copies of their sacred gospels and hid them wherever they could, often sealed in pottery jars. The gospels of Gnostics found near Nag Hammadi and at Alexandria—both in Egypt—were prime examples, and she knew there were others, a vast quantity of material that had been omitted from the *Bible*. Dixie Lou, like her council members, knew this very well. Amy Angkor-Billings had spoken often of the troubling history, referring to it as "herstory."

It was like ancient times now. Dixie Lou and her council had taken the necessary steps in order to keep the eleven authentic she-apostle gospels from being stolen and relegated to the forgotten burial grounds of history. In the vast scheme of things a falsified twelfth gospel was inconsequential, and easily justified. She had been considering putting the remaining councilmembers to death for what they knew, but she leaned toward letting them rise or fall with her.

Developing important plans of action provided Dixie Lou with some measure of control over the intertwined problems that pummeled her. But an unresolved—and perhaps *irresolvable*—matter remained, potentially the biggest and most dangerous of all. This one was explosive.

The trouble was, she didn't know exactly what it was herself, couldn't get a handle on it, a clear view of it, other than a terrible sense of fear and foreboding, and a suspicion that it had something to do with Lori Vale and the strange vision the two of them had shared of a bright form hovering over Lori, and a baby crying.

Is Lori truly dead?

Doubts assailed her.

And something lurked in the most inaccessible archives of her mind, something to do with a knife, and stabbing sleeping forms to death. If she could only remember the details, she might formulate a sensible plan.

But the information seemed to be too deep in her consciousness to retrieve. It was bubbling down there in a cauldron, like lava about to erupt and inundate her.

* * *

Several hours passed, and across the world it was early evening. Vice Minister Styx Tertullian sat alone in a room, staring at the blurry shapes dancing in front of a VR-TV screen. There were no lights on, just the unfocused glow of the machine. He felt depressed. This entertainment room for the Bureau had been set up for executives to use on their breaks, but he was the only one in the entire building now, except for security personnel roaming the corridors. Everyone else had gone home.

A remote control had been built into an armrest of his chair. He pressed buttons, but got only more of the same. Everyone in the world wanted to know about the mysterious women who produced the stunning *Holy Women's Bible*. The introduction to the book referred to reincarnated she-apostles, perhaps the strangest claim in the long history of world religion. It sounded more like creatures in a horror movie than reality. But millions of gullible people wanted to see these she-apostles in the flesh. The introduction was signed by Dixie Lou

Jackson, Chairwoman of United Women of the World, the UWW. The public was clamoring to find out who she was.

News stories on Jackson were sketchy, and no one had yet stepped forth publicly to talk about her past. That was about to change, because Tertullian knew something about her from Bureau intelligence reports. He knew she'd been a prostitute, and so had at least one of the "she-apostles" featured in the *Holy Women's Bible*—Mary Magdalene, in her original lifetime. He even came up with a phrase to counter the disinformation that the UWW was producing: "She-apostles—the figments of a whore's imagination."

Feeling his pulse race in anticipation, Tertullian glanced at his watch, then switched to the program he'd been waiting to see, the Tony Drew Show. It was a panel discussion featuring two participants, a mustachioed older man with a bald pate and a blonde young woman. The smooth-faced interviewer, Drew, sat in between them.

To Tertullian's surprise, the program was already in progress. He glanced at his watch again. It showed the top of the hour, but must be running slow. Removing the timepiece, he tossed it toward a wastebasket across the room and hit it dead center, giving him only the smallest measure of satisfaction.

The older man was talking, his tone condescending and pedantic, like a tired school teacher. Beneath him a caption read:

Ronald Friese-Greene

State Department Official

"It's obvious to anyone with half a brain," he said, "that the Unholy Women's Bible is a complete fabrication. Why, some of the—"

"*Holy*, not *Un*holy!" the woman interjected. A caption beneath her indicated:

Villial Luciano

University Professor

"But Madame, there is only one *Holy Bible*."

"And only one *Holy Women's Bible*."

The moderator said, "I must inform you, Miss Luciano, that we're getting thousands of responses on the worldwide net, and it's only running twenty percent in favor of the *Holy Women's Bible*. Most of the world believes it's a fraud, and that the UWW is a crackpot organization."

She bristled. "First of all, it is *Ms.* Luciano. Secondly, how many responses are you talking about?"

"Uh, three hundred twenty-four thousand."

"How interesting, and what, pray tell, is the population of the world?"

"Seven billion, maybe eight. I'm not sure."

With a toss of her long blonde hair she said, "Your tiny sample is meaningless."

"I wouldn't say that."

"I would. Aside from the minuscule sample, isn't it true that most of the responses came in by computer?"

"Mmmm, ninety percent, and the rest by fax and phone."

"Consider this, then. Many of the women who can be helped by the *Holy Women's Bible* don't even own computers, phones, or fax machines."

Tony Drew leaned forward. "Then why did the UWW publish it over the Internet?"

"Speed of dissemination. E-books were the best place to start, but it was only that, a start. Hardbound and softbound copies, as well as holo-recordings, are being distributed now, available free to everyone."

"It's all hogwash," her opponent said, rubbing his pronounced chin. "From page one to the end. Every word of it."

"And have you read the book, sir?" she inquired, in an erudite tone.

He cleared his throat. "Not directly, but reports reaching my desk indicate the events described in it could not possibly have occurred. The ridiculous assertion that twenty-four apostles attended The Last Supper, for example, and the claim that the male apostles were jealous of their purported female counterparts. Everyone agrees it's all absurd, of course."

"Keep it up," Tertullian murmured to the television, because he had paid Friese-Greene a substantial fee to debunk the female bible. Now the young woman could be heard in the background, trying unsuccessfully to get in a word.

Friese-Greene, who had once been a radio announcer, kept talking, building up a righteous head of steam. In his dominant, resonant voice he quoted a number of biblical verses in rapid succession, and then another, "The only true word of God is in the *Bible*. Verse 7:17 of the Book of Matthew says that every rotten tree produces worthless fruit."

"You're misquoting!" Luciano screeched, so loudly that the camera cut away from Friese-Greene and focused on her. Her eyes were piercing. Her prim little chin quivered with anger. Over the protestations of her opponent she howled, "All of your quotes are distorted or taken out of context to suit your purposes. What about the rest of Matthew 7:17?"

"It is of no help to you."

Tertullian groaned in displeasure as the woman continued to assert herself. "The entirety of Matthew 7:17," she howled, "goes like this: 'Even so every good tree bringeth forth good fruit; but a corrupt tree bringeth forth evil fruit.'"

"So what?" the older man said. "I don't see—"

She was shrieking at him to be heard. "Don't you get it? The UWW is a good tree producing fine fruit! Matthew 17:18 goes on to say, 'A good tree cannot bring forth evil fruit—' Mister Friese-Greene, the framers of the *Holy Women's Bible* accept the King James version of the *Holy Bible* for the most part, including the passage I've just quoted. Other passages have been corrected so that they more accurately reflect the loving attitude of Jesus toward women."

"*Corrected?* What temerity! One does not correct the *Holy Bible*!"

"I'm not a member of the UWW; I'm just quoting what I read in their sacred book. Only portions of the *Bible* have been rewritten, those that are adverse to women, and counter to the actual teachings of Jesus Christ. According to the gospels of the she-apostles, political forces in the centuries after the crucifixion of Christ twisted the truth, altered scriptures to suit their purposes—their *male* purposes. The resurrected companions of Jesus are speaking the true word of God."

Watching the debate from afar, Styx Tertullian wanted to press buttons on the remote control and blow off the blonde woman's head, splattering it all over the camera lens. He also didn't think much of Friese-Greene's knowledge of the *Bible*, or his debating skills. He should he quoting from Revelation at the very end of *The New Testament*, that God would inflict plagues on any person adding to the gospels or taking anything away from them.

The sputtering Friese-Greene, an increasingly hapless and pathetic figure, finally attempted to assert his dominance by raising his voice as much as he could, so that he thundered over his opponent, that crafty little female demon. Smirking, she finally fell silent and allowed the roar of Friese-Greene's voice to fill the studio and the speakers of every television set tuned to that channel. He looked like a red-faced fool. Finally he attempted to compose himself and asked, "What's the name of that UWW leader—Johnson?"

"Dixie Lou Jackson," the moderator said. He tugged at an earlobe.

"Whatever," Friese-Greene snapped. "Why is she hiding? Who is she and what is her organization all about? Do you know, Ms. Luciano?"

"Dixie Lou will answer for herself in due course," came the reply, in the calmest of tones. "And as for the organization, the UWW seeks to further the cause of women, who have been downtrodden for centuries. The UWW deals with women's issues."

"What a pile of rot. *Issues*? Women have no issues! Your gender is always complaining, always whining, always crying about something."

"A typical sexist comment," Luciano said.

"And that's a cheap shot," Friese-Greene countered. "People like you use buzz-words to play on the emotions of women."

"Another sexist comment," she said. "You criticize women for having an abundance of emotions, but you seem entirely unable to carry on a rational conversation yourself."

As Tertullian listened to the give and take, he dredged up a thought that occurred to him from time to time. If he could only figure out a way for humanity to get along without women he'd do it in a heartbeat.

Women are the Devil's Breed.

He wondered when Friese-Greene would drop the bomb that Styx had sent with him. He seemed to be waiting too long. Then, as if the paid man could read the thoughts of the BOI leader, he said, "What about the fact that Dixie Lou Jackson worked as a prostitute on the east coast?"

"That's a lie!"

"I have proof that it isn't." He held up a printed document that had been provided to him by the BOI, but which bore no marks to that effect. The camera zoomed in on it. The document, as far as Tertullian knew, was authentic, an arrest report on Jackson when she was twenty-one, including her fingerprints and three photographs.

"You've falsified that!" the woman protested.

"This report can be easily authenticated—unlike the fraudulent *Holy Women's Bible*—which is why Jackson and her co-conspirators are hiding like rats."

"I'm not a member of the UWW. In any event I'm certain they aren't hiding from anyone."

"Then why haven't they surfaced? And why don't they make the purported she-apostles available for inspection by neutral parties? Why is the UWW hiding the children that are so central to their claims?" He stared at the camera. "Dixie Lou Jackson, shame on you for manipulating and abusing children for your perverse purposes!"

"As I said, I'm not in the UWW, but I know they aren't abusing anyone. They're just striking back at male injustices."

"Then come out and tell us what we want to know. Let us examine the children and question Jackson." Friese-Greene stared into the camera. "Dixie Lou Jackson, come forth and face your accusers."

"There are security concerns," Luciano said. "People who oppose the BOI have been known to disappear."

"Nonsense. If people have disappeared it's by their own choice, with some nefarious design in mind."

Luciano glared. Beads of perspiration glistened on her forehead. "Men have been murdering women for thousands of years, but from now on out that's going to change. Women will no longer lie down and accept rape—in any form."

"Mark my words, young woman, the *Holy Women's Bible* is going to set womanhood back a thousand years. I'm not at liberty to reveal details yet, but the UWW's so-called sacred texts are being examined at this very moment. There are grave inconsistencies, questions—"

"Why don't I believe you?" Luciano said, with a sneer.

"I've been listening to both of you," the moderator said, "and I've tried to be impartial. But I must agree with this gentleman to an extent." The camera zoomed in on Tony Drew and he looked directly into it, saying, "Dixie Lou Jackson, where are you?"

"Come out, come out, wherever you are," Friese-Greene added.

Chapter 14

The destructive, catastrophic acts of men are endless. One has only to see a documentary of war, read a newspaper, or listen to the evening news. One has only to read history to see the centuries and millennia of violence. Wars are created by men, for men.
—The Reflections of Lori Vale (unpublished manuscript)

To Lori it seemed an odd juxtaposition of cultures as she watched three Arab women approaching her camp in the middle of the day, their arms laden with electronic equipment. She recognized Malia in the lead, carrying a flat-screen television receiver. One of her companions toted a satellite dish, and the other had control boxes and loops of wire and cable.

"Dixie Lou Jackson is about to go on the air," Malia announced. "We thought you might like to see your enemy's worldwide broadcast."

Unaware of this development, Lori felt a surge of curiosity. "Thank you. We have a satellite television aboard the helicopter, but we don't want to be tracked if we turn it on. You can get that working out here?"

With a smile, the woman said, "You doubt our proficiency?" Quickly, she added, "Just watch us."

The desert women moved quickly, setting up the television receiver on a tarpaulin that the pilot had left on the sand. Only moments before, Rea Janeg had tested the engine and pronounced the helicopter fit for travel—although Lori had not decided to take off yet. She didn't want to be detected by Dixie Lou or her companions.

In only a few moments, the old TV screen flickered to life. Malia operated a control device. "It's searching for the most clear channel now," she said. "Ah, here it is."

On the screen, news reporters discussed the broadcast, which was scheduled to begin in only a few minutes.

* * *

The Chairwoman stood off to one side, watching a young female reporter and her small crew set up camera equipment in the dining tent. It was midday, the air warm and dry. Dixie Lou wore a black pants suit with a green-and-orange collar, the same outfit she'd worn in the escape from Monte Konos. It was clean, though, having been washed with sea water that had been desalinated with equipment on board the helicopter. Each day she showered in the processed water, too, and even though it was fresh she never quite felt clean from it.

"I'm so excited to finally meet you," the reporter gushed. She had olive skin, and short brown hair. "I've long been an admirer of United Women of the World. I was even in a goddess circle last year, and used to wish I could be just like Amy Angkor Billings."

"How nice," Dixie Lou replied, concealing her displeasure at the remark.

"You replaced Amy?"

"Yes."

"She retired?"

"You might say that," Dixie Lou said, with inward glee. "Of course we can't discuss internal, organizational matters. Privacy is essential to us."

"So I've heard. Even with the release of the *Holy Women's Bible*, I'm surprised you're granting an interview."

"Times are changing," Dixie Lou said.

When all was ready, the two women sat in inflatable chairs, separated by a small table. A gray screen stood behind them. No windows or structural details were shown. The camera picked up the women in profile.

"Welcome to Global News," the reporter said. "I'm Joanne Gazzara, broadcasting a live special report from somewhere in the desert, at the secret headquarters of Dixie Lou Jackson, who is with me now. Her aides brought me here blindfolded, and I'm not permitted to describe anything seen off-camera."

"It's nice to be here," Dixie Lou said.

"Your new *Holy Women's Bible* is an absolute sensation!" the reporter said. On her lap she held a glossy white paperback copy, with raised-gold lettering on it. Turning several pages she added, "Here in the introduction it says the she-apostles are alive today. Where are these special people?"

"Would you like to meet one?"

"Right now, you mean?"

The black woman nodded.

"An unexpected pleasure. Millions of people in our audience are waiting breathlessly!"

After gesturing to someone off-camera, Dixie Lou announced, "She's being brought in now."

A white-uniformed woman, with exotically dark features, came into view, carrying a blonde-haired baby. The child had an oversized head in relation to the body, even for an infant.

* * *

Watching from her own encampment, Lori Vale shook her head. It was the fake Martha, and her eyes were dull and glazed over, undoubtedly from sedation. It was child abuse, pure and simple. The teenager seethed, wished she could do something to help the child. But she was helpless to do anything, except watch. . . .

* * *

"This is Martha of Galilee," Dixie Lou said proudly, and then recited the concocted tale of her life: "In ancient times she was an apostle of Jesus Christ. Prior to that she'd been an employee of a wine shop in Jerusalem, working for her father. Upon hearing Jesus speak for the first time, she gave up her job and family and joined the holy entourage, even leaving her fiancée behind. Some said she wanted to marry Jesus, and that may have been her hope for awhile. But soon she realized that the holiest of men was not available for betrothal or any sort of physical relationship with a woman. Still, a bond of affection and trust formed between them, and Lord Jesus made her an apostle, one of the twenty-four."

"That's one of the most startling assertions of this book," Gazzara said. "There are so many new stories here. I haven't had time to read all of them yet, but I have some preliminary observations. You depict the fair sex in an entirely new, much more favorable light. There is no portrayal of the slavishly obedient wife here, or of the woman who cannot speak out in church, or of Eve as sinner and seductress, or of Mary Magdalene as a prostitute. In their time—the age of Jesus—decent, intelligent women were as important to the Savior as men."

"As we will be in the future," Dixie Lou said, "for all of humankind. Now that the message is out."

"What do you have to say to the people who think you're a crackpot? You've seen the opinion polls, I presume?"

"I have, and I could care less what people think of me personally, or of my organization. We do not seek approbation or popularity. When we compiled the *Holy Women's Bible* we did it as a service to *women*. It was a labor of love by my devoted staff, collecting and organizing the remarkable stories of the twelve she-apostles. If modern women choose to accept these truths and take them to heart for their own good, that is to their benefit—but if the opposite happens, I cannot account for stupidity."

"Harsh words."

"But true. Men have written history, molding it into their own story. But what about '*her*story?' What about *female* traditions? In the years after Christ, our gospels were stolen from us and destroyed. Our gospels were omitted from the *Bible*. It was a terrible crime."

"This is incredible," the reporter said.

A wild glaze filled Dixie Lou's dark eyes. "Listen to me carefully. Listen as a *woman*, not as a reporter, not as a pawn of the manipulators. The manipulators are out in force now, trying to put a spin on our message, seeking to distort it. They speak of us as false prophets, as servants of Satan, as child abusers. If women choose to believe such distortions, they are easily deceived, as they have been for millennia." Looking directly into the camera, Dixie Lou added, "Isn't it time for us to smarten up?"

* * *

At the edge of camp, a tall brunette guard spoke to Alex in a low tone, telling him what she had just learned about a female television correspondent who had been brought in blindfolded to see Dixie Lou, and about one of the she-apostles who was with them.

"Your mother is already broadcasting something," the guard said. The day before, she'd told him her name was Annette Tormé.

"Any idea what?"

She shook her head. "The Chairwoman is an interesting woman. And most unpredictable." The guard's large blue eyes bore another message. They danced whenever Alex met her gaze. She seemed to want their relationship to go further, but Alex didn't think he could do that. He could not get Lori out of his mind, couldn't stop worrying about her safety. Where was she?

Pensively, Alex rubbed the back of his neck. He wore a light-green shirt, only buttoned halfway up, and faded khaki chinos. "I appreciate you telling me this," he said.

"Perhaps you would care to look in on the broadcast?" Annette said.

"If I can do it without her noticing me."

"Why don't we go take a peek right now?" She pointed toward a cluster of tents, whose tops were flapping in a light breeze.

When they reached the tents and made their way silently past them, Annette suddenly stopped and put a finger to her lips. Alex stopped beside her.

Voices could be heard inside one of the nearby tents, off to his left. Two women conversing in low tones. One had a husky, throaty voice and sounded older, while the other, apparently younger, spoke in smooth, silky tones.

The elder was speaking. "The *Holy Women's Bible* is a sham. I can't stand the thought of it."

"Calm down, Deborah," the younger one said. "Only one of the gospels was improvised. The rest of the holy book—"

"That's Nancy Winters," Annette whispered. "She's talking with Deborah Marvel, another councilwoman."

They continued eavesdropping, but tried to look as if they were just standing there. A guard on the other side of the camp glanced at them, but looked away, apparently unconcerned.

"I just don't like it," Marvel said. "I know, I voted with the rest of us to falsify Martha's gospel, but—"

Alex and the guard exchanged surprised glances.

"There's nothing we can do about it now," Winters said. "The book's been released on the Internet. It's done. If anything leaks about this it will seriously damage our cause."

"I know, I know, but what we did—"

"It bothers all of us, especially Dixie Lou."

"I wonder if that's true. She never mentions Amy anymore. It's like she never existed. It's like *we* never existed. We're not mentioned by name in the *Holy Women's Bible*, either. Dixie Lou only referred to the 'council' in general."

The voices faded, and as they did, the pair of eavesdroppers moved away. "Do you realize what this means?" Alex whispered excitedly to the guard. "If Martha is a fake, that means one she-apostle is still missing."

"I wonder where she is," the guard said. Then, without warning, she planted a kiss on Alex's lips.

"You shouldn't do that," he said, pulling away.

"I've been wanting to since the first moment I saw you," she said. "But I must admit, I never liked your mother."

Suddenly she hurried away without explanation, and disappeared around the side of a tent.

Curious, Alex walked in that direction himself. He passed the councilwomen who had been talking, but who were now silent. They continued on, and so did he, scuffing up sand and dust. Moments later he was on the west side of the encampment, separated from the dining tent by one of the camouflaged helicopters.

For several moments as Alex watched, Annette stood outside the dining tent. Then she ran inside, past a male news crewman who tried to stop her.

* * *

Startled, Dixie Lou and the young reporter looked up at her. Nearby stood a playpen with a baby in it, a child Annette had not seen before. On her right she saw a Global News television camera with a red light on it. The camera was directed toward Dixie Lou and the child.

"Oh, are you interviewing our Chairwoman on live television?" Annette asked, nervously. "I'm sorry to interrupt."

The reporter stared at her blankly.

Dixie Lou's expression changed to anger. Her dark eyes simmered.

"I have something to say," Annette announced, moving to the side of the baby, in front of the camera. She felt warm air blowing in from the desert, through the open tent flaps.

"Turn off the camera," Dixie Lou demanded, glaring at the reporter.

But the camera's red light remained on, making a live broadcast.

"Is there a camp emergency?" Dixie Lou asked, of the guard.

"It goes beyond this camp," the tall guard said.

"Turn off the camera," Dixie Lou said again. "Whatever this is, it isn't part of the broadcast."

"Tell her about this *fake* she-apostle," Annette demanded. She gestured toward the baby.

The child didn't seem to notice the tension in the air, and sat in her pen playing with a dark-skinned doll.

"Guards!" Dixie Lou yelled. "Then, with a sweet smile, she looked into the camera and said, "Her charge is preposterous, of course. She can't prove it." Her eyes, however, were filled with fear.

Annette struggled to remain calm. "We—I—overheard two of your councilwomen discussing Martha. They were in a tent, didn't know I was listening." She didn't want to implicate Alex if she could avoid it, because she really cared about him.

Dixie Lou's gaze didn't waver from the rebellious guard. "Who did you supposedly overhear? Did you see them?"

"No," Annette admitted. "I didn't. But I know who they are. I just don't want to get them in trouble." She felt uneasy, way over-committed.

"You're very young," Dixie Lou said calmly, "and you have much to learn. Would you admit that you could be mistaken? The she-apostles are—quite understandably—a subject of intense debate all over the world. Perhaps the women were merely discussing that, and you misinterpreted."

"I don't think so." Annette's mind whirled, seemed incapable of focusing. She glanced at the camera, with its steady red light, its unblinking, probing eye. Her cheeks felt hot. Was this interview actually being transmitted live? She'd assumed so when setting up her impulsive plan—based upon what she had heard. There was supposed to be a direct satellite news linkup. But now she wasn't so certain.

It occurred to her that she was debunking the entire *Holy Women's Bible* by calling only one she-apostle and the Chairwoman into question, and this could cause the whole women's movement to flame out, just as Councilwoman Marvel had feared. Because of this concern, Marvel and the other councilwoman had backed off, and maybe Annette should do the same, considering not only herself but the welfare of her fellow women. She hadn't considered the far-reaching consequences before bursting impetuously into the tent. She'd only thought of her righteous rage at this terrible woman—Dixie Lou Jackson—and the way she was ruining the legitimacy of the women's movement.

"She doesn't *think* so," Dixie Lou said, a sarcastic tone. "With all her *vast* years of experience this guard doesn't *think* so."

The baby in the playpen began to fuss and whine, causing a white-uniformed matron to hurry in. "What is it, Martha?" she asked. "Too hot for you?" Blocking the child from the camera, the woman removed a shirt and long pants from the cherubic-faced child, exchanging them for a pair of pink shorts, with no top. The baby curled up as if to go to sleep, and the matron left.

"Guards!" Dixie Lou shouted, again.

This time they heard her, and two guards appeared. One was the short redhead with whom Annette often shared duty, Lipia Picard, with her usual stern expression.

"Remove her!" Dixie Lou commanded, pointing at Annette. "She's completely lost her mind." After this was done, Dixie Lou looked at the reporter and asked in a dulcet voice, "Now, shall we continue?"

"Is this some kind of a publicity stunt?" the reporter asked.

"Just a little bump on the road to women's rights," the Chairwoman said. "I've been facing and surmounting obstacles all my life, fighting for the truth, struggling for women to achieve equality with men."

"Some would claim that you seek *superiority* over men," the reporter said. "What do you say to that?"

With a smile, Dixie Lou countered, "But women *are* superior to men. In a future broadcast, perhaps I will list a hundred ways, or five thousand. But today, we are here to discuss little Martha of Galilee, and the astounding *Holy Women's Bible*."

* * *

Standing in front of the flat-screen television, Lori Vale shifted uneasily, kicking up a little cloud of sand at her feet. She stretched her arms, and spoke to Fujiko without looking to the side at her. Malia was smoking a cigarette, talking to her companions off to one side. Some of the smoke drifted Lori's way, and seemed to follow her whenever she shifted position. Since quitting smoking, she didn't like the smell of cigarettes, but didn't want to be rude by saying anything to Malia.

"That's why Martha didn't come to me with the she-apostles," Lori said to Fujiko in a low tone, "and why we only have eleven, not twelve. She's a fake."

"Dixie Lou didn't have her talk on camera, because the kid doesn't know a word of ancient Aramaic."

"I feel sorry for the child, whoever she is," Lori said. "She looks like she's been drugged, undoubtedly to keep her from saying much of anything at all."

Fujiko narrowed her gaze. "Dixie Lou must be going crazy, losing eleven she-apostles. I'll bet she doesn't know they're with us, doesn't even know if they're still alive."

"She probably doesn't know where the last child is, either," Lori said. "And neither do we."

The last child, Lori thought.

She recalled the shared vision she'd had with Dixie Lou, and the baby Lori held in her arms at the end of it, with Dixie Lou backing up in terror. Could that child, with auburn hair like Lori's own, be the twelfth she-apostle? Was Martha of Galilee waiting to be born?

And am I supposed to be her mother?

A shiver ran down her spine.

As Fujiko continued to talk, Lori didn't really hear her words. They were just disjointed sounds, floating in the air between them. With all of the problems and uncertainties assailing her, Lori wished she had her best friend Alicia Koppel around, to obtain her advice. Alicia, while not well-read, had an innate, natural intelligence, and always knew the smart thing to do.

Looking over at Fujiko and hearing the kindness in her voice, Lori wondered if the two of them might ever become close like that, so that they could confide in one another. But Lori was not ready for that, not yet.

* * *

In the commotion, Alex Jackson slipped over to the tent of Liz Torrence and Siana Harui, which was temporarily unguarded. Both of them were inside. "Come with me!" he said.

"Where to?" Siana asked. A petite young woman, she had short-cropped black hair and the attractive Asian features of her mother.

"Do you care? It has to be better than this place."

"He has a point," Liz said, as she slipped into her shoes. Slender and pretty, she had large green eyes.

The three of them broke into a run across the open sands, heading in the direction of the Arab village. They struggled to the top of a dune and tumbled down the other side, then regained their footing and kept running.

Alex had hoped to locate a trail marking the route of the Arabs, but wind had blown the sand completely smooth.

* * *

A tornado of blind fury stood in the open doorway, ready to enter the tent and destroy all inside it.

"That was pretty cute today," Dixie Lou said, a barely controlled growl from the storm of her face. She brandished a large, gleaming knife, and her gaze riveted on Annette Tormé, who lay on the fabric floor, her hands and feet shackled.

"Thought you'd surprise me with that little trick on live television, didn't you?" Dixie Lou said. Hellfire burned in her eyes. "And while you were there, three prisoners escaped."

Aloud, Annette prayed to the She-God for salvation.

With a quick motion, Dixie Lou plunged the knife into the guard's chest, then watched as life flowed out of her.

Chapter 15

The name Jesus is not intrinsically male or female. Derived from the Hebrew word Yeshua, it means "Jehovah is salvation."
—Editor's unpublished notes, the *Holy Women's Bible*

Western coast of Mexico . . .

Everyone else had gone to bed, but Raffaela Inez was restless, unable to sleep. She kept thinking about the young Mexican woman, Consuela, and her unusual baby. Raffaela had spent time with the child each day, listening to her babbling . . . and trying without success to understand her. In her medical studies, including research into the communication patterns of babies, Raffaela had never encountered anything like this before.

Consuela said "bad doctors" were after Marta. Preposterous. Or was it?

It was a warm evening, and Raffaela sat on a wicker settee outside, in the yellow illumination of a porch light. Medical journals were stacked next to her, along with the most recent Doctor's Journal, forwarded to her by a colleague who knew she wouldn't want to miss it, even while on vacation. Moths hurled themselves at the light and fluttered about, darting in front of Raffaela's face, but she paid little attention to them.

Instead, she stared blankly at a current journal article on new prosthetic devices. Unable to focus on it, she put it down. Then, absent-mindedly, she flipped through the pages of the other journals, scanning old headlines and articles. Nothing of interest. With a sigh, Raffaela was stacking the journals neatly, when one of them fell on the floor and opened to an article she had not noticed earlier, under the heading, MYSTERIES OF LANGUAGE.

In the article the author—a German doctor named Werner Hinkel—summarized what was known about the means of communication employed by various animals, including elephants, dolphins, whales, and dogs. He said they showed emotions and intelligence beyond the range of human comprehension or interpretation, since humans tended to make the mistake of using their own experiences and reference points for everything, thus creating filters that blocked vision.

The doctor went on to assert that even plants had intelligence, and cited the example of a wooden fence that was being overgrown by ivy. A small boy, after playing near the fence, returned to his mother in her rose garden and said, "The ivy spoke to me." The woman, trying to humor her child, replied, "That's nice, dear. And what did the ivy say to you?" Without hesitation, and in a tone that she found eerie, the child said, "It wants to wreck the fence. It doesn't like the fence there." His words were barely out of his mouth when a large section of the structure slumped to the ground, under a strangling snarl of ivy.

"Children understand these things better than we do," Dr. Hinkel wrote. "They are much closer to the vast mystery of existence than we are, having more recently emerged from it in the process of birth."

The concluding sentence particularly intrigued Raffaela: "Mothers, the next time your baby babbles at you, with sounds that make no apparent sense, try looking at it in a different way. Maybe it's not gibberish after all; maybe it's something else—the intelligent language of another dimension."

Setting the article aside, Raffaela envisioned the innocent face of little Marta, who lay asleep inside the house, and she wondered what unknown thoughts were going through her mind.

* * *

Rashid Ali Khan was feeling better. Upon arriving at his Bedouin camp in the middle of the night, he'd been so ill with fever that his men had strapped him to a camel's back, to prevent him from falling off. He remembered someone carrying him into his tent, and seeing his number-one wife Malia in flickering lantern light, hovering over him and assuring him he would get better soon. How many hours or days had passed since then? He wasn't certain, but knew from the warm temperature in his tent that it was not morning.

Someone had opened the window and door flaps so that desert breezes could blow through, and as he awoke he had no bed coverings over him. The thin woolen blankets had been tossed aside. He'd probably done it himself in his sleep. His wife's side of the low bed had been made up neatly. This large tent of the caravan leader had partitions inside, and a high ceiling so that a dozen men could stand in the reception area or sit comfortably for meetings and meals. The walls were hung with carpets and cloths with graceful Arabic designs.

As he sat up he stared at his small prayer rug, which someone had left rolled up at the foot of his bed. He wondered how many holy prayers he'd missed during the fever. He heard the rapid voices of women outside, but not of Malia. One of them said the men were on the nearby beach, fishing. Rashid's laptop computer sat on a low table in one corner.

Dressing hurriedly in white pants and a white shirt, he went outside and washed his hands in a laving basin near the tent, then laid down his prayer rug and knelt in the shade for his first prayer of the day, facing east toward Mecca. To make up for the time he had been asleep, he spent extra time communing with Allah, asking for God's infinite mercy upon his pitiful mortal soul.

As he finished, Malia appeared. "I am so pleased that you are feeling better," she said.

He started to stand up, but wavered, and she helped him to his feet. "Guess I'm not as strong as I thought," he admitted.

She supported him by one arm as he walked back to the tent. There she served him a meal of falafel, hummus, and wheat pocket-bread, with a bottle of warm beer. Afterward she left him alone, suggesting that he get more rest. Instead, he went to the laptop computer and switched it on.

Within fifteen minutes, after reviewing news reports, he had the full text of the *Holy Women's Bible* in front of him, casting an amber glow in the half-light of the tent. The cover page said it was an Arabic translation of the original English version. A whistle escaped his lips as he read on and learned that the new book—released only a few days ago—had already been translated into virtually every living language in the world. Technology amazed him.

He scanned the Gospel of Martha, the last of the book, which asserted that Jesus had twelve female apostles and an equal number of male apostles. The "she-apostles" were named, and some of their long-ago family members as well. A number of the women, according to the text, tried to warn Jesus about the treachery of Judas, but Jesus wouldn't listen, a fateful decision that led to his execution.

The Bedouin leader read the last pages, the final lines of verse. Taking a deep, agitated breath, he gazed through the open doorway of his tent toward the bright sky. Criminal women had written this . . . liars who did not believe in Allah the Magnificent. Something more troubled him. He scrolled through the screens, couldn't figure out why. What was he looking for?

Pausing, Rashid closed his eyes and tried to think, struggling to remember something that had barely tickled the edge of his consciousness. At the fringe of his awareness his fingers moved, as if in possession of a mind of their own.

When he opened his eyes he found himself staring at the answer: a series of tiny hieroglyphics across the bottom of the last page, including an Arabic anagram of Malia's name. The *Holy Women's Bible* had originally been transmitted from her e-mail address! The flaw in her computer program had not been repaired yet.

But she is not Christian!

Rashid was certain of this. There was no more devout Muslim woman than his favorite wife.

The western women are liars . . . full of devilish tricks. What have they done to my Malia?

His heart grew cold. An arctic wind blew through his soul.

He called Malia in, and when he pointed to the hieroglyphics on the screen she began to shake. "What have you done?" he thundered.

"They didn't tell me what they were transmitting. I didn't know."

"Where are the infidels?"

She pointed with a long, slender finger. "Beyond the rock outcropping, in two camps. They arrived in four aircraft, which are camouflaged."

"How many women?"

"Around thirty adults, plus children."

"The she-apostles," he muttered.

"Yes, my husband." She omitted some details, particularly the rift between Lori Vale and Dixie Lou Jackson.

"Get away from me," he commanded, raising a threatening hand toward Malia, "for I do not wish to hit you."

"I'm sorry, my husband. I didn't know." With her head lowered in shame, she hurried from the tent.

In a matter of seconds Rashid e-mailed the police in Tripoli, the nearest city. Within five minutes he received a response. The police were on their way. He was ordered not to contact anyone else.

* * *

Inside her camouflaged helicopter, Dixie Lou and her council sat in seats that had been swiveled into a simulated conference room.

"Maybe Katherine was right about Martha," Deborah Marvel suggested. "This is trouble."

"How did that guard know Martha wasn't a she-apostle?" Dixie Lou demanded. Her wilting gaze settled on Nancy Winters, who looked away. "Who do you suppose she overheard talking in a tent?"

No one volunteered a confession.

"Maybe your son had something to do with this," the heavyset Bobbi Torrence suggested. "I only mention it because he's missing."

"Perhaps I should have drowned him at birth," Dixie Lou mused.

"He has behaved suspiciously," Bobbi said, "ever since that Lori Vale showed up."

"Now they're both gone," Deborah said. "And good riddance."

"I was lenient with Alex," Dixie Lou said. "In fact, I've been lenient with a lot of the people around me." She glowered around the compartment, added in a low, menacing tone, "Two of you aren't as loyal as I had thought. Maybe we should get by with a smaller council." She stood up and removed the Sword of She-God—sheath and all—from a bulkhead bracket behind her.

"This is no time for us to squabble," Marvel said. "We need to put all of our heads together—for damage control."

Dixie Lou grasped the sword by its jeweled hilt and unsheathed it, revealing the gleaming steel of the exquisitely tooled blade. Intricate designs were worked into the steel.

"It sounds to me like the guard should be executed," Nancy suggested, "but we're short-staffed."

"With rookies," Dixie Lou muttered. "Just our luck." She held the blade surface close to her face and peered deeply into the distorted reflections of its surface. Her eyes took on a wild, insane cast. "As for the guard, she has already been dealt with."

The women murmured nervously among themselves. Opening a window for air, Dixie Lou heard the agitated voices of her inexperienced guards outside, hyperactive from the events of that afternoon.

"There is much to work through," Dixie Lou said.

"We will need to be more vigilant," Bobbi Torrence added.

Hearing the increasing noise of aircraft, Dixie Lou peered out a porthole, and beyond a waving flap of desert camouflage fabric she saw an approaching air squadron, darkening the sky.

Aided by Malia and her makeshift Arab technology, Dixie Lou had sent coded messages to operatives around the world, instructing them to take precautionary actions through narrowly defined chains of command. With the *Holy Women's Bible* published, Dixie Lou had felt it necessary to take this additional risk. She couldn't remain out in the desert indefinitely, had to reach out and let them know where she was, and ask them for military assistance. In a few moments she would know the results of her gamble.

"I have something bold in mind to gain public support," Dixie Lou said, noting the agitation of her councilwomen as the aircraft noise increased. "Remain seated, please."

Nervously, Dixie Lou replaced the sword in its sheath and wall bracket. During the moments remaining before the arrival of the airborne forces—which she hoped were friendly—she quickly sketched a plan to her council that had been fomenting in her mind, one their adversaries would never expect and would keep them off-balance.

"That might work," Deborah Marvel said, after listening to her commander's ideas.

As Dixie Lou listened to the comments of the other councilwomen she noted that they were, like Deborah, being extremely careful in their choice of words. Dixie Lou's proposal was bold, but none of them dared oppose it. Everyone was too afraid of her. Exactly the way she wanted it.

And they only knew *part* of the plan . . . the part she wanted to reveal to them.

Emerging from the makeshift conference room, Dixie Lou breathed a sigh of relief as she saw seven black VTOL gunships on the ground, their tilt-rotors spinning. More were landing nearby, disgorging armed UWW commandos in pale gold uniforms. She recognized two of her female officers as they ran across the sand from their gunships—disguised aircraft that bore no UWW markings.

* * *

But another squadron of aircraft rose over the desert coastline south of Dixie Lou's camp, four brown police helicopters and a military escort of eight more. In the lead craft, Police Commander Raoul Tirez, in charge of the assault, was startled at what he saw. Hundreds of troops on the ground, unmarked aircraft taking off and landing. Who were these people?

Orange tracer fire skimmed his windshield, and Tirez heard an explosion, one of his companion craft turned into a fireball.

"Turn back!" he shouted into a hand-held radio. He was attempting to send a message back to the city of Tripoli when a missile tore through his helicopter. In less than a minute, all of the Libyan aircraft had been destroyed.

Part Two

THE SHE-JUDAS

Chapter 16

For the indignation of the She-God is upon all nations of men, and her fury upon all their armies; she hath utterly destroyed them, she hath delivered them to the slaughter.
          —Isaiah 34:2, as amended in the *Holy Women's Bible*

During the arrival of the UWW military force and the battle against the Libyans, Dixie Lou made her move. "Hurry, hurry!" she exhorted the councilwomen, guards, translators, and matrons—and the one child they had to watch among them.

In the midst of it all, Deborah Marvel stuffed her own things into a pack. She didn't have much in the way of possessions, just a small travel bag and a toiletry kit grabbed hurriedly during the escape from Monte Konos, along with a paperback novel that had been given to her by one of the pilots.

Angrily, Dixie Lou hurled a rock at a burly female soldier she didn't think was working quickly enough to gather up camp supplies, hitting her squarely in the chest. The woman, who had dark facial hair and a scowl set deeply into her features, quickened her pace.

Carrying her pack and camp supplies to the command helicopter, Deborah grimaced, but knew to keep her opinion to herself. For years she had been Dixie Lou's staunchest ally, voting with her at council meetings almost all of the time—believing in Dixie Lou's vision for the UWW and for the welfare of women. As a reward for this support, Dixie

Lou had promised to make her second in command in the UWW, the most powerful of all councilmembers and answering only to the Chairwoman herself.

But Deborah was beginning to wonder if she had made a Faustian bargain, if she had sold her soul to the devil. Dixie Lou had changed for the worse since replacing Amy, and had become increasingly brutal. The way she left Katherine Pangalos and five other councilwomen back at Monte Konos—all women with a history of voting against Dixie Lou in council matters. Hardly a coincidence, and they were probably all dead now, in the BOI military attack. Deborah also didn't like the way Dixie Lou treated the she-apostles, using cruel forms of persuasion on them.

For now, Deborah was committed, though she would keep her eyes open.

She saw the fires of downed aircraft out on the desert. The Libyans had not sent enough firepower, at least not this time. Something exploded in the distance, and everyone hurried into the UWW vessels. Moments later Deborah was airborne, sitting with Dixie Lou aboard the command aircraft. Through the porthole the troubled councilwoman saw the blinking lights of scores of planes and VTOLs, all sleek and black in an assortment of shapes.

Inside some of them were children who had been brought along at Dixie Lou's command, in all a dozen females around the ages of the authentic she-apostles, including the phony Martha of Galilee. They were human props to be used by the Chairwoman in the next stage of her plan.

Human props, Deborah thought, agitated by this. *Am I one as well?*

Sitting alone in the forward section of the passenger compartment, Dixie Lou was working on a speech, looking at herself in a mirror attached to a seat-back and using a recording cube to play back her own words. The speech, at least the parts Deborah overheard, concerned the creation of the *Holy Women's Bible* and the "glorious" future of women. But the Chairwoman seemed to be in an even edgier mood than usual, and made a number of rude remarks to her aides and councilwomen, who subsequently tried to avoid her.

* * *

As the aircraft lifted into the afternoon sky, the Arab woman Malia came into Lori's camouflaged camp, and said it was Dixie Lou leaving with a large UWW force. Malia also described the battle with Libyan forces. Lori's first reaction was that this freed her up to take off herself without being detected, but she wondered if it could be a trick.

"Where is Dixie Lou going?" Lori asked, noting other Arabs milling about at the edge of the camp.

"North," Malia said. "Out over the Mediterranean."

"Toward Europe? But why?"

"I've brought someone who might know," Malia said, nodding toward the robed people who had accompanied her.

At a gesture from Malia, one of the group stepped forward and tossed back the hood of his dark gray robe. Lori did a double take, then squealed with delight as she made the recognition.

"Alex!"

They ran to each other and hugged. She felt the hardness of the young black man's muscles, lifted her lips to his and they kissed. Behind Alex, she saw Liz Torrence and Siana Harui, and she smiled at them. Crying out with happiness, Fujiko rushed to her daughter. "My baby! My baby!" Fujiko said.

"And you're a baby, too," Alex said, grinning at Lori, "still too young for me."

"But now we have a chaperone," Lori said, glancing over at Rea Janeg, who was serving a plate of figs and dates to the she-apostles, food that had been brought to the camp by nearby villagers. "She looks pretty tough, eh?"

"We'll need her," Alex said, giving her a playful nudge.

"How did you get away?" Lori asked, watching the little towhead Candace holding a fig, chewing around the edges of it.

"We ran off when they weren't looking. The Arabs found us this morning." Lori saw him gazing at the departing aircraft. She could barely hear their engines and rotors.

Alex updated her on the events in the other camp, including the conversation he overheard between Deborah Marvel and Nancy Winters, and how they did not like the idea of a fake twelfth she-apostle, because it could severely damage the UWW cause by discrediting it. He also told Lori he didn't know where his mother was going, but said, "At last we're free of her."

"I'm not so sure about that. I have a bad feeling."

* * *

Lori knew that she could not remain in the desert any longer, not after the battle in which Libyan aircraft were destroyed. Soon the authorities would be crawling all over the place, searching for evidence, making accusations.

But she had another important decision to make. Which direction should she go? Rea Janeg had assured her that the helicopter—with its long range fuel tanks—could still fly a considerable distance. Rea even drew a radius on a map, showing how far they could go with their remaining fuel. If necessary, they could fly to Spain, Germany, Turkey, or south into the heart of Africa, as far as Lake Chad.

While considering the options, Lori spent time that evening with the eleven she-apostles. Together, they walked out on the sand beneath the starlight, a short distance from the helicopter.

As one, they paused and formed a line, gazing to the north, in the direction the UWW aircraft had taken. Lori stood in the middle, with five children on one side and six on the other. As Lori knelt and held hands with the toddler Mary Magdalene and the baby Abigail on either side of her, she remembered what the latter had told her three days ago: "To speak the special tongue of the she-apostles you must learn to think without words. . . ."

All of them linked hands. Moments passed, and without the exchange of words, the answer came to Lori. She would leave first thing in the morning and follow the same route, across the Mediterranean. They were going to Rome.

Afterward, when she returned to camp and separated from the children, Lori had her doubts about the decision she had made. It had not been at all logical; in retrospect she could think of many reasons to take an entirely different route, getting as far away from Dixie Lou

Jackson as she could, finding a safe place for the children. But that portion of her brain, with its capacity for sound reasoning, could not see into the realm where she needed to find such answers.

The whole concept of safety is an illusion, she realized.

* * *

For several days, Raffaela and Arsinio Inez had been vacationing, a welcome respite from the rigors of their professional lives. Time and time again, however, their conversation turned to the young peasant woman staying with them, and her most unusual child.

"We need to consult with someone on this," Arsinio said one day, as he and his wife stood at the living room window, gazing out onto a tropical, sunlit yard. It was late morning, with the moisture of recent rains evaporating from the broad green leaves of plants, forming a mist over the jungle. "You know some people at the university who should be able to offer good advice."

She shook her head. "We need to be extremely careful about this. Let's just assume for a moment that she's right." A woman who did not mince words, Raffaela was brilliant, with a unique ability to identify and hone in on important points. "Just think about that for a moment."

"All right."

The baby was asleep in the guest bedroom while Consuela was out with the boys at the beach, where they were teaching her how to ride a surfboard. For the occasion, Raffaela had taken the young woman into town the day before and purchased a swimsuit for her. Consuela had never owned one before, but said she knew how to swim, since she'd grown up near a lake where she'd gone swimming nude with other children. In the swimsuit she had looked quite lovely, with a pleasing figure. Gilberto and Jose had been only too happy to act as her beach escorts.

Arsinio cleared his throat, as he often did. "OK, I thought about it. Let's just assume for a moment that she's right. What are you driving at?"

"Just listening to Consuela," Raffaela said, "it's difficult to believe what she's saying, her outlandish story of a harrowing escape from death when she and her baby were attacked inside a church. *In a church?*

Impossible, my mind tells me. Her words are not convincing enough, not even with her terrified demeanor. But when all of this is added to the peculiar, even bizarre behavior of her baby, it gives me pause."

"You're saying it all adds up to something?"

The large woman nodded. "My darling, we lead sheltered lives. Each day you go to your office and decide what to export and how much to charge, while I go to the university and lecture students. But beyond our safe cocoons, our sheltered, predictable social life and pleasant vacation trips to the coast, there is a more dangerous realm, where strange and inexplicable events occur."

"You're saying you believe her, that she's really being chased by 'bad doctors?'"

"I don't know, but you have to admit her baby *is* unusual. That could mean something. I'd like to hear a translation of what little Marta is saying. It doesn't sound random to me; I hear a rhythm and a cadence, like a language. From a child who is only seven months old! And her eyes are so alert, so probing."

"All right," Arsinio said. "Let's assume for a moment that bad people—real doctors or doctors in disguise—want this child. For what, I can't imagine."

"I can."

Surprised, he looked at her.

"While we were in town, I bought a newspaper. A story on page two jumped out at me. It's about the new *Holy Women's Bible*. You said something to me about it the other day."

"Just what I overheard at the *mercado* about some crazy women who put together a heretical book. The Pope says it's evil, that no good Catholic should look at it."

"Did you hear about the children?" she asked.

He looked at her blankly.

She handed the newspaper to him, folded open to the story. "Read the part I circled first."

Her husband did so, studying three circled paragraphs. "Could it be?" he asked, as he finished. "They babble in a strange language—" He looked toward the bedroom where the child slept.

Raffaela nodded.

"But the UWW already has twelve she-apostles, it says here."

"Not exactly," she said. "I heard on the radio that a guard accused Dixie Lou Jackson of using a fake she-apostle, of falsifying part of their *Holy Women's Bible*. If one of them is fake, it leaves eleven real ones. Or, there are really thirteen of them."

"Don't get drawn into this, Raffy. The *Bible* says there were only twelve apostles, and all were men."

"We're already drawn into this, *mi esposo*, and we need to be extremely careful. Consuela said a woman attacked her in the church, firing a gun. I don't think we should tell anyone about the baby yet."

"Well, the boys aren't talking. Consuela pleaded with them not to, and they're taking her seriously. For now, the secret is safe."

"Yes, but for how long? I'm very worried about this, Arsinio, very worried."

* * *

After a four hour flight, the formation of aircraft landed at a private airstrip near a large city, the twinkling lights of which Deborah Marvel could see across an expanse of water.

The passengers disembarked and hurried into black, shiny motor homes, said by a UWW officer to have stealth capabilities, as did the aircraft in which the group had flown here. Dixie Lou entered a large vehicle, while Deborah and the other councilwomen were escorted to a smaller one, accompanied by a muscular female driver. Deborah sat in the back, a plush blue velvet enclosure with leather bucket seats. The air smelled factory-new.

Security was everywhere, heavily armed women in pale gold uniforms with UWW patches on their lapels and sleeves. With Dixie Lou's motor home in the lead, the caravan rolled toward the city specified by Dixie Lou when she described her plan to the council.

Roma . . . Rome, Italy.

The motor homes slipped into underground parking slots, beneath a television station building. Dixie Lou, wearing a heavy black coat, boarded an elevator, followed by her entourage of women carrying twelve imitation she-apostles.

She had an appointment for a recording session.

Chapter 17

Nothing is more destructive than righteous energy.
—Finding of the U.S. War Commission, a non-profit think-tank

Pope Rodrigo stepped back from the videophone image as loud, angry words poured across the connection, like a shrieking storm. Even though he was the most powerful, most influential religious leader in the world, he still had to endure this—his aged, senile mother in one of her moods. He closed a folder, pushed it to one side of the wide desk top and looked at the image of his tiny, stooped mother.

This was the office of one of his cardinals, who had gracefully loaned it to him while remodeling work was being performed in the papal offices. It was one of the last renovation tasks in an extensive schedule of construction and rearranging that had been ongoing for more than five years, throughout Vatican City. The changes had been controversial, as some purists criticized altering the arrangement of furnishings and art works that had been untouched for centuries, except for cleaning and repairs. But Pope Rodrigo had ignored the naysayers, and all of the cardinals agreed with him that the world headquarters of the old church needed to be refreshed. During the work, the catalogue of art pieces was continually updated, as were the Vatican maps, so that the public could keep track of where priceless artworks were now being kept.

"You're such a big shot now," his elderly mother said, in her native Catalonian Spanish, which her family had spoken for centuries. "You don't come and see me anymore, so I always have to take the train to Vatican City. That's a long way for an old lady to travel."

He responded in the same dialect. "Mama, I'm busy. You know how it is. I've tried to explain so many times." Nervously, he spun an ink pen on the high-polished mahogany and inlaid-pearl desk top. The office was dimly illuminated by porcelain table lamps. Through his window he saw the lights of Rome, outlining the modern and ancient structures. The "Eternal City" that had survived for so many centuries, and seen so many political changes.

"How many mothers do you have, Rodrigo?"

"You know the answer to that."

"Do I? For all I know, with your influence upstairs you have another mother on order, to take my place. A nice old lady, she'll probably bring you *bollos*, the little sweet cakes you love."

"Mama, you know that's not true. You're my one and only."

"Then come to Segovia and visit me."

He sighed. "I will."

"Do you promise?"

"I promise. I'll check my schedule." With the pen, he doodled on a piece of parchment, occasionally dipping the writing instrument in an inkwell for replenishment.

"Rearrange things if you have to. Cancel the President of France and the Prime Minister of Canada. Come and see your mother instead. I may not have much longer to live."

"You're in perfect health."

"Perfect health for a ninety-eight-year-old lady isn't so great. When may I expect you?"

"Soon, Mama, I promise."

As he completed the call and shut off the connection it occurred to him, as it had before, how much she resembled the outlandish, Gaudi-designed apartment building in which she lived. An art piece to some and an eyesore to others, it had molded stucco walls without any perceptible uniformity and a fantasy park on the rooftop. He disliked the bizarre place, but she refused to leave it.

Emerging from the office into the mosaic-tiled reception area, he saw Sister Meryl sitting on a bench, with a thick, rough-bound book open on her lap. A tiny woman with large eyes, she wore a black habit with white trim around the hood.

He cleared his throat in an indignant fashion.

Startled, she closed the book and stood up. "Your Holiness, I brought the heretical material you requested. It has been printed from the Internet. I was just checking the page numbering to make sure it's all here."

"It looked like you were reading it."

"I would never read blasphemy, Your Holiness."

"Oh? And *I* would?"

"I didn't mean it that way. It's just that everyone knows that this *Holy Women's Bible* is ungodly. Everyone's talking about it."

"Then it's your sacred duty not to listen."

She bowed, and handed him the heavy volume, which had an unmarked cover.

As the Pope hurried to his office he took a deep, agitated breath. Previously he'd seen only a packet of draft pages obtained for him by a Greek priest, a computer printout comprising only a portion of the profane tome. Now he was anxious to see the complete version. He wouldn't read all of it, just enough to select the most sacrilegious sections, which he would publicly condemn from the steps of St. Peter's Basilica.

He collapsed into the leather chair at his immense desk and wished God had never permitted the hadean invention of computers. The devices were causing a lot of trouble, especially when combined with the Internet, making the Pope's job much more difficult. He'd never learned to operate one himself, and never would, especially after this. Perhaps with prayer, God would find a way to rid the world of them.

The *Holy Women's Bible* lay in front of him, an ominous presence. He flipped it open to the title page, then looked away. That nun had been behaving strangely. Should he have her investigated? She was a *woman*, after all, and these days a man—even a servant of God—could not be too careful. A lot was at stake.

For long moments, seeking inspiration, he stared at a fifteenth century painting of the bearded Jesus. *No*, he finally told himself. *I'm just acting paranoid. It has nothing to do with Sister Meryl.*

He glanced down at the desktop, at the folder he'd been reading before his mother called. His fingers tapped the gold Vatican seal imprinted on the cover. Inside was a letter. One of those arriving periodically on his desk, it had been scrutinized at lower levels of the church bureaucracy and referred higher and higher, each time with a comment sheet and recommendations, seven of which were now in the folder. Another problem . . . so many of them nowadays.

He reread the suggestions, then scanned the letter again, which had been written by President Markwether's brother. Odd sort of fellow, Zack Markwether, and most peculiar that he would send the letter directly, instead of passing it through channels. This had not come from the President of the United States, as it bore no cover letter from that office. Filled with recommendations to tighten security, the letter had at first annoyed the Pope, and then—after further study—he had been frightened by it. Could the allegations possibly be true? Were there really gaping holes in Vatican security, dangerous oversights that were large enough to steer an ocean liner through? Such impertinent wording, but what if the man was right?

He sighed, looked at a medieval sculpture that depicted the Virgin Mary and the infant Jesus. The gaze of the Madonna seemed to be focused directly on him, and for the first time her eyes were not filled with compassion and love. Instead he saw—or *thought* he saw—worry in them, and fear.

With a smooth stroke of the pen, the Pope wrote an order to the Chief of Vatican Security, Aldo Gasperi. Then he turned to the other problem, the book of heresy.

Chapter 18

Brain researchers know that women generally use two sides of their brain at once, while men only use one. Consider, does this suggest greater potential for women, or for men? It might be argued either way, with women claiming that their brains operate more efficiently, and men insisting that they have accomplished much more than women using only half of their brains. But what have men really accomplished? Haven't we had enough of their destructive male energy?

—Amy Angkor-Billings, *Discourses*

"We're over Palermo now," the pilot announced to Lori, who sat beside her in the cockpit. They'd left early in the morning, and had been flying for a couple of hours. The weather had been mild and warm, with almost no wind.

Outside her window, the teenager saw the white buildings and churches of the Sicilian city below the helicopter. Another time, perhaps in another lifetime, she might have enjoyed exploring the picturesque, byways down there, purchasing food and crafts from street vendors, dining in charming outdoor cafes. But today, with her destination lying farther to the north . . . the Italian mainland . . . she had other things on her mind.

Lori felt like a bloodhound on the scent of a fleeing felon, but it was not a redolence in the traditional sense. Rather, she followed a trail through the sky that was revealed to her almost instinctually, a visceral sensation by which she discerned the spoor left in the air by Dixie Lou Jackson. It was an extension of the information she had gleaned earlier while holding hands with the she-apostles, when she learned that the UWW leader was bound for Rome. This was a confirmation of that fact.

Though she had these had two linked processes providing her with the same information, Lori still didn't understand exactly *how* she knew where Dixie Lou was going, but she *knew* nonetheless, and she was as certain of this as she was of the breaths she took and the thoughts that rushed through the neural pathways of her brain. It was a wordless truth.

In one sense this pursuit was a compulsion for her, driven by a subconscious impulse that could not be ignored. Certainly it must have something to do with her personal dislike for Dixie Lou, especially for the Chairwoman's part in the death of Lori's mother, Camilla Vale.

In considering this, however, Lori took a deep breath.

The force driving her with such intensity involved much more than personal animus. She needed to stop Dixie Lou for a larger reason. Lori had eleven she-apostles with her, but where was the twelfth, Martha of Galilee? Had Dixie Lou killed her? Lori needed to find out. She needed to expose the frauds of this abominable woman, and the homicide she had committed at Monte Konos. That murder, witnessed by Lori and Alex, was undoubtedly just the tip of the iceberg.

Since the attack on the goddess circle, events had been going at a breakneck pace. Through it all, trying to keep up, Lori sensed a change inside of her, a strange feeling that she was very old. Even so, this did not fatigue her. In a conversation with Alex earlier in the day, she had told him she felt energized, stronger and wiser.

Now, feeling a powerful impulse, Lori went to the jump seat at the rear of the cockpit and switched on the small flat-screen television set, mounted on a bulkhead. She turned up the volume, heard a female announcer say that the enigmatic leader of United Women of the World was about to deliver a speech that would be telecast all over the world. News of the impending address by Dixie Lou Jackson had been on every satellite news station for hours. It was not live; the announcer said she had recorded it the evening before.

The screen flickered, and Dixie Lou Jackson appeared, dressed in the long gold vestment of a priestess. Around her neck hung a golden sword-cross on a chain. Looking very distinguished, she stood at the podium of a studio theater, gazing into the camera. The Sword of She-God, never far from her, rested on a stand at her side. Behind her stood matrons holding small children.

The Chairwoman cleared her throat. "I am in Rome, Italy, broadcasting from an unnamed studio. For the moment, security does not permit me to say any more than that. Sadly, I have enemies who wish to do me harm. I am like all of the women who have ever been threatened by men, except I am taking steps to fight back."

I was right, Lori thought. *She's in Rome....*

Dixie Lou's elegant robe, which Lori had never seen before, bore the green-and-orange UWW emblem on each side of the collar. Draped over one shoulder was a colorful stole adorned with twelve boxes, each of which, Dixie Lou explained to her television audience, contained an artist's rendition of the face of a different she-apostle, as that child appeared during the creation of the sacred *Holy Women's Bible.*

Looking on, Lori noted that one of the boxes contained the face of the counterfeit Martha of Galilee, and the other eleven faces were phony as well. None of them were the actual she-apostles.

One by one the compact black woman introduced all of the supposed she-apostles personally, from the toddlers (Veronica, Mary Magdalene, Priscilla, Sarah, Kezia, Candace, and Lydia) to the babies (Esther, Hannah, Abigail, Rhoda and Martha). These children represented all the major races of humankind, she said, and Lori thought that their appearances looked remarkably close to the authentic she-apostles. Some of them were nearly exact replicas, in fact, she thought as she looked closer. Dixie Lou must have had makeup artists perform changes to those children's faces, because the real ones had already been seen in public.

As Dixie Lou introduced the children, matrons brought them forward. To her disgust, Lori noted that all of the she-apostles appeared to have been given sedatives. They looked listless, ready to nod off. Dixie Lou said each child was born with a different name in modern times, but revealed their apostolic appellations as soon as they began speaking in ancient Aramaic.

A story that was based in truth, but which applied to the wrong children.

Presently, Dixie Lou motioned for the matrons to step back and continued her speech, in her Southern drawl. Her often tense mood was exactly the opposite now, as she quipped about the purported she-apostles' antics, bantered with them and announced to the women of the earth the great joy of the *Holy Women's Bible* that had sprung from the reincarnated minds of these children. Somewhat correctly, she related the history of the book, how it included not only the *Testament of the She-Apostles* but also *The Old Testament* and *The New Testament*, edited to give the correct view of women.

Holding up a bulky, leather-bound copy of the holy book, Dixie Lou exclaimed, "These are the only true gospels!"

Wild applause ensued, but to Lori it sounded canned, since there was probably no studio audience, other than a few trusted associates of the Chairwoman.

Gesturing with her thick arms for emphasis, Dixie Lou said, "Some of you might wonder about the guard who interrupted my last broadcast, charging that we have a fake she-apostle."

Intrigued that she was even bringing the subject up, Lori leaned closer to the screen. Dixie Lou was confronting the matter head-on, an unexpected move.

Following a pause, Dixie Lou smiled confidently and said, "Not a word of it is true. That particular guard has a history of mental illness, which she concealed from us when she was hired. We've posted details on the Internet. But today I have a much more important message, of the utmost importance to every woman on the planet, and to the men who love and support those women."

You're the biggest liar in the world, Lori thought.

The Chairwoman took on a deadly serious expression, while calling for an end to abusive behavior by males in every nation of the world, and for the cessation of atrocities against women that were occurring at that very moment. Dixie Lou spoke of cowardly men who beat and murdered smaller and physically weaker women in brutal attempts to control and misuse them.

With her voice rising in angry crescendo, she described bride burning in India, women in China who were compelled to have abortions because of the one-child-policy, girls in the Middle East who weren't allowed to go to school, teenagers in Southeast Asia forced into slavery and prostitution, beautiful young Bangladeshi woman burned with acid by rejected suitors, and the genital mutilation of female children in Africa.

The catalogue of atrocities was masterfully delivered.

As she concluded her speech, she went to the purported she-apostles and lifted the redheaded "Apostle Mary Magdalene," one of the toddlers. Cradling the mock she-apostle in her arms, she rocked her back and forth and said, "This is the way of women, nurturing and loving, helping young minds and spirits grow. Unlike our male counterparts, women have not widely embraced the way of violence in the past, but this has to change for awhile. Each of us must be willing to fight for our She-God-given rights, for the sake of our granddaughters."

She paused, then continued in a determined tone, "Women of the world, take control of your lives! Do whatever is necessary, and when it is complete the earth will be a better place. Use a knife, a frying pan, a rolling pin, your man's golf putter or his gun to drive him back, whatever it takes. That man is bigger and stronger, so get yourself an 'equalizer.'"

The unseen, canned audience clapped and cheered. On the screen, Dixie Lou Jackson raised her arms in front of her and smiled.

* * *

As she watched her own recorded broadcast that morning, the Chairwoman recalled her secret reason for smiling. Prior to the speech, computers had sprayed coded Internet messages to clandestine UWW paramilitary forces in her vicinity, moving them into position, focusing power. Gunboats were speeding to a rendezvous point on the western coast of Italy; underground equipment had been brought out and was being transported by cargo plane; armed female soldiers were gathering.

Messages also went out to operatives in key positions—sleeper agents—summoning them to action.

The BOI would never suspect what Dixie Lou had in mind next, and would not be able to prevent it.

* * *

Hearing something behind her, Lori swiveled her chair and looked into the eyes of the redheaded toddler who stood there, looking up at her. Mary Magdalene's eyes glowed like bright little suns, so that Lori wondered if she could continue to gaze at them without blinking. But she did nonetheless, transfixed.

Mary dipped a small hand into a pocket of her robe and brought out a handful of sand. Holding her palm flat in front of her, the sand began to shimmer bright silver, and floated in the air. The tiny grains floated around the room, over the head of the pilot (without her seeing them) and back into Mary's hand.

With a smile, she put the handful of sand back in her pocket and returned to the passenger compartment.

Lori tried to comprehend what she had just seen, but the more she tried, the more elusive the truth became, as if it were dancing away from her. It fled understanding, concealed itself in shadowy, cosmic reaches. And she realized how pointless it was to make any attempt to understand the phenomenon, at least on the level at which her brain was accustomed to operating. For answers, she needed to go deeper, into an alternate realm that remained largely unavailable to her, an awareness that she could not force open.

The timing had to be right, she realized. In due course it would come to her if she was meant to know it, like understanding the arcane language of the she-apostles.

Lori was certain of one thing, though. She needed to catch Dixie Lou and stop her.

* * *

A half hour later, as they flew northward over an aquamarine sea . . .

Lori wandered back down the central aisle of the passenger compartment, heading for the aft galley. The pilot Rea Janeg had flown nonstop across the Mediterranean, but hadn't slept well the night before departure. She kept going on what she called "repeated injections of caffeine," cups of strong coffee brought to her by Lori.

While Lori filled yet another paper cup with coffee, she watched three she-apostles toddle into the galley single file . . . Priscilla, Lydia, and Candace. They looked sleepy-eyed.

"A bit young for coffee, aren't you?" Lori asked, with a smile. The helicopter bumped through turbulence, and she grabbed a side bar to hold on, spilling some of the coffee.

The children had better "air legs" than she did, and maintained their footing much more easily. They rubbed their eyes and yawned.

"Can you make sand dance in the air like Mary Magdalene?" Lori asked, as she fitted a plastic lid onto the cup. She spoke English to the children, wondered if they could understand. Their eyes were alert and inquisitive.

Bending down, Priscilla picked up an empty paper cup from the deck, and tossed it in the air. Just as the cup was about to hit the floor in front of the children, it floated back upward, hovering in front of their faces. Lori saw a shimmering disturbance in front of the children, and heard buzzing in her ears.

The toddlers gathered around the cup, and with their mental energies tossed it back and forth among them in the air, making a game of it. All the while, they kept glancing over at Lori, as if for approval.

"That's a pretty neat trick," Lori said. She slipped by them, carrying the coffee forward along the aisle. Glancing back, she saw the children having trouble keeping the cup in the air. It tumbled to the deck, and they couldn't get it to float anymore.

After making the delivery, Lori peered back into the passenger compartment. Apparently giving up on the game, the children returned to their seats, where Alex, the translator, and a matron were taking care of them. Soon the three toddlers joined the other she-apostles in sleep.

Alex was asleep himself, holding the slumbering baby Esther in his arms, wrapped in a blanket. Lori smiled at how cute he looked holding the child, whose skin was a beautiful shade of light black, a mixture of races. Earlier, Lori had seen him speak to the fussy baby in a gentle, calming tone that immediately caused her to quiet down.

For a long while, Lori sat on the jump seat, trying to comprehend. The she-apostles had an interesting telekinetic power, but didn't seem to have endurance with it, as if they needed to develop their mental muscles more. Perhaps that would come with age.

She wondered if this power might develop into something other than a parlor trick, and contemplated something else as well. Did her own presence have something to do with their telekinesis, perhaps through a force field that they shared? In the days to come, she wanted to explore such a possibility—but something told her to do it away from the inquisitive eyes and interference of adults.

If Lori had something to do with their abilities, this suggested another interesting possibility, a quid pro quo: Did the she-apostles also impart something to her, the mysterious tracking ability she seemed to have? Had the children somehow inspired her, permitting her to tap into internal resources she never knew she had until now?

She tried to slow the racing of her mind.

Chapter 19

It is natural for any organized religion to consider the new gospels heretical. How could they take any other position, since their entire power structure is based upon something entirely different? Change is very unsettling.

                         –Lori Vale, *The Psychology of Religion*

Before arriving in the "Eternal City" of Rome, Lori had been forced to deal with several problems, which she solved with the enterprising assistance of Fujiko Harui while they were still in flight. First, Fujiko arranged for them to land at a small private airfield outside the city that she'd learned about through her own extensive network of personal contacts. It was a field where they would not be scrutinized by the Italian police or customs officials, and which the UWW would not know about, either.

Next, she called a tourist office and arranged to rent the entire top floor of an apartment building in the Manzoni district of the city. The facilities were expensive, and so were the airfield arrangements, but they had plenty of money onboard the helicopter, and this was a legitimate expense for the she-apostles.

Fujiko also reported that the apartment complex had connections with the operator of a large private van, which could transport all of them from the airfield in one trip, and that the apartment superintendent had promised complete privacy and security . . . in exchange for additional payments, of course. Pursuant to Lori's instructions, Fujiko told the superintendent, an elderly woman, that they would have fourteen terminally ill medical patients with them when they arrived—eleven children and three adults. Under the concocted tale, they were all going to receive experimental medical treatments in Rome.

The three adult "patients" were actually the prisoners Wendy Zepeda and the two guards. The troublesome trio could not just be left on the helicopter, not even under supervision, because that might result in unwanted attention from outsiders. Fujiko had once been a doctor, so half an hour before landing she did as Lori instructed, administering soporific injections to them from the helicopter's medical kit, causing them to pass out. The prisoners would be removed from the aircraft on stretchers.

It was an offbeat fabric of lies, but told to the driver and the apartment superintendent in such a convincing fashion that they said in broken English that they wanted to do everything possible to help. Lori thanked both of them, and asked them to say prayers for the safe recovery of the patients.

This pleased the two Italians, especially the energetic old woman who ran the apartment building, Mrs. Capo. "*Si, si*," she said, wiping her hands on a food-stained apron, and then touching a silver cross that she wore on a chain. "I will pray to Jesus for your success." She and the driver then took Lori and Fujiko by elevator to the top floor, and showed them the connected apartments they would be renting.

"I must emphasize something very important," Lori said, handing separate wads of hundred dollar bills to the superintendent and the driver, funds from the money cabinet on the helicopter. Lori and her confidantes now had all of the funds in valises and other bags carried off the aircraft, and were keeping hidden how much they had. She was trusting the two middle-aged matrons, the pilot, and the scholarly translator now, in addition to Alex, Fujiko, Liz, and Siana.

"Anything," Mrs. Capo said.

"*Si*, anything," the driver agreed, counting the bills with considerable pleasure.

"As my friend told you when she made the reservation, we require complete privacy for our medical program, and you must not discuss us with anyone. No one is to even know that we are here, not your other tenants, nor anyone else. This is essential for the complete recovery of the patients. You would not want to do harm to these patients at such a vulnerable time in their lives."

"*Sì, sì,* absolute privacy," the manager promised. "We will be available for all of your needs."

The driver of the private bus, who had introduced himself as Domingo Petrovese, nodded and agreed as well.

Mrs. Capo had other duties to perform, but instructed the driver to help her new tenants with whatever they needed. That morning, Petrovese helped transport the three stretcher-bound women, the children, and personal articles up to the top floor, the seventh. He said he was a close friend of the superintendent, and that he lived in the building himself. Lori asked him where in the building he lived.

"I live in Mrs. Capo's apartment on the floor beneath you," Petrovese said, with a big grin.

"Oh."

"I am Mrs. Capo's special friend. I do handyman work, anything she requires.' He leaned close and whispered, "Do not tell her I told you we are roommates. She is a very proper Catholic woman, and would be embarrassed."

"You have my word of honor," Lori said with a smile.

"And you have mine," he said, moving a forefinger across his own lips, like a zipper. "Our secrets are safe with each other."

* * *

For three years, Aldo Gasperi had been Captain of the Swiss Guard, responsible for the safety of the Pope and for the security of the holy shrines of the Vatican. At the age of fifty-six, this balding little man occupied a small but comfortable apartment in Vatican City, shared with a fluffy white cat that had black paws. The large female cat, named Shag Rat by Aldo's English cousin who brought her from London, was adept at keeping the apartment clean of not only rodents but of any other pesky intruders (especially flies and moths) that might foolishly dare to trespass. Shag Rat took her guard duties seriously, as her master did.

While sitting at a kitchen table with his cat curled near his feet, Aldo reread a handwritten note that had been delivered to him that evening, less than an hour ago. The note, written on heavy, gold-embossed papal stationery, instructed him to follow up on each of the recommendations made in a preposterous letter written by the brother of the President of the United States—a transmittal that criticized the security systems of the Vatican and made recommendations for improvement. Aldo felt his blood pressure rise as he again looked over a copy of the American's letter. The nerve of that man! Why couldn't he mind his own business? And why did His Holiness Pope Rodrigo take the comments seriously? Was he losing faith in Aldo? It was disturbing, most disturbing.

Somehow he felt he had let the Pope down, even though His Holiness had not expressed any criticism in his note. Pope Rodrigo was a man of infinite patience, and an excellent judge of human character. He knew how to draw out the best in people. Aldo, like so many others on the Vatican staff, adored this most perfect of all men, and would do anything to please him.

The Pope had only written, "Please look into this" on the note, but now Aldo felt he needed to prove himself to his boss—actually to *re-prove* himself. It wasn't fair, really, since Aldo done so many things well over the years. Once, he'd even been responsible for saving the Pope's life by apprehending a clever assassin who had scaled a wall of the Vatican Palace with climbing gear, during a short period when the alarm system went down. Aldo, ever vigilant, had increased the surveillance of the grounds while the alarm system was being worked on, placing the entire guard force on duty. As it turned out, the assassin—a Turkish Muslim who was wanted for crimes in his own country—had been hired by an insider, who had disabled the system. Through an intensive internal investigation, Aldo had discovered the Vatican staff member who had initiated the assassination attempt, and had begun the process that led to the conviction and incarceration of both men.

Tears welled in the guard captain's eyes, but he tried to steel himself. Even though this was not fair, having to answer a letter from a meddlesome American, who was Aldo to question such things? After all, as His Holiness often said in his pronouncements, each person must constantly face challenges in life, all in accordance with God's Plan. So it must be with this unexpected letter. He sighed and felt a little better as he placed himself in submission to God's will. A heavenly calmness swept over him, and he was pleased with this, for it allowed him to think more clearly.

For many decades, Aldo's family had worked for the Vatican, in a variety of positions. His mother Gina had been a cleaning woman and later a cook in the cafeteria, and his talented sister, Malvi, had helped in the restoration of an old mural. Beto, his father, had been on the guard force, but had been killed in an automobile accident when Aldo was small, living with his parents in Vatican City.

Later Aldo had been scrutinized and tested by the school nuns who decided that he would be a good candidate for the prestigious papal guard force—one of the most elite organizations of its kind in the world. Stringent security and psychological tests ensued, and the young man—at the age of eighteen—had gone into intensive training. As Aldo advanced to captain of the force over the next decade, the Pope came to know him by his first name, and became a father-figure to Aldo, who had lost his own father so tragically. On Aldo's twenty-first birthday, he, his sister, and their mother had even been invited to dine with His Holiness. Aldo's mother was gone now, having passed away the year before, and his sister had moved to Florence, where she was working on the restoration of priceless murals.

Reviewing the Pope's note and the Zack Markwether letter that precipitated it, Aldo resolved to prove himself again to this Pope who had been so generous and loving to him, and prove himself as well to the master of them all, the Holy Father himself. Aldo would begin investigating the allegations this very evening.

* * *

The Mediterranean seaside town of Cerveteri, northwest of Rome . . .

Olivia Puccini sat up in bed, listening to the familiar sleeping sounds of her corpulent, black-mustachioed husband, who lay beside her. Outside an open window, a nightingale cried.

Making love to her husband that evening had been more of a chore than usual, and she had taken a long, hot shower afterward. Now he was asleep beside her, his body stinking with the sweat of a hot, fat man. Swarthy and hairy, he was General Cosimo Puccini of the Italian Army, and this was their bedroom in the family villa, high on a terraced hillside overlooking the sea.

By her own mother's standards she should be happy in her position, but she had rarely felt that way, not even before the televised speech of Dixie Lou Jackson and the encoded e-mail message she'd received. For centuries women had been treated poorly by men, as she had learned through her secret association with united Women of the World. Advances, while occurring over the centuries, had come too slowly.

That was about to change.

As General Puccini slept, she unlocked his desk and reviewed the contents, all the letters and other documents proving he'd been stealing weapons and munitions, and selling them on the black market. She also had evidence that he'd been maintaining mistresses, a common enough habit for Italian men, but one she didn't appreciate herself. In an adjacent office she made six copies of the documents, then sealed five of them and the originals in separate envelopes, which she addressed and stamped. They would go to her personal lawyer, to her sister, and to others whom she could trust.

Keeping one copy with her, she hid the thick envelopes.

A short while later she nudged the General awake with the barrel of a .44 magnum handgun.

He stared wide-eyed at the big weapon, and then at her oval face and large olive green eyes. "Olivia, my sweet, what are you doing?"

"You're going to move your troops away from Rome," she announced with a flutter of her thick eyelashes. "I'll provide you with the details."

He laughed, but stopped suddenly when she tossed a packet of papers on his bare belly. Opening the bundle, he found the photocopy evidence of his transgressions.

"I have the originals in a safe place," she said. "From now on you will do as I instruct. If you don't, or if any harm comes to me, everything will be published."

"You're kidding, my sweet."

"Am I?" She spun the chamber of the gun, so that he could see it was full of bullets. "I'm not alone, *my sweet*. I have six friends."

Silently she handed him another document, instructing him to split his Rome garrison and move the troops to three training grounds in the countryside. "We'll be spending a lot more time together from now on," she said.

* * *

Few people in Vatican City gave the tiny nun in the black-and-white habit any notice as she flitted between offices, delivering and picking up messages. Little did any of them know that Sister Meryl had a "higher calling," as she liked to quip to her covert associates. Her clandestine assignment: gather intelligence on the comings and goings of officials in the Roman Catholic Church and report to United Women of the World.

In a vaulted corridor she passed Captain Gasperi of the Swiss Guard, but he gave her only a passing glance, without his customary smile. Such a pleasant man, far too nice to be in his position. He seemed preoccupied this evening, upset about something. He carried a little hand-held recorder or transmitter of some sort, and was speaking into it, words she couldn't quite make out. She paused to watch him as he inspected a number of locked doors, doing things his men customarily did. Why was he doing it himself this evening? She'd seen the men on duty a short while earlier. Gasperi rounded a corner and disappeared.

It was late now, approaching midnight. She reached her tiny, nondescript office, where she would ostensibly organize her schedule for the following day, as always. Calmly, she sat facing the door, with a painting of the Madonna and child on the wall behind her. It was an arrangement of furnishings under which no one could sneak up behind her and look over her shoulder.

Something big was in the air, though she had not been made privy to any details. For days her superiors in the UWW had been after her for more frequent reports, and she'd been providing them dutifully: a steady stream of photographs, computer microcylinders, and minirecordings. As a trusted employee of the Vatican, she had no difficulty obtaining the information and disseminating it. No one would ever suspect a nun of committing espionage.

With her curiosity peaked, Sister Meryl used a precision tool to adjust a digital camera smaller than her fingernail, then slipped the camera into her pocket.

Chapter 20

The truth can be a dangerous commodity.
—Lori Vale

Raffaela and Arsinio stood on the porch of their vacation home, using binoculars to watch fishing boats and pleasure craft out on the water. They heard something crack in the garden, then noticed a gray gull land. The bird began pecking the meat out of the a broken clamshell it had just dropped on a rock.

Beside them, the brown-skinned baby sat on a porch swing, propped in position by large pillows on either side of her. She held a bright blue toy boat on her lap, and uttered words occasionally, stringing a few together.

The Inez boys were out with Consuela again, having fun on a double date. They had departed only a few minutes before. Consuela was with the older boy Gilberto, three years her junior, while José was with a pleasant, though plain, girl he'd met at the beach, the daughter of a wealthy local farmer.

The shadows of early evening had set in, with the young people having just departed. A crab and lobster casserole, prepared by Consuela, was cooking in the oven of the wood-burning stove. Mouth-watering aromas filled the house and drifted out onto the porch. In an hour, Raffaela was supposed to turn the oven off and let the dish cool, then refrigerate it. Consuela had an unusual way of preparing it, said she had learned it from her old *abuela*, her grandmother.

But Raffaela and Arsinio were not thinking about dinner. They were only biding their time, making sure the young people weren't going to come back for something they had forgotten.

"It's time," Arsinio finally said. He set the binoculars on a wicker table and lifted the baby into his arms.

They entered the living room, and from her purse Raffaela removed a recording ball marked *Holy Women's Bible*. She inserted it into the VR-TV.

Classical piano music played as credits rolled. The music faded and a gold-robed woman appeared in three-dimensional form in the middle of the room. She delivered a short introduction, followed by the close-up projection of a toddler with bright green eyes.

Identified as the Apostle Veronica, the child sat in a tall chair and spoke rapidly, with a translator speaking over her voice in Spanish. The translator said this was a recording made months ago, at the since-destroyed retreat of Monte Konos.

Excitedly, Marta pointed at the images that floated in the air, and let go of her toy boat. She began babbling rapidly, as if talking directly to Veronica. Though Raffaela could not understand anything, she picked out some of the same sounds and phraseology being used by both children.

Glancing at her husband, she saw his stunned expression. They exchanged uneasy glances. Consuela had been telling the truth, and it meant all of them were in extreme peril.

* * *

The following afternoon, vans and buses moved into position on the surface streets of Rome around Vatican City, where they disgorged female soldiers disguised as tourists. Inside the holy city, four nuns and two disgruntled priests—all of whom believed strongly in women's rights—were UWW operatives, sworn to do the bidding of the Chairwoman. Each of them had a separate assignment, without knowing who the other operatives were. Alarm systems were being compromised and security doors were being disabled in the tunnels and catacombs beneath the buildings, so that they could not be locked.

The Swiss Guard stationed at the Vatican numbered only a few hundred men who went about ceremonial duties for the most part. At the main entrances of the major tourist attractions they maintained tight security—in particular for St. Peter's Basilica, the Sistine Chapel, the Vatican Palace, and the Vatican museums.

Nonetheless, armed UWW operatives were able to slip undetected into the immense Piazza di San Pietro and the surrounding porticos, where they sat on the steps or stood around, talking and waiting. Finally several of them approached St. Peter's Basilica, the most sacred church in all of Christendom. Atop nearby buildings, yellow-and-white Vatican flags flew, displaying the papal emblem: staff, tiara, crossed keys.

At five minutes before one o'clock in the afternoon, at the height of the tourist onslaught on the Vatican, the UWW operatives heard automatic weapons fire from the basilica and knew the subterranean assault squad was emerging from the tunnel system into the sacred building. All across the square, disguised tourists brought out automatic rifles and snapped them together.

Snipers picked off guards stationed at the church. Alarm sirens sounded frantically, in the foreground and distance.

* * *

Captain Aldo Gasperi had not slept well the night before. During the lunch break he had closed the door of his Vatican office in order to lay his head on the desk top, intending to take only a short nap. Soon, however, he slipped into deep sleep, and nearly an hour passed. When the alarms sounded he heard them, but at first he didn't move, thinking it was only a dream.

Suddenly, as the shock of realization seeped through the layers of consciousness, he sat up and bolted for the door.

Chapter 21

Biologically and intellectually the human female is the most advanced creature on earth, with her body containing thousands of complex connections and interactions dedicated to the creation and maintenance of life.

—BOI Archives, suppressed medical report

Just before the gunfire, Deborah Marvel, other councilwomen, and all of the counterfeit she-apostles (with their matrons) had been waiting at the main entrance to the Vatican, while Dixie Lou bustled about nervously, talking to uniformed UWW guards. At the same time, more uniformed guards had appeared, and UWW soldiers with them, seeming to flow out of shadows on the street, making Deborah wonder why the Chairwoman was bringing so much security. The whole situation had seemed odd to her, bringing such a large entourage and so many guards for a meeting between Dixie Lou Jackson and Pope Rodrigo.

Back in Libya, Dixie Lou had outlined her plan. Following the satellite broadcast from Rome, she said she was scheduled to meet with Pope Rodrigo, to obtain his blessing for the UWW and the plight of disadvantaged women all over the world. Dixie Lou claimed she intended to plead her case to the Vicar of Christ and try for his political support.

Then the gunfire had begun, and explosions had rocked the Vatican. Dixie Lou ran into the fray shouting, "It's She-Time!"—but none of her councilwomen knew what she meant.

* * *

White House Cabinet Room, shortly after 2:00 PM, EST . . .

Zack Markwether sat at the table beside his brother, with the members of the cabinet. As they watched a VR-TV on one wall, they made moans and mutterings of displeasure. Dixie Lou Jackson was holding a bizarre press conference, transmitted all over the world by satellite.

"I still can't believe this kooky lady is holding the Pope hostage," Secretary of State Harold Gravidovitch said. "How did she ever pull it off?" He was a small man with a pointed nose. His checkered yellow and brown tie was loose at the collar.

"You tell us," President Markwether said, leveling a hard stare at him.

With a shrug, Gravidovitch responded, "It just happened. What do you expect?"

"Do not take that tone with my brother," Zack interjected, his tone almost menacing.

"You're not even a Cabinet Minister," Gravidovitch countered. "I don't take orders from you."

"Please, gentlemen," President Markwether said. "We don't want to be at each other's throats. Remain calm, so that we can think this through."

On the screen, Dixie Lou Jackson continued to speak. Several Cabinet Ministers snickered when she said the babies with her were the female apostles of Jesus . . . reincarnated. But others present, including Zack and the President, remained silent.

"I'm speaking from the Papal Altar," Dixie Lou said, "designed and built by the famed artist Gian Lorenzo Bernini in the seventeenth century." The camera zoomed back to display the priceless altar for the viewing audience. "Isn't it magnificent?"

Zack ground his teeth together, then stood and stared at the virtual-reality TV, with Dixie Lou and her surroundings seeming to float in the air in front of the television screen. He wasn't a Catholic, but his mother had been. He was thankful that she wasn't alive to witness this sacrilege, the kidnapping of the Pope. It was an outrage! Military forces had been sent to Italy by NATO, but they were not attacking. The wacky high priestess had her own forces, and the Pope, three cardinals, and the sacred Vatican were her bargaining chips.

Dixie Lou Jackson continued. "I've learned the most interesting historical facts. Directly beneath this altar are the bones of St. Peter, but the body has no feet. Most intriguing, wouldn't you agree? But this was taken as one of the proofs of identity of the remains, since religious martyrs were typically crucified, and victims were often cut down from their crosses the quickest way—by slashing off their feet at the ankles, with a sword. The bones . . . found in a purple garment . . . date from the first century AD.

"Many of you are concerned about our presence here, in the holiest of Christian shrines. But let me assure you that we would never consider defiling this lovely place, which more than a billion Roman Catholics consider blessed. There is no cause for concern whatsoever. First of all, we are not a violent or destructive organization. On the contrary, we are peaceful and only seek to rebuild what was destroyed by men. Secondly—and this is a crucial point—we also consider this shrine holy, for we are devout Christians, followers of the beloved Jesus Christ, who counted women among his apostles. We have proof, however, that the men who led the early church discarded our holy gospels, even destroyed them, so that women could be kept in their place.

"We're putting men on notice. Never again will we be quote unquote 'put in our place.' At this moment my forces completely control Vatican City, and we are prepared to annihilate everything here—all the priceless treasures of art and antiquity—if NATO attacks us. We have taken these steps in order to draw worldwide attention to our cause, the cause of freedom and equality for all women."

"Where's the Pope?" shouted one of the television reporters in the great cathedral.

"In comfortable quarters."

"How do we know you really have him?"

"If I don't have him, I hereby challenge him to make a public appearance. He will not appear, ladies and gentlemen, because he is not able to. Not without our permission."

"Is it true you've wired the Vatican with explosives?" another reporter shouted, a man with long gray hair.

"Regrettably, yes, though I take no pleasure in admitting this. But I assure you, my friends, the end does justify the means! For too long, religious women have been kept under the yoke of cruel, uncaring men. It takes a radical event like this to turn things around."

"But what do you say to those who accuse you of being a common criminal, of attempting to blackmail the Christian world?"

"I warn you: Do not challenge me, or you will not like my response."

The press corps fell silent.

"Scary lady," Zack said. Upset, he left the Cabinet Room.

* * *

At BOI headquarters in Washington State, Styx Tertullian threw a paperweight at his own VR-television, smashing the receiver and shutting it off with a fizzle and a spark. His startled Vice Ministers and other staff members, seated around the conference room, stared at him without saying anything.

"I'm going away for a few days, " Styx said, "to consult with someone important."

"With whom?" Vice Minister Kylee Branson asked.

"I'll let you know when I get back. For now, you're in charge, Kylee."

Revealing no more, Styx hurried into his office to shut down his computer terminal. Fifteen minute later, he was in a subterranean hangar, boarding his personal jet.

* * *

"We're leaving for Mexico City tomorrow," Raffaela Inez announced. She and Consuela stood on the brick floor of the kitchen, mixing unsweetened chocolate into a dark *mole poblano* sauce that bubbled in a pot on the wood-burning stove.

Consuela dipped a finger into the sauce, tasted it. "A little more chicken broth would be good," she suggested.

Raffaela poured in the amber broth, stirred the mixture. "We want you and your baby to come with us. You will be safe there in our home. We've been without a live-in maid and cook for months now, and we are very tired of eating ready-made meals." Actually, she had much more than that in mind, something she was not revealing. Steps had already been taken; they had sent a letter to Rome.

"You want me to cook for you? And clean? You're offering me a position?"

Raffaela smiled. "You're very good in the kitchen and ever so neat. We would certainly appreciate your help. For your services you would receive room and board plus two hundred pesos a week. Well, what do you say?"

Tears overflowed the girl's lower eyelids and streamed down her dark cheeks. Touched by this, Raffaela moved close. Placing an arm around her, the older woman said, "We also want to talk with you more about the bad doctors. You may have been right about them."

Consuela wiped the tears from her cheeks. "Thank you, *Señora*. God has sent you to help us in our time of need."

Chapter 22

The she-apostles are arisen;
The she-apostles are among us.
—Mantra, United Women of the World

In the connected apartments, Lori and Alex tried to find out from the she-apostles how Candace had performed her vanishing act at Monte Konos, and how they had performed the telekinetic tricks onboard the helicopter. But whenever they asked the children about these mysterious occurrences, they acted as if they didn't understand, and never repeated the feats—not even when Lori showed them a paper cup, particles of sand from the pocket of Mary Magdalene's robe, and even a handful of bullets, to represent the hail of gunfire that Candace had eluded by vanishing for an instant and then reappearing when the danger was past.

After a couple of attempts, Lori left Alex with the children, since he was so good with them. . . .

Back in her apartment, she returned to another matter she had been contemplating, the reason she had come to Rome. Initially she had wanted to dislodge Dixie Lou from the leadership of the UWW and the harm this was doing to the cause of women. Now she had an additional reason to bring her down, because of the Vatican pulpit she had taken so forcefully, in such an ignominious fashion. None of this was doing women any good.

Deep in thought, the teenager thumbed through an international newspaper that Fujiko and her daughter Siana had obtained, reviewing all news on the Vatican takeover. Breathing a long, exasperated sigh, she finally folded the paper and set it aside, with a photograph of the imprisoned Pope Rodrigo on top. Her gaze lingered on the pontiff's kindly face briefly, without fully focusing on him. Then she thought of something to do. It would involve changing the story she had made up about the terminally ill adults and children in her care.

It would require telling the truth, to a lot of people. And the payment of more money to Mrs. Capo and Domingo Petrovese.

* * *

Styx Tertullian was slow to awaken. He had always been this way and invariably it upset him. He was the kind of person who wanted to get to work right away since he had so much to do, but his body was uncooperative, requiring two cups of espresso every morning to prime its biological engine.

In the kitchen, situated next to his bedroom, he heard Mrs. Bonham scuffling around as she used her walker. He remembered coming to stay her in West Seattle a short while ago, for a visit with the octogenarian who had been his mother's closest friend. He did this for a few days of much-needed vacation where no one would bother him, in a hideaway where he couldn't be located and hounded for decisions. After all, he didn't know what to do about the heretical UWW women who had taken over the Vatican. All options seemed woefully inadequate to him, and his brain had been fatigued from the unending meetings, the long hours, the steady stream of crises.

His arms felt heavy. He tried to force himself to sit up, and in doing so he heard the disturbing rattle of chains. Something was secured to his wrists! Looking down without his eyeglasses, he saw the fuzzy images of his wrists in handcuffs, connected to the bedposts by chains and padlocks. He noticed his eyeglasses on a side table, but could not reach them.

"Good morning, young man," the elderly Mrs. Bonham said pleasantly, as she shuffled into the room, gripping the rails of her walker.

The walker had a basket in front, containing a folded newspaper, a white-and-gold book, and a plate of fudge squares.

The angular old woman stopped at his bed, and he saw that the book was a softcover copy of the *Holy Women's Bible*. He swore under his breath, and his pulse raced. A little over a week had passed since the blasphemy had been published on the Internet.

"What are you doing?" Styx demanded. "Release me immediately!"

"For what purpose?"

"I need to get back to my office, of course. Have you gone mad?"

She extended the plate of fudge, to within his reach. "It's fresh out of the oven."

"I don't want any," he said, pushing the plate away.

"Too bad for you. It's the last treat of a condemned man."

"What do you mean, you crazy old woman?"

Placing the *Holy Women's Bible* on his lap, she said, "Read Psalm 37:40, and then I'm going to have to kill you."

"Just because I won't eat your fudge?"

"Hardly. What a shallow thing to say."

"But why?" Tertullian whined. "I thought you were my friend."

"You have no *female* friends," the old woman said. "Not even me." Something bulged in the pocket of her dress, and she brought it out. A large, heavy meat tenderizer. She raised it overhead, with the teeth of the tenderizer block pointed toward him.

"No!" he said.

"Read the scripture!"

"I need my glasses!"

Setting the kitchen tool down, she slipped his wire-rimmed eyeglasses onto his face.

The lenses were smudged, but in a quavering voice he began reading: "'The She-God shall help us and deliver us from wicked men, because we trust in her.'"

He looked up. "But this isn't Psalm 37:40! It's been changed!"

"*Men* changed it first! We only restored it, and this is the way the sacred text shall read evermore!" She had the meat tenderizer again.

"God is not female!"

"Call upon your God to protect you then!" the old woman howled, raising the improvised weapon high above him.

He began to pray, a feverish outpouring. On a table just beyond his reach sat his black leather briefcase, containing a laptop computer that could connect him to BOI military forces around the world. If only he could find a way. . . .

With demonic strength Mrs. Bonham swung the tenderizer repeatedly, ripping Styx's pillow open with the sharp teeth, but not striking him. A cloud of goose quills fluttered all around.

He whimpered and cried and cowered, and spit goose quills out of his mouth. With trepidation, he opened his eyes and peered at her.

Finally the old woman set the heavy object aside. "Now," she said, breathing hard. "Won't you reconsider having some fudge? I get so upset when people won't eat what I cook."

"OK," he murmured, barely able to speak.

* * *

In the Piazza di San Pietro, Dixie Lou assembled all of the nuns in their black habits, along with female office workers, a small army of bishops, cardinals, and other male Vatican officials. It was a brisk evening, and the crowd shivered in a cold wind. New green-and-orange banners fluttered on the buildings, replacing Vatican flags that had been taken down. Somewhere in the throng was the nun who had smuggled information out to the UWW, but Dixie Lou didn't care to deal with her any longer; she was of no more use to the cause.

As she stood above the plaza on a dais that was bathed in light, Dixie Lou wore a black-and-gold robe. Speaking into a microphone that floated by her face, she said, "All of you nuns and other women will be happy to learn that you are, from this day forth, free of the yokes of your former masters. I'm liberating you! As for most of the other women and the men who have been on staff here, I'm *firing* you. I want all of you to leave the premises, immediately."

To enforce her bidding, UWW guards began prodding the crowd, guiding them all toward the main entrance of the square. Dixie Lou smiled as she watched them depart in disarray. She only needed the Pope, her own soldiers and guards, computer experts, and a skeleton crew of Vatican employees to run the place—along with the Pope's construction crew, which she intended to put to her own uses. This made the situation more manageable for her. . . .

* * *

"I think we should put the Pope on TV," Bobbi Torrence said, after clearing her throat. "Get him to assure more than a billion Catholics that he's unharmed and we're treating him well." A special evening meeting of the council was just getting underway.

"Maybe we could actually bring him on board with us," Nancy Winters suggested. "We might be able to convince him that all twelve of our she-apostles are authentic. If he goes on the air and makes that announcement, it would be a huge victory for us."

"The Pope?" Dixie Lou Jackson snapped, incredulously. "Don't be ridiculous. We don't need him!"

Inside St. Peter's Basilica, she sat high on the bronze Throne of St. Peter, where she had been lifted by two of the guards, despite the protestations of her council, who had expressed concern about defiling sacred objects. The most holy relic of United Women of the World, the sacred Sword of She-God, lay across her lap.

Not saying much so far today, Deborah Marvel sipped a cup of Lapsang Souchong tea, already her fourth of the day. She heard construction noises from nearby offices, an extensive remodeling project that the Chairwoman had ordered right after their arrival, to accommodate her twisted view of reality. The work was being performed by contractors who were under constant guard, and Dixie Lou said she intended to convert the Vatican into the world headquarters for United Women of the World.

Deborah felt dismal, didn't like this Vatican situation at all. The UWW had over-extended itself, and was in danger of alienating most of the civilized world and destroying the cause of women for centuries. But Dixie Lou Jackson thought things were going well, having cited volumes of supportive e-mails and letters, and demonstrations taking place all over the world in support of her. She had tunnel vision in this regard, however, as she ignored wide-scale, mostly peaceful, protests against what she had done.

"Bring the Pope on board with us?" Dixie Lou said, continuing her response to the council. "The man who won't allow women in the priesthood or in the College of Cardinals? The man who opposes abortions and who treats nuns as his personal servants?"

"I just thought we might try to explain ourselves to him," Nancy said, her tone apologetic. "I've heard that he is a good man, and he might understand the plight of women." The council members stood around the apse, gazing up at Dixie Lou.

"*There are no good men*, you fool! Explain ourselves to him? It is *he* who must explain himself to us! Are you daft?"

"I guess I am. Pardon me."

"Well, what about the Pope, then?" Deborah Marvel asked. "What are we to do with him?"

"Actually, I've been thinking about executing him," Dixie Lou responded, in a wintry tone. Casually, she flicked a fly off one of the ornate bronze arms of the throne.

"We can't do that!" Deborah exclaimed.

All of the councilwomen voiced alarmed concurrence, and Deborah pointed out the strategic mistake of such a radical course of action, since a captive Pope gave them bargaining power. In reality, Deborah wished she'd been able to raise a voice of objection before the UWW attack, but that had been impossible at the time, since she hadn't even known what Dixie Lou had in mind. She felt like a piece of flotsam in a tidal wave, unable to extricate herself.

"You don't think Vatican City, with all the greatest art treasures and books in the universe, gives us *bargaining* power?" Dixie Lou thundered, so that her Southern drawl carried out of the throne apse and onto the nave of the immense church, the largest in the world.

"Of course," Deborah agreed, but–"

"Anyway," Dixie Lou interjected, staring at her own fingernails with a spoiled, displeased expression. "If I eliminate him I intend to do it quietly, so that no one will know."

Shifting uneasily on her feet, Deborah said, "You can't—uh, you shouldn't do that without the advice and approval of the council. We must consider each action carefully, weighing all possible consequences."

"Maybe you're right," Dixie Lou said. A cruel smile worked at her mouth, and she said, "And maybe you're wrong." She fiddled with the hilt of the sword on her lap.

"Pope Rodrigo should have more suitable quarters, don't you think?" Deborah said, nervously chewing at the inside of her mouth.

"Where is he now?"

"Exactly where you instructed. At the Vatican Palace, locked inside the Pauline Chapel."

"Oh yes, his private house of worship, the one containing those wall paintings."

"Two magnificent frescoes by Michelangelo," Deborah said. "The Conversion of St. Paul and The Crucifixion of St. Peter."

"I thought it would please him to be there," Dixie Lou said. "He can pray all day and all night." She looked bored with this line of conversation, as if she was only humoring the council members by making them think she was considering their opinions.

Deborah found herself seeing the Chairwoman from a new angle, detecting things she hadn't noticed before. The woman was a full-blown lunatic, a candidate for the asylum. But she had set up safeguards preventing anyone from attacking her. She had a force of guards and soldiers, as well as an explosives detonator that she carried on her person all of the time. If she ever activated that, it would blow up Vatican City.

"He's sleeping on a mattress on the floor and using a porta-potty," Deborah remarked. "Shouldn't we arrange for something nicer?"

"Oh, all right," Dixie Lou said, in an irritated tone. "I'm putting you in charge of him from now on. Just make sure he's watched closely. Popes are tricky."

* * *

"But this must be so expensive," Consuela said, upon learning what her benefactors had in mind. She sat in the back seat of the boys' dune buggy, a converted motorcar with oversized tires, holding her child on her lap. Raffaela sat beside her as they bounced over a rough section of road, with her sons in the front, Gilberto driving. They followed the red Alfa Romeo driven by Arsinio.

"Don't worry, we can afford it," Raffaela assured her. "Mexico City is too far to drive with the baby. This will be more comfortable for both of you."

"But you have two cars. There is plenty of room for all of us."

"No, dear. We insist."

The cars pulled onto the gravel parking area of a small airfield and came to a stop by a sleek black jet that gleamed in the afternoon sun. This and other private planes were parked at the edge of the runway.

"Your airplane," the peasant girl said, breathlessly. "It is so beautiful."

"My parents leased it with a pilot," José said as he opened the passenger door and tilted the bucket seat forward." Gilberto and I are driving the cars to Mexico City."

Consuela climbed out onto the gravel and looked up. "I'm going way up in the sky with my baby?"

"That's the general idea," Gilberto said.

"I've never been in a metal bird before."

"Don't worry, dear," Raffaela said. "It's perfectly safe. We fly all the time."

They would spend several days in Mexico City, while Raffaela and Arsinio made arrangements for an overseas flight to Rome. It could be dangerous, but they had to do it.

Chapter 23

The reputed "sins within our skirts" are nothing in comparison with the shameless mass violence of men, much of it conducted through the cover of their religions. Thousands of years before the Christ, goddess religions ruled the earth, and peace reigned supreme. It was only later, when the male-dominated religions took hold, that the mass killings of warfare and genocide began, invariably "in the name of God." Such hypocrisy! To kill in the name of God? Jesus was the Son of God Almighty, speaking for God, but he preached love. It is no accident that when Jesus Christ rose from the dead, he appeared before the women first, including Mary Magdalene.

—Amy Angkor-Billings, Monte Konos dedication speech

The next morning, Lori made a holo-recording, and had it delivered the largest television station in Rome. For security reasons, she could not go there personally, especially not with all of the she-apostles that she wanted to appear with her in a major public announcement. To solve this concern, Alex Jackson left a parcel in a park near the studio, and then notified them where it was, and the subject of it. He also told them that they had only three hours to make the broadcast—a major news announcement—or Lori Vale would contact another station.

While waiting to see what they would do, Lori went to Mrs. Capo and Domingo Petrovese in her apartment, to tell them the truth. She had Rea and Fujiko with her, and both were armed, just in case. Domingo greeted them at the door, and invited them in.

Mrs. Capo's apartment was filled with expensive antique furnishings, and she had several glass fronted bookcases in her main living area. She sat in a rocking chair with a shoebox of old photographs on her lap. Domingo took a seat on the couch near her, where he had left a newspaper. They had their robes on, and china cups of coffee sitting on tables by them.

"I've been going through my photographs," the old woman said. "Trying to sort them out. It's quite a formidable task."

"I can imagine," Lori said. Standing with Rea and Fujiko behind her, the mature teenager got straight to the point. "In a short while, the world is going to learn the truth about us, and about the children. We're here to discuss that with you."

Mrs. Capo arched her gray eyebrows. "The truth?"

Lori went into considerable detail, revealing that they had eleven authentic she-apostles with them, and that she was going on the air to announce this to everyone. Looking stunned, the old woman and her companion listened without saying anything.

"We don't like the lies that Dixie Lou Jackson has been telling," Lori said, "and we're going to do something about it. We're also deeply disturbed that she's taken Pope Rodrigo hostage, and is defiling the sacred Vatican. It is a sacrilege."

"A sacrilege," Mrs. Capo said. "Yes, it is a terrible thing."

"What can we do to help?" Domingo asked. He smiled. "We are Catholic."

"I thought so," Lori said, because she had seen both of them wearing crosses. "You can help by not telling anyone where we are. No one. It's a bigger secret than before, and we're willing to pay you more, a lot more."

"Helping you and the children is not something we should be paid for," Mrs. Capo said.

"And stopping a sacrilege," Domingo added. "We will accept no additional payment, and will guard your privacy with renewed passion."

"Thank you," Lori said. She felt tears coming on, and wiped her eyes. "This means a lot to me. It means a lot to the world. Believe me, this is very important."

* * *

Upon viewing the recording, the station manager rose from his desk and, in a loud voice, he exclaimed, "Put this on the air immediately! *Mama mia*! In all my days, I have never had such a scoop!"

Within an hour, he preempted all programming, and a white-robed Lori Vale appeared on hundreds of thousands of television screens in and around Rome, some in flat resolution and others in the more expensive, but highly popular, virtual reality version. She said she was speaking from an undisclosed location in Rome, Italy.

Lori addressed not just the Italian audience, for she knew that the story she had to tell was big enough to be picked up by international news organizations. For the holo-recording she looked directly into the camera, grasped a crucifix of the Savior Jesus Christ in her right hand, and in an unfaltering voice spoke to the entire world.

"My name is Lori Vale, and I'm fifteen years old. Despite my youth, a great responsibility has been placed on my shoulders, and I take it very seriously. Like millions of people around the world, I am outraged at the actions of Dixie Lou Jackson, for defiling the Vatican and taking the Pope prisoner. She has not advanced the cause of womanhood at all, as she claims. The only thing Dixie Lou Jackson cares about is herself, not oppressed females or the idealistic members of United Women of the World. While I have never been a member of the UWW, I am still inspired by the exploits of its martyred leader Amy Angkor-Billings, an outstanding woman who would *not* have condoned the actions of her successor."

Gesturing to her right and left, Lori said, "Now I would like you to meet the *authentic* she-apostles who are here with me, not the fakes being exploited by Dixie Lou Jackson. So far, we have located eleven. One, the real Martha of Galilee, remains missing." The camera zoomed in on the children's cherubic, innocent faces.

Lori provided some of the background about how the she-apostles were located, and the creation of the *Holy Women's Bible*, emphasizing that only one of the gospels had been falsified, not the entire book . . . and that all references to a She-Judas had been deleted, about a woman who was said to have conspired against Jesus.

The bold teenager didn't hold anything back, not the death of her mother that she blamed on the Chairwoman, or Dixie Lou's murder of the guard at Monte Konos, or the strange visions Lori had experienced. She held hands with two of the children, while some of the others alternated to speak ancient Aramaic on camera, repeating scriptural passages that had already been transcribed and published. Michelle Renee explained this as the toddlers and babies spoke, and translated their words.

"These she-apostles speak Aramaic," Lori said. "The children with Dixie Lou do not."

Immediately following the broadcast, an esteemed local professor of ancient languages telephoned the studio. His comments were played over the air live, as he gushed about the miracle of children speaking the ancient tongue so fluently. His confirmation of the Aramaic gospels added a nice touch of authenticity to Lori's version of the story, and gave credibility to the disparaging comments she made about Dixie Lou Jackson.

Across Rome, as Lori watched the broadcast from her hidden apartment, Fujiko said to her, "You have a way with words, my young friend, a nice way of turning phrases."

Lori nodded and thanked her, but she was thinking of something else, of the secret communication methods of the she-apostles. She saw them using it on the air, in their expressions and in the veiled movements of their lips. She was only on the periphery of their universe.

* * *

At home in suburban Washington DC, Zack Markwether leaned over his computer, reading an e-mail message from his sister, Jennifer. Fighting a bout of food poisoning from a restaurant, he had not been at the White House for two days, and had slept for fifteen hours straight. It was the middle of the morning, and he wore a blue robe over his underclothes.

"Sorry you haven't been feeling well," her e-mail said. "I had that myself last year, and it's not pleasant. Please see the attachment, which I recorded for you. Maybe it's just a coincidence, but the girl has the same name as your missing daughter, Lori Vale. Since she's has been all over the news, I'm sure you've already seen this, but just in case—"

Lori?

Feverishly, Zack brought up the attachment, and it began to play a television program on his computer.

Transfixed, he stared at the screen. A pretty young woman in a white robe was challenging Dixie Lou Jackson, asserting that all of the she-apostles with her were fakes.

My Lori? Zack's heart skipped a beat. His memory tried to fit pieces into place.

As he heard the girl's voice over his computer, memories poured into his consciousness, as if a flood valve had been opened on a dam, pouring a great river of information into his skull. Unsure if this was the same person, he remembered carrying his two year old daughter on his shoulders thirteen years ago, and her infectious laughter.

He also remembered her mother, a young woman with light brown hair and a ready smile. Employed in the Pentagon secretarial pool, Camilla Vale had been one of the civilians who had passed stringent security checks. Of all the women he'd known (and there had been many), he'd never married any of them. With respect to Camilla, it may have been the biggest mistake of his life. When their daughter was almost three, Camilla gave him an ultimatum, a deadline for marriage. When he didn't meet it, continuing to avoid commitment, she disappeared with the child, leaving Washington, DC for parts unknown.

It had left a deep void in his soul, one that had never been filled. He had gone through a series of relationships with other women following that traumatic split, but none of them had been the same. He lived a life of regret for not marrying Camilla, for not promising to care for her and their unborn child. He should have been stronger, should have tried harder to find them.

Studying the girl on the screen, with her heart-shaped face and long auburn hair, Zack wondered if this could possibly be his lost daughter, whom he had not seen for more than twelve years. Since the original broadcast was in virtual reality, he was able to obtain three-dimensional views in his computer, in color. Examining her face from several angles, he thought he saw a resemblance to Camilla in the eyes, and to himself in the nose and chin, but feared that this might only be wishful thinking.

During the first couple of years of his relationship with Camilla, they had clicked—everything had worked. Their relationship had seemed bullet-proof to Zack, filled with passion and laughter. They had the same interests, enjoyed going to folk music concerts, baseball games, and Impressionist art exhibits. There were bicycle rides, hikes into the Appalachian back country, sailing trips in Chesapeake Bay and even quiet times spent reading poetry aloud—Theodore Roethke, Ezra Pound, Elizabeth Barrett Browning. The words of a favorite Browning poem came back to him, and he murmured them, "'Love me, sweet, with all thou art. . . .'"

He fought back his emotions as the rest of the poem came back to him, and choked him up. As close as he and Camilla had been, he hadn't thought she would ever leave him. He had called her bluff, and had lost. According to a news announcer, Lori Vale was from Seattle. While Zack had never been there himself, this bit of information gave him a rush. Camilla's mother had been named Lori, and Camilla had been brought up in Seattle. They had discussed her hometown often, had spoken of taking a trip there together one day.

As moments passed, Zack became more and more convinced about the identity of the girl on the computer screen. Even her voice sounded familiar, with the soft, intelligent tones of her mother.

Catching himself, he backed up and tried to rethink the situation.

From a desk drawer he brought out a color photograph of Lori taken when she was a year old, one of the few photos he had of her. Rummaging around in the drawer, he brought out another picture, this one of the toddler standing between himself and Camilla. The child was around two in this one. The shape of her face looked right, although the heart shape was more accentuated now. The eyes looked right, too.

On impulse, he e-mailed the photo to Fred Siegenthaler, a police detective in Washington, DC. He explained the situation and asked him to do a rush projection on the baby's face, to see what she might look like at the age of fifteen. Knowing he had to wait at least until the next morning for an answer, Zack went into the living room and watched several television news programs, on different channels. His sister was right. Stories on both Dixie Lou Jackson and Lori Vale dominated the communication networks, along with special reports on the mysterious United Women of the World.

Hearing a loud beep from his computer room, he rushed in there. To his surprise, it was a message from Siegenthaler. Bringing up the attachment, Zack stared in disbelief at a projected image that looked like a twin sister to the teenager he'd seen on the television program. There were minor differences, in the thickness of the eyebrows and the length of the neck, but the detective had told him he was more than ninety-nine percent sure it was the same person.

My daughter!

As if with new eyes, with all doubts removed, Zack saw the truth of this in the features of the girl on the screen, in the unmistakable identity markers of the Markwether family, a lineage that went back to the pilgrim founders of the American nation and to European conquerors before that. Lori had his tallness, nose, and firm chin. The eyes were lavender and widely spaced like his own mother's.

Zack had suffered tremendous guilt over losing contact with his daughter, and in the first couple of years after Camilla disappeared with her, he had made some attempts to locate them. All to no avail, and he had given up. Now he was elated.

I can't believe it!

In a daze, he sent a coded e-mail to his brother, the President of the United States. "You'll have to get by a little longer without me," he wrote. "I'm on my way to Rome." He summarized what had happened, and then sent separate notes to his sister and to the detective.

Shortly after breakfast, Zack's videophone rang. It was his brother calling from the Oval Office, his image projected over the secure land line. The President had been gaining weight recently, as he was prone to do from all of the state dinners. Soon, as usual, he would go on another diet and the pounds would fall off. He could gain and lose weight amazingly fast.

Zack filled him in with more details. After listening in astonishment, President Markwether said, "You can't go to Rome!" His reddish-brown eyebrows lifted in displeasure.

Feeling his face flush hot, Zack snapped, "What do you mean?" Reconsidering his tone of voice, he added in a softer tone, "I mean, what do you mean, *sir*?"

On the video image a slight smile lifted the corners of his brother's mouth, but it was ephemeral. "You can't risk it. As a *nation* we can't risk it. NATO is involved, and may take military action to liberate the Vatican. Those crazy women might even have nuclear weapons, could destroy the entire city of Rome."

"Then I need to get Lori out of there. She's your niece, too."

President Markwether paused. "Even so, I don't want you interfering with NATO."

"Can't you see I *have* to do this? Don't talk to me like one of your staffers, Mr. President. Talk to me as your brother. I ran from my responsibilities before, didn't marry Camilla. Now I have a chance to reconnect with my daughter."

The most powerful political leader in the world rubbed his chin thoughtfully. His normally rock-hard, blue-eyed gaze wavered.

"You'll have to put me under arrest to stop me," Zack said, "or take away my passport."

"I wouldn't think of doing those things."

"And you won't try to stop me in any other way?"

President Markwether swiveled his chair and looked out a window of the Oval Office, at the perfectly manicured gardens. "All right, *go*," he said, "but you know what our position is if you're taken hostage."

"No deals in exchange for my life."

"Right. We won't even return a phone call."

* * *

"What about the accusations Lori Vale made?" Nancy Winters asked.

"Shouldn't we respond right away? If we're not careful, our credibility will be harmed." The narrow-faced councilwoman sat in an ornate Vatican conference room with her peers and Dixie Lou Jackson. It was mid-afternoon.

It's already been harmed, Deborah Marvel thought, seated across the table from the Chairwoman. Deborah wanted a way out of this, wished she could find a way to slip out of the Vatican. Reconsidering, she decided that she must be here for a reason. Fate. Being here, she could make Pope Rodrigo more comfortable, and might even find an opportunity to free him.

For several long moments Dixie Lou appeared lost in her own thoughts, then said, "Deborah, I want you to orchestrate a propaganda campaign against Lori Vale, to reduce her stature. Not that she has that much to start with, but we can't be too careful. Portray her as a headstrong girl, with a history of past drug and alcohol abuse, and too much sexual activity."

"That's all true anyway," Bobbi Torrence said, "from what she's told others."

"I know; play it up. Then we'll filter other information out, disputing everything she says. In fact, write me a speech and I'll go on the air with it tomorrow morning."

"I'll get started right away," Deborah said, moving to the doorway.

"I never had any doubt of that," Dixie Lou said, staring through narrowly slit eyes at her subordinate.

* * *

Deborah Marvel didn't like turning against Lori, and only did so in order to keep from incurring Dixie Lou's dangerous wrath. The councilwoman wrote the speech for her superior and delivered it to her that evening. Then, working long into the night, she set the Internet propaganda mechanism in motion. She only caught a few hours of sleep afterward.

Early the next morning, she awoke at her normal time anyway and continued a physical conditioning routine she had developed . . . as much to keep her troubled mind in shape as her body. Every day she worked out, either in the papal gymnasium or by jogging around the Piazza di San Pietro. Sometimes she ran up the interior steps of the great basilica to the top of the domed ceiling.

Dressed in dark blue shorts and a tight tee-shirt, Deborah ran laps around the square this morning, at a surprisingly brisk pace. Then she darted into a portico and drank a bottle of water she had left on a bench. She felt a little better, as the beta endorphins generated by exercise percolated through her brain, driving away the fatigue.

As she drank, she gazed up at the magnificent dome of St. Peter's Basilica, arguably the holiest structure in all of Christendom. Events had been occurring too fast, and now the world was faced with the greatest religious confrontation since the crusades . . . except this time it was Christian against Christian.

Dixie Lou Jackson was like a storm from hell, moving so fast that no one could keep up with her . . . or stop her. Feeling increasingly desperate, Deborah needed to come up with something, even if she died in the attempt. Purposefully, as a small act of defiance, she didn't attend the Chairwoman's morning speech.

Chapter 24

She-God shall rebuke the nations of men, and they shall flee far off, and shall be chased as the chaff of the mountains before the wind, and like a rolling thing before the whirlwind.
    —Isaiah 17:13, as amended in the *Holy Women's Bible*

After moving into the top floor of the apartment building, Lori considered what to do with the three adult prisoners in her custody, who were being kept in an improvised cell in one of the units. She had taken care to have Fujiko keep administering drugs during the trip here, and afterward, using her medical skills.

Lori had been considering allowing the prisoners to take guarded walks around the top floor, and perhaps guarded trips to parks, too, where they could get more exercise. But there were security issues involved with taking them off premises, and even with keeping them here. She needed to come up with a humane way to deal with the trio, so that they did not suffer unnecessarily.

She, Alex, and Fujiko sat on black wicker chairs in a common living area they had set up for their apartments, discussing the situation. From the street below, horns honked impatiently, tinny sounds that rose above other traffic noises. A window-mounted air conditioner whirred behind Lori, but didn't cool the room enough to suit her. Being from Seattle, she wore shorts and a thin blouse, while her two friends had on heavier clothing, and looked perfectly comfortable.

Ever since Lori made her television broadcast, the worldwide controversy over the she-apostles had intensified. Millions of people believed in her, but even more believed in Alex's diabolical mother. Despite what the Chairwoman had done to the Pope and the Vatican, she had the UWW behind her, and its proven advocacy of women's rights, including the publication of the powerful *Holy Women's Bible*. To millions of women, that was a compelling factor in her favor, but Lori felt certain that Dixie Lou's popularity could not hold, because she was relying on a foundation of lies.

After consulting with Alex and Fujio, who were her closest confidantes, Lori had decided to remain here in Rome for a while longer. With all of the furor surrounding the she-apostles, it would be too risky to move them.

"Our prisoners have no idea where we are," Lori said, "so I think we should take them out and release them in another part of Rome, so that we can focus on more important matters. We can do it tonight, after their medication wears off."

"Maybe we should have killed them," Fujiko said. Annoyed by a gnat in front of her face, she swatted at the tiny insect, but it escaped.

Feeling the hairs bristle on the back of her neck, Lori exclaimed, "You don't mean that! I would never consider doing anything so dishonorable, not for any reason!"

Meeting the teenager's hostile gaze, she responded, "I just wanted to see what your reaction would be, Lori."

Annoyed, Lori said, "A test of my character?"

Fujiko nodded. "Something I wish I'd been able to do with my last superior, Dixie Lou Jackson. Actually, Lori, I agree with you, and do not believe in taking human life."

"I didn't think so! As a doctor you must have taken the Hippocratic oath."

She nodded. "Now we need to borrow Domingo Petrovese's van, or rent a vehicle ourselves."

"All right."

"I'll go talk to Domingo," Fujiko said, rising to her feet. "I'm an excellent driver, but I'll have to be careful in Rome, the way these Italian men drive." Again, the gnat got in front of her face. This time, by clapping her hands sharply, she got it, then flicked the victim off one palm.

"Not part of the Hippocratic oath," she said, with a grin. The Japanese woman went out the door and down the outside stairs.

Lori and her companions had covered their tracks well, and didn't think anyone dangerous would discover where they were staying, not even if Wendy Zepeda and the two guards—when released—filed complaints with Italian authorities. No one would know where to look.

Of utmost importance to Lori, she always made certain not to do anything morally wrong. She had not harmed the prisoners, and only had them under soporific medication temporarily. To her credit, she had removed eleven she-apostles from the clutches of the dangerous and unpredictable Dixie Lou Jackson—and she had told the truth to the world.

A few minutes later, the diminutive Fujiko returned. "We can use the van," she said. "And Domingo won't take any additional money for it. He even went out to fill it up with fuel for us."

"OK. We need to pick a safe place to drop our patients off. Not only safe for us, but for them. This evening should be a good time, when their drugs have worn off a little."

"Right," Fujiko said. "I'll monitor them as they come back to awareness, and tell them we're taking them out blindfolded to let them go, but only if they don't raise a stink."

"I don't know what I'd do without you."

* * *

Lori, Fujiko, and Rea Janeg waited until darkness had settled over the city, then took the prisoners down to the parking garage underneath the building. Rea had her gun drawn, and remained behind the others. Fujiko noticed that Wendy Zepeda was slow to come out of her induced sleepiness, and was much more sluggish than the two guards with her. At first Lori wondered if that might be because the councilwoman was thinner than the other two women, but Fujiko said she had already taken that into account when administering the dosages.

They were discussing this while getting into the van, when Zepeda suddenly struck Rea Janeg in the nose with her fist, stunning her and knocking her gun away. Rea went to her knees, groaning in pain.

Reaching down, the councilwoman tried to grab the handgun, but Lori kicked Zepeda in the forehead and sent her sprawling. Rea, her nose bleeding, grabbed her weapon again and motioned the guards back into the van, while Fujiko and Lori pounced on Zepeda. They held her down, and tied her hands with a length of rope. Then they secured the hands of the guards in the same manner.

"You OK, Rea?" Lori asked, as she shoved Zepeda onto the rear seat between the guards.

"I've been hit harder, but never in the nose," she replied. Rea slipped her gun into a shoulder holster under her coat, then used a cloth to wipe away the blood. "Yeah, I'm too tough to let a lowlife like her take me out."

Fujiko slid into the driver's seat, with Lori and Rea in the back to watch the prisoners.

"I told you we should have killed them," Fujiko said, looking over her shoulder and winking at Lori. She started the van and pulled out of the garage onto the street.

Zepeda turned red, apparently not noticing the wink. "Are—are you going to kill me?"

"Would you like us to?" Lori asked. "I'm sure we could talk Rea into it, for your little trick."

"I'm sorry—I just panicked."

"We told you we're going to release you," Lori said, with rising anger. The van picked up speed. "Did you think we were going to take you somewhere and dump your bodies?"

"I wasn't sure. You and Dixie Lou are enemies, and I didn't know what you'd do."

"You took the wrong side," Lori snapped. "Wendy, we're not going to harm you. When we gave you our word, we meant it. Unlike your inglorious Chairwoman."

As the van rolled through the nighttime city streets, Rea stuffed a gag in Zepeda's mouth and secured it with a scarf tied around her face. She did the same to the other two.

In half an hour, Lori and her loyal friends drove the prisoners to a dark alley four blocks from the Vatican. Removing each of them from the van, they placed them gently on the pavement, lying on their sides.

"In a few minutes we'll call someone to come and get you," Lori said, as she stuffed hundred dollar bills into each of their pockets. Wendy, if you're so loyal to Dixie Lou, go back to her."

"And good riddance," Fujiko said.

As Lori climbed into the front passenger seat, she heard a man shout something in Italian.

"He said to halt," Rea said, jumping in the back of the van and closing the door. "He's wearing a uniform—looks like police or a security guard."

Fujiko leaped into the driver's seat, and backed the van through the alley, toward the street.

Since it was a warm evening, they had the windows open. Lori heard more shouts in Italian, and through the windshield she saw two men running toward them, with guns drawn.

"They're threatening to shoot," Rea said. To Lori's shock, the stocky brunette unholstered her handgun and was about to lean out the side window with it.

"No shooting!" Lori said.

As they reached the street, Fujiko spun the van around and pressed hard against the dashboard-mounted accelerator. The van screeched out into the street, throwing Lori against the side door. No shots were fired.

"Well, I guess that saves us the price of a phone call," Fujiko said.

Lori and Rea didn't laugh at the comment until they pulled into the garage of their apartment building.

* * *

Spring arrived a few days early in Washington, DC, with cherry blossoms budding on neatly trimmed trees all over the city. Gentle breezes wafted the delicate, pleasing scents of flowers through the air, mingling with the fragrance of the Rose Garden. It was an overcast day.

Deep in thought, President Markwether walked along one of the garden paths, his hands clasped behind his back, looking down. In one of the raised flower beds a gardener knelt on loamy soil, using a trowel at the base of a Princess Diana rose bush, one of the First Lady's favorites. Sometimes she even worked out there herself, since it calmed her to immerse her hands in the earth. The President couldn't relate to any of that. He didn't like to get his hands dirty, in any sense of the phrase.

Problems. There were so many of them in his position, and they had an irritating way of piling up at the same time. Now his brother was heading into danger, having taken a flight to Rome that morning. Zack's daughter, if he really had one, was at risk as well. It was hard for the President to imagine his bachelor brother with a child, and even more difficult to imagine him caring about one born out of wedlock. Over the years, Zack had been with many women, and only rarely did a relationship last more than a few months. He must be maturing, at long last.

He hoped Zack stayed safe, and the young woman, too. He wished he could do something to help them. It was frustrating having to wait, not being able to use the vast powers of his office. Why hadn't his advisers, or the Pope's, seen this coming?

* * *

Using her walker, lifting it and scraping it across the hardwood floor, Mrs. Bonham made her way to the front door, where her prized bird-song door chime had just warbled. Holding onto her walker, she stood sideways at the peephole and peered through. The magnifying lens of the viewer showed two men in suits on her doorstep. Nice looking young fellows. They wouldn't harm her. Still, in the pocket of her house dress she felt the reassuring heaviness of a small caliber pistol. She was not entirely defenseless.

Opening the door part way, she looked through the narrow opening, squinting in sunlight.

"Mrs. Bonham?" the shorter of the pair inquired. He held a wallet open, displaying his identification. She couldn't quite make out what it said. He snapped the wallet shut, slipped it back into the vest pocket of his suit coat.

"Yes." She offered her sweetest smile, the one she always used when handing fudge or cookies to someone.

"I understand you're a friend of Sylvester Tertullian?"

"Oh yes. Fine young man. I knew his mother, you know. Poor, sweet soul."

"We got your name from a computer file. You haven't been answering your phone."

"I don't always hear it ring. What can I do for you?"

"It seems that Mr. Tertullian is missing."

"I hope nothing's happened to him." Her eyes brightened. "But if you haven't found a body, maybe he's all right."

"When was the last time you saw him, ma'am?"

"A long time. I'm not sure. I'm old, and my memory isn't what it used to be." She heard something fall in the other room.

"Just my cat," she said. "I'll have to see what mischief she's gotten into. If that's all, would you excuse me, please?"

"Of course." He handed her a business card, added, "Please contact us if he turns up."

After their departure, Mrs. Bonham scuttled into the guest bedroom, on the main floor of her tidy little house. She found Styx hanging off the side of the bed, struggling at the end of his heavy chain. The duct tape she had placed over his mouth remained in place, and he was grunting angrily.

"You'll have to get out of that yourself," she said. "I'm just a fragile old lady."

His eyes sparkled with rage. Styx put one foot on the sideboard of the bed, lifted a shoulder onto the night-stand and rolled back onto the bed, where he lay on his backside, breathing through his nose with difficulty.

Leaning over him, she pulled the tape from his face with a hard jerk designed for maximum pain, then ripped the tape off his mouth. "I don't want to kill you," she insisted, "but I will if you're not nice."

"What would you do with my body?"

"I'd drag you into the garage and cut you up into bite-size pieces—for my kitty."

"Your little cat is going to eat me? Don't make me laugh."

"I have a big freezer, silly, and lots of plastic bags to keep everything neat. As for your bones, I used to be a chemist, so I just might have some acid around here someplace. Would you like me to look?"

"You run a real house of horrors here. How many bodies are buried under the porch steps?"

"Oh, that's a good idea. Would you dig the hole for me if I give you extra fudge tonight?"

"Don't play games with me."

"And don't play them with me. For years you've been acting like Mr. Upstanding Citizen, when in reality you were ordering your BOI henchmen to kill innocent women."

"The women you speak of were not innocent. They were the sworn enemies of God."

"That's not the way I hear it. You've been a monster, Sylvester. The things I've learned about you—" She sighed. "Too nasty for a sweet old lady to speak of. Still, I knew your mother, and she would want me to watch out for you."

"She would appreciate it," Styx said.

Chapter 25

United Women of the World, founded with such lofty ideals, might have accomplished so much more for women if its leadership had only remained rational.

—From a confidential White House report

Three days passed, and it was early morning.

The Cabinet Room of the White House overflowed with faces familiar to President Markwether, most of them male. The Prime Minister of Great Britain, the President of France, the Premier of Russia, and five other world leaders, along with the Supreme NATO Commander and the entire US Cabinet. Most looked bleary eyed, and took large gulps of strong coffee to awaken their minds. Throughout the capital city, cherry trees were in full blossom, splashes of cheerful pink that contrasted with the somber moods of the people in this room.

The dignitaries were silent as they watched two wall-mounted VR-TV sets on opposite ends of the large room. Dixie Lou Jackson, dubbed "the Black Priestess" by news announcers, was presenting arguments, legal and moral, for her shocking takeover of the Vatican. For nearly an hour she'd been citing evidence of misdeeds against women committed by the Roman Catholic Church, which she listed at the very top of organizations that were committing offenses against women. Finally she paused and looked to one side, toward a dozen nuns who filed into the room and stood behind her.

"Look at these women," she said, as the camera panned over the plain, serene faces. "For centuries, virtually all the clerical and housekeeping duties of the Vatican have been performed by nuns, while slovenly men ruled—the Pope, his cardinals, other male officials. From the top down—not just the Vatican, but secular governments and corporations, too—it's been this way since time immemorial. Doesn't that sound familiar, ladies? Isn't it this way everywhere? Aren't you fed up with it?" Her Southern drawl became more pronounced, and she added, "Massah man, we ain't gonna carry yo' water no mo', we ain't gonna change yo' dirty sheets, we ain't gonna cook yo' meals."

With a sigh of disgust, President Markwether touched a button on the table, turning off the sets. "These women are out of control."

With his brother headed into the dangerous situation in Rome, he was worried. The President's thoughts drifted back, to games of pool he and Zack had played in the White House game room, and the important talks they'd had, long into the night. The two had always been close, remaining in touch no matter where they were. Whenever they traveled far from one another, there were usually postcards, one or two a week. But in this case, he wasn't sure what to expect. It was not a vacation, by any stretch of the imagination.

The British Prime Minister, Livingston Bramble, cleared his throat, hawked and swallowed something foul. A paunchy man with huge, quivering jowls, he said in a basso voice, "This is intolerable. The blasted worldwide web is spreading their message like the plague, moving faster than we can counter it. I think we should shut the whole thing down."

"We can't do that," Markwether protested. "It would only make matters worse."

"I heartily disagree," Bramble said. "Look at public opinion polls. The UWW is over the thirty percent approval mark, more than a ten point jump in only a few days. We thought the Vatican takeover would backfire against them, but instead it's boosted their credibility. The mad women are multiplying like flies. They have discussion groups on the web, even computer war games in which mythical female armies annihilate male armies."

"Maybe not so mythical," NATO Commander Kenneth Selkirk said, from his chair beside Markwether. A gray-mustachioed man with a strong Scottish brogue, Selkirk spoke in an agitated voice. "For at least fifteen years the UWW has been trying to achieve nuclear capability. We've known about it, but haven't taken enough action against them."

"Don't blame my government," Bramble said.

"We're all at fault," admitted Nicholas Prodinsky, the Premier of Russia. He glared at the President of France, Antoine Villerny. "You French, too, and the Australians."

"I had nothing to do with it," the French President protested, vehemently, and then went into a diatribe, reeling off a number of high level witnesses who supposedly would support his assertion. A man with widely set eyes and thinning blond hair, he made hammering motions with one hand for emphasis.

"In any event," Prodinsky said, "as long as the BOI was superior in firepower, the women weren't considered much of a threat. In hindsight this was an error, the consequences of which we need to deal with now. Following the publication of the *Holy Women's Bible* and the takeover of the Vatican, the UWW has made disturbing military advances, in addition to their gains in public opinion. Bolstering the forces they already had arrayed around the world, they have been infiltrating other military and paramilitary organizations, taking control by subtle means. It happened in Italy, when General Pucci's wife not only persuaded him to withdraw troops from Rome but subsequently induced three more Italian generals to make equally foolish blunders."

One of the few women present, US Treasury Secretary Tillie Armbruster, said, "Women do not always need to fire shots in order to achieve their ends."

"How true." NATO Commander Selkirk touched a button in front of him, and the television screens went back on, showing estimates of UWW military strength in various regions of the world, which he described for those present. Due to successful cloaking procedures instituted by the troublesome women, NATO could only make estimates of the UWW's war materiel, based on intelligence reports. "I estimate that they have the military capability of a small nation now," Selkirk said.

"We have a real problem here," President Markwether said, in what may have been the understatement of all time.

* * *

In the Oval Office, President Markwether stood and shook hands with two BOI men in dark blue suits.

"Thank you for granting us your valuable time," said the shorter of the pair—Vice Minister Tommy Lee Chang—as he took a seat in one of the chairs on the blue-and-gold carpet bearing the Presidential seal.

"Any sign of the Acting Minister?" Markwether asked.

Chang hesitated, since the United States had no authority over the BOI. "Nothing yet," he said, presently. "Tertullian had to consult with someone important, that's all we know."

"It's suspicious that he hasn't surfaced. Have his bank accounts been checked?"

Chang nodded. "No unusual activity." After a moment he added, "With your permission, Mr. President, your time is precious, so may we turn to another subject?"

"Don't tell me. You need more money."

Chang nodded.

President Markwether flicked a small fly off the wall, wondered where the insect came from. The White House looked spotless throughout. He sighed. Nothing was perfect, it seemed.

"We need another five hundred million."

The President stiffened with displeasure, shook his head. "New information has surfaced. Charges against the Bureau of graft, fraud, and misuse of funds."

Chang's brow lowered on his unlined face. "All false."

"Perhaps, but an investigation is necessary."

"We are international, not under your control."

"Maybe so, but if proof turns up we can notify others who have been filling your coffers."

Chang shook his head. "We're too big to worry about that."

"Even with your Acting Minister missing?" He studied his visitor closely.

Considerable agitation was apparent in the twitches of Chang's facial muscles, in his constant shifting of position, in the nervous tapping of his fingers on an armrest. "You didn't take him, did you?" Chang asked.

"Don't be insolent. As for the money, we're not giving you any more this year. Congress won't authorize the funds."

Chang's face darkened. "Our financial needs are not negotiable. You know that Mr. President."

"Times have changed."

Abruptly, the Vice Minister and his companion rose to their feet and stalked out of the Oval Office. "You haven't heard the last of this," Chang vowed, but the President was not concerned about the threat. Already his military forces were moving into position for decisive strikes against the Bureau . . . and against the pesky women of the UWW.

* * *

Standing on the checkerboard marble floor of the Vatican Library it seemed to Deborah Marvel that the magnificent ceiling, the arches, and column frescoes imparted an Islamic feeling to the elongated room, with a predominance of golden brown hues, like those of the desert. This struck her as curious, especially in one of the most sacred cities in all of Christendom, headquarters of a religion that for much of its history had considered Islam its number one enemy.

Then she recalled from her studies of religion that Christianity, Islam, and Judaism had all sprung from the desert cultures of the middle east, and all shared certain religious stories. In her mind's eye, she substituted Arabic scepters and Islamic crescent moons for the large Christian crosses on the columns and arches, and they seemed to fit.

From either end of the library, UWW guards watched her on their night shift, but only out of curiosity, not suspicion. After all, despite her feelings of misgivings about Dixie Lou's actions, Deborah remained second in command of United Women of the World, as the highest ranking councilwoman.

In here, she had been asked by the aged curator not to touch certain priceless books without his assistance and the aid of the library's specialized technology, since they could be damaged. Actually this was only a request from him, since Chairwoman Jackson had let him know in no uncertain terms that the UWW was in charge now and would make all decisions about the disposition of art objects, jewels, books, codices, manuscripts and the like. Though Deborah had authorization from Dixie Lou to use the library in any way she wished, she wouldn't think of touching any books that were exceedingly old or fragile, such as the twelfth century incunabulum she had been admiring.

A rosy-cheeked, nervous little man, the curator approached her. "It is important to treat all of the treasures in this library with reverence," he said. "God is watching us."

Smiling pleasantly, Deborah asked to look at the thick leather-bound volume, which was in a glass case. Taking utmost care, the curator put on plastic gloves, then touched a button on the side of the glass case, causing the lid to open and an atmosphere-control bubble to appear around him. Deborah had heard about the technology, but had never seen it firsthand before this. The bubble, faintly visible around the curator as he lifted the book out and carried it to her, matched the humidity and temperature inside the glass case, so that priceless books did not decay whenever they were read.

As the curator walked toward her, the atmospheric enclosure stayed with him. He set the tome on a table, and motioned for her to take a seat.

When she hesitated, he said, "Go ahead and step into the bubble. It won't hurt you."

Deborah did so, and sat down. She didn't think much about any difference in the air. Her gaze was riveted on the beautiful old book.

He moved the volume closer to her, and she noted a soft patina on the dark brown cover. "There are no other copies of this book in the entire world. It was assembled almost nine hundred years ago, centuries before the Gutenberg Bible."

"I assume you're going to turn the pages for me?"

"Yes, that would be best." He turned the thick parchment pages slowly, said, "It describes ancient Roman sites in the vicinity of the Vatican. The text is Latin, which I assume you don't read?"

"That's correct."

Translating into English, he read some of the book for her, including information on the very spot where the library now stood. The copious original illustrations, in illuminated gold, were exquisite, unlike anything Deborah had ever seen before.

She spent two hours there, a pleasant respite from the insanity surrounding Dixie Lou Jackson.

* * *

Just before midnight, the private jet set down at Rome's Leonardo da Vinci Airport and taxied to a hangar. A long silver limousine waited on the tarmac, by the hangar. It was a humid evening, with a heavy downpour of rain pummeling the aircraft.

"You're sure my baby will be safe here?" the peasant woman asked, in an agitated voice. Consuela had argued with the Inezes on the plane when it became apparent to her that their destination was not Mexico City, and she had only calmed down a little when she realized there was nothing she could do about it. But she remained agitated.

"You have to trust us," Raffaela said.

"Where are we?" Consuela rested a hand gently on her sleeping baby's shoulder. The child slept on the seat beside her.

"Rome, Italy."

"Where's that?" she asked, for she was not educated in geography or world affairs.

"A long way from home," Arsinio answered.

He and his wife exchanged uneasy glances. After discovering that Consuela's baby had a special connection with the she-apostles who had dictated portions of the *Holy Women's Bible*, they had decided to contact Dixie Lou Jackson, leader of the women's rights group that published the book, and were sponsoring the children. The UWW's takeover of the Vatican had given Raffaela and Arsinio pause, because they were good Catholics. But they had watched the numerous speeches of the Chairwoman, and found her credible enough to send her a letter anyway, saying they had another she-apostle, and providing details of the baby's behavior.

But they had been careful in the letter, not providing their real names, or any information about where the child was. They signed the letter with the names Roberta Muñoz and Maria Aguilar, fictitious women, and said they would contact Dixie Lou again when they arrived in Rome.

The couple had mixed feelings about what they were doing, a strange compulsion to take the child to Rome, and concern over the safety of the mother and child. Consuela had said that a woman with a gun had chased her before the Inezes met her, and she had narrowly escaped with her baby. A *woman*. Very strange. The Inezes had also known that a guard had accused Dixie Lou of faking the twelfth she-apostle, whom she called Martha of Galilee. The Chairwoman had denied this in a convincing fashion, but something kept nagging at the minds of the Inezes, telling them to be cautious.

While they were in Mexico City, making travel arrangements to fly to Rome, Lori Vale had made her astounding claims and charges against Dixie Lou, and the controversy over the she-apostles had escalated. Now there were two conflicting camps of she-apostles. And, just as the Inezes had done earlier while she-apostles were speaking passages from the *Holy Women's Bible*, they again put little Marta in front of the television set—this time while the she-apostles with Lori Vale spoke what she said was ancient Aramaic. The Inezes did this while Consuela was at the market, shopping for fresh fruit and vegetables—and as before, Little Marta spoke excitedly to the television set, a stream of strange sounds that sounded very much like the language the children on television were speaking.

Now Raffaela and Arsinio were glad they had taken precautionary measures. Surreptitiously, they had done additional checking on the children with Dixie Lou Jackson, from tapes of her broadcasts—and little Marta had no response when those children made sounds. Only when Consuela's baby saw the original she-apostles speaking passages from the *Holy Women's Bible*, and when Marta saw the children with Lori

Vale, did she respond. That meant that the bold young woman had the original she-apostles, and Jackson did not. It was a very curious turn of events, indeed.

And it meant the Inezes were still going to Rome, because that was where Vale was, and where the real she-apostles were—the eleven others. Little Marta would be the twelfth. They didn't know where Vale was, but had put out inquiries ahead of their arrival, and would look more intensely when they were there.

Certainly the Inezes had deceived Consuela Santos, the ignorant peasant woman, but they were convinced that their actions would not harm her or her child. Important issues were at stake. In the days before departure they'd rushed a photograph of Consuela to a contact in Mexico City, where a false passport had been prepared in a fictitious name.

Now, with everything in place, the Inezes passed through Italian Customs in Rome as Mexican tourists on vacation, accompanied by their "maid" Rosario Juarez, and her baby.

Chapter 26

We knew about the transgression of the She-Judas, and her part in the betrayal of the Savior. But her connection to the murders did not emerge until much later.

—Lori Vale, *Revelations*

The morning was pleasant, with a bright orange sun rising over the ancient buildings of Rome. On the terrace of the Vatican Palace, Dixie Lou Jackson sipped a glass of robust, deep red Chianti while waiting for her breakfast to arrive. Casually she tossed bread crumbs to a pigeon, and the creature ventured close enough that she was able to give it a good kick. The bird squealed and flew off.

She laughed at the small deception she had accomplished.

A letter—delivered the day before through her own clandestine channels—lay open beside the Chairwoman's plate. The contents were most interesting, and exceedingly gratifying. A Mexican peasant woman claimed to be the mother of a thirteenth she-apostle, and said she was bringing the baby to the Vatican right away. The letter had been postmarked in Mexico.

Being suspicious by nature, Dixie Lou's first thought was that it was a fake, some sort of a trick. There had been other women, and men, saying they were the parents of she-apostles. It further concerned her that the two women signing the letter—Roberta Muñoz and Maria Aguilar—had not revealed where they were at the moment, only that they would contact Dixie Lou when they arrived. The Chairwoman had put out inquiries to places where they might be staying in Rome, but thus far she had not learned anything more.

Now, as she ran her fingers over the words in the letter and studied the handwriting, Dixie Lou hoped the women were being truthful, and were right about the child. The missing Martha of Galilee *had* last been reported in Mexico, but the mother had run off, eluding the armed pursuers sent by the UWW. The mother's name had been Consuela Santos, but that name was not mentioned in the letter, nor did the two women signing it say who the mother of the purported she-apostle was.

It was all very peculiar, and thus far there had been no further message from them. But as soon as they contacted her again, Dixie Lou would grant them an audience, while taking every precaution against assassination. All of them, including mother and child, would be searched, scanned, turned inside out and put back together again. After all, a bomb could be hidden inside the baby.

A baby bomb.

She rather liked the concept, but didn't particularly want to depart this world in quite that manner.

The sojourn into black humor, and the pigeon incident, had put her in a good mood. She assumed that her recent speech accusing Lori of lying about who had the real she-apostles had been successful, along with the propaganda campaign that Deborah Marvel had set in motion.

Maybe it was all the work of a greater power.

Dixie Lou smiled to herself, for she saw immediately how to put the child to use, if she was in fact the elusive Martha of Galilee.

* * *

In their hotel room near the Villa Borghese, Raffaela and Arsinio Inez sat with Consuela Santos, who held baby Marta on her lap. A breakfast tray sat nearby, with dirty dishes on it. Raffaela didn't particularly like the Roman coffee, but drank it anyway, for the stimulation of caffeine. She and her husband wore pajamas, while Consuela had arisen with the dawn and was already dressed for the day.

The elegant old hotel had no televisions, since the owners prided themselves on presenting an authentic nineteenth century atmosphere. A charming structure built around a garden court of flowers, the establishment seemed like a journey into the past. But the Inezes were not there on vacation.

While Raffaela sipped her coffee, Arsinio tended to his personal computer, on which he was playing a recording of Lori Vale's broadcast, in English with Italian subtitles. Because they spoke English, the Inezes were translating selected sentences for the illiterate young woman, choosing what they wanted to tell her and embellishing the rest as they went along.

"That young women, and the eleven special children with her, are the reason we've brought you here," Raffaela said to Consuela in Spanish, as she pointed at the screen. "Lori Vale can help your baby. She knows all about special children like yours."

"She's a good doctor?"

"You might say that," Raffaela said.

"She is quite young, though, isn't she?"

"She must be older than she looks."

"Lori Vale does have a nice face," Consuela admitted, "and a pleasant voice, even if I don't understand her words, or the words of the children. But the children do sound like Marta."

"We aren't sure exactly where Vale is," Arsinio said, "only that she and the children are here in Rome. We're looking for her; we've hired people to find her."

The Inezes were not certain what Lori Vale's relationship to the UWW was, and it was one of the things they wanted to find out, to make certain that Dixie Lou Jackson did get anywhere near Marta. While they had originally believed in the Chairwoman, when they reexamined the facts carefully they found that she had no credibility at all, and they had come to the opinion that she was insane.

But prior to that woman's involvement, they had seen great merit in United Women of the World. The Inezes had long been feminists, contributing money to various groups promoting the advancement of women. For years there had been rumors of an umbrella organization for women's rights, but shortly after the Mexican couple learned its name—United Women of the World—the group went into an even higher security mode, making it difficult for Raffaela to join. It required extensive background checks and interviews that she didn't have the time for then, though she'd hoped to go through the process when she could.

The couple had wanted to participate in United Women of the World in the most meaningful way possible, drawing them out of the ruts their lives had fallen into. They had the money and the time to do whatever they pleased, and they'd felt they were overdue for a change. Even Arsinio, though not of the gender that would ever allow him to join the UWW formally, had wanted to do what he could for the cause.

Now that had all changed, because of the disturbing situation in Vatican City. The *Holy Women's Bible* seemed to have great merit, elevating the historical and religious stature of women. But somehow, a good cause had been hijacked by a madwoman.

The Inezes still wanted to be involved in the cause of women's rights, and to do that they had become convinced that they needed to go through young Lori Vale and the eleven unusual children with her. The Mexican couple also felt as if they were on an important religious mission, filling them with the Holy Spirit. They felt compelled to take baby Marta to her she-apostle sisters.

Beside them, Consuela cradled her precious baby, and hummed a mountain *indio* lullaby that her own mother had sung for her when she was small.

* * *

Dixie Lou Jackson enjoyed moving her council meetings around the Vatican. There were numerous large and fabulous rooms in the holy city, and an incredible number of them were filled with treasure. It had to be the most stunning concentration of wealth in the entire world, and now all of it was under her control. This morning she was holding a session in one of the Vatican museums, at an Italian Renaissance map table with the chairs of past popes removed from their display positions and pulled up to the high table. The Sword of She-God lay in front of her on the polished surface.

Through a window she could see military equipment arrayed at the perimeter of Vatican City, as NATO attempted to intimidate her with tanks, armored personnel carriers, artillery pieces, and thousands of troops. She smiled to herself. They didn't dare attack because of all the explosives she had placed, and besides, she had faith that UWW sympathizers within NATO ranks—male and female officers, and even enlisted personnel—were gaining influence.

Her fingers touched the explosives detonator in a pocket of her elegant robe. It was a comforting feeling, reassuring her that she could not be defied, or she would blow up the Sistine Chapel, St. Peter's Basilica, the Pope, and everything else. The electronic device was a little insurance policy that she carried around with her. She touched the safety cap over the detonation button, but did not slide it off.

"Just a moment," she said to the councilwomen, who were beginning to take seats. Rising from her chair at the head of the table, she went to a massive teak-and-glass display case containing the holy papal scepters, a case she attempted to open. It was locked.

"Curator!" she shouted. "Come and open this for me!"

Presently an elderly, silver-haired man hobbled toward them across the marble floor. Alberto Carducci was one of the Vatican officials in charge of the various collections. In addition, since he had a special knowledge of passageways to get in and out of the Vatican, she used him as a courier. He carried a large brass ring of jangling keys.

"This one, madam?" he asked nervously, designating the display case beside her.

"Are you dense, man? Of course, this one."

He began trying keys in the lock, but couldn't seem to locate the right one.

"Hurry up, hurry up," she demanded. "Can't you see we're in the middle of an important meeting?"

"Yes, ma'am." He fumbled with the keys, dropped them with an embarrassing clatter, picked them up.

"Move faster, you idiot!"

But the poor Italian was too upset. Perspiration covered his face. His hands shook so badly that he nearly dropped the keys again.

"Here, give me those," Dixie Lou snapped. She grabbed them from him and swung their bulk against the glass, smashing the case open. Alarms went off. She stepped back to avoid falling glass, and kicked it out of her way.

Through the broken glass Dixie Lou retrieved a golden scepter with a jeweled cross on top—of rubies, sapphires, emeralds, and diamonds. "Have these jewels removed," she said to the cowering man.

"I beg your pardon?" Clearly he was stunned by the command.

"You heard me." Glancing sidelong, she noticed disapproval on the faces of some councilwomen, particularly Deborah Marvel. This disappointed her.

"But this is a holy relic, from the Second Crusade," Carducci said.

The alarm continued to sound.

She slapped him hard across the face, leaving a red mark on his cheek. "I'm not going to quibble with you. These jewels are to be removed and worked into the hilt of my sword—replacing the cheaper ones already there." She pointed to the weapon on the table. "I want the finest craftsperson in all of Rome for this project. Do you understand?"

He nodded.

"Furthermore, the work is to be completed here, under my supervision. I will show where the stones are to be worked into the hilt." She gave him a hard shove, and he almost fell over. "Now go shut the alarm off."

In a fluster of terror and sweat, he retrieved the keys and scurried off to do her bidding.

"Some of you have expressed concerns to me," Dixie Lou said, as she laid the holy scepter on the table, next to the legendary sword. "You want to know how my plans fit into the goals of United Women of the World."

She looked from face to face, then calmly added, "Have I summarized your concerns adequately?"

"Yes," several women murmured. Others nodded, carefully. She saw fear in the eyes of some, perplexed curiosity in the eyes of others, and hard, almost disapproving stares from two–Kaiulani Maheha and Bobbi Torrence, who sat next to one another. Kaiulani, a large Hawaiian woman, had always been an ally of Dixie Lou in the past, the reason she had been included in the evacuation list from Monte Konos. But Bobbi Torrence, shorter and heavyset, had only swung over to Dixie Lou's side under duress, because of the kidnapping and sedition charges against her niece. These councilwomen would bear close scrutiny.

"I think you're afraid I've slipped a bit off course," the Chairwoman said.

"Oh no," the councilwomen said, almost in unison.

"We realize you are following a carefully considered plan," Kaiulani said. "It's just that we don't understand what it is."

"Yes," Bobbi agreed. "Is it true you may have located the actual twelfth she-apostle?"

The black woman's eyelids narrowed dangerously. "Time will tell. The mother hasn't brought her in yet."

"But what good will she do us if she proves to be authentic?" Bobbi asked, "since Lori has the other–" Her words trailed away as she seemed to think better of questioning her superior.

"I don't have to answer that," Dixie Lou said. In her own mind, she didn't know what she would do with Martha of Galilee if the two of them ever came face to face. She only knew that she wanted to know what the little brat had to say. She *had* to know.

"Do you plan to use her for more leverage?" Kaiulani asked, her voice tremulous.

"Perhaps," Dixie Lou said, nodding. "Let me assure all of you. I have not slipped off course, and at the proper time I will explain everything to you."

"Yes, Chairwoman," several women said.

Privately, Dixie Lou felt the weight of these concerns, and many more. She stood up, and carrying the papal scepter and the sword, she marched from the room.

* * *

Late in the afternoon . . .

Deborah Marvel stirred her gin and tonic, took a thoughtful sip. It was strong, but she preferred it that way. Some of the other councilwomen in the room were beginning to show the loosening effects of alcohol from their after-dinner drinks,: letting down inhibitions, talking more. In Deborah's private apartment an open bar had been set up, and all of the remaining councilwomen were present: ten, including her.

"As you know," she began, raising her voice, "Dixie Lou doesn't know about our little side-session, but there's nothing wrong with it under the UWW Charter."

"Can we discuss her—mmm—behavior?" Bobbi Torrence inquired. She gulped her drink, glanced around like a nervous bird watching for a predator. "That incident this morning with the holy scepter was really bizarre. Ordering jewels removed from a sacred relic?"

"That's one of the topics," Deborah said, thus far concealing her own opposition to what the Chairwoman had done. "Checks and balances, remember?" This was a complaint she had expected to hear, the reason she'd called the side-session. Some of the councilwomen had been acting edgy in recent days, and she needed to deal with the situation, needed to cut the tension before it erupted. Dixie Lou would want to keep the tensions under control.

"And no one will report what we say to her?" Bobbi looked extremely worried. Her puffy face seemed to have aged ten years recently.

"Title 6.19.2," Deborah said. She held up a copy of the charter.

"Well," Bobbi began, "do any of you agree that Dixie Lou has been acting rather, uh, egocentric?" Clearing her throat, she stared at her drink. "I mean, she hardly mentions Amy in any of her speeches, and we're *never* mentioned. All the work we put into the holy book, and it's like we don't even exist."

"Is that what this is all about?" Tamara Himmel asked, with uncharacteristic fervor. "*Credit?*" Her pinched face tightened.

"No, that isn't what I mean, but there is such a thing as graciousness, and I think she's forgotten about it."

"Women are supposed to have finishing school manners, right?" Tamara said. "We're the civil, polite ones while men are barbarians?"

Most of the councilwomen laughed. Deborah noticed that two who didn't were Bobbi Torrence and Kaiulani Maheha. Those two were conversing privately in low, anxious tones.

"I think Bobbi has a point," Kaiulani finally said, looking up. "Dixie Lou avoids giving credit to anyone except herself in public. Face it, ladies: our beloved leader has become addicted to power and fame. Look at the way she doesn't honor holy relics, and her odd habit of carrying the Sword of She-God around with her, everywhere she goes. She seems more than a little nuts to me. At first I thought she might be struggling to out-do Amy's achievements, but now she's way beyond even that."

An uncomfortable silence fell over the room, like a foul mist settling over a graveyard. Ice cubes tinkled in glasses. Someone coughed. Paper rustled.

"No one can ever replace Amy," Deborah said, at last. "I'm sure Dixie Lou never tried to do that, and she isn't letting power go to her head. It's just that she's so passionate about the cause, the important work we're all doing."

"Why is she doing things without our approval?" Kaiulani asked.

"Good question," Bobbi said.

"She's making executive decisions," Tamara Himmel suggested. "Remember, it wasn't that long ago that we barely escaped from Monte Konos. She's just taking steps to ensure security."

In a sharp tone, Bobbi said, "The Vatican attack—without our knowledge or approval—didn't exactly do that, did it? Now in addition to the BOI against us, it's the armed forces of NATO and most of the civilized world."

"Maybe we should go over her unilateral decisions one by one," Tamara suggested. "Let's see how we would have voted on them. If she would have carried our vote anyway, it's a moot point to argue. I suggest that we begin with the downloading of the *Holy Women's Bible*. And I'm still not sure how all of you feel about this Vatican situation. Only a couple of you have openly voiced opposition to it." Her gaze focused on Deborah for a moment, then drifted away.

"You're missing the point," Kaiulani snapped. "The *point* is, Dixie Lou should have consulted with us, should have opened the issues up for discussion and debate." The pudgy woman had her own copy of the charter, bound in green and orange leather. Flipping through it, she said, "Here, look at this, Title 3.14.6: 'The Chairwoman must obtain council approval for all important decisions.' *All*, not some. *All*. We're the council. And here, 4.12.1: 'The council shall consist of sixteen women.' We only have ten. Presumably the other six were killed at Monte Konos. When will they be replaced?"

"Maybe never," Bobbi said. "I brought it up to Dixie Lou the other day, but she wasn't interested in discussing it."

"Isn't it convenient how she left all of her political opponents behind?" Kaiulani said. Slapping the charter down on a table with a loud thump, she added, "Amy Angkor-Billings must be turning over in her grave." She gazed from face to face. Most of the women looked away, obviously uneasy.

But one, Tamara Himmel, thought, *Dixie Lou will be pleased to learn the details of this meeting.*

With nothing more to be said, the side-session broke up.

That evening Bobbi Torrence and Kaiulani Maheha disappeared, reducing the council to eight members. A more manageable number for Dixie Lou Jackson.

Chapter 27

I knew I had to make the attempt, no matter the odds against success, and no matter what it cost me in terms of my career, or my life. No force on earth could have kept me away from Rome.

—Zack Markwether

He hadn't expected Rome to be warm at this time of year, so it surprised Zack Markwether when he stepped off the plane and found the air sweltering. As quickly as he could he removed his uniform coat and strapped it to the outside of his leather carry-on luggage, the only bag he had brought in his rush to leave Washington, DC. He wore a khaki uniform shirt (thankfully it was short-sleeved), puffy jodhpurs, spit-polished black shoes, and rakish aviator glasses.

Zack needed to find Lori, and had made advance contacts, looking for her. The private detective he hired in Rome, Trig Arnold, was supposed to leave a message for him at the hotel, and they were scheduled to have dinner together that evening. Arnold, retired from military intelligence, lived in Italy now and did freelance investigations for high-level clients. The two of them had served in the army together more than ten years ago, when Zack was his commanding officer.

The airport bristled with security, much more than Zack had seen the year before when he visited Rome with a congressional delegation. Uniformed soldiers toting machine guns eyed every person in the terminal suspiciously, sizing them up, watching for indications of trouble. The illumination inside the terminal was an eerie pink, from wall and ceiling-mounted scanners washing over the crowds, looking for known criminals and other suspects. In this atmosphere of tension and fear, he hoped that NATO didn't have to attack the Vatican. That could have disastrous results, spilling out into Rome, making the entire city a war zone.

With almost no knowledge of the Italian language, Zack picked up only a few words he had learned from a pamphlet the stewardess had given him. As he wandered through the crowded terminal building trying to interpret signs, a rotund man in a black tee-shirt appeared. "You are looking for a taxi, mister?" the man inquired, in a thick accent.

"Yes, I am."

"You are in luck, *signore*, because I am a driver. I take your luggage to the taxi." Grabbing the leather bag, he began to walk toward one of the terminal exits, and said, "Follow me."

The American considered this peculiar, but reminded himself he was in a different country after all, where it might be customary. On his previous visit he'd been transported in a private limousine. He felt isolated now, without the power and influence of the White House. They couldn't help him here.

He followed the man outside, just as it was beginning to grow dark. Some vehicles on the street had their headlights on. Horns honked as aggressive drivers darted in and out of traffic. At the curb the man said, "My taxi is just down the street. You wait here, and I'll be right back."

Carrying the luggage, the man disappeared into a crowd.

Zack's thoughts drifted. He wondered if Lori would even consent to see him, or if she would turn him away. She probably had a lot of security around her, having become such an important public personality.

Minutes passed, and with a sense of mounting dread it occurred to Zack that he had been taken for a ride without ever having gotten into the taxi. Despite his own knowledge and naturally suspicious nature, he had been more concerned about finding his daughter than anything. Cursing his own stupidity, he looked around for a police officer, and soon spotted a pair of them, toting black machine guns. They were busy arresting a man at gunpoint, so he didn't approach them.

A loud horn honked, and looking to his right, he saw the taxi driver pulling up to the curb. Zack breathed a sigh of relief.

The man was laughing. "I bet you thought I stole your luggage, eh, mister? I'm sorry, the traffic is terrible these days."

The American climbed into the back seat.

"Where to, mister?"

"The Hotel Lucrino, just off Via degli Scipioni."

"Oh, I can't take you there, mister. It is too close to the Vatican, where there is so much trouble. The streets are blocked off, but you might be able to get in on foot."

"The hotel didn't say anything about that when I made the reservation."

"They just want your credit card number, *signore,* to put a charge on your account. Now, if you do not show up, they will charge you anyway."

"That's the least of my problems. OK, get me as close as you can."

The driver made the sign of the cross on his chest and forehead, then pointed to a photograph of Pope Rodrigo taped to the dashboard. "We all pray for His Holiness, that those crazy women will let him go."

"How close can you get me?"

"Maybe ten blocks. You'll have to walk the rest of the way."

"Let's go."

* * *

When Zack walked to the hotel that evening, following the driver's directions, he had to pass through two checkpoints, each one a machine gun nest set up on a corner with sandbags around it. He had to show his identification, which they scanned into a data system, along with his retina prints, fingerprints, and a snip of his hair. Rome had become a war zone.

Like a lost tourist in a foreign city, he turned the wrong way on a side street, except this had potentially more serious consequences, because it forced him back to one of the same checkpoints. But an Italian soldier was helpful this time, and he finally got the right directions.

The Hotel Lucrino, with flower boxes in every window, would have been perfect if Zack really had been a tourist, but he wasn't here for that. He barely checked into the room and then went down to the bar in the lobby, where he met the detective he'd hired, Trig Arnold, a tall man in a suit and black shirt, with no tie.

"Did you find her yet?" Zack asked anxiously, as they sipped glasses of white Tuscano wine.

He shook his head. "No, but I have some interesting leads to tell you about." The detective excused himself for a moment to use the restroom.

The wine had a sour, rough taste to Zack. Not that he was a wine snob; he wasn't. But he had hoped to calm his frayed nerves with something that went down smoothly. Maybe the taste had to do with how upset he was by the whole situation, how worried he was about the safety of the young woman he thought was his daughter. He pushed the glass away.

Arnold had been the top sergeant in an Army unit commanded by Zack. They'd served together in the Fourth Iraq War, where Arnold had been wounded and was sent home. He still had a scar on his chin from shrapnel, and Zack knew he had even more evidence of past wounds beneath the clothing. He was lucky to have survived them. Now he was a private investigator, working in Rome and Milan. His name was not Italian, but he always said he was of that ethnicity anyway, and that someone had gotten it wrong on his birth certificate.

"My parents said I was Irish but I never believed them," he used to say when they served together. And then—invariably after a couple of drinks—he would go off on a wildly humorous tangent, making up his own life history, relatives, and all sorts of details that never actually happened. In the past it had been entertaining, but now Zack didn't want to hear any of that. He needed hard facts, and hoped his old friend was as good as his professional reputation. If not, Zack would need to take someone else into his confidence.

Trig Arnold returned and sat down. He leaned across the table, and spoke in a conspiratorial tone. "A couple of nights ago, three bound women were dumped in an alley near the Vatican, a strange incident in which no one was hurt. The women, all Americans, refused to press charges, said it was just a practical joke."

"What does that have to do with Lori? She wasn't one of them?"

"No. I'm getting to that. From my contacts at the police, I have a videotaped incident report, and I discovered that one of the women is a member of the UWW council."

"Dumped on a street?"

"Right. The police didn't make the connection and released her along the other two women. I have good sources, though, with access to the most advanced facial recognition technology; they tell me the councilwoman's name is Wendy Zepeda. And get this: I found out that Zepeda was aboard one of three helicopters and a VTOL plane that escaped from a military attack in Greece. Dixie Lou Jackson was aboard the lead helicopter in the group, and Zepeda was on the same helicopter as your daughter."

"Where is Zepeda? Have you been able to question her?"

The detective shook his head. "No one knows where she is."

"So this is a dead-end?"

"I don't know. I'm still working on it."

They ate dinner in the bar, but Zack hardly touched his. When they parted that evening, the detective seemed remarkably sober, even though he had consumed almost two bottles of wine. "Don't worry," he said. "I'll be on this first thing in the morning."

But Zack did worry. He worried a lot.

* * *

A surprise lay behind Mrs. Bonham's tidy little bungalow, a secret English garden with fragrant lavender and thyme shrubs, and vines of ivy and wisteria snaking over a high stone wall. In bright sunlight the old lady shuffled with her walker along a crushed shell path, just behind Styx Tertullian. In his hands he carried a length of heavy chain connected to his ankles, so that he could only take short steps. He also carried a copy of the *Holy Women's Bible*. At a wrought iron bench, with elegant fern patterns in the metal work, she commanded him to sit.

He did so, grumbling and clanking.

"Now secure the chain," she commanded. "Just like yesterday." She wore a floppy straw hat, shielding her sensitive facial skin from the sun. From the pocket of her daisy-print house dress she brought out a padlock, which she tossed to him. It landed on the path.

He leaned over and picked it up, then completed the familiar routine she had forced on him, looping the chain through the ironwork of the bench and securing it in place with the lock. Behind him loomed a twisted, drooping willow tree with an antique birdhouse perched on a lower branch.

As before, she sat on a bench at the opposite side of the path, where she could watch him from a safe distance. Her aluminum-framed walker stood in front of her, on the path. From a pocket she brought forth a .25 caliber automatic pistol, which she set on the bench beside her.

In a dark mood, Styx stared at the white, leather-bound book on his lap.

"Open it," she commanded.

Reluctantly, he complied. "Which passage today?"

"I want you to select a verse that best reflects the error of your ways, and memorize it."

Exasperated, he began flipping through the pages, searching, taking deep, anguished breaths. The paper rustled and crackled.

"Show more respect for the holy word," she cautioned. "Don't bend or tear the pages, or you'll be in big trouble."

"Bigger than now?"

"Don't be sarcastic, young man. I'm trying to rehabilitate you."

Styx found a passage that he thought she would like, and began memorizing it, mouthing the heretical words with great distaste, making whispers of sound.

Within a few minutes Mrs. Bonham's eyelids grew heavy and she fell asleep in the warmth of the sun. Her head tilted to one side, and the floppy hat seemed about to fall off, but somehow it didn't.

Carefully, trying not to rattle his chains or make any other noticeable noises, Styx rose to his feet and began dragging his bench across the path toward the old woman, a few centimeters at a time. Having been waiting for this opportunity, he didn't take his eyes off her.

She shifted on the bench. Her veiny eyelids flickered.

He held his breath.

Mrs. Bonham began snoring, her head still slumped to one side, the gun beside her.

The desperate man dragged the bench closer, finally getting to the middle of the shell path. Only a few minutes had transpired, but it seemed like much longer, and sweat ran down his face, stinging his eyes. Stretching to the limit of his chain, he thought he could almost reach the weapon now, but first he needed to move her walker out of the way.

Slowly, watching the chain all the while, he reached out and grabbed hold of the top bar of the walker. The aluminum frame wasn't heavy, and he lifted it easily.

Suddenly he heard screeching from behind him. Turning, he saw a white Persian cat and an orange tabby facing off, claws bared, tails erect. Several feet above them, atop the birdhouse in the tree, a black crow looked down and cawed, as if refereeing the fight between the felines. The cats separated, ran off in different directions.

When Styx looked back at Mrs. Bonham, she was sitting straight up, and had the gun pointed at him. She shook her head sadly. "I've tried to be nice to you," she said. "Really, I've gone out of my way to give you every consideration. But you're an impossible man."

"I'll try to do better," he promised.

"Read the sacred word and feel the holy She-Spirit!" the old lady commanded. "Read, and ye shall be saved!"

It was the absolute worst time of his entire life.

Chapter 28

The good leader recognizes the difference between power and responsibility. It is the difference between taking and giving . . . the difference between personal interest and the welfare of the organization.
—Amy Angkor-Billings, *Axioms on Leadership*

Dixie Lou had intended to use Alberto Carducci to arrange for the Mexican women and the child to get into the Vatican. They still had not contacted her to let her know they were in Rome, but in preparation Dixie Lou wanted the curator set up the details required to get visitors past NATO security, and get ready.

The silver-haired Carducci, in addition to being a curator by profession, had talents getting in and out of Vatican City through little-known underground passageways, and he had been performing courier duties for Dixie Lou. He had agreed to do all these things for her, however, in exchange for her promise that the Vatican treasures would not be harmed, with the exception of the papal scepter that she insisted on destroying for its jewels. The confrontation over the scepter seemed to have soured him, even though he tried to conceal his feelings. But his agitation had been apparent, as his usually cool demeanor crumbled when she broke into the display case.

Trust no one, she reminded herself as she spoke with Carducci now, on the main floor of St. Peter's Basilica. Behind them towered Gian Lorenzo Bernini's magnificent Papal Altar, with four twisted columns—

like the four gospels of *The New Testament*—supporting a bronze canopy.

When Carducci had her complete instructions, just as he bowed to her and was about to turn and do the preparatory work, she summoned her guards, with a shout that echoed throughout the huge, ancient chamber. As the armed women ran to her, boots thumping on the floor, she removed the Sword of She-God from its scabbard and looked at her own reflection in the shiny steel blade.

Like a movie suddenly put on hold, Carducci froze. "Ma'am?" he said. "Is something wrong?"

"We'll see, won't we?"

Four huge female guards ran up, their weapon belts banging against their hips.

"Strip search him," Dixie Lou commanded.

"Here, Chairwoman?" the sergeant of the guards asked, a woman with the blackest, most pure skin that Dixie Lou had ever seen, bringing to mind African royalty.

"No, dunderhead, take him into the men's room so he can have privacy. Yes, do it here and do it now. I'm busy and I don't have time to waste."

As the old man sputtered in indignation and protested to no avail, the women removed his clothing, revealing a gnarled, wrinkled body. He stood shivering on the intricately designed marble floor while Dixie Lou looked him over disdainfully. A silver crucifix hung from his neck, the only thing he had on now other than a silver ring bearing the classic facial image of Jesus Christ.

"What is it we're looking for?" the black guard asked, as her companions searched through his pockets, bringing out common objects that an old man might have in his possession.

"Something hidden." Stepping back, she swished the legendary sword through the air, and marveled at the clean, whistling sound it made. Such a magnificent piece, and she deserved to wield it.

"There's nothing here," the guards reported, one by one. "Only these things." One of them showed her a pocket watch, a money clip with bills folded inside, and a string of black rosary beads. Dixie Lou examined them, dropped them on the floor by Carducci.

"May I get dressed now?" he demanded.

Ignoring him, Dixie Lou said to the black guard, "Rip out the lining of his jacket."

Carducci's face went ashen, and when the guards brought out a piece of white cloth with words written on it in black lettering, he fell to his knees in front of Dixie Lou. "I'm sorry," he said. "I didn't know what to do."

The sergeant passed the piece of cloth to Dixie Lou, saying, "Obviously, he didn't use paper to keep it from rustling."

Reading the words, Dixie Lou scowled, and felt blood rush to her face, making her cheeks and forehead hot. For some reason he had written a summary of what Dixie Lou had been told about the Mexican mother and her child.

"Let me see," Dixie Lou said, placing the tip of the sword against Carducci's quivering chest. "You brought this along as your notes, in case you forgot something. You are an old fellow now, and things just naturally slip away."

As pale as a ghost, Carducci didn't respond. Instead, he stared beyond Dixie Lou, to the immense crucifix of Jesus that rose high in the chamber.

"What did you intend to do with this summary? Who were you going to give it to?"

"Please don't be angry with me, Chairwoman. I'm just trying to do what is right with the Lord, and I thought Lori Vale should know about the last she-apostle. I was going to send a note to her, that's all, thinking the two of you would be back together someday anyway."

"We'll never be back together. *Where is she?*"

"No one knows yet. Please don't be angry with me!"

"Oh, I'm not *angry* with you," Dixie Lou said, as she thrust the Sword of She-God through his heart.

With his last burst of energy, he grabbed the rosary beads from the floor, and died clutching them.

* * *

When one curator dies, there is invariably another to take his place. So it was that Dixie Lou brought in a younger man, who had previously been in charge of a special collection of illuminated medieval manuscripts. Early that afternoon, she spoke with Giancarlo Veron beside the blood-spattered body of Carducci, and told him what she would do—not only to him, but to the precious manuscripts—if he ever tried to deceive her.

To his credit, the muscular, black-haired Veron looked her directly in the eye and didn't seem overly nervous; he was not like a person trying to get away with anything. "I will set everything up for when the Mexicans contact you again," he promised, in his slight accent. "It will be very smooth. I know the same route in and out of the Vatican that Carducci used, a 'secret stairway' he discovered."

"I warn you again, don't try to get away with anything, or you *will* be caught."

"I am not a man of tricks," he responded. "I am a man of God."

"And don't make any other mistakes. Everything must be done with extreme attention to detail."

He looked down in a subservient fashion. "I will take care of everything to your satisfaction."

Raising the threat level, she said, "If you care about the Vatican and the Pope, you will not fail me."

"I understand, ma'am. You can count on me."

After he left, Dixie Lou sent out urgent inquiries through her encrypted Internet network (which her computer experts assured her had not been compromised), ordering an exhaustive search for the Mexicans and the baby they had with them. She'd only received their letter two days ago, but she was running out of patience. Now she intended to find out where they were, assuming the letter had not been a complete hoax.

If they were in Rome, she would find them. There couldn't be that many arrivals from Mexico in the last few days. . . .

* * *

The day after his meeting with Trig Arnold, the detective called Zack to let him know he had a much more solid lead on Lori's whereabouts. He'd discovered that the three bound women who had been left near the Vatican (including Wendy Zepeda) had been taken there in a van, and he had traced the license plate to an apartment building in the Manzoni district. He'd done the research independently; the police didn't know anything about the lead.

Arnold provided the address, and Zack hurried over there by taxi. He wore his Army officer's uniform and white gloves, but had not paid his usual attention to keeping himself spotless and pressed.

He did not see any guards stationed on the perimeter of the seven-story building, not walking around, in vehicles, or in adjacent buildings, none of the usual methods that he, as an expert, could recognize. If Lori and the she-apostles were in there, perhaps she thought that concealing herself in a typical Roman neighborhood was enough, and she didn't want visible signs of anything unusual going on that might alert people, causing them to ask questions. But the apparent lack of security troubled him.

Crossing the street and climbing the stairs to the main entry, he noticed a brunette just inside the lobby, visible through a glass door. Rather stocky and buxom, she wore dark slacks and a long black jacket, and he noticed the characteristic bulge of a shoulder holster on one side, pushing one of her arms away from her body.

The door was locked, so he rapped on it. She looked at him suspiciously through the glass, but said nothing and did not move to assist him.

"I'm here to see my daughter," he said in a loud voice, choosing simplicity and truth. "Lori Vale." He spoke in English.

The woman's eyes narrowed. Then, as if realizing she might have revealed something in her expression, she took on a placid, almost emotionless countenance. He saw her take a deep breath. Some agitation there, and a twitch around the mouth. She shrugged, extended her arms to the side with palms up, as if she could not speak English. She certainly did not look Italian to him, didn't have tan skin or black hair, but he knew this did not necessarily mean anything.

"Can you get someone to help me?" he asked. This time, he slid a small color photograph under the door. "That's Lori when she was two. My name is Zack Markwether." He chose not to mention that he was the brother of the President of the United States, as that could make her think he was a kook. If she understood English, that is, which he suspected she might.

Again, the woman shrugged. But she picked up the photograph and studied it, her expression still bland.

"That's me with her, and the woman beside me is Lori's mother, Camilla Vale."

Taking the photograph with her, the brunette turned and entered an elevator. After the doors closed, the indicator light showed that it stopped at the fifth floor, but he doubted if that was really where she was going. She was probably taking the stairs up or down to the real floor.

* * *

"He says he's my father? What's his name?"

"Zack Markwether," Rea said. "He's tall and distinguished looking, in an American Army officer's uniform. He gave me this picture."

Studying the photograph, Lori was stunned. It showed her mother with a uniformed man, and Lori as a child standing between them, holding hands with the adults. She was a toddler, around the age of the older she-apostles.

"And this man is downstairs in the lobby?" she asked, pointing at the picture. She had never seen a photograph of her father before, since her mother had destroyed all of them, but she thought she detected similarities in the face to her own. She felt her pulse quicken.

"I'd say it's him, yes. Or his exact double. Of course, he's aged and the picture hasn't, but I think it's him. Even so, this could be one of Dixie Lou's tricks, a doctored photo to see if you're really here."

"One way or another, the very fact that he came here proves our cover is blown," Lori said, "I have to see him, don't I?"

"Yes. I'd better take Fujiko with me, and Alex, and we'll all be armed. We'll bring the man back up. Keep that .38 handy, all right?"

"OK, but if he were really dangerous, being a military type and all, he would have sent an assault squad to take over the building, don't you think?"

"Makes sense to me, but we need to be careful. . . ."

After searching him for weapons they brought him upstairs, a tall, powerfully built man in a brown and khaki military uniform with puffy jodhpurs and white gloves. He had curly, reddish-brown hair and a rugged but heart-shaped face—wide at the forehead and narrow at the chin.

"He's unarmed," Fujiko said. But she and the others remained close by, watching his every move. Standing in the middle of the air-conditioned living room, Lori had her own coat on, so that she could conceal her snub-nose .38 inside a pocket. With both hands in her pockets, she felt moisture on one palm as she gripped the handle of the weapon.

The man paused and stood just inside the doorway, studying her with a bemused expression on his face. His blue eyes twinkled. She saw the brass edge and dark lens of a pair of sunglasses, tucked into a an outside pocket. He seemed familiar, almost comfortable, but she didn't want to let her guard down.

"I'm your father, Zack Markwether."

Lori felt a shortness of breath. As she had noted from the photograph, the man's face resembled her own, and he had hair close to the color of hers. The eyes were different—dark blue instead of her lavender—but like her he was tall, a characteristic her mother had revealed about him, but in a complaining way, as she always did when it came to him. Her mother had never, in fact, said a solitary positive thing to Lori about him. He had a strong, even arrogant face, but as he stood there she saw emotions seeping into his features, bringing moisture to his eyes.

"Well, aren't you going to give me a big hug?" he asked, moving closer to her. He stopped, a couple of meters away.

"How do I know who you really are?"

"I'm the real McCoy all right—or should I say, the real Markwether? You're a Markwether, too."

"Maybe, maybe not." She returned the photograph to him.

"That child is you," the man said, pointing at the toddler in the picture. "And that's your mother."

"Pictures can be altered."

"Shall we take DNA samples and have them analyzed?"

She looked him the eye. He held steady. "Where was the photo taken?" She released her grip from the hidden gun, brought both hands out of her pockets.

"Washington, DC, near the Pentagon. Your mother was in the clerical pool when I was a Captain in the Army. One afternoon I needed a letter typed, and dictated it to her. We hit it off right away, as if we'd known one another for a long time."

"I found rent receipts from Washington, DC in my mother's papers," Lori admitted, feeling a bit more relaxed with him. "She was upset with me for getting into them."

"Just like Camilla. She always wanted her privacy, didn't like anyone poking around or questioning her."

"She's still that—" Lori hesitated as she remembered the terrible truth that her mother was gone forever, except in the memories of those who knew and cared for her.

The teenager's eyes filled with tears, and she felt herself drawn closer to this man. Under the watchful eyes of her friends she hugged him, but uncertainly. Desperately, she wanted to believe in him, but even if he really was her father there were potential problems. What if her mother had been telling the truth about him, and he wasn't a good person? Camilla Vale had alluded to his improper behavior, but had never provided details.

"We have a lot of catching up to do," Zack Markwether said.

The pair sat on a sectional sofa and talked awkwardly, since they didn't know one another. "One thing I have to tell you," Lori said after several moments. "Mom is dead."

Sadness consumed his face. "I was afraid of something like that when I couldn't reach her. How did it happen?" He seemed genuinely anguished, blinked away tears. Lori noted deep creases around the corners of his eyes, and a high forehead. He had the same last name as the President of the United States–Markwether–but she assumed it was just a coincidence.

"Mom was shot by uniformed men who attacked a goddess circle. I'll tell you more about it later, but I was there. At first she was injured but still alive, and might have been saved if Dixie Lou Jackson had obtained proper medical care for her."

"I haven't heard anything good about that woman yet," he said, in a bitter tone.

"You have nerve, finding me like you did," the teenager said, her doubts almost gone. "Maybe that's where I got mine. *Maybe.*"

The comment seemed to please him, and he beamed from ear to ear. Placing an arm around her shoulders, he drew her close to him.

She considered pulling away, but her recently acquired ability to detect falsehoods–at least she thought she had it–told her he was sincere and honest, that he really was her father. She didn't think DNA tests were necessary. She desperately wanted him to really be her father.

"We lost so many years," he said, "but I hope it's not too late for us to start again."

"Maybe you really are my father, but I don't know if we can ever be close, not after what Mom said about you. She said you were a bad husband and father. Why would she say that? I want the truth."

"It had nothing to do with you."

"So it's none of my business? Well whatever you did–or whatever she thinks you did–involved me, because I lost my father over it, and that's pretty serious."

"I'm sorry, Lori. You're right. It's a familiar story, I suppose. I'm not proud of it, but I didn't dedicate myself to your mother, not in the way she deserved."

"What do you mean?"

After a long pause, he replied. "We were never actually married, though she told people we were. I didn't want to make the commitment. We were together for almost four years."

"Now I see why she didn't forgive you," Lori said, "but she had no right to keep me away from my own Dad. No matter what you did, you're not a murderer or anything. I wish you had stayed with her, but—" She paused in midsentence.

"Are you all right, Lori?"

She'd almost said, "—I love you anyway," but had second thoughts.

"I'm proud of you, Lori."

"I'm still not sure if you really are my father," she said, just to test him a little. "I've been thinking about what you said, and it doesn't match what I already know." This wasn't true, but she wanted to see how he reacted.

Glancing at him, she noticed that he looked hurt, that her comments had burned through to his heart. She felt badly, but reminded herself that he had refused to marry her mother, that he had made a decision that led to the dissolution of their little family.

"Tell me what doesn't seem to add up," he said, "and I'll deal with it. Your mother's apartment in Washington, DC was on "M" Street SE, near the Washington Naval Yard. She had a small patio with a table and chairs on it, and a fluffy white kitten that liked to sleep out there in the sun. Do you remember that?"

She hesitated. "I'm not sure." Actually, Lori recalled the cat very well. She used to nuzzle her own face into its warm fur.

"I realize I hurt your mother and you, and I'm deeply sorry. Losing you and Camilla was the biggest mistake of my life, a tragedy, and I'm deeply sorry. Can you ever find it in your heart to forgive me?" Tears streamed down his rugged face. "I'm so terribly sorry."

Lori couldn't help herself. He was telling the truth, and she forgave him completely. As she hugged him, their tear-streaked faces touched.

Chapter 29

One explosion leads to another.

—Anonymous

It had been so easy to locate the Mexicans that Dixie Lou regretted waiting two days to send out her inquiries. As she'd suspected, there had been very few arrivals from Mexico in recent days, only fifteen people, to be exact—and she'd found the ones she wanted in a hotel in Rome, near the Villa Borghese. Their names were different from those on the letter, but one of her operatives had spoken with a hotel maid, who reported hearing a baby in their room, making sounds she'd never heard from a child before.

Dressed in police uniforms, Dixie Lou's four-woman commando squad had removed a man, two women and a baby from the hotel that afternoon and put them in a stolen police car. At this very moment, the Mexicans were being brought to her via the narrow subterranean passageway that the late Alberto Carducci had discovered.

Dixie Lou could hardly wait.

* * *

Having been summoned to her office by the Chairwoman and briefed on what was happening, Deborah Marvel slipped into a deep cushion emerald green chair on one wall. One of Dixie Lou's translators stood off to one side, a woman with platinum hair and eyes that peered through narrow slits. The oversized chair, soft and comfortable, made

Deborah feel small, as did this imposing office, formerly occupied by a cardinal, and subsequently by Pope Rodrigo, while his own office was undergoing an earlier makeover. The Mexicans had not yet arrived.

The councilwoman identified some of the changes Dixie Lou had made since taking over the Vatican. The desk was the same, but little else. Green and orange proliferated, with gold accents, and the woman's touch in decorating was evident, with lace curtains and pillows, and crystal vases filled with flowers.

Almost paradoxically, military pictures lined the walls, showing fictional victories of women over men. A brass plaque labeled each. Perhaps one day they would be replaced with real scenes, depicting the capture of the Roman Catholic Pope and the final defeat of the Bureau of Ideology.

Feeling more sad than at any time since Dixie Lou Jackson took over the helm of the UWW, Deborah thought of all the great Popes who had worked in Vatican offices over the centuries, furthering the ideals of love and humanitarianism embodied in the *Bible*, and how everything had come to such a dismal point. Without overlooking the shortcomings of Catholicism, she saw the takeover of their holy Vatican City as a clear reversal for mankind. The treatment of women in the Church and in the world, while inconsistent at times, had been on a broad, if gradual, upswing. Then this had happened.

She shook her head, but only a little, so as not to be noticed.

Moments later, four commandos dressed as Italian policewomen entered, with two women, a man, and a baby, all brown-skinned. At Dixie Lou's order, the commandos stood off to one side, to act as guards.

The captive adults looked visibly upset to Deborah, and seemed disoriented.

"Do you know who I am?" Dixie Lou asked. She had a golden barrette in her braided hair and wore a formal robe, a very businesslike look, Deborah thought.

"Yes, Madam Chairwoman," the man said, in accented English. His gaze flitted around nervously.

"In my presence, the woman always speaks first." She looked at the older woman, said, "You are Raffaela Inez, and this is your husband Arsinio?"

"Yes." The Mexican woman looked at her defiantly.

"Why did you send me a letter using phony names? Didn't you think I had the capability to discover your lies?"

"We didn't use our real names because we weren't sure about you."

"And are you sure about me now?" Dixie Lou smiled cruelly. Her dark eyed gaze was piercing, but the woman did not flinch under it.

"Sure about you, yes, but in the wrong way. Are you insane? How dare you have us forcibly removed from our hotel room? This is an outrage!"

Be careful, Deborah thought. She shifted uneasily in her chair.

"I will define the outrages here." Dixie Lou rose and walked over to the peasant woman, who was shaking visibly. Her eyes were downcast, filled with fear as she held her child tightly against her bosom. The brown-skinned baby was fidgeting and kicking her way out of the blanket around her, but had not made any sounds yet.

Deborah wished she could do something to stop this.

Putting her face very close to the poor woman, Dixie Lou said, "And you are Consuela Santos, with your daughter Marta. We have been searching for you for a long time. Thanks for coming to me; you've made it much easier. But is your child an authentic she-apostle?"

The peasant woman looked confused, didn't understand until Raffaela spoke to her in Spanish. Then Consuela glowered at Dixie Lou, showing her own courage. Deborah was impressed by the strength of both women, but worried about their safety.

Speaking without being asked to, Raffaela said, "Consuela says her baby is illegitimate, and the father ran out on her. She also says that when she heard the strange words only days after the baby was born she wondered if she was in the presence of a demon. The mother prayed, but received no sign from God."

"It's not God," Dixie Lou snapped. "It's *She*-God." Poking at the blanket around the baby's face to get a better look, she asked, "How old is the child?"

"Seven and a half months," Raffaela answered, in her accented English.

"You must understand," Dixie Lou said, "we're contacted by kooks all the time, women claiming we have the wrong she-apostles, and that their children are the actual ones. It's absurd, really, but we make every effort to be polite." She touched the child's hand. "Perhaps you are mistaken about this child, and–"

Suddenly Dixie Lou withdrew and fell silent, as the baby screamed and issued a stream of indecipherable words that to Deborah sounded angry. With a very hostile expression, the brown-skinned child–her face fully out of the blanket–glared at Dixie Lou, all the while issuing a flow of apparent invectives. Dixie Lou seemed to cower, and moved back to the papal desk.

Finally the baby ceased the torrent of words, her large brown eyes open wide and looking directly at Deborah now, hypnotically. Somewhere Deborah had heard that children this young weren't necessarily looking at you when they appeared to be, since they couldn't focus their eyes very well. But if this really was a reincarnated she-apostle. . . .

Consuela Santos began talking fast, in Spanish. Tears streamed down her face.

Raffaela interpreted: "She wants to leave, says her baby doesn't like it here."

"Tell her we don't hurt mothers and children," Dixie Lou said.

Moments later, Dixie Lou took her translator aside and said within Deborah's earshot, "Well, what do you think?"

The platinum-blonde woman had her arms folded across her chest. She nodded. "The child spoke ancient Aramaic," she reported, keeping her voice low. "She is a she-apostle for sure, the Martha of Galilee you have been searching for."

"Exactly what did she say?"

"You haven't made a very good first impression on her, Madam Chairwoman. She said, 'The vengeance of the Lord will fall upon you.'"

Dixie Lou took on the most serious expression Deborah had ever seen. "Is that so? Well, we'll see about that."

And in a harsh, commanding voice she had one of the commandos remove the child from its mother's arms. Consuela wailed in Spanish and the baby screamed and kicked and made noises that sounded like words, but Dixie Lou Jackson had made up her mind, and when she made up her mind, no one could change it.

The translator stood by Dixie Lou, telling her in a low voice what the child was saying, a steady stream of insults against the Chairwoman, and threats for retribution by the Lord. . . .

* * *

Dixie Lou had the two older Mexican adults placed in the Vatican jail until she decided what to do with them. She decided to allow the mother, Consuela Santos, to have access to the child, but only when accompanied by a matron. She also assigned two translators and half a dozen guards to the baby. The Chairwoman needed to consider how best to handle this situation, wasn't sure if she wanted to touch Marta herself again.

A translator had told her that Marta was the Spanish equivalent of Martha, but this in itself was not proof, and only led to more questions. None of the previously authenticated she-apostles had been given the same (or essentially the same) names at birth as they had in ancient times. Why, then, would Martha?

Was it another sign that she was somehow distinct from the others? Dixie Lou watched the kicking, screaming baby as she was taken away, and realized that if this child had special information, she might be worth more than the other eleven children Lori Vale had, and more than the Vatican, the Pope or anything else in all of Christendom.

The Chairwoman wondered if this child was the key to the entire puzzle, but she wasn't certain if she wanted to know the answer.

A chill ran down her spine.

* * *

"Do you have any idea what I've done for you?" Dixie Lou said. Wearing maroon slacks and an oversized black blouse, she stood in the doorway of Deborah Marvel's office, leaning in. The Chairwoman held a large glass of red wine, almost spilled it.

"Eh?" Deborah said, startled at her demeanor and the rhetorical question.

"You should be more appreciative."

"I don't know what you mean." Deborah had been going over printouts of military reports, none of which were particularly favorable. Papers were strewn across her desk. She held a pen in her hand, with which she'd been making margin notes in red ink. Receiving these reports through clandestine means, the UWW leadership had learned of the destruction of numerous bases and offices all over the world, and the disappearance of key personnel.

But not at the hands of the Bureau of Ideology. Instead, allied nations were turning against both the UWW and the BOI, trying to eliminate each of the extremes. In doing so, they were risking the wrath of the unstable Dixie Lou Jackson, who could blow up the Vatican and kill the Pope at any moment. So far, NATO was not attacking her in the holy city, but they were undoubtedly working on contingency plans.

"The truth, Deborah. You know better than to lie to me." Noticing her glass tilting, Dixie Lou straightened it, without spilling the wine.

"Looks like you've found the Pope's private stock," Deborah mused.

"*My* private stock now."

"So it is. As for what you've done for me, Dixie Lou, I didn't join United Women of the World for personal recognition or advancement."

"As long as I permit it, you are one of its highest officials."

"You seem intent on reminding me of the power you hold over me. Is something bothering you? Have I failed you somehow?" Deborah heard vehicle noises outside, and crowd noises.

"I'll ask the questions around here, not you." Dixie Lou took a gulp of wine, but did not appear to be drunk. Her dark eyes were alert, her speech concise. "I've done a lot for you, for all of the councilwomen.

And I have every right to expect loyalty in return. Is that too much to ask?"

Pursing her lips, Deborah responded, "Perhaps not."

"Then why do you speak about me behind my back?"

"I don't. We had the one private session that you seem to know about—a meeting that was permitted under the UWW Charter—and that was all. Surely, Tamara Himmel told you that she and I defended you at the meeting. Did she?"

A slight smile touched the Chairwoman's mouth. "I do not reveal my sources of information."

"The only councilwomen who spoke against you at that meeting are probably dead," Deborah said. "Isn't that true? You want to speak of truth, what about that? Where are Bobbi Torrence and Kaiulani Maheha?"

"We both know where they are. In hell."

Deborah was not afraid. "Another decision you made without our consultation."

The Chairwoman stared at her.

"When you aren't around, Dixie Lou, I try not to say negative things about you, only positive. Everyone knows that I've been troubled by your takeover of the Vatican, which you did without consulting with us. But I've tried not to criticize you personally, and I've tried to make the best of the situation."

This was true to an extent, for Deborah had been keeping most of her thoughts to herself, considering them too dangerous to reveal to anyone in the UWW. It seemed clear to her that Dixie Lou was on a slippery slope, losing touch with reality. The last two councilwomen to express such an opinion could no longer be counted among the membership, or among the living. Tamara Himmel had seen to that, ingratiating herself to Dixie Lou.

Another sip of wine. "And you expect me to believe that?"

"You asked for the truth." The crowd noises outside were louder, and Deborah wanted to look, but the window was behind her and would require opening a drape.

A savage smile rippled along the Chairwoman's mouth. "And I can always expect the truth from you. Isn't that the case?"

"I know I've irritated you sometimes, saying things you don't want to hear. If you want only yes-women in your new organization, I'll turn in my resignation right now."

"Not quite yet, Deborah. I'll notify you when—and if—you're no longer of any use. All right, tell me something I don't want to hear."

Lifting a sheet of paper, she responded, "The military reports aren't getting any better." She provided details.

After listening, Dixie Lou said, "Why didn't you come in to tell me earlier?"

"I just learned about it, and I've been preparing an analysis."

Dixie Lou finished her wine in one large gulp. "No matter, we have more important prizes here."

"There is some good news in these reports. Our approval rate just ticked up to thirty-two percent, and money is pouring in from sales of the *Holy Women's Bible*. We have a huge bestseller on our hands."

"Maybe I should do a book tour," Dixie Lou mused, showing evidence that the wine might be having some effect on her after all.

"I think we should negotiate with NATO," Deborah said in a firm voice, "We can't remain here forever, and will eventually lose the siege."

"I disagree! Despite the short-term reversals, eventually we could infiltrate every army, navy, and air force in the world. We can rule the planet, Councilwoman Marvel! Think of the power we would have!"

"We should be thinking in terms of responsibility, not of power."

"Don't quote Amy to me," the Chairwoman said, referring to a limited edition handbook written by Amy Angkor-Billings. "I don't need a conscience." She stared into her empty wine glass.

A great clamor arose outside, bullhorns and crowd noises. The two women hurried to the office window and pulled open a heavy drape, providing them with a vantage of the eastern approaches to Vatican City. At the NATO barricades thousands of people were milling, stretching as far as the eye could see. Some stood atop cars and trucks, and more packed the rooftops.

Dixie Lou threw open the window, allowing her to hear chanting from the crowd.

"Dixie Lou! . . . Dixie Lou! . . . Dixie Lou!"

Leaning out of the window, the most famous woman in the world shouted ecstatically to the throng, the front edge of which was perhaps a hundred meters away. They noticed her, and the crowd noises increased, and became more unruly. Sirens began to whine in the distance.

In the mass of people, Deborah saw a number of anti-Dixie Lou Jackson signs, and more of them streaming toward the front of the throng, like a river in their midst, pushing people out of the way. Fights broke out.

Seeing only what she wanted to see, the Chairwoman exclaimed, "Today the Vatican, tomorrow the world!"

Chapter 30

There are dead people in her past.
    —From a BOI report on Dixie Lou Jackson

The following day, Dixie Lou Jackson presided over her council from the bronze Throne of St. Peter, inside the cavernous basilica. She held the unsheathed Sword of She-God on her lap, a weapon with newly fitted rubies, sapphires, emeralds, and diamonds.

Looking up at her, Deborah held an old fashioned clipboard, with a document attached to it. "I have the provisions report you asked for," she said. "As you know, Chairwoman, we're under siege, and it's not the first time that's occurred here. In 1082 Pope Gregory VII held out against King Henry IV of Germany, and in—"

"Don't waste my time with useless information!" Dixie Lou thundered. "Who cares about the history of the Vatican?" She rapped the sword on the bronze arms of the regal throne. "Just give me what I ordered."

"We have enough food and water for at least seven years, and enough wine for eternity."

"The Catholics do like their grape juice, don't they?"

Tight smile. "Yes, they do."

"Seven years," Dixie Lou mused. "That's a lot of time."

"Not historically. They may just decide to wait us out, and we can't extend our time by anything appreciable. If we try to move provisions in through the hidden passages, they're sure to be discovered and shut down."

"If NATO pushes this siege, we destroy everything—the Dome of St. Peter's, in the Sistine Chapel, all of it." She brought out the detonator in her pocket and held it up in the air. "Boom!" she said. "And they all fall down."

"Your other bargaining chip—Pope Rodrigo—may not last that long. He's seventy-nine and deteriorating under stress."

"Well, get him a doctor. Pump wine into him intravenously. Whatever it takes to keep him going." She stared at the detonator for a moment, then put it back in her pocket.

Deborah didn't find the Chairwoman funny. She was in a particularly cruel mood, cracking facetious jokes. Deborah herself had engaged in a number of conversations with the Pope and liked him, despite his tendency to sermonize. If the truth be told, she enjoyed his company a lot more than that of Dixie Lou, and always tried to make him as comfortable as possible. A distinguished gentleman with impeccable manners, he seemed to appreciate her efforts.

"Incidentally, I think those battle reports we've been getting are a fraud," Dixie Lou said. "Someone has broken our Internet encryptions. I'll bet our forces are actually winning."

"But our codes are unbreakable."

Pursing her lips, Dixie Lou nodded in resignation. "You're right, so it must all be true, and true that the allied nations are attacking the BOI, too. What do you hear about the submarine we have under construction in India?"

"It's behind schedule. Trouble getting parts, and costs keep going up."

"Tell them hurry up. I want to load it with nukes."

"We don't have any nuclear capability," Deborah said, startled. "It's only a conventional submarine."

"I was just kidding," Dixie Lou said.

But the comment bothered Deborah, making her wonder if this crazy woman had secret nuclear weapons somewhere, and she was trying to get a delivery system for them. There had been rumors, and she was clearly insane.

"We need to be very careful not to make any public comments that sound threatening," Deborah said. "We've gained slightly in public opinion polls, but we probably can't get much above our present thirty-two percent, not with all of the inflamed Christians. It's bad enough what we've already done, but if we start talking about nuclear weapons we'll be universally loathed. Everything we've worked for: the *Holy Women's Bible*, better lives for women, all will be lost. . . ."

Although Dixie Lou appreciated Deborah's wise counsel, she didn't always appreciate her directness, which sometimes bordered on lack of respect. "We should put our approval rating on a wall graph," Dixie Lou said. "I want to see it rise. Do you understand?"

"Yes, Chairwoman."

In her mind's eye, Dixie Lou tried to envision how her Vatican adventure would play out for history . . . for *her*story, as she liked to say it in public now, having purloined credit for the phrase from Amy Angkor-Billings. The way Dixie Lou Jackson held out in the holy city against overwhelming NATO forces would become as legendary as her time spent in the desert, or as the years she devoted to Monte Konos. She began to think about a name for the Tunisian desert place where she'd fled with the she-apostles, and about a new name for the Vatican—appellations that would extol the virtues of the women's movement and especially of herself.

Returning to awareness, she noticed Deborah Marvel gazing up at her, awaiting her command. This would be a good time for Dixie Lou to pull one of the surprises she enjoyed so much.

"Hereafter you shall be known as Cardinal Marvel," the woman on the throne announced, in her most somber tone. "Step forward."

Perplexed, Deborah did so.

Leaning down from the high chair, Dixie Lou touched the tip of the Sword of She-God to Deborah's forehead, and said, "There, it is done."

"What is this all about, Madam Chairwoman?"

Like a scolding teacher, Dixie Lou shook her head. "Henceforth I am to be referred to as Grand Messenger of the Holy She. The UWW is disbanded, in favor of this new, more appropriate umbrella organization. The Holy She. Has a nice sound to it, don't you think, infinitely better than the Holy See they used to call this place?"

"I had no idea you were contemplating such a change. Shouldn't we discuss it more, consider the public relations consequences and other aspects?"

"You sound like a scratched record, repeating the same thing over and over." Her voice took on a mocking, mimicking tone: " What will the public say? Shouldn't we discuss it in council? Don't you want additional opinions? The charter requires this or that—But Deborah, has it occurred to you that there is no charter, because the UWW no longer exists? It's a whole new ballgame, Cardinal, and you'd better get used to it."

"I don't mean to question your decision, uh, Grand Messenger."

"Then go forth and announce it to the other seven. They are all cardinals, too, and you are first among them."

"I appreciate that, Grand Messenger."

"That's all," the Grand Messenger said, noting that Deborah was staring blankly at her, with her blue eyes glazed over. "I must prepare for a proclamation this afternoon, notifying the world of my decisions."

"Yes, Grand Messenger," Deborah said..

As the newly appointed Cardinal departed, Dixie Lou told herself that she didn't entirely trust her, despite her years of loyal service. If she'd learned anything at all in her lifetime, the self-anointed Grand Messenger knew that things changed, and often not for the better.

* * *

The blonde woman ran up the narrow interior staircase that led to the Dome of St. Peter's Basilica, five hundred thirty-seven steps. She wore purple jogging shorts, a matching tee shirt, and a headband. As a jogger, Deborah Marvel saw a lot of the Vatican that most people never saw. She enjoyed exploring nooks and crannies.

Reaching the outdoor viewing deck on top, she was breathing hard. She ran in place while a female soldier watched her from a rocket launcher position, one of three on this level. The other two were out of sight, around the curve of the deck.

Gazing out at the smog-choked, pewter-blue sky of Rome, Deborah saw the NATO military encampments along the Via della Conciliazione and other streets leading to the Vatican. Tanks and artillery pieces had high-caliber guns aimed at St. Peter's, and she wondered if this revered holy site—built so many centuries ago—would be destroyed, tragically. An artillery shell could blow off the top of the Basilica at any moment, killing her instantly, along with the UWW soldiers in the defensive nests up there.

Actually she might welcome death, to free her of her problems, especially her own feeling that she should have done more to prevent Dixie Lou Jackson from wreaking such havoc on the world. But she didn't know what she could have done, and her own death would only make Dixie Lou worse. Sometimes the woman did listen to Deborah, though examples of that were diminishing.

And I can't attack her physically, Deborah thought, *or she could set off the explosives.*

At the sound of something behind her, she turned and was surprised to see Dixie Lou herself, dressed in running clothes, emerge from the stairway and reach the viewing deck. Earlier Deborah had seen her jogging in the Piazza di San Pietro, but thought she didn't want to undertake the steep climb to the top of the cathedral.

"Not bad, eh?" Dixie Lou said, breathing hard. "You didn't think you could outdo me, did you?"

"No, ma'am. I've never considered anything like that."

"I wonder, old friend. I wonder."

Deborah tried to put on a cheerful expression, but her mind was filled with troubling thoughts. Atop this holiest of all Christian shrines, stretching toward the heavens, she considered the fate of her soul, and of Dixie Lou's, and of the Pope's. Their time on this earth might be over soon. It had been a terrible mistake for the UWW to attack the Vatican, a sacrilege.

"What are you thinking about?" Dixie Lou asked.

"Nothing much. Just clearing the cobwebs out of my mind. That's why I like to jog."

"Cobwebs? You have nasty spiders prowling through your brain?"

"Once in awhile," Deborah admitted, knowing she could never hope to conceal all of her thoughts from this prying, intelligent woman. Better to admit small flaws than to put on a face of perfection, which would make her look suspicious.

Deborah looked away. She wanted more than anything to push Dixie Lou off the top of St. Peters, avenging what she did to Katherine Pangalos, and preventing her from harming any more people. But she didn't know if she could accomplish it. The little black woman looked strong.

"I have a few cobwebs myself," Dixie Lou admitted. "Exercise is good for the mind and the body, and I want you in top form. We have important work to do."

The Chairwoman turned and started back down the stairs, with Deborah Marvel following.

Chapter 31

Truth can kill the soul, or resurrect it.
　　　　　　　　　　—Amy Angkor-Billings

All day long, two translators had been working with Martha of Galilee, but the brown-skinned baby had not revealed any new gospel details. While she had ceased an initial onslaught of fussing and crying, she was refusing to cooperate in any other manner.

Despite being only a little more than seven months old, she could walk already, and now she was pacing the room with her herky jerk walk, acting like an adult jammed into that tiny, unformed body. She was talking rapidly, as Dixie Lou stood with the translators, watching her.

"What's she saying now?" the Grand Messenger demanded.

"More bad things about you, I'm afraid" replied a translator who had a dark brown pageboy haircut. She made several entries in an electronic unit, then showed Dixie Lou the transcript screen.

As the black woman read, she felt so much rage building inside that she wanted to take the baby and fling her against a wall . . . or out a window. "What sort of garbage is this? She calls me a murderess? A murderess? It is a lie!"

"Of course, Chairwoman," the other translator, a platinum blonde, said. "We know that."

"I'm no longer the *Chairwoman*," Dixie Lou said, slapping the woman across the face with the transcript unit, and then following that up with a bare hand. "I'm the Grand Messenger of the Holy She!"

"I'm sorry. Of course." The woman backed up. "I was so focused on this difficult child that I forgot."

"A murderess!" Dixie Lou exclaimed. "The same thing that lying teenager said about me on television." A moment later, she grinned viciously. Do you suppose Martha watches television?"

"I don't think so, ma'am. Not here, anyway. And her mother is so poor that they probably didn't even have electricity in Mexico."

Dixie Lou watched the child as she paced the room, moving at a surprising clip despite her awkwardness. Abruptly, Martha stopped and looked up at Dixie Lou with feral eyes that almost seemed to blaze reddish brown instead of brown. She walked toward Dixie Lou. The Grand Messenger backed away, and for some reason remembered touching Lori Vale and seeming to share a peculiar vision with her, like a dream version of Lori having a baby. But this was not Lori's child. This was another one, the missing twelfth she-apostle.

Martha spit words out in a sharp tone, then turned her back on Dixie Lou and marched off.

"She called you a murderess again," the brunette said. "And a liar."

Working late that evening Dixie Lou inflicted what she considered a mild form of discipline on the child—withholding food, milk, and sleep, in an attempt to obtain a new gospel from her. But the rude, stubborn little creature refused to say anything at all. She just glared with fiery, hateful eyes.

* * *

Since the Acting Minister was off consulting with an important, unnamed person, that left Kylee Branson in charge of the Bureau of Ideology. Some of the Vice Ministers theorized that Styx was meeting with high-level officials in the US government, using the diplomatic and political clout of his position. The timing of his trip seemed strange to most of the BOI people, however, especially the way he refused to take any of them into his confidence.

It was mid-afternoon. Branson sat in Tertullian's windowless office with the lights out and only the computer on, casting an amber glow across the office. The headquarters complex was filled with people—virtually all of the employees and every Vice Minister except Tommy Lee Chang The optimum time to do what he had in mind.

He tapped deep-access keys and brought up the military codes.

Kylee had always been fiercely loyal to the Bureau of Ideology. As one of the most efficient managers, he had risen rapidly through the ranks, attaining an appointment as Vice Minister of Construction & Transport before the age of thirty. The nine Vice Ministers, while each bearing the same rank, were actually not equal. His first ministry had been the lowest, and gradually, as opportunities became available, he reached the lofty position of Vice Minister of Doctrine & Faith, second among vice ministries only to the Department of Minority Affairs, under Styx Tertullian. That was the way the departments had lined up under Minister Culpepper, anyway . . . and so far under his acting successor. In previous regimes, the departments had lined up differently, depending upon the political needs of the time and the priorities of the Minister. As a career bureaucrat, Kylee understood these things very well.

His path to the Bureau of Ideology had been, to say the least, an unusual one. Born Kaylee Branson (and not Kylee), the journey to his present position involved more than dropping the "a" from his given name. Considering all of this, the Vice Minister sighed at the memories of physical and emotional pain, including the sex change operation he underwent at the tender age of fourteen. Born a bouncing nine pound girl, Kaylee had—at her own insistence—been altered to a boy.

Just before her operation, the fights with her parents had been fierce, but ultimately Kaylee had won out by making a case to them that she didn't feel comfortable as a girl, that she had always longed to be a boy instead. Besides, she pointed out quite correctly with her logical mind, it was easier for a man to succeed in business and politics than for a woman to do so. And, contributing to her decision, she was quite tall for a girl anyway, well over six feet. Thus there were practical and emotional reasons for the transformation. Her parents had finally assented, and had agreed to pay for the surgery.

Thus in a short period of time, Kaylee became Kylee.

Kylee's father Lawrence Branson, a school district commissioner, then secretly changed school computer records to make it appear that his *son* had gone through school, instead of his daughter. A couple of well-placed bribes ensued, resulting in the alteration of county statistics as well, showing that a boy named Kylee had been born to the Branson family. That left school mates who remembered the girl, but she had been a quiet person, easily forgotten, and such memories faded with time. Kaylee went away to a boy's boarding school under her new name, never returning to her home town. . . .

The Vice Minister thought about such things every day. His sexuality was at the core of his being, affecting virtually every decision he made. Now, as he sat at the computer, he voice-activated a code known only to three people—the Acting Minister, the Vice Minister of Military Affairs, and himself. It was to be employed only in cases of extreme emergency, to prevent Bureau secrets from falling into the wrong hands. He heaved a deep, agitated sigh.

During his rise through the ranks of the Bureau of Ideology, Kylee had experienced new feelings, new longings. Though he struggled to conceal it from everyone around him, something of his old female self had been resurfacing, a remnant that had been dormant and was now coming back. It was a subject he never dared to discuss with anyone, and to some extent he had been able to set it aside. He had worked extremely hard to get ahead in the BOI, the world's pre-eminent bastion of male supremacy. On a subconscious level this might have been so that he could destroy his feminine side once and for all.

When Minister Culpepper died, however, things began to change. Kylee didn't like the way Styx Tertullian treated him, always yelling and casting blame on him unfairly. Kylee was certain that Styx resented him for his superior breeding and Ivy League education, too, since Tertullian's background had been blue collar. But that was only part of the problem. Maybe Tertullian—a self-proclaimed misogynist—sensed something hormonal about Kylee, that he wasn't what he appeared to be. That could be dangerous, if he ever ordered a close scrutiny of school and county records and something turned up . . . a loose bit of incriminating information that had been overlooked. Or if he ordered a probative medical examination.

In recent weeks, Kylee had been having second thoughts about what he'd done to his own body, deep regrets and feelings that he had betrayed all of womanhood by abandoning them. This was quite a quandary, especially for a person in his position—now second in command of the Bureau of Ideology. It was during this time that he decided to take a drastically different course, to make up for what he had done, what *she* had done. Thousands of people would die in the BOI headquarters because of the action she was taking now, but it could not be avoided. Sometimes it was necessary to make a statement, and perhaps the She-God had placed her here for that reason.

A woman could outperform a man after all, and Kaylee was proving it.

She tapped a single key, and three seconds later heard the first blast, followed quickly by another, and then another, like deadly dominoes. There were explosives wired into the headquarters complex, designed to protect BOI secrets when no other options remained. She only counted three blasts, because the next one took her—and the remainder of the BOI headquarters facility—with it. . . .

* * *

When Mrs. Bonham returned from grocery shopping, her house was no longer there. And neither was her house guest. Unknown to the old woman, Kaylee Branson had tracked Styx down and made her last BOI management decision, taking care of an essential detail. In fact, the two explosions that Kaylee originated had occurred simultaneously, timed meticulously to avoid harming an innocent old woman.

Too bad, Mrs. Bonham thought, picking through the rubble and finding a piece of the chain that had been holding Styx Tertullian down. Once, he had been such a sweet boy, and in time she might have salvaged something of the old personality.

Chapter 32

Males are not permitted into the new priesthood. Any man wishing to participate in religious affairs shall do so with his wife or his female companion, under her supervision.

—By Order of Dixie Lou Jackson, Grand Messenger of the Holy She

The following morning . . .

At a brisk pace Dixie Lou crossed the foyer outside her holy office in the Vatican, the heels of her gold boots clicking on the green marble floor. In recent days, her construction crew had begun the extensive job of remodeling the papal offices, utilizing stored building materials and valuable articles from the museums and other repositories of holy Christian treasures. Despite the shut-down of the UWW, she still liked the green-and-orange colors of the old organization, so they were used extensively here. The result pleased her, especially a row of enlarged photographs of herself that lined the foyer, in various heroic poses. In each, she wore what she had on now, one of her elegant white-and-gold robes.

Inside her office, television cameras were being set up for another worldwide broadcast scheduled to begin in a few minutes. She had just supervised the production crew. It was the same format as the afternoon before, when she'd proclaimed herself the Grand Messenger and spoken for half an hour.

Opening the door of Deborah Marvel's outer office, she strolled in, past the male private secretary who slouched at a desk. He hurried to stand as she swept past. An ugly little man with coke bottle-thick eyeglasses. Why didn't Deborah get a good-looking, well-built stud knight, as the other newly appointed cardinals had done? Now it occurred to Dixie Lou that Deborah had never utilized stud knights, even though she professed to be heterosexual. The Chairwoman could not recall for certain, but thought Deborah had once mentioned to her that she had been married, and was either separated or divorced. No matter. Dixie Lou didn't care one way or the other.

Though Dixie Lou had considered watching Deborah Marvel more closely, she had never done much of anything about it. That might have to change. Deborah was still in charge of caring for the Pope, which put her in a position to cause trouble. Perhaps it was time to order an updated report on her. But she found the thought jarring.

What am I thinking? Deborah has always been my most trusted ally. If I can't trust her, who can I trust?

Dixie Lou realized that she would have to kill all of the remaining councilwomen and start over if she continued along her suspicious line of reasoning. And this was not a good time to do that. She needed their help, relied on their support. She decided that she was only imagining that Deborah needed to be monitored.

I'm being paranoid.

Dixie Lou strode into her chief subordinate's inner office. Seeing her, Cardinal Marvel, attired in the new green-and-orange vestment of her position, stood and bowed. A steaming cup of coffee sat on her desk. She resumed her seat, but not until she saw the Grand Messenger slipping into one of two brown leather chairs fronting the Cardinal's cherry wood desk. This desk and all furnishings were identical to the office amenities for the seven other cardinals, set up by Dixie Lou so that all appeared to be treated equally.

A close examination of the layout revealed favoritism, however, as Deborah's office was nearest to the impressive papal office that would soon be occupied by Dixie Lou, and the others were strung out from there–leading to a small council chamber. In accordance with a blueprint drawn up under Dixie Lou's direction, a second, much larger council chamber was under construction on the main level of the Vatican Palace. It had been interesting to hold council meetings in various chambers around the religious city, but they needed a secure, permanent facility for the world-renowned organization that the Grand Messenger envisioned.

The Holy She.

"We have a few minutes before my speech today," Dixie Lou announced, "and there are some things you and I need to discuss. I think I know what to do, but I'd like to run my ideas past you. I've decided not to answer NATO at all."

"You know that distresses me, because I'm afraid it will make them unnecessarily agitated, and perhaps cause them to attack. We must respond to them."

"Nonsense. They don't dare attack the Vatican, for fear that we'll blow up the priceless art treasures and kill everyone here, including the Pope and the cute little she-brat, Martha of Galilee. I have some ideas about her, too."

"With all due respect, can't we please discuss this more?"

"No time. I'm on the air in fifteen minutes."

With her hand trembling, Deborah lifted the coffee cup to her lips and drank. Her blue eyes simmered, but she said nothing more about the matter.

Deborah doesn't dare do anything against me, Dixie Lou thought. *She still disagrees, but I have her under control.*

"Initially," the Chairwoman said, "I thought the eleven she-apostles were dead, and Lori, too. So I went on the air with twelve fakes."

"Then Lori Vale surfaced with eleven real ones," Deborah said. "And the Mexican Martha showed up."

"Exactly. And now I'm going to contact Lori."

"Why?"

"I thought about telling her we're going to kill the real Martha if she doesn't bring the other eleven she-apostles to us. Give her a deadline and then crucify the kid out in the square."

"*Crucify* a child?"

"Pretty dramatic, huh?"

"But that would make you look bad to the public. You'll never be an admired world leader if you murder an innocent child!"

Taking a deep breath to calm herself, the Grand Messenger said, "You should listen more carefully, Deborah. I told you I only *thought* about giving Lori that ultimatum. I have something else in mind entirely. I want you to handwrite a letter to her for my signature, and this is what we'll say. . . ."

Awkwardly, apparently since she wasn't accustomed to being treated like a secretary, Deborah scribbled notes, then asked, "You want me to write this up for your signature?"

"No, I want you to throw the notes away, and I'll dictate it to someone else all over again. Yes, I want you to write it up! It's a matter of utmost urgency and security! Why do you think I'm having you handle it?"

She nodded, deferentially. "I'll take care of it right away. Go deliver your speech. I'll have the letter for you within the hour."

"What do you think of today's speech? You read my draft, I presume?"

"Of course. Well, this is your second speech in two days, and–"

"*Our* second speech."

"Yes, of course, *our* second. Yesterday you–I mean *we*–announced the formation of the Holy She and officially ordered the destruction of all religious texts other than the *Holy Women's Bible*."

"And fires lit up all over the world." Dixie Lou's eyes took on a wild glaze. "You saw the burnings on TV, the way the VR-flames seemed to be right inside the room? I leaped up and rubbed my hands in the burning light!"

"I saw the news. But your–our–next proclamation may be a bit severe. I don't know if we should issue it. Anyone discovered with a heretical publication is subject to summary execution?" She shook her head. "I think it's too harsh, and unenforceable. We're confined to the Vatican, after all."

"*Confined?* On TV and over the Internet, we can call for Holy She vigilantes to take care of the details."

"If we issue a proclamation like that, I guarantee you the Internet will be cut off, NATO won't permit any more reporters in here, and no more couriers will get in or out. The order to burn holy books is bad enough, and there may be repercussions from it." Deborah started to say something else, but fear crossed her face and she fell silent.

Dixie Lou's eyes flashed. "They don't dare cut us off, unless they want to see the Pope's bloody corpse in the Piazza di San Pietro."

"Alive, the Pope is a bargaining chip. Dead, he has hardly any value."

"Maybe you're right." The Grand Messenger paused, and her wild eyes seemed to settle down. "All right, I won't order executions yet. We'll discuss it in council first." She glanced at her watch. "I need to go on the air now."

"Wait. What are you going to say?"

"I'll wing it. A few platitudes against men, and brief 'bios' on the she-apostles. I'll come up with something. Mmm, maybe a little religious history, putting things in perspective."

"No proclamations, OK?"

"Agreed. For today."

On the way back to her office, Dixie Lou considered the future and the past, and how she might go about linking them. Certain passages in the authentic gospels of the she-apostles were intriguing to her, suggesting a dual nature to Jesus, in which he incorporated both male and female aspects. This could be the basis of a future speech.

She set such thoughts aside. The camera crew awaited her.

Sitting down at her desk, Dixie Lou smoothed her exquisite robe, and straightened a golden sword-cross dangling from her neck. Notes were arrayed in front of her, but only for effect. She wouldn't read them.

"It has come to my attention that the Roman Catholic Church has established a temporary papal office in Avignon, France," she began, as she spoke into a tiny microphone speck that floated, almost invisibly, in the air beside her. "Students of religious history know that the papacy was located there for much of the fourteenth century, when there were two competing popes—one in Avignon and one in Rome. Perhaps the Church intends to set up a second pontiff now, but that is not necessary, because Pope Rodrigo is in fine fettle. No one has thrown him from the top of St. Peter's yet."

Dixie Lou chuckled at her facetious remark. "Now that I have your attention I'll tell you more about the Holy She. Our message is sweeping the globe. Millions of women are rushing into the fold. . . ."

* * *

Though she tried to conceal it, Deborah had been growing increasingly upset with Dixie Lou Jackson, and deeply disturbed by her actions. After Katherine Pangalos and five other councilwomen were left to die on Monte Konos, Dixie Lou told Deborah it wasn't intentional, that Katherine must have been meeting with her council friends at the time of the attack, and all of them were just unlucky. It might have happened that way, but circumstantial evidence said otherwise. The subsequent disappearances of Bobbi Torrence and Kaiulani Maheha said otherwise, too, immediately after both of them voiced opposition to Dixie Lou. She had as much as admitted killing them, saying both of them were in "hell" now.

Now Deborah could hardly remember why she and Dixie Lou had been friends and political allies in the first place. The woman's strange behavior went back to the death of Amy Angkor-Billings, when she began to act as if the whole world revolved around her. Dixie Lou was increasingly losing her grip on reality. More and more she was living in a fantasy realm.

Giancarlo Veron showed up at Deborah's office while she was writing Dixie Lou's letter by hand. He said he had been commanded to take it back to the Grand Messenger right away for her signature, and then he was supposed to deliver it to Lori Vale. The Curator of Medieval Manuscripts, he said he knew his way through the secret stairway and narrow passageway that Alberto Carducci had used previously—a route that Dixie Lou kept guarded.

But as Deborah chatted with the dark-haired Veron while finishing the letter on Vatican stationery, she could tell that he was displeased with the tasks the Chairwoman had given him to do, not only because he was loyal to the Papacy, but because he had been a friend of the murdered Carducci. In earlier conversations, Deborah had explored Veron's thoughts, and felt he was a person whom she might trust.

I have to take the risk, she thought. *I have no choice.*

"Get her signature," Deborah said, handing the letter to him. "Then meet me at my apartment before leaving Vatican City, and say nothing of this to the Grand Messenger."

The curator's black eyebrows arched in surprise. "But she will want the letter delivered right away."

"There is a matter concerning the security of the Vatican that I must discuss with you first," she said. "Just between the two of us. Do you understand?"

Apprehensively, he looked at her, his dark brown eyes seeming to search for something. "Just between the two of us," he agreed.

Then he spun on his heels and left.

* * *

Standing in what was formerly a royal guest room of the Vatican Palace, Deborah thought it must have housed the most famous people in the world when they came to visit the Pope, seeking his blessings. Presidents, kings and queens, premiers, industrialists, musicians, intellectuals, sports heroes. Their names would be familiar to millions. It was quite an old building, dating back centuries, from appearances. She wished it had a visitor's book that she could peruse.

Original oil paintings adorned the walls, depicting church officials of the past. She didn't recognize their names. One of them was a scarlet-robed cardinal, tall and regal, with a wide nose and pale green, penetrating eyes. Another depicted the soft-featured Leo X (Giovanni de' Medici), who was Pope when Martin Luther began the Protestant Reformation. Between the paintings a pair of alcoves had been notched into the walls, with a bronze Christian statuette inside each. The doors— one to the hallway and another to an adjacent room—were hand-painted, with miraculous religious scenes on them.

With a deep sigh, Deborah thought of her own impoverished beginnings in America, and how she had once been a housewife. In recent weeks, events had been moving so fast, at breathtaking speed. First the *Holy Women's Bible*, then Dixie Lou's first satellite broadcasts, then the takeover of the Vatican and the kidnapping of the Pope. All of them astounding, earth-shaking events.

Deborah pulled a chair out from a Louis XV writing desk and sat down. The desk, with an inlaid marble top, leaded glass cupboards, and rosewood carvings, stood on tapered, carved legs. She removed stationery and an ink pen from one of the shallow drawers. The heavy, textured paper was gold embossed, with a Christian cross at the top.

She began to write, but the pen, which seemed to have no ink, scraped on the paper. After examining the instrument's tip, she noticed a small ink reservoir just above it. In one of the pigeonholes of the desk she located a crystal ink bottle, opened it. Dipping the pen inside and pumping ink into the reservoir, she found that it provided her with an adequate supply of smooth-flowing ink. In a short while she had written a brief letter:

Dear Lori Vale:

I am at great peril saying this, because Dixie Lou will surely kill me if she finds out. But I must do what is right, especially for the special children. I will do what I can to bring that madwoman to justice. I offer to help you, Lori Vale, in any way possible. The real Martha of Galilee is in the Vatican Palace, on the third floor, at the southwest corner. While I have been assigned to care for the Pope, another councilwoman—Dalal Karim—is in charge of Martha. My ability to help you is limited, but perhaps this bit of information will enable you to rescue her.

Do not trust Dixie Lou's offer, but be careful how you respond. She may kill Martha of Galilee, Pope Rodrigo, and blow up the Vatican, in an attempt to have her demands met. So far, I have talked her out of such radical courses of action. Although it is hard to imagine anything more radical than her takeover of this sacred religious facility, it could be worse. If her wild rages take control of her, it *will* be worse.

I beg of you. Act prudently, and act quickly. This is a critical moment in history.

Deborah Marvel

For several moments Deborah stared at the letter, rereading it, whispering it aloud to see how it sounded, how it might be received and interpreted by the recipient. There were messages between the lines . . . fear, remorse, her desire for redemption and for the forgiveness of God.

Her note was strong enough, she decided, the precise tone she wanted to convey. She would leave it as is.

Just as she completed it, she heard a rap on her door, and went to answer.

With baited breath, she opened the door, half expecting to be arrested by Dixie Lou's military police. Instead, Giancarlo Veron greeted her, holding the earlier letter she had written for Dixie Lou's signature. With a smile and a sigh of relief, she motioned him inside.

Chapter 33

Women, who have been deceived, dominated, and excluded by men for centuries, suddenly find themselves at the crest of a holy tidal wave.
—EBC News account

Another day passed, and on the streets of Rome surrounding the Vatican, black-robed Catholic priests delivered simultaneous open air sermons to sectioned-off crowds of men, women, and children. The solemn onlookers wore their best clothes and held palm leaves, with some wearing broad green foliage in their hair and on their clothing. This was in honor of the upcoming Palm Sunday, a day long ago when Christ the King entered Jerusalem, and ancient spectators strewed palms in his path.

From her room, Deborah heard the metallic blare of loudspeakers, and with a sinking sensation understood their significance. Though she'd tried to embrace Catholicism in her youth, she had been stymied by an unsupportive family, and had never gotten as involved as she would have liked. Still, she felt the pain of the people outside, and wished Vatican City had never been contaminated by the fanatical Dixie Lou Jackson. So much harm had been done, not only to this sacred city, but to the credibility of the entire women's movement.

Deborah wore a white bathrobe. Her blonde hair was still wet from the shower she had just taken—the second of the day, since the weather was so warm and sticky. On occasion, showers also helped her relieve stress, but this time she could not find a way to make herself feel better. As days passed, she found herself listening more and more to sounds outside, waiting for something even more terrible to happen. At any moment, NATO commandos could come roaring into the compound, with helicopter gunships firing bullets and rockets. In reaction, Dixie Lou would begin setting off the explosive charges she had ordered planted in all of the major structures. It would be a cataclysm, and Deborah hoped with all of her heart that it could be averted.

Having told Dixie Lou that she wasn't feeling well—true to a degree—the despondent Deborah had avoided sitting with other so-called female cardinals at today's television broadcast from Dixie Lou Jackson. The Grand Messenger liked to call them her "church-side chats," and she was making one each day.

Grand Mess is more like it, Deborah thought.

Glancing at her watch, she wandered into the parlor, where the closed-circuit VR-TV had just gone on automatically. Large, three dimensional letters projected out into the room: STAND BY FOR A SPECIAL ANNOUNCEMENT FROM THE GRAND MESSENGER. The pompous coronet music of the Holy She sounded.

In a three-dimensional projection into the parlor, a half-size Dixie Lou Jackson seemed to float in the air in her regal robe, with the large golden sword-cross about her neck and a familiar copy of the *Holy Women's Bible* in her hands. She stood in the Grand Messenger's office, in front of the immense desk formerly used by the Pope of the Roman Catholic Church. The music subsided.

The Grand Messenger smiled in a benign way, and proclaimed, "Do you know what Vatican means? It is derived from 'vatic,' which pertains to prophecy. It stems from the Latin *'vaticinator'* for a prophet, or *'vaticinatrix'* for a prophetess. Hear this, and listen carefully. I am the prophetess of modern times, and millions flock to my word. I speak to you from Vatican City, now the She-God's pulpit on earth."

She paused, while from somewhere applause and theme music sounded. When the noise subsided, she continued. "After long consideration, I have decided not to change the name of the Vatican, or of any of the holy structures here. They will remain as links between past, present and future, to remind earth's inhabitants of where we have been and where we are going. The Holy She does not seek to tear down the Christian Church; rather, we are building upon its foundation, adding new information that for centuries has been suppressed."

Disgusted with the contrived public image Dixie Lou was portraying, Deborah paced the room, waiting for the unbearable speech to conclude—a public address that the television set would not allow her to turn off. She had tried. Even the volume setting could not be adjusted, and there was no way to disconnect it from the power source. Finally the broadcast concluded, and the quiet of the room was as welcome as a cool breeze on this sweltering day.

* * *

Afterward, Deborah changed into black sweat pants and a gray sweatshirt, with a small cross on the lapel and a photograph of Michelangelo's "Last Judgment" on the back. A couple of days ago, she had obtained the shirt at a gift shop on the grounds of the Vatican, surprising the clerk by actually paying for it, and full price.

"But why are you paying?' the gnarled little man had asked. Only in his late twenties or early thirties, he appeared to have a birth defect that caused his back to hump outward. "Your comrades in arms always take whatever they want."

"I'm not one of the soldiers," Deborah replied, although she fell short of telling him that she had not even known in advance about the UWW attack on the Vatican.

"But even the other councilwomen such as yourself–" The man stopped, as if suddenly understanding. "You don't approve of the takeover?"

"I didn't say that, did I? We're not councilwomen, either. Dixie Lou has changed us to cardinals."

"You've all become Catholic?"

"Not exactly . . ."

As Deborah thought back on the gift-shop conversation now, while jogging across the huge central square, it almost seemed amusing to her, the way the poor man had looked so befuddled when she left him. She had said as much as she could say to him, had danced along the edge of loyalty as deftly as she could in an attempt to maintain her own sanity in an insane situation.

The afternoon sky glowed pale blue, with swollen clouds floating through the air, like immense cream pastries lifted by the wind. She saw construction crews at work in the papal offices, which Dixie Lou was having remodeled to suit her elaborate tastes and needs. The heavily guarded crews were operating around the clock, in no small part because Dixie Lou liked to brandish the Sword of She-God at them, constantly urging them to work faster.

Deborah felt better after the run, but only a little. She took her third shower of the day.

Chapter 34

No matter the exalted or favorable positions we attain, we are but transients passing through portals of life, constantly entering chambers and trying to stall our inevitable exits.
> —Lori Vale, *Reflections On A Life*

In the Manzoni district of Rome . . .

After watching Dixie Lou Jackson's broadcast, as she did each day, Lori suffered through a children's program on another channel, this one also sponsored by the newly named Holy She organization. In cartoon form, the show described how young girls should grow up to serve She-God, for the betterment of womankind. Coronet music played in the background, which a chubby cartoon lioness explained was the new military anthem for the Holy She.

Sitting with her, Liz Torrence and Siana Harui expressed their own contempt for the daily Grand Messenger propaganda, and for the manipulation of young minds through cartoons. Since escaping with Alex, the two young women had been inseparable. Siana was by far the happier, since she was reunited with her mother, while the slender, pretty Liz continued to worry about her aunt, who (as far as she knew) was still under the control of Dixie Lou. Lori had a bad feeling about the fate of Bobbi Torrence, but didn't want to say anything about it. A nagging sensation of unease. . . .

She wondered why NATO permitted Dixie Lou to make any broadcasts at all. It must be because they didn't want to upset her, not until they exhausted their efforts to negotiate with her, and completed their backup preparations to attack.

The teenager did not feel at all inspired by Dixie Lou's television programs. She loathed that woman and everything associated with her, wished more than ever that she and her mother had never gone to that ill-fated goddess circle near Seattle. It seemed like so long ago to Lori, and a universe away.

A window in her line of sight, just past the darkened VR-TV set, was being pelted by windblown rain, darkening her mood even more.

As Liz and Siana left, Alex entered the room, and exchanged only a few words with Lori when the videophone interrupted them with peculiar buzzing and hissing noises, as if it were an insect or a snake. Lori's father had arranged for the special phone—a secure line—using his military contacts. Zack had also arranged for armed guards to discreetly protect the building.

She snapped her fingers, and the phone receiver floated in the air by her face, without activating the video feature. "Lori?" a male voice said. "You there?"

"I'm here—Zack." She had considered calling him Dad, but didn't feel comfortable being that familiar yet.

He paused, as if disappointed with her choice of words. "NATO was contacted by Dixie Lou Jackson today," he said. "By one of her representatives, anyway, a Mr. Giancarlo Veron. He says he has a message for your eyes only."

"Why is that?"

"He wouldn't say. Anyway, NATO referred him to me because they know I'm your father. I'm very proud of that, Lori."

She felt moved by his words, but remained silent.

"I'll bring Veron to you," he said, "but it will be my way, so that he never knows where you are."

They set up a time, and made other security arrangements.

* * *

The "secret stairway" that the late Alberto Carducci discovered, and which Giancarlo Veron now negotiated, was really an ancient set of worn rock stairs that led from the Vatican into a narrow underground passageway, and ultimately to a doorway into a Rome subway station. He carried a thin valise.

In some places the way was so narrow that s muscular man such as Veron had difficulty getting through. Perhaps it was designed for small people in the old days, or to prevent military attacks via that route. Or perhaps earthquakes moved things around a bit. He noted that the rock and concrete walls were cracked and patched, and had a dark patina of age.

He exited the subway station onto street level and made his way down an alley to the meeting place. A short while later a dark sedan pulled up, and Veron climbed into the back seat, alongside a tall U.S. Army officer wearing aviator sunglasses. The car had tinted windows.

"We will take you to Lori Vale," the officer said. He patted the man down for weapons, searched his valise, and then placed a blindfold over his eyes. The streets of Rome were clogged with traffic, and it took nearly forty minutes to reach their destination.

The officer removed Veron's blindfold when they were inside an elevator. Glancing up as the doors opened, the black-haired curator saw that they were in a shadowy hallway on the seventh floor . . . information that was of little use to him, and only of slight interest; he had no intention of betraying Lori Vale. . . .

In her sitting room, with the curtains drawn for security, Lori greeted the messenger, while her father and Alex stood off to one side, looking on. This was only the second time that the two most important men in her life had met, and she'd been worrying about her father's attitude toward Alex, because he had previously expressed reservations about him.

She saw no sign of acrimony between them now, which pleased her. She had assured her father that Alex had made it abundantly clear to her that his own intentions were honorable, and that he was too old for her. Though she didn't know her father well yet, she had decided that he was not prejudiced against Alex because of skin color, and that his initial coldness toward the young man was only the natural tendency of a father to be suspicious of anyone who might potentially get involved with his daughter.

"Have a seat, please," Lori said to Veron, motioning to an overstuffed chair.

"I'd rather stand," he said, shifting the valise in his hands. "I have a chronic back problem that is acting up today, and when that happens it is difficult for me to sit. You should see my office, the custom furnishings, the way my desk is set up." He looked at her nervously. "But that is not what we are here to discuss."

"I imagine not," she said, standing with him. She was a little taller.

"Please believe me when I say that Dixie Lou's takeover of the Vatican is a dreadful sacrilege," he said, "a calamity of historic proportions. Horrible, horrible, just horrible." He gestured excitedly with his hands as he spoke, and his olive skin reddened. "The good Pope Rodrigo does not deserve this. They call him 'The People's Pope,' you know, because everyone likes him."

"I know," Lori said. "A lot of people agree with your feelings."

Taking a deep breath, he told her about the murder of his aged friend Alberto Carducci at the hands of Dixie Lou Jackson, and how upset he was about that. He also described the secret stairway route he had taken, which Carducci had discovered at a very young age, while breaking through a subterranean wall with a Vatican construction crew.

"Interesting," Zack said. He obtained details on where it ran, then asked, "Is that the route Jackson used when she attacked the Vatican?"

"I'm not sure. Could be. I only know what I heard, that somehow she used the underground tunnel system. The old-timers say there are lots of passageways down there, but I'm only familiar with the one I used today."

"And the reason you came to see me?" Lori asked.

Veron removed a letter from his valise, and passed it to her. "The Grand Messenger forced me to deliver this message," he said. "It's absurd, really."

"I know that woman, only too well."

"There is another message as well," he said, withdrawing a second letter from its hiding place in the lining of his case. "You cannot tell Dixie Lou that you know about this second one." He paused. "I was not searched before leaving, so this was not discovered—but only because of the identity of the person who wrote it, and the arrangements she made for my safe passage."

Her curiosity peaked, Lori accepted the second letter.

"If I may suggest," he added, "read them in the order I gave them to you?"

Nervously, Lori slit sealing wax from the first letter, and began to read. On Vatican stationery, the handwritten letter from Dixie Lou Jackson said:

> Lori, an interesting person arrived on my doorstep, speaking in the words of the ancients, going by a name familiar to both of us. That individual has undergone extensive tests for the purpose of identity confirmation. As you can imagine, this has immense potential repercussions.

Does she have the real Martha of Galilee? Lori wondered. *This is written so that it doesn't incriminate her for the fake twelfth she-apostle.*

Lori continued reading:

> You and I need to work together, for the benefit of womankind. Let bygones be bygones. Bring back our little friends, and come with them. I will make you my High Priestess.
>
> Sincerely,
>
> The Grand Messenger of the Holy She

Our friends. The eleven authentic she-apostles.

"She's inviting me to be her High Priestess," Lori said, angrily. "She wants me to join a pack of murderers and kidnappers who shot their way into the Vatican and took the Pope hostage! What future is there in that? She's insane. Let bygones be bygones? She allowed my mother to die! I'll never forgive her for that!"

"May I?" her father asked, reaching for the letter.

Seething, she handed it to him, then noted the messenger staring at her with a pained expression on his face.

It occurred to Lori that she should delay answering, to avoid provoking the insane woman into harming Martha of Galilee, or Pope Rodrigo The teenager knew that the twelve children should be together, but it made no sense at all to allow Dixie Lou to control all of them. That would only risk the other eleven. But Fujiko Harui and the she-apostle Abigail had told her that Martha was essential, a key to the puzzle of these remarkable children.

And Dixie Lou had the key.

Now Lori turned to the message from Deborah Marvel. "It's in the same handwriting," she said, "but the two letters are signed by different people."

"Dixie Lou ordered Deborah to handwrite the first one for her signature."

"Oh." As she read the second letter, the comments surprised and astounded her. Deborah referred to Dixie Lou Jackson as a "madwoman," and offered to help Lori "in any way possible." Lori had not expected anything like this. Deborah had never shown her any indication that she opposed Dixie Lou in any way.

Do I have a new ally? Or is this only Dixie Lou's trick, an attempt to lull me?

She passed the Marvel letter on to her father, too, and noted the perplexed expression on his face as he read it.

"Do you have responses?" Giancarlo Veron asked, of Lori.

"None that a young lady should utter," she said, with a tight smile. She glanced at Zack. "At least, not in the presence of my father."

He smiled in return, but his eyes were narrow and intense.

"My first inclination is to address her as the Grand Murderess," Lori said. "And tell her I won't discuss anything with the 'Holy She' until she is completely out of the picture."

"I think my daughter needs time to think about this," Zack said.

"Will twenty-four hours be long enough?" Veron asked. "Shall I return tomorrow?"

"All right," Lori said, as her father nodded. "Come back tomorrow at this time."

"You will respond to both Marvel and Jackson at that time?"

"We will discuss it more tomorrow," Lori said.

"If I may caution you, Miss Vale, do not respond to Ms. Marvel in writing. Tell me what to say and I will repeat it faithfully. Only write to the Grand Messenger."

"That sounds wise."

* * *

For the rest of the afternoon, Lori, her father, and Alex discussed the letters. Previously, Lori had filled Zack in on her life since the goddess circle, and told him how much Alex had helped her, and how he despised his own mother. "I trust him completely," Lori had said. She had also told him in a firm voice that she intended to include Alex in the important decisions she had to make, as one of her key advisers. Her father had argued.

Now, after reexamining the letters, Lori said, "I'm not sure how to respond."

"Do you think Dixie Lou really has the missing twelfth she-apostle?" Zack asked, "the one that supposedly knows things the others do not?"

"I don't know," Lori said, "but if Martha is there I want to rescue her. Maybe that tunnel route is the way to do it."

"It's sure to be heavily guarded," Alex said. Wearily, he passed a hand through his crop of unkempt, curly black hair. He had dark circles under his eyes, looked as if he needed to catch up on his rest. Earlier, he had said he'd been sleeping poorly because of all the commotion, and that he had decided to take sleeping pills until things settled down.

Lori gazed at the ceiling for several moments, trying to sense whether Dixie Lou really had the last she-apostle. She held the first letter on her lap, and passed her fingers repeatedly over Dixie Lou's signature, without picking up any strong sensation, one way or the other. Likewise, she couldn't get any particular sensation from the other letter, which was signed by Deborah.

Finally, she said, "I want to go in. We have to assume Martha's there."

"You don't mean you want to go into the Vatican?" Zack asked.

"I told you about the small telekinetic tricks the she-apostles do when I'm around, things they can't seem to do when I'm not there. Why do you suppose that is?" Lori asked.

Zack shrugged.

"It's because we have a connection," Lori said. "I feel it in my soul, that my life isn't worth anything without those children—without all twelve of them. I need to get to Martha and protect her."

"If you go, I'm going too," Alex said, rising to his feet for emphasis.

Zack glared at both of them. "Both of you are out of your minds. NATO can take care of this without either of you. They'll nab the kid and bring her out."

Shaking her head, Lori said, "They won't find her so easily, if Dixie Lou hides her, or keeps moving her around. But I can find Martha, wherever she is, the same way I figured out where Dixie Lou was going when she was flying away from Libya, heading across the Mediterranean. It came to me when I was holding hands with the she-apostles, and afterward when I seemed to be following the Chairwoman's spoor, and I knew she was going to Rome. I just *knew* it without anyone saying so, and I turned out to be right."

She paused. "I have an extrasensory link with the children, you see, and perhaps a link with something even deeper. Look—Dad—I need to be involved in rescuing Martha. You know the miraculous story of the she-apostles, and if you believe that, it's not a stretch to believe more, that I'm somehow part of their destiny."

"I don't know what I believe," he said. "I'm just worried about you."

"We should both go with her," Alex said.

"And you should get some sleep," Zack said, looking at him. "You look as if you're going to fall down."

He stood there, as if too tired to even walk into his apartment.

Taking a long, deep breath, Lori said, "Dad, you apologized to me for all the years we lost together; you said you hoped it was not too late for us to start over. This is incredibly important to me, more than I can ever express to you. I hate to say this, I hate to put it this way, and I wouldn't if I didn't have to, but if you don't help me now, if you don't get us into the Vatican with the NATO assault force, you and I will *never* have a relationship."

The tall officer looked miserable. He shook his head sadly. "I don't want you harmed, Lori. I'd rather save your life, even if you never speak to me again."

"If you let me down on this, you can count on that."

"And why do you want him to go with you?" Zack shot a laser glance at Alex. "He's one of your key advisers, you said; he's not a military operative."

"I believe in him completely," she said. "Assuming he gets some sleep. I told you about him, all the ways he helped me when his mother was so awful to me."

"Anyone else you want to bring along?" Zack asked. "Your friends from high school, maybe? Some street people from Seattle?"

She glared at him.

"All right," he said, "I'll see what I can do."

He grabbed his officer's hat and coat, and stalked out.

"I need to be alone," Lori said to Alex. She gave him a peck on the cheek, and he shuffled off to his own quarters.

* * *

By herself in the sitting room, Lori brooded over the situation.

Closing her eyes, she envisioned the faces of seven she-apostle toddlers: Veronica, Mary Magdalene, Priscilla, Sarah, Kezia, Candace, and Lydia . . . As each face came to her, she paused to examine it, in all of its details. Four she-apostle babies came into view: Esther, Hannah, Abigail, and Rhoda. Eleven she-apostles were familiar to her, in all.

Now she remembered the frightening vision she and Dixie Lou seemed to have shared involving Lori's own future baby, a child with auburn hair like her own. Previously, Lori had wondered if this might be the real twelfth she-apostle, Martha of Galilee, but now Dixie Lou said she had her at the Vatican.

Suddenly, the visage of a brown-skinned, black-haired baby came into focus, but faded quickly. She struggled to bring the image back, but unsuccessfully. It had been so ephemeral that she couldn't recall the facial details, only the skin and hair color.

Martha of Galilee?

Lori opened her eyes wide, but they wouldn't focus. It was as if she was looking through a tinted window that increasingly darkened, moment by moment.

Her fingers transmitted a texture to her, something they were touching. The letter from Deborah Marvel. She focused on the ending words: *This is a critical moment in history.* Deborah was right.

The self-proclaimed Grand Messenger was moving ahead with a curious sort of determination, cranking the engine of her organization to full speed ahead. Her surprise takeover of the Vatican had been shocking, and would certainly earn her a place in the history books, albeit an ignominious one. This was big and getting bigger. The attention of the world was riveted on Rome.

Lori wondered about her own place in the history unfolding around her, how much she would be able to influence it. She didn't care about credit for herself. She only hoped everything would turn out all right, and vowed to do whatever she could to make certain it did.

As her eyes focused, or seemed to, she saw the eleven she-apostles standing in front of her chair, looking up at her. She tried to determine if this was in her mind's eye, or if the children really stood there. Somehow, it didn't matter to her. The important thing was, she had a connection with them.

Lori stared at the eleven children, reached out her hands and touched some of them—or seemed to—and asked them what she should do about Martha of Galilee. They only looked at her with their expressive eyes, without saying anything, and without seeming to communicate with her in any other manner. This time it was as if they had the answer but would not share it, as if Lori needed to figure out what to do on her own. Frustrated that the children were not sharing information with her, Lori felt irritated, but only for a moment before she had second thoughts, before she realized it was another example of wordless interaction.

It was a test, pushing Lori to her limits, making her use her own abilities to figure things out for herself. If she didn't succeed at this, she realized, then she could not possibly advance, could not possibly understand the secret realm in which the children lived.

Odd, she thought. *Children teaching an older person. But they are "old souls," the term Dixie Lou likes to use.*

To Lori, it was also odd the way they were communicating with her, in their ancient, secret language that involved spoken and unspoken words. Perhaps when she no longer considered such methods strange, then she would understand.

"What will happen when all of you are with Martha of Galilee?" Lori asked, looking at each of the children, her gaze drifting from face to face.

In unison they smiled, in a way that gave her tremendous hope.

Chapter 35

I don't need to negotiate with my enemies; they are rotting away.
—Dixie Lou Jackson, Grand Messenger of the Holy She

It seemed the worst sacrilege in the history of the world to have Dixie Lou Jackson—surely a pawn of Satan—in charge of the holy Vatican City. This woman had, after all, been raised in the poverty of the inner city and supported herself for years through prostitution. How could she be dislodged? To President Markwether, the problem seemed almost insurmountable, but he and his advisers were determined not to rest until it was solved.

NATO had decided upon a multi-pronged approach, one that had been instituted with the cooperation of its member nations. Thus far, Dixie Lou had refused all offers from the allies to negotiate. In London, Paris, Rome, and other major cities around the world, potential emissaries were being interviewed by diplomats and psychologists, with an emphasis on finding just the right women and men who did not sympathize with the criminal Holy She, but who understood their deviant thought patterns and motivations. That focus formed the first NATO prong, under the direction of the N-1 team.

The second prong—a propaganda campaign involving the Internet, television, radio, and print media—was already spreading negative information on the Holy She and its leadership. This effort—designated

N-2—was under the supervision of the flamboyant and outspoken Rickson Prentiss, an egotistical Australian media mogul.

The United States, by agreement with the others, was responsible for N-3, the violence option, involving military force and/or assassination. That put President Markwether in charge of N-3.

In the fitness room of the White House, the President sat inside a fat-melting electronic field that shimmered all around him. Standing nearby were Harold Gravidovitch and Argan Smits, the Secretaries of State and Defense respectively, who were delivering their reports one at a time.

The President had gained fifteen pounds in a matter of weeks, and now he was embarking on a crash diet and "exertion program" to knock the weight off. He never actually worked out, preferring the comfort and ease of automatic devices. Markwether's skin tingled from the pulsing, penetrating field; he was red-faced and breathing hard, with perspiration pouring down his brow. He wore a khaki shirt with "US ARMY" emblazoned across the chest, and had a small towel bearing the presidential seal draped over one shoulder.

While he had never served in any branch of the armed forces himself, he had run for office on a policy of strong support for the military. His brother, an Army colonel, had advised him closely on this. He wished Zack could be here now, to guide him through the difficult decisions he had to make. He wasn't accustomed to relying on these two cabinet ministers—Gravidovitch and Smits—and they knew it. An awkward tension hung in the air.

The President hadn't told them his brother was in Rome, and could be in danger if NATO decided to attack the Vatican. It seemed best to keep that information to himself, and to avoid worrying about it, if he could. Affairs of state always took precedence over individual or familial concerns.

"You asked me to report on the possibility of getting an assassin close to Dixie Lou Jackson," Gravidovitch said. The small man wore a wrinkled suit, reflecting long hours of work without going home. He had removed his tie.

"*Close* to her?" Markwether snapped. "We need to get *closer* than close, you bumblehead! I want her stabbed, shot, poisoned!"

"Yes sir, but we must determine her patterns first. We have all the Vatican entrances under video surveillance, watching who they allow in and who they don't. We're also trailing people who emerge from the complex, and we have parabolic microphones trained on all possible windows, picking up whatever we can of the words that are being spoken in the rooms."

"So you don't have an answer for me yet?" Markwether said, an edge to his voice. He studied the digital readout of the calories he was burning, and increased the intensity of the electronic field.

Gravidovitch shook his head. "This is not a normal situation. We're breaking new ground here. While we have FBI and CIA files on United Women of the World, the information on Dixie Lou Jackson is somewhat limited, just the poverty and prostitution facts being used for propaganda by Prentiss in N-2. We actually developed the information first and gave it to him. In turn he shared it with the N-1 people."

"You did what?"

"Uh, we told Prentiss about Jackson's unsavory background."

The President's face became stony. "I've never liked that guy, and I'd rather he found it out for himself, but all right, you didn't do anything wrong. We're on the same team with him, trying to defeat the Holy She.'""

""We're working on getting more details about Jackson and her people, trying to find a weakness to exploit."

Markwether wiped perspiration from his forehead. He didn't think much of these two members of his cabinet. Consulting with them was not like working with his own brother, and he wished he hadn't allowed Zack to go to Rome. As President of the United States he could have taken steps to prevent it. The trip couldn't have come at a worse possible time.

"Sorry, sir," Gravidovitch said.

President Markwether increased the setting of the electronic field again. He imagined the fat rolling off his body.

"OK, what about N-1?"

For a moment, Gravidovitch looked confused. "The psychological analysis on Jackson and her top advisers, sir? We only have preliminary information so far. A few more days, and they should have a better report."

Secretary of Defense Smits folded his arms across his chest. "I wish we could just bomb Vatican City and get it over with." A bulky man with effeminate mannerisms, Smits had tiny, pale green eyes and a mole on his chin.

President Markwether stopped pedaling. A scowl creased his face.

"Don't be ridiculous," Secretary of State Gravidovitch said. "Even conventional bombs would destroy Michelangelo's masterpieces, the Sistine Chapel, the sacred Basilica—" He shook his head sadly. "—and kill everyone."

"If necessary we could do that," Markwether said, finally. "But only as a last resort."

"It's almost Holy Week for the Roman Catholic Church," Gravidovitch added, "and the celebration of Easter. We can't even consider such a sacrilege."

"If I say we consider it, we consider it," the President snapped. "Believe me, I don't like it any more than you do."

"But such an attack would also kill the she-apostles. Innocent babies and toddlers."

"Maybe they're only phonies," Smits said. "Lori Vale claims she has eleven real she-apostles herself, and Dixie Lou faked the ones with her."

"But they're still children!" Gravidovitch insisted.

Secretary of Defense Smits shook his head. "There's only one good way to deal with an enemy."

With a solemn nod, Markwether added, "Sometimes there is no other way." But memories of his brother intruded, when the two of them were small, playing in vacant lots and school yards. He fought to suppress the thoughts. Hopefully Zack wasn't anywhere near Vatican City.

"Children are not our enemies, sir," the Secretary of State said, daring to argue with the President. "This is the toughest part of our assignment. Dixie Lou Jackson may be a crazy woman, but I'm starting to think the *Holy Women's Bible* has merit."

"Are you daft?" Markwether thundered. Astonished at what he was hearing, he stepped off the bike and wiped his forehead with a towel.

"I've been reading it carefully myself," Gravidovitch admitted, "and some of it does make sense."

"*What???*"

"I have to agree with our esteemed Secretary of State," Smits said. "I'm especially intrigued by the Gospel of Abigail, in which she—"

"Don't ever say anything like that to me again!" Markwether boomed. "And the next time I summon the two of you I want to hear a plan of action. Not studies, not guesses, not a bunch of generalities. I want it all laid out in detail."

"Yes, sir," both of them said.

"Now get out of here and go to work."

The two US Secretaries left hurriedly, with their proverbial tails between their legs.

* * *

Outside Lori's apartment building, her father paused and spoke with one of the plainclothes guards stationed to protect her. This man was Trig Arnold, the private investigator he had hired to locate Lori in the first place. Now Trig was in charge of the guards assigned to her.

"You said in your e-mail that you've been inside the tunnel that leads from Vatican City to Castel Sant'Angelo," Zack said, "one of the routes used by popes centuries ago to get to the fortress castle if the Vatican was ever attacked."

"Yeah, that tunnel used to be a big secret, but one of my contacts got me in on the Castel Sant'Angelo side last year."

"Can you get in again? I found information that there's a second tunnel route down there, and it has a hidden intersection point with the main tunnel." He handed the man an underground map that had been provided by the CIA, with the source information redacted.

As Trig looked the document over, he nodded. "This looks right for the main tunnel, but I'm not sure about the other one. I've heard about the secondary route, but this is the first time I've seen a chart it. A hidden intersection point, eh? How is it hidden?"

"I don't know, but can you get into the main tunnel again?"

"Maybe, but it could be dangerous. The rumor mill says the UWW sent its attack squad through the tunnel system."

"Main or secondary route?"

"Not sure."

"In any event, I'm sure they're out of the tunnel system by now, and have buttoned up everything on the Vatican side."

Trig nodded.

"Be discreet about this, but see if you can get me more information. It's important." He handed a wad of high-denomination U.S. currency to him.

"I'll go down there myself and see if I can find any sign of the hidden intersection point of the two tunnels." The investigator scowled. "I wish this drawing was to scale, though."

"It's the best I can do," Zack said. Putting on his aviator sunglasses, he added, "Do this as fast as you can, OK?"

Lori's father spent the rest of the day pursuing military contacts, asking for drawings, histories, anything they could put their hands on. Because of his security clearance, he obtained thick piles of printouts.

* * *

Each evening, Deborah tried to spend time with Pope Rodrigo at his apartment in the Vatican Palace. She was impressed with him, not only for his great charm and intelligence but for his courage in the face of tremendous adversity. The apartment had no bugging devices in it, so Deborah Marvel felt confident saying whatever she wanted here.

"I worry about the Vatican employees that are still here," the tall, distinguished old man said, "and I pray for them to the Lord Almighty." He paused, and looked around, his eyes moist with emotion. "This apartment is my velvet-lined prison cell. The riches here are but a microcosm of the treasures of the Vatican, the greatest religious art the world has ever seen. To me, and to all Catholics, this city is a living entity, and a testimony to great achievement."

"I've been trying to convince Dixie Lou not to harm you, little Martha, or the Vatican," Deborah said. "A living entity. Yes, I am not Catholic, but I believe that is true. If Vatican City is destroyed, it would be a murder, wouldn't it?"

"You are a sensitive woman."

"And you're wondering how I ever became involved with Dixie Lou Jackson. She wasn't like that at first; power changed her. I originally joined United Women of the World for the ideals espoused by Amy Angkor-Billings. Like yourself, she was a great and inspirational leader. Of course, the UWW never had the riches or influence of the Vatican, but it had a strong moral footing, like Catholicism."

"I do not agree with your *Holy Women's Bible*, as you call it."

"Well, the Gospel of Martha was falsified, but the rest—the other eleven gospels—are divine scripture, except for deleted references to a She-Judas."

He shook his head.

"For a great religious figure such as yourself, it might be an impossibility to ever accept the new gospels. But you are a learned man. You know that there were political decisions made in the early centuries after Christ, when church authorities decided what to include in the Bible and what to omit from it."

"They only omitted that which should have been omitted, and they included the real gospels."

"Real gospels, yes. We agree on most of that. But there were other gospels that were—forgive me, Eminence, for saying this—stolen from women." She looked away. "I speak too directly to you. I mean no disrespect."

"It is obvious that you believe what you are saying. I sense a goodness in your heart, that you mean no harm, that you intend no blasphemy."

She gazed at him, and felt comforted by the gentle, beatific expression on his face. Such a kind man, with such a depth of understanding. This must be the most difficult time of his entire life.

"I will help you in any way I can," she promised, softly. "I would give up my life for you, sir."

"My life is not my own," he said.

Deborah felt that she needed to do more to help this great man. It was not enough to hold her tongue around Dixie Lou and attempt to persuade her not to harm people or treasures. She wanted to do more, and hoped Lori Vale would accept her offer. She gazed out a window, at the vast military force arrayed around Vatican City, and wondered if anyone would still be alive here after the fighting stopped.

Chapter 36

I am fascinated by the interplay of conscious and unconscious memory, and how the human mind cannot always retrieve information in its "databanks."

—Amy Angkor-Billings

This evening was not the first time Dixie Lou Jackson had lost sleep, especially since taking over the reins of the most radical women's rights group in the world. With so many moving parts in her organization and so many things that could go wrong, she often found herself going off on what she called "negative jags," in which her mind filled with nothing but bad things and she could not go to sleep, not even with medication.

When she joined United Women of the World, and began working with Amy Angkor-Billings, she used to be an optimistic person, a believer in her own abilities and inevitable triumphs. In those days, she still killed people secretly or had them killed, or did whatever else needed to be done, but always with a sense of bright purpose around her, as she basked in a rising tide of good fortune.

Her state of mind had changed drastically, and as she considered this in detail, she realized that it went back even further than her ascension to the top spot. It went back to her first encounter with Lori Vale. The teenager was like a Jonah, a shipmate who brought bad fortune to a voyage. While she wished Lori had never appeared, she also felt very strongly that it had to happen, that it was a destiny carved out for her by a power much greater than herself.

In the middle of the night, Dixie Lou wandered through the Vatican Palace, carrying a large, powerful flashlight, playing its beam off the paintings of the masters and the antique statuary. Angrily, she swung the flashlight and broke a statue, without caring what it was. She could turn the building lights on, but had ordered them shut off this evening for her personal enjoyment, despite the advice of her security people to the contrary.

She preferred darkness, and as a black-skinned person she sometimes thought this was her realm to rule. She had first thought of this as a ten-year-old child, playing in the basement, moving around in the midst of clutter and then switching off the lights, going faster and faster, testing her ability to avoid running into anything. At times, it seemed as if she could actually see in the darkness like a nocturnal animal.

One time when she was scurrying around downstairs, her mother came down and turned on the lights. "Child, what are you doing in here?" she asked.

"I'm Queen of Night and Shadow," Dixie Lou had said. "With my black skin, I slide through darkness. I command the dark forces."

Her mother was a large, profoundly religious woman, and hearing such blasphemy, she put on her most stern countenance. "Don't talk such craziness! You act like black folks are allied with the devil, and that just ain't so. We're as good as any white folks, better than most of them. We believe in the Lord Jesus, not in any dark forces."

With those words, which Dixie Lou never forgot, her mother grabbed her by the arm and dragged her upstairs. She then locked the basement, and forbade her from ever going down there again.

It also led to her mother forcing her even more than ever to read the *Bible*, and to memorize passages. Every day, the child had to demonstrate her learning through recitation, which she only did to stay out of trouble.

In her adulthood, Dixie Lou came to believe that Jesus Christ existed as a historical figure, but she never felt an affinity for Him, the *Bible*, or anything to do with Christianity. She only used religion to enhance her own career. In public and in council meetings she put on one face; in private, she whispered entirely different things to herself.

Now, as Dixie Lou stepped into Martha's room, ever so silently so as not to awaken the mother in the next room, she shut off the flashlight. Moving like a black cat, she made her way across the room, until she heard the breathing of the child. Her eyes adjusted to the low light, and she saw the shadowy form of the sleeping baby.

Reaching down, she lifted Martha and carried her out into the hallway. "If I can't sleep, you won't either."

She took Martha to one of the translators in an adjacent building, and rousted her from bed, too. By this time, half a dozen of Dixie Lou's guards were following her with their own flashlights, concerned for her safety.

The translator, a woman with platinum hair and squinty eyes, tightened her robe as she answered the door. "Yes, ma'am?" she asked. Light from her room flowed into the hallway.

"Make her talk," Dixie Lou said.

Abruptly, as the Chairwoman was handing Martha over in the doorway, the child began to babble, and then fell abruptly silent. The translator's eyes grew large, and her jaw dropped.

"Well, what did she say?"

"She made no sense at all, just gibberish."

"I heard words, and my own name repeated. What did she say? Tell me!"

"Uh, forgive me for saying this, Grand Messenger. In ancient Aramaic, the child said, 'So many murders you committed, Dixie Lou Jackson, and such a devious, cowardly way you did them, creeping in like a thief in the night and stealing lives–'" Nervously, the translator said, "Forgive me for repeating such madness, but that is exactly what the child said. Of course, it is nonsense."

"Get her out of my sight!"

"Yes, ma'am. I'll return her to her room." Leaving her own door open, the translator ran down the hallway, carrying the child. Two guards broke away and accompanied her.

After ordering the other guards away from her, Dixie Lou stood alone in the corridor, in the light from the translator's open door. The Grand Messenger of the Holy She felt a surge of panic and intense guilt, a sensation that she had been discovered, that her most closely guarded secret has been revealed. But she had no memory of it.

Dixie Lou realized that Martha wasn't referring to the guard that she shot in the back of the head, or to the curator she had impaled on the Sword of She-God, or to any of the other murders she remembered, going back to her youth. No, the last she-apostle was referring to something else entirely.

It was as if the strange baby had tapped into a nightmare from the Grand Messenger's subconscious—from the cimmerian recesses of her mind—and it was something Martha could recall but Dixie Lou could not.

I'm not remembering because I don't want to, she thought. *Because I would rather forget.*

* * *

In the morning, Zack used his presidential security clearance to gain access to the NATO Commander's office, on the top floor of an old building on Via del Corso. He brought Lori with him, and introduced her as his daughter.

"I am familiar with Lori Vale from the news reports," General Kenneth Selkirk said, in a rolling Scottish brogue. Only in his early forties, he had a smooth face but gray hair and a matching mustache. He wore a tan uniform shirt with three gold stars on each side of the collar. Through the window behind him, Lori saw the gold-and-gray dome of St. Peter's Basilica.

"To insanity," Zack said, as he and Lori dropped into a pair of Italian Renaissance chairs fronting his black onyx desk, an odd juxtaposition of styles. "Not mine—Dixie Lou Jackson's."

"Yes," he said. "That's what brought me to Rome myself. But war is always madness, isn't it?"

"Since Dixie Lou isn't willing to negotiate, you're going to have to attack the Vatican, aren't you?"

"I could speak to you about such matters because you are the President's brother, but—" The General looked at Lori.

"I trust her completely. You can speak freely."

Selkirk hesitated, then nodded. "The only question is, when to attack Vatican City, and on what scale. We've done the psychological analyses on Dixie Lou Jackson and have battered her reputation with propaganda. The only thing left now is to use force."

"We have new information that you should know," Zack said. On the desk, he placed a document that described details of the secret route that couriers had been using to get in and out of the Vatican, including its terminus in one of the subway stations. "Study this, General Selkirk, and you'll see that it is very interesting information. I got it when a courier delivered a letter."

The Commander examined the papers, then looked up. "It says here that Dixie Lou Jackson knows about this route, but your source is not sure if she used it in her takeover of the Vatican."

Zack nodded. "It's a potential escape route for her, so I thought you'd want to incorporate it into your attack plan."

"You're right; we'll add this to our tactical information. There is also the matter of how Jackson's assault forces got into the Vatican in the first place. Presumably not by this courier route, because it's so narrow and is accessed from a public place—although I suppose they could have entered it surreptitiously, concealing their weapons."

"There's a honeycomb of old passageways and chambers beneath Rome and Vatican City," Zack said. "Have you investigated any of them as a means of getting our assault forces in?"

"Not seriously. They're old and disused, not suitable for modern assault forces. We're thinking more of parachuting commandos in."

Zack handed him another document, the original CIA diagram. (His private investigator had not been able to develop any additional useful information.) "This describes two more subterranean routes that may be of interest to you. I've done my own research, and there are two tunnels that ancient popes used to use, and which have been closed off for some time now. They run from Vatican City to Castel Sant'Angelo in Rome."

Selkirk looked it over, while Zack added, "These routes were used in centuries past to protect the pontiffs and cardinals in a variety of ways—for their personal safety in the event of an attack, and to permit them to sneak lovers in and out."

"You say a courier delivered a letter to you?" the General asked.

"Actually, there were two letters from the Vatican, both written to my daughter." He glanced over at her.

"Oh?" Selkirk set the documents aside.

Lori reached across the desk with the letter from Dixie Lou. "This is one of the letters," she said. The paper made a crinkling sound.

After reading it, the commander said, "So, the Grand Messenger will talk to you, Miss Vale, but not to NATO?"

"She's not offering to give up the Vatican," Lori said, "or to return the Pope." Her chair had a hard cushion, with an unfortunate lump in the middle. She shifted to one side, trying to get more comfortable.

"I noticed," the NATO Commander said.

Next, Lori passed Deborah Marvel's letter to him. "This tells us where Martha of Galilee is being kept, on the third floor, at the southwest corner of the Vatican Palace."

Lori explained how she had eleven authentic she-apostles in her care, while Dixie Lou had a dozen fakes, and what sounded like one real one, Martha of Galilee. While the girl spoke, the General nodded and said he knew all that, then read the Marvel letter.

"I wonder if this woman is lying," General Selkirk said, as he finished the letter and set it down. He rubbed his mustache thoughtfully.

"I don't think so," Lori said. "I think she's telling the truth and we need to move fast, before the information gets stale."

Selkirk gazed at Lori across the desk's black, gleaming surface.

"I just sent Dixie Lou a message saying I needed twenty-four hours to reply," Lori said. "I didn't respond to Deborah Marvel at all."

Clearing his throat, General Selkirk said, "Tomorrow, I want you to send the Grand Messenger a note that her proposal is acceptable, but tell her you and the she-apostles can't get through NATO lines, because you're being watched too closely."

"Acceptable? But I don't want to be High Priestess of the Holy She! I just want the she-apostles safe, all twelve of them."

"He's right," Zack said to his daughter. "We need to reply or she might do something crazy." He grimaced. "As if she hasn't already proven herself a nutcase."

Selkirk leaned forward, his elbows on the desk. "This is just a delaying tactic, Miss Vale, so that we can make full preparations."

"For what?" Lori asked. She fidgeted in her chair, couldn't seem to get comfortable.

"For our best attack option," he said, in a tone that she found irritatingly patronizing, as if he were talking to a child.

"We need to protect Martha of Galilee at all costs," Lori said, "so I want you to include me when your assault squad goes into the Vatican."

General Selkirk's eyes opened wide. "Out of the question."

"Hear me out," she insisted. "*Please*. Let me explain."

The Scotsman looked imploringly at the teenager's father, but Zack said, with a bemused expression, "I can't keep her under control, if that's what you're wondering."

"Martha of Galilee is incredibly important to the Christian community and to all of humankind," Lori said. "We are at a critical turning point in history, where the child's death could have huge, catastrophic consequences. Much more is at stake than the loss of the Vatican or the Pope. I'm talking about something else."

Catastrophic? the General said. Admittedly, it would be tragic for the child to be killed, but catastrophic? I can't see why."

"I'm only beginning to understand what's going on myself," Lori admitted, "so it may be difficult for me to explain. But the phenomenon of the she-apostles is real, not a circus sideshow act or a scam. The gospels of eleven she-apostles in the *Holy Women's Bible* are real, and Martha of Galilee has the final gospel, the information needed to complete this momentous and pivotal holy book. If she dies, her secrets go with her, and there may never be another opportunity to find out."

"You are well spoken for your age," Selkirk said, "but I don't believe any of that garbage about female apostles of Jesus. However, just for the sake of discussion, I'll suspend my disbelief for a moment. Let's suppose that they really are *reincarnated* apostles. If Martha dies, can't she just be reincarnated again?"

"General, it took almost two thousand years for these reappearances! It could take another two millennia for them to come back, or this could be our only opportunity at salvation."

"What about the male apostles, Peter, John, Matthew, and the others. Why haven't they come back?"

"I don't know. I only know that these are the women who followed our Lord Jesus." Lori's voice grew passionate, louder. "They're here to tell the true story of women, the story that has been suppressed by powerful men, the story that needs to be told today. Women are finally ready to hear it. The world is ready to hear it!"

General Selkirk shook his head. "We have a mission to accomplish here, and we can't be distracted by a teenage girl getting in the way. We can't divert any resources to worrying about your welfare."

Gripping the arms of her chair, Lori said, "You need to rescue the Pope, right?"

He hesitated. Then: "Right. And save the antiquities."

"What about the children that Dixie Lou has in there?" Lori asked. "And the skeleton Vatican staff? I assume you have contingency plans to protect innocent lives."

"Of course. We'll try to save everyone we can."

"Aren't the children more important than antiquities? Isn't Martha of Galilee more important than *things*?"

"Maybe the antiquities should come first. They are priceless, you know. Especially the Michelangelo and Bernini sculptures and paintings. It depends on how you look at it."

"You didn't hear anything I said about Martha, did you?" Lori said, ignoring the hand her father placed on her forearm.

"Now wait just a minute, young lady. I'm granting you my valuable time because your father is the President's brother. Yes, I'm listening, but I have to make the final decisions."

"Martha is essential to the future of Christianity," Lori said. "The Pope is a great and good man, and he needs to be saved, along with the last she-apostle."

"So many problems," General Selkirk said, gesturing with his hands for emphasis. "The greatest art treasures in the world, the Pope, and a reincarnated apostle of Jesus. How much pressure can be put on me?"

Zack flashed his own identity card, a hard piece of glittering, electronically impregnated film. "I'm Special Adviser to the President of the United States," he said. "I want my daughter included in this mission, and I'll pull whatever strings necessary to get it done."

Lori looked at him appreciatively.

Rising to his feet, the General said, in a biting tone, "Is your brother going to call from the Oval Office and order me to include his niece when we go into the Vatican?"

"If I ask him to. I am his older brother, you know."

"Don't get all worked up, Markwether."

"Are you completely out of touch, Selkirk? Don't you watch the news or read intelligence reports? My daughter is no ordinary teenager!"

"I know who she is, I know who you are, and I know the stories about paranormal events. Just give me some time to think about it. I'll let you know tomorrow morning."

Lori and her father rose to their feet at the same time, and she said, "We need a special unit to rescue Martha, giving her equal priority with the Pope."

"You don't ask for much, do you?" the beleaguered Commander said, as he escorted his visitors to the door.

Chapter 37

There are ways within ways, secrets within secrets. If you dig deeply enough to solve any problem, you will always find an answer.
—The Quotations of Lori Vale

Built in the second century AD as the Roman Emperor Hadrian's Mausoleum, in medieval times it was converted to the impregnable papal fortress, Castel Sant'Angelo. An immense, thick-walled citadel, it became the fortified home of popes, and a sanctuary whenever the Vatican found itself in danger of military attack. Multiple corridors connected it to Vatican City, a few blocks away—one an overhead, covered walkway—the *Passetto Vaticano*—and the much more arcane subterranean passageways.

It was through the tunnel system that Pope Gregory VII may have escaped from King Henry IV of Germany, who in 1082 took control of St. Peter's and the Vatican and installed the unelected Pope Clement III as his puppet. That was the original St. Peter's—predating Michelangelo's church. When the new cathedral was built in the sixteenth century, the passageway was left open and the secret of its existence zealously guarded. In modern times, the tunnel was blocked off, by order of Vatican authorities.

Now, operating through intermediaries to conceal who was doing it, NATO arranged for Castel Sant'Angelo to be temporarily closed to public tours, under the guise of performing construction work required by life safety codes. Large trucks began arriving, and onlookers were kept at a distance. Out of sight of the public, contractors and engineers exited the trucks and filled the lower levels of the building, hurrying through corridors that led past ancient dungeons and torture chambers, taking with them the tools of their trade.

Lori, her father, and Alex were in their midst, and only partially because of Zack's relationship to the President of the United States. That morning, a sheepish General Selkirk had admitted to Lori's father that his own wife had demanded the teenager's inclusion. "Don't you realize how important she is?" the wife had shouted at him. "Do whatever she wants!" So, to maintain the peace of his household, he consented to Lori's inclusion in the mission, along with the two men.

He also ordered a reconnaissance mission to check the subterranean routes between Castel Sant'Angelo and the holy city. . . .

* * *

Beneath the streets of Rome, half a dozen engineers faced a wall built of tightly-fitted stones, streaked in black, brown, and green. The men, culled from various allied armed forces, wore different national uniforms. The area was illuminated by their powerful helmet lanterns.

NATO Commander Kenneth Selkirk stood off to one side with armed soldiers. In a thick Scottish brogue, he asked, "What's the probe say?"

A young American engineer pressed an electronic device against the wall. "Might be a hidden tunnel here, sir, but if so, it's been closed off. I can't read what's on the other side. The wall's too thick, or it has something to do with materials behind these stones. I don't think anyone installed masking electronics here, not with a wall this old."

"Don't assume anything," a grizzled, paunchy engineer said, in French-accented English. "There are ways of making things appear old."

Looking on, Lori considered what she had learned from her father: Over the centuries, Vatican authorities had intermittently closed and reopened the secondary Sant'Angelo escape tunnel, but the research that Zack did was only of limited utility. Twenty centuries after Christ, only church leaders had the records of exactly where the hidden tunnel was, and how to open it back up.

Now, staring at the wall where the tunnel might be located according to the instruments and documents, the engineers shook their heads and muttered among themselves. "We don't know how much material we have to break through," the Frenchman said. The other engineers called him Marseille, but that might have been a nickname based on the French city, perhaps his hometown. Sometimes Lori liked to speculate on things like that. Another engineer, who conferred frequently with the Frenchman, was a US Army sergeant.

"Bust through anyway," General Selkirk ordered. They were several blocks away from the Vatican, and he was not worried about making noise yet.

It took almost an hour for their construction crew to drill into and knock down part of the wall, enough for people to get through. They probed with flashlights, and a short distance away they encountered a second wall, this one built of oversized, reinforced bricks. A pair of large rats squealed and scurried out.

In another half hour, they penetrated that barrier, too. The French engineer stepped through first, then the others. Following them, Lori saw that the tunnel curved to the left.

"Goes in the wrong direction," Marseille said, splashing the illumination of his powerful flashlight ahead. He'd been checking his compass. Warily, the reconnaissance team proceeded through the passage, and presently the tunnel widened. Soon, they encountered what appeared to be three blocked tunnels. The Frenchman cursed in his own language.

Checking his compass again, he said, "None of these tunnels point in the right direction."

"Which way now?" Selkirk asked.

As the men studied the available documents, without finding anything of help, Lori felt a strong impulse. She went to a place on a wall and touched her open palms on its cool, damp surface of rock and mortar, then pressed the side of her face against the ancient wall.

Strange images filled her mind, pulsing amorphous shapes in human form. Startled, she pulled away, and her mind cleared. Summoning her courage, she again pressed herself against the wall, and the images returned.

"What's she doing?" a man asked.

Another: "Not sure."

"Leave her alone," Zack said.

Lori moved down the corridor a ways and touched her hands and face to the wall several times, without achieving the same result. Then she returned to the original spot on the wall that she had first selected, and the strange visual experience returned, even more sharply this time. She envisioned the tunnel open on this spot, and people hurrying through it in white, purple, and red robes, like phantoms from the past.

"Punch through," she said, with a feeling of absolute certainty. She moved to one side, folded her arms across her chest and stared at the French engineer.

With a ferocious scowl, Marseille said, "But that's not even one of the blocked tunnels."

"I suspect tricks," Lori responded, "set up by the Popes to throw their enemies off, to confuse them." She tapped the wall. "The real tunnel lies on the other side."

"My daughter may be right," Zack said, obviously trying to be supportive, although she detected doubt on his face. "This could be a clever labyrinth of barricades and false passageways set up to protect the Vatican, to keep the Pope's backup escape route from being accessible to attack."

Another rat ran by, squealing.

"At least the rats seem to know their way around in this maze," Alex quipped. This elicited chuckles, but they quickly tailed off as the group considered the predicament.

"There's only one way to find out," Zack said. "Break through the wall."

"Do it," General Selkirk said.

The section of wall, which on this side had appeared to be as thick as the others they had encountered and was impervious to electronic probing, proved to be only half the thickness. As the construction crew took the stones apart, Lori thought it was designed to be easy and quick to open, in the event of emergency. A tunnel opened up on the other side.

"You were right, lassie," Selkirk finally said to the teenager, patting her on the shoulder. "You're our new secret weapon."

She smiled.

This time a heavy iron door lay a short distance into the tunnel, with a rusty lock mechanism. They broke it open, and beyond that found a long passageway that they hurried into, excitedly. The way curved around to the right, then straightened.

The Frenchman checked his compass as the squad proceeded, with helmet lights showing the way. "*Oui*, now we are going in the correct direction!" he exclaimed.

Finally the tunnel turned to the left for a short distance, then sloped slightly upward and widened as it came to an end. Four heavy iron doors lay ahead of them, each much larger than the first one they had encountered, with more elaborate lock mechanisms.

"Whew!" one of the engineers said, as he examined the obstacles. "These babies are *built*. We'll have to use muted explosives."

"Which door do we go through?" General Selkirk asked.

All eyes looked at Lori. As the men turned, their helmet lights focused on her, bathing her in a pool of illumination.

The teenager hurried forward, pressed her open palms against each of the old doors, and then touched the side of her face against the surfaces. She hesitated, trying to decide between the two at the center. Both were important passageways, filling her mind with phantoms from the past.

"This one," she finally said, designating the one on the right.

"You're sure?" Selkirk asked.

She took a deep, excited breath. "This is this way we want to go," she said. "No doubt about it."

"Sir, we're almost to Vatican City," the American sergeant said, to General Selkirk. "Maybe we shouldn't go any farther today?"

"You're right. We'll break through when we're ready." He looked at Lori and her father, and said to them, "I like this. It gives us the element of surprise. Obviously the women didn't examine this tunnel system, because it hasn't been disturbed for a long time. We'll mobilize at Castel Sant'Angelo and pour through the tunnels, with airborne commandos and other forces standing by, ready to go at the right moment."

"Good," Zack said.

"We're calling it Operation Deliverance," General Selkirk said.

While the engineers took photographs and scribbled notes, Lori thought back to the sensations she'd felt when holding hands with she-apostles, and afterward when flying from North Africa toward Rome, and she'd known the correct way to go, without knowing exactly why. Now she wondered if this was similar. Was she following a scent of a different sort now? Had Martha of Galilee been taken this way, through a tunnel? In view of the obstacles they had encountered so far, she didn't see how that could be possible. Still, she was sure it was the best route to the child, the best way to rescue her.

But how do I know that?

Lori felt her consciousness opening up, making neural pathways available to her that she had not known existed before. Somehow, her ability to detect lies while interrogating Wendy Zepeda and the two guards was linked to this burgeoning ability.

Truth without words.

In her mind, Lori Vale could envision a subterranean pathway on the other side of the door, a stairway, and a corridor that led to the Vatican Palace, where the corrupt women were keeping Martha of Galilee.

And Lori couldn't wait to go.

Chapter 38

The Sword of She-God is said to impart superhuman strength to its user.

—Davida Lewis, *Legends of the UWW*

Following a meeting with her council, Dixie Lou Jackson hurried off, to inspect construction work in the papal offices, which she was impatient to see completed. Under constant pressure from her, Vatican work crews were laboring like ants energized by caffeine, running back and forth with building materials, hammering, drilling, sawing. They were going around the clock, in twelve-hour shifts.

During the afternoon session, members of her council had asked her to accept an offer General Selkirk of NATO had made to them that day, but she told them she was going to refuse it. In the offer, NATO gave them seventy-two hours to accept amnesty for Dixie Lou and the rest of the Holy She leadership, in exchange for the release of Pope Rodrigo, Martha of Galilee, and the return of the Vatican. NATO also offered to establish a new world headquarters for the women, and to assist them in providing security for it. If Dixie Lou didn't accept what he called a "generous offer," the General threatened unspecified "dire consequences."

"He's bluffing," Dixie Lou had said, as she tore his letter to pieces and scattered it around the chamber.

"But what if he isn't?" Deborah Marvel asked.

"I was wondering about that, too," Nancy Winters said.

"Just leave the important decisions to me," Dixie Lou snapped. And then she called the meeting to a close. . . .

Now, with great satisfaction, she watched two men installing green-and-orange wallpaper inside her large new office, as yet unoccupied. Artisans had erected a splendid work of art behind the location for her desk, a pair of sculpted female hands with their palms upturned, where she would place the sacred Sword of She-God . . . the legendary weapon that she intended to employ any time she found it necessary.

When the men glanced at her nervously, the Grand Messenger smiled inwardly. Undoubtedly, their extra effort had something to do with the gleaming sword, which she brandished whenever she gave them orders.

And when they were finished with all of the offices, she had other work for them to do, a number of remodeling projects to the Vatican City buildings.

But little did she know that the ongoing noises would soon muffle subterranean activities under the streets near Vatican City . . . the approach of an army.

* * *

Two days passed, and it was Palm Sunday. . . .

"You are more comfortable here?" Dixie Lou inquired, in the most polished tone she could muster. Holding the Sword of She God, she stood in an apartment of the Vatican Palace looking down at the angular, elderly man who had not risen to greet her. A hall guard closed the door and remained out in the corridor. It was more than a week since she'd had the Pope moved out of the Pauline Chapel into this heavily guarded apartment, which had previously been servant's quarters.

Substantially better than the earlier, rudimentary quarters she had provided for him, this was still far beneath the style in which he was accustomed to living. But it was as good as he was going to get, since she wanted him to remind on a daily basis that he now occupied a station subordinate to her own, because she had vanquished him.

I could make this 'Servant of Christ' my own attendant if I wished to do so, she thought. *He might even make a suitable butler, with his snooty ways.*

Dressed in a simple white robe, Pope Rodrigo sat at a *vargueño*—a seventeenth century Spanish writing cabinet—that had been brought from his former office, which Dixie Lou was remodeling for her own use. The mahogany cabinet, containing numerous interior drawers and compartments and (known only to its owner) a hidden storage drawer for an old family crucifix, was decorated with geometrical pieces of ivory and mother-of-pearl. With the drop-down lid open, the Pope had been writing something.

Barely looking at her, he continued scribbling with a black-and-gold pen, which he occasionally dipped into an ink well. He had a fresh piece of palm frond pinned to one lapel of his white robe, in honor of Palm Sunday. With only a week until Easter, the pontiff felt empty inside, and frustrated at the course of events. Why did all of this have to occur right before the holiest of all Christian holidays, the celebration of the resurrection and eternal life of Jesus Christ? Pope Rodrigo sighed in reluctant acceptance. The ways of God were not always clear, not even to him.

"It is customary to show respect for one's superior," Dixie Lou said.

"*Es verdad*," he replied. *It is true.* But still he did not rise.

Dixie Lou felt her face heat up. "I am the Grand Messenger of the Holy She! You don't consider me your superior?" With great fanfare, she flourished the magnificent sword, and examined the hilt with the priceless Vatican jewels embedded in it.

"You are carrying on a conversation with yourself, making your own assumptions."

"I will excuse your impertinence this time, Pope Rodrigo. What are you writing?"

His gaze slid casually to the sword, then away. "A letter to my mother in Segovia. She turns ninety-nine next week."

"You'll be that old one day, too, but only if you cooperate with me."

With a disdainful expression he continued writing, making broad pen strokes on the heavy parchment paper. Despite his own age, his black hair remained thick, with only a few streaks of silver.

"Don't try to sneak any code phrases into that. We'll catch you if you do."

"Did you come here to tell me that?"

"A couple of days ago we received an 'offer' from NATO."

"I am aware of it," he said. "Amnesty for you and your fellow criminals if you relinquish control of the Vatican and release the hostages. They are also offering to help you establish a new headquarters. Perhaps Monte Konos can be restored."

"How did you—"

"God and I have long conversations," the Pope interjected. "I am praying for your soul, but I must inform you, your activities are interfering with the sacred duties of the Roman Catholic Church."

"Such as?" She swished the sword through the air to within a meter of him, but the irritatingly brave Pope seemed unconcerned by it.

"Oh, many things. I should be delivering a sermon today, in honor of Palm Sunday. Tomorrow I was scheduled to perform a sainthood ceremony for Benito Sanchez, the brave South American priest who was murdered by a police death squad. This is Holy Week, and next Sunday is Easter. You profess to believe in our savior Jesus Christ, so you should understand."

With a scowl, Dixie Lou said, "Jesus existed, but he was not *my* savior. I'm a *woman*, pledged to She-God Almighty." Although Dixie Lou believed in Jesus Christ as a historical figure, she didn't believe in God or even She-God; she was just playing a part, a much more complicated one than her thespian-like son had ever attempted. Unlike him, Dixie Lou vowed, she would succeed in concealing her true self from others. A tributary of this thought jarred her, an awareness of something else in her past that she could not quite remember, but which clung to her nonetheless, like the stench of death. What was her true self?

"This should be a festival week for Catholicism," Pope Rodrigo said, "and instead you have turned it into sadness. But our faith is strong, and this is but another travail."

"How about me?" Dixie Lou said. "When are you going to make me a saint? Has a nice sound, doesn't it?—Saint Dixie Lou."

Pope Rodrigo set down his pen and folded the letter carefully. "You are *not* Catholic, madam, not even close."

"You would prevent me from converting?"

His face was parched, wrinkled. It revealed little emotion, not even in the dark-green eyes, which now gazed up at her dispassionately. "I didn't say that."

"You're a tricky one, aren't you? Popes must be trained that way, or born that way. I read about some of your predecessors, the double lives they led, the sexual liaisons, the intrigues, the political murders. One of them may even have secretly been a woman, Pope Joan."

He didn't respond.

She glared at him. "The Pope Joan story might just be a legend, but I bet you have the records around here somewhere to prove it one way or the other, don't you?"

Again, no response.

"As for the Vatican," she said. "I feel secure here, much more than at Monte Konos." She scratched her chin. "I know what! You and I can share Vatican City, under my jurisdiction, of course. I'll permit you to perform occasional ceremonies here. We'll coordinate our schedules. You can either do that, or become my personal manservant."

"Preposterous." His face reddened. "I am the Pope of more than a billion Roman Catholics!"

"And I'm Dixie Lou Jackson, the most important woman on earth." She paused, and smiled tightly. "Come to think of it, there are billions and billions of women on this planet, so my influence is greater than yours. In fact, women form a large share of your membership, and they're already flocking to my cause."

"Earth is but a way station," the old man said, "an inglorious realm of pain and suffering."

"God told you that, did He? Well, tell Him this for me. Tell Him I don't accept NATO's offer."

* * *

In the deepest darkness of night, a squadron of stealth bombers took off from a US Navy aircraft carrier in the eastern Mediterranean. The electronically invisible aircraft took separate courses, each with an assignment from NATO.

Within an hour seven direct hits were reported, three against underground bases operated by the Holy She . . . in Sicily, southern Albania, and Greece. Additional strikes took out Bureau of Ideology assets: a communication station in Germany, a paramilitary training facility in Morocco, and a satellite launch pad in Spain.

Chapter 39

All popular religions feature miracles. The essential question to answer is this: Are the supernatural occurrences real, or counterfeit? And who is to tell the difference?

    —Amy Angkor-Billings, private journal

NATO's seventy-two hour deadline came and went, like a ticking time bomb that did not go off when the clock struck zero.

At shortly before dawn the next day, Zack Markwether pounded on his daughter's bedroom door, then turned the handle and pushed. The door stuck against a tight jamb, finally opened. "Thirty minutes to get out of here," he said.

"Only thirty minutes?" Lori said to her father, as she swung out of bed.

"Operation Deliverance is set to go."

"I'll be ready." But she didn't feel ready.

"Dress warmly," he said. "It's cold in the tunnel." He turned and left.

So, it's now, she thought, rising uncertainly to her feet. . . .

Lori had slept fitfully, having felt ill during the night, as she did now. A couple of hours ago, she had hurried into the bathroom and vomited. Upon coming out, she had encountered Alex in the hallway. "Are you all right?" he had asked.

"Sick to my stomach. Case of nerves, I guess, or a touch of the flu."

He had looked at her oddly, with a half smirk. "You're not pregnant, are you?"

"Are you kidding?"

"Sorry, I'm half asleep myself, don't know what I'm saying."

"You certainly don't. No, I'm not pregnant! I've never been with a man." This was not entirely true, because she was not a virgin. The year before, she had slept with a boy her age in Seattle, certainly not a *man*. That liaison had been so long ago that she could not possibly be pregnant.

During her conversation with Alex, the she-apostles had come out of the two rooms they shared, and had watched her silently. One of them, Mary Magdalene, had stepped forward and communicated with her in an ancient, secret way. Not spoken words, just a concise expression on the she-apostle's face that shocked Lori.

You are with child, the she-apostle had told her. *The Child of God.*

Since then the teenager had been lying awake, thinking back, trying to comprehend, wanting to believe that Mary Magdalene's words had only been a dream. . . .

Lori dressed hurriedly. She had been wondering when the NATO attack would occur. There were rumors that General Selkirk had given Dixie Lou a deadline, but neither she nor her father had been able to find out for certain. This morning, fearing Zack would prevent her from going on the mission if he knew she wasn't feeling well, she resolved to say nothing about this to him—and quickly told Alex not to say anything, either.

With her hair wild and her teeth hardly brushed, Lori accompanied her father and Alex to the basement parking garage. Zack, his overcoat open at the front to reveal his uniform, handed out coffee in covered paper cups. The three of them piled into the back of an unmarked van. Their NATO driver—wearing a coat over his own uniform—made sure they were in, then sped out of the garage.

On the way, Lori sipped her coffee silently, hoping it would keep her alert for this important day. She already had a head full of monumental concerns, and new events were sure to crowd in. She felt as if she were in the middle of a great, swirling storm, and it was thrusting her forward to an uncertain future, intensifying moment by moment.

Pregnant?

She took another sip of coffee, and nearly choked on it from her worries.

"Are you all right?" Zack asked.

"I'm fine," she said, lying. She coughed several times, having aspirated the warm liquid.

The driver of the van, an Italian sergeant, looked back, then focused on negotiating the streets. It was just getting daylight, and only a few cars and trucks were out. They passed a sidewalk market, where vendors were arriving with fruits and vegetables, setting up their stands.

It all became a haze to Lori, because ever since Mary Magdalene's startling assertion she had been thinking of the vision of light that had entered her desert tent and taken her away for the briefest of instants, so ephemeral that the experience had been like a dream, but a very vivid one. Where had the strange light taken her, or seemed to have taken her? She could not recall, but did remember feeling the powerful, protective presence of the Lord during the journey. The visitation had lasted for only a few seconds . . . maybe even less than that.

Now an intense sensation came over her, a powerful epiphany that could not be denied. The event had been as *real* as real could be, and she had journeyed a long way, indeed. Of that she was certain, with sudden clarity. It had *not* been a dream, nor had Mary Magdalene's unspoken bombshell only hours ago.

Truth without words, she thought.

Another presence had been in the vision as well, a cold, inky darkness behind the light, larger than the light. Lori shivered, and began to tremble. Supernatural pregnancies did not occur—with one exception, to her knowledge.

Mary, Mother of Jesus.

But if such a conception could possibly occur to Lori, if it was true, why was she learning of it today, of all days, when she was scheduled to accompany the NATO assault force? She and her companions were heading toward the center of the city and a fateful confrontation with a madwoman. The van turned onto a main thoroughfare, merged into traffic.

Admittedly, there had been physical indications suggesting the possibility of pregnancy. Lori had not menstruated at her regular time this month, and now she had suffered her first bout with morning sickness, which continued to embroil her innards. She should go to a doctor. There might be an explanation other than pregnancy, a medical condition she had never considered. Maybe it was even psychosomatic, and she had only imagined the vision, and what Mary Magdalene told her.

In memory, Lori saw Mary's eyes shift just a little, and the quiver of her lips. Such a startling contention that Lori didn't want to believe it, didn't want any distractions from the important business of this day. With God's grace, and a considerable amount of luck, all twelve she-apostles would soon be reunited.

I'm at a turning point of history, she thought. *Of herstory.*

As the van plunged forward into the future, Lori tried to put the troubling thoughts out of her mind, at least setting them aside for another day. Now, she needed to focus all of her attentions on her mission: the rescue of the last she-apostle.

Chapter 40

Thy holy cities are a wilderness.
                —Isaiah 64:10, *The Old Testament*

At the rear of a force of uniformed NATO soldiers, Lori ran through the tunnel. Bright lights illuminated the way from the helmets they all wore. Staccato boot steps echoed off the ancient rock walls.

Having demonstrated a proficiency with weapons to General Selkirk (and to her own father), Lori carried an automatic pistol in a shoulder holster, and wore black, lightweight body armor that had been issued to her. Zack and Alex, also in body armor but carrying more powerful automatic rifles, ran just ahead of Lori.

When the attack force embarked, and after the earlier reconnaissance mission, a NATO captain had briefed Lori on military imperatives, telling her to follow orders and to stay out of the way. "When we find Martha," he said, "she will be given to you."

Lori had nodded her head. Whatever it took to be included.

Upon reaching the Vatican, they would divide into squads, each with a different assignment. Lori's group had responsibility for Martha of Galilee, while another was assigned to rescue the Pope. Yet another, larger, force would track down Dixie Lou Jackson and her co-conspirators. In the midst of the battle, helicopters would land, disgorging soldiers to protect St. Peter's Basilica, the Sistine Chapel, and the most priceless antiquities.

Zack and Alex, overcoming tension between them in the beginning, seemed to like one another now. Lori had been noticing similarities in both of them, especially the way they were so dedicated to protecting her. Neither of them seemed to have any fear, despite the tremendous dangers. They were like knights . . . real ones.

Lori had important matters on her mind, huge questions to answer and unknowns to face. She might even have a more mighty protector than the gallant men who ran with her . . . the Lord Almighty. But even the Sovereign of the Universe, the mightiest champion of them all, was known to have a formidable enemy . . . Satan. And in this subterranean region beneath the streets, Lori would remain especially alert; she had no fear for her own personal safety, but needed to survive for the sake of Martha.

The tunnel sloped slightly upward and widened, and they came to the four heavy iron doors they had reached on the earlier reconnaissance mission . . . and the door Lori had already selected as the route to take. This was a point of great danger, because none of them knew for certain what lay beyond, not even Lori with her apparent second sight, though she didn't want to admit her flickering doubts to anyone. Instruments told the soldiers they were near the Vatican Palace.

Any moment could be the last for all of them. Just opening the door, or blasting through, could set off explosives that Dixie Lou claimed to have planted all around the Vatican.

We need to trust in a higher power, Lori thought.

A demolition team began drilling into the door and surrounding wall, and inserted muted charges into the openings. They set up a protective shield, and ordered everyone back.

Lori had been told that the charges were a new, almost entirely silent technology, with very little wasted energy. The charges, when activated, created muffling buffers all around them, and then went off inside those protected areas.

Explosions knocked the heavy door off its hinges.

The NATO force, with Lori at the rear, surged through the doorway. . . .

* * *

Even though they were supposed to be close to the Vatican Palace now, known to be one of the most protected buildings in the holy city, this subterranean region did not appear to have been visited by human beings for centuries. Lori smelled a mustiness that wrinkled her nose, and unpleasant companion odors that she thought might be dead rats and sewage.

Just ahead, soldiers were forming into mission squads, while others shined helmet beams up two staircases, leading in different directions on either side of the passageway. Lori heard the clicking of rifles and handguns as the men checked their weapons. She checked her own, slipped it back into the shoulder holster.

"Can't see the tops of the stairways," an officer said.

"Martha is that way!" Lori said, pointing to the stairs on the left.

Pushing past them, she ran ahead, up the worn rock steps. Her father and Alex called for her to stop.

The steps under Lori's feet were slick and damp, which she saw in the illumination of her helmet lamp, so she had to watch her footing. She heard men running behind her, saw their lights coming up the stairs behind her.

One of the men said, "We may as well go with her. Can't tell which way to go anyway."

Another man agreed. "She has a sixth sense."

At the top of the stairs, Lori tried the lever handle of a door, but it didn't budge. The stubborn barrier would not move.

"I'll take care of it," a soldier said. "One side, please."

The demolition expert set the charges and activated them, creating a soft percussive thump. The door gave way, and Lori ran into what looked like the basement of a large structure, with a corridor that extended for hundreds of meters.

A soldier beside her fiddled with his compass, trying to determine the direction of the southwest corner of the third floor, where Deborah Marvel had said the last she-apostle was being kept. He was having trouble with it, some sort of magnetic disturbance, he said. Bringing out a plan of each floor, he studied it.

Even though she had never been here before, Lori knew which way to go without looking at the plan. It was as if this ancient maze was as familiar to her as her own home. In her mind's eye she saw a complete diagram of the palace and surrounding structures, every floor, every passageway and staircase.

* * *

Dressed in a gold robe trimmed in black, Dixie Lou Jackson carried the legendary Sword of She-God. She strode into a third floor room that centuries before had been the bedroom of a papal mistress, and which now contained a white wooden crib where the baby Marta Santos lay sleeping beneath a blanket. Morning light seeped into the room, and table lamps were on, left that way by the child's mother, who had a Mexican superstition that Marta should not sleep in darkness, lest evil spirits take her away. The matron assigned to watch the woman reported that she had been terribly upset one night, when Dixie Lou turned off the building power and wandered the darkened corridors and rooms for her own personal enjoyment. She might do that again, if she ever felt like it.

For now, the Grand Messenger locked herself inside the room, and sealed off the door to the adjoining room as well, where she had permitted the mother to live, under supervision of the matron and the guards. A small kindness that no one gave Dixie Lou credit for. She set the Sword of She-God on a table, heard ongoing construction noises in the background.

Gliding silently to the crib, Dixie Lou held the smoothly painted top rail and listened to the barely audible breathing of the child. She could smell the perfume of baby powder, evidence that the mother took good care of her. Such a sweet smile on the little brown face, dreaming unknown delights. So innocent in appearance, but Dixie Lou sensed something extremely dangerous about her. She was at once fascinated and terrified.

After taking a deep breath for courage, she touched—timidly at first, then firmly—the side of the child's neck, intending to obtain the elusive truth, no matter the pain she had to endure to do so.

From somewhere far off, but seemingly within the child, a subtle trembling began, and moment by moment it intensified, like an earthquake but not quite like one, because it was not sudden and not external. When the vibrations became so severe that Dixie Lou thought she could endure no more, a reverberating, rumbling shock knocked her loose and hurled her across the room, slamming her into a wall. She hit her head hard, nearly passed out.

The mother was awake now, pounding on the side door and chattering hysterically in Spanish.

Her head throbbing, Dixie Lou shouted, "Shut up, you fool! The baby is fine!"

But the women kept up the commotion, to the point where Dixie Lou felt like killing her, until she heard the voice of the matron in the other room, talking to the peasant woman. The Grand Messenger tried to focus on something else, on the reason she had come to this room in the first place.

Crossing to the crib, she knelt beside it and stared through the slats at the baby, who was awake now and stared back at her with intelligent brown eyes.

The child smiled in a condescending manner, as if in possession of secrets that were unfathomable to Dixie Lou. She found this deeply disturbing. Then, through an opening in the slats, the baby reached out and touched the back of Dixie Lou's hand. This time their skins seemed to lock together and meld into one. The trembling resumed and intensified, but now it drew Dixie Lou deep into the memory of this child-that-was-not-a-child, to the ancient time of Jesus Christ and Pontius Pilate.

"I must know the truth," Dixie Lou murmured.

Long dormant thoughts and word fragments filtered into Dixie Lou's brain in ancient Aramaic, but which she understood in a translation process that she could not explain. An adult female voice announced, "You are forgiven."

"*Forgiven*? What are you talking about?" Inexplicably, Dixie Lou felt a terrible guilt, but about what?

"I am the true Martha of Galilee, Apostle of Jesus," the voice said. Then she kept talking, explaining scenes while they reeled across Dixie Lou's awareness liked the damaged copy of a movie, forming unclear images: the Savior at the Sermon on the Mount . . . at the Sea of Galilee . . . in the Garden of Gethsemane. These images, though of poor quality, were electrifying to Dixie Lou.

Excitement and fear surged through her. This *was* the twelfth she-apostle! But the images remained clouded, and Dixie Lou hungered to see more, to *know* more.

Suddenly all went black, and Martha's adult voice stopped.

Her mind roiling in confusion and terror, the Grand Messenger withdrew from the child. Questions surfaced, important ones: Why had she experienced a vision of Lori having a child? That conflicted with what she'd just been told. If this truly was Martha of Galilee, the missing she-apostle, who would Lori's baby be?

And why did Dixie Lou feel such intense personal guilt, that she had done something horrible and unforgivable?

A loud explosion jolted her to awareness, and she ran alone into the corridor of the palace, shouting for her guards. Unnoticed by her, a brown-skinned woman stepped out of an alcove and slipped into the room, closing the door behind her.

Chapter 41

For everything a person senses, there is always more, just beneath the surface. This is true for all people, no matter their extrasensory abilities. It is like this with every aspect of life, and accomplishment. You can always do better, can always attain more.
—Lori Vale, *Philosophies*

Deborah Marvel had expected NATO to attack the afternoon before, the moment the seventy-two hour deadline expired. When it didn't happen and the evening passed, she slept poorly all night, wondering when they would come, or *if* they would come at all. Had they only been bluffing?

Just as she finally fell asleep in the wee hours of the morning, she awoke at a loud noise, and came to consciousness with the feeling that she was emerging from a bad dream. Hearing another loud noise, this one like an explosion, she bolted out of bed and dressed hurriedly.

Carrying a handgun, the blonde woman lunged into the corridor on the fourth floor of the Vatican Palace and sprinted toward the Pope's room, faster than she ever jogged, rounding corners so fast that she almost fell down.

At his door, she passed through the saffron light of an identity scanner. The wooden door opened and she and burst into the room. Gunfire sounded downstairs, perhaps on the ground floor of the palace.

"It has begun," he said, calmly, in his slight Spanish accent. Pope Rodrigo was fully dressed, wore a simple white robe. He held a *Bible* open, which he now closed and slipped into an oversized pocket. Through a window behind him, orange flashes lit the morning sky. Deborah heard a fusillade of machine-gun fire outside, and the shouts of women in the palace.

"Come with me, Your Eminence," Deborah said. "I don't think you should remain here."

He looked at her inquisitively with his old green eyes, and smiled. "Where do you intend to take me?"

"To safety, Your Eminence. Please, we need to hurry."

"Leave your weapon behind, please."

"It's only set to stun, can't really hurt anyone."

His eyes looked deeply into hers. "All right," he finally said, and rose to his feet. She was struck by what an elegant, infinitely calm and emotionally centered old gentleman he was, especially in his terrible time of trial.

She led him into the corridor, where partially dressed councilwomen, matrons, and servants were running and screaming. As Deborah and the Pope approached a stairway, two burly female guards emerged from it, brandishing snub-nose assault rifles.

"Come with us," one of the guards yelled. "We have standing orders from the Grand Messenger to take the Pope to her office."

"I have a better place for him," Deborah said. She recognized the guards.

"Sorry, ma'am," the other guard said, lifting the barrel of her rifle, but only a little. She looked warily at Deborah's pistol. "We have our orders."

"You know who I am," Deborah said in a level tone, "and you will do as I say. My orders override any standing orders. It's not safe to take Pope Rodrigo that far."

The guards looked at each other. One of them tried to grab the Pope by the arm, but he pulled away.

Deborah fired twice, one stun pellet at each of the women. The projectiles hit them squarely in their torsos, and both of them fell backward onto the top of the stairwell, crying out and dropping their weapons. Then, abruptly, they became rigid, with their eyes staring and unfocused.

Obviously concerned, the Pope knelt over one of the guards, felt the carotid artery on her neck.

"They won't be able to move for about five minutes," Deborah said. "Don't worry, Your Eminence, they aren't seriously hurt."

He rose to his feet, but looked very worried, and anguished.

Grabbing the guards' assault rifles, Deborah shouted for Pope Rodrigo to follow her down the stairs. The pontiff murmured a quick prayer over the motionless guards, then caught up with her.

At the first landing, Deborah halted, and with the barrel of her pistol she pressed on the wall, near a corner. A panel slid open with a hard thump, and she led Pope Rodrigo inside, closing the panel behind them.

Entering a narrow corridor that ran parallel with the wall, a passageway barely wide enough for one person to get through, she led him to a low-ceilinged, windowless room. "We are between floors now," she said.

"You've certainly done your homework," Pope Rodrigo said, hunching over since he was taller than the ceiling. "But you may not know that I also have access to this area from my apartment, even though it is only servant's quarters."

"I didn't know that."

"Every apartment in the palace has access to safe rooms such as this one, for those who know about them."

"You and the Roman Catholic cardinals?"

He nodded. "The most trusted of the trusted know about these secret passageways and rooms."

The Spartan chamber, whose ceiling was only an inch or two above Deborah's head, featured two beds, a pair of chairs with thin cushions, a simple kitchen, and a toilet, seen through an open door.

Deborah slumped into one of the chairs and dropped the weapons on the hardwood floor beside her. "I'm sorry we did this to you," she said. "I don't want to make excuses because I am part of the organization, but I didn't know Dixie Lou intended to capture the Vatican and kill your people in the takeover. None of the councilwomen knew. She only told us that she had a meeting with you, and then all hell broke—Pardon my language, Your Eminence. It is all so painful."

"I do not blame you, my child."

"I'm also sorry I had to stun those two guards, but I needed to protect you."

His face filled with sadness. "I abhor violence."

"Of course you do," she said, "but sometimes it is necessary."

"There may be historical examples to support your view," he admitted, "but I think we should take every possible step to avoid harming anyone."

With a scowl, Deborah picked up one of the assault rifles, and slid it across the hardwood floor, to him.

He stared at it blankly. "As a man of peace, I could never accept that."

"You could become a man of *pieces* if you don't defend yourself."

Shaking his head stubbornly, he said, "You see only my corporal form, not my eternal soul. I shall never touch a gun, or any other weapon. God will protect me."

With a rueful smile, Deborah said, "I didn't expect to see you running into the plaza with an assault rifle." She sighed. "OK, I'll do the fighting for both of us."

* * *

Reaching the third floor of the Vatican Palace, Lori ran for the southwest corner, knowing which way to go without looking at a compass. Unholstering her automatic pistol, she released the safety and rested her forefinger on the trigger guard. There were women in the corridor, running this way and that, emerging from doorways, disappearing into them. Some were barefoot, in their night clothes. As if playing a video game or undergoing a test in a police academy, Lori focused on each as they popped into view, and made an instantaneous decision as to whether or not they were a danger.

No enemy combatants appeared to be among them, and no visible weapons. As she rushed forward, the women got out of her way, and out of the way of the uniformed NATO soldiers who ran just behind her, their helmet lights still glowing.

Abruptly, everything changed. Lori felt herself freeze up, for only the briefest of moments, but it was almost too long. As she and her comrades rounded a turn, the way was blocked by soldiers of the Holy She, in pale gold uniforms.

"Get down!" Zack shouted. He pushed Lori to the floor and knelt in front of her, firing his automatic rifle, just as the enemy opened a barrage.

Then, like a warrior hurling himself into battle, Alex ran ahead of the others, firing his gun. Lori cried out to him, but her words were drowned out in the din of combat. To her horror, her father took a bullet, and fell back over her, grabbing his shoulder. But he didn't let go of his rifle, and climbed in front of Lori again, firing non-stop. With her own pistol Lori fired past him herself, and thought she knocked one of the female soldiers down. Then her gun jammed, and she couldn't get it to work. She re-holstered it.

With NATO soldiers right behind him, Alex waded into the midst of the female fighters, firing right and left, hitting them and knocking them down. He seemed invulnerable, refused to fall and didn't appear to take a hit. Despite his own injury, Zack jumped to his feet and fought beside Alex. The NATO forces were driving their opponents back.

"Go ahead!" Alex shouted to Lori. "Get Martha!"

Seeing an opening, Lori ran past the men, leaping over fallen bodies and scattered weapons. At the end of the corridor, she saw a door that looked as if it belonged on a church, covered with raised gold religious carvings. She ran straight to it, through a wash of saffron light, and tried the handle, but it would not open.

The light changed color, began to flash pink. The identity scanner had rejected her.

Her eyes focused on a control panel mounted on the wall, and she visualized the override code, numbers and letters dancing in front of her eyes. Lori tapped the proper keys, and the thick door opened. She pushed it shut behind her. Just before it closed, she heard Alex shout to her that he would guard the door.

* * *

As Dixie Lou Jackson ran through the hallway, shouting at her elite guards, ordering them to follow her, she thought they behaved clumsily and stupidly, that none of them were qualified to do what needed to be done. She was the most important woman in the history of the world, but found herself surrounded by a garbage dump of humanity.

Much of this was her own fault, she realized. If she had been using good sense, she would have kept Martha of Galilee and Pope Rodrigo in living quarters adjacent to her own (moving them during the day to keep them close to her) so that she could make her last stand, using both of them as hostages. But deep in her consciousness, in that portion of her soul that could only be dealt with truthfully, she knew that she deserved this state of affairs, and a lot worse. She deserved the fate that awaited her when NATO soldiers finally got her in their sights and opened fire. Helpless as a moth, she could only flutter into the flames.

She had the detonator in her pocket, but could not bring herself to activate the explosives that had been rigged all over Vatican City. Something prevented her from taking that last, final step. She did not want that to be her epitaph, that she had failed, and had taken so much down with her.

Maybe, just maybe, she could still figure a way out of this.

Upon hearing the signs of an attack, her first impulse was to run for the Pope and leave the child behind. She could have carried Martha to the Pope's quarters, but Dixie Lou had been terrified of the little she-apostle, and took the first excuse to get away from her, even if it cost her important time and leverage.

I didn't want to know what Martha would say next, didn't want to learn what lay next around the corner of my own memory.

Now she tried to tell herself it didn't matter leaving Martha behind. Pope Rodrigo was the biggest prize anyway, and he was just down this corridor, through the wooden door at the end, in the servant's quarters.

Passing through the light of a security scanner, she and seven elite guards surged into the apartment. But it was empty. The Pope was not there.

Running back out into the corridor with her guards, Dixie Lou encountered a group of Holy She soldiers, some wounded, who described a violent confrontation one floor down, outside Martha of Galilee's room. Her guards and soldiers surrounded her in a protective cocoon. The officer of the guard asked her what they should do.

"Wait out here," the Grand Messenger commanded. And she reentered the apartment.

Chapter 42

Jesus had a brother, James, and three sisters. The sisters' names, in order of birth, were Susanna, Ruth, and Phoebe. The youngest died before her first birthday, while the older sisters were present at the crucifixion of their brother, and wept inconsolably.

—Gospel of Hannah 12:24–25, the *Holy Women's Bible*

With great trepidation, Lori approached the crib, then stopped as she heard a scream, and saw a blur of movement on her left. A brown-skinned woman emerged from an adjacent room and ran directly at her.

Anda! the woman shouted. *No toca la niña!*

Lori braced herself to take a headlong charge. But, abruptly, the woman stopped, only inches from Lori. Looking past Lori, into the crib, the woman said, "*Marta? Qué quieres, mi querida?*"

In the crib, the child was reaching out . . . reaching for Lori.

"Are you the mother?" Lori asked, glancing at her.

Nodding, she said, "*Si, si. Yo soy la madre.*"

"I won't hurt your daughter," Lori said, placing a comforting hand on her shoulder. "I came to save her. Please trust me."

The woman, her face torn with emotions, nodded, though she obviously did not understand all of Lori's words. She pulled away from the teenager and took a step back.

Taking this as a sign of approval, Lori lifted the baby out and sat with her on a settee. She felt no sensation of change, but realized she had not been touching Martha's skin, only her clothing. With bated breath, Lori pressed the baby's tiny hands between her own, and gradually the sounds of conflict from the corridor faded.

Suddenly a powerful current tugged at Lori, causing her entire body to tingle. She felt herself drawn into an infinite void, and gradually the unpleasant feeling subsided, to a smooth, even hum. In only a few seconds, she was no longer Lori Vale of Seattle. A blur of faces appeared before her, creased and darkened from an unrelenting desert sun and searing hot, dry winds.

Though Lori's eyes were open, she saw nothing of the palace room, and she was instead transported to a faraway place in a long-ago time. She sat beside a young woman—a brunette known to her as Martha of Galilee—on a bench in a rooftop garden, with the whitewashed buildings and narrow streets of a familiar city visible in the distance.

Roman Jerusalem.

The realization shocked and terrified her, and she wanted desperately to withdraw. She tried to break contact, but could not. She could only look and listen. Everything stood out in sharp focus, and she seemed to actually be in that ancient city. The sun was too bright and hot, and she needed relief from it. A warm afternoon breeze carried the fragrance of the garden to her, but it was not a pleasant scent, and somehow gave her excruciating pain.

In a faltering, almost dreamlike voice, Martha spoke in an ancient tongue, but Lori understood completely. Martha told of the apostle Judas Iscariot, who was her lover, and the man with whom she had betrayed Jesus Christ for a mere thirty pieces of silver. Her voice breaking with emotion, Martha said she never would have committed such an atrocious act if Judas had not lied to her about Jesus, convincing her that he was an instrument of Satan, a false prophet, and that God wanted him destroyed.

Quoting from the Fifth Book of Moses, Judas had said to her: "'But the prophet, which shall presume to speak a word in my name, which I have not commanded him to speak . . . that prophet shall die.'" All the while, Judas had concealed the real reason from Martha, that Jesus had rebuked him after the apostle Matthew—who had experience with monetary matters—proved that Judas was a thief.

From across the centuries, while these things were revealed to Lori in the timeworn Vatican room, she listened with rapt attention, as if she were caught up in a powerful whirlwind. . . .

"Most of the terrible events have not occurred yet," Martha said, "but they are predestined, and there is nothing I can do to stop them. Jesus knows what is about to happen to him and to those around him, episodes so frightful that I can barely describe them—" Her voice broke, and she fought back sobs. . . .

The images shifted, and Lori found herself looking through Martha's eyes instead of her own, while Martha resumed speaking to her: "Today is the day after Judas accepted the thirty pieces of silver. He and I are summoned to appear before the Sanhedrin, the high tribunal of the Jews. In a large chamber, we face High Priest Joseph Caiaphas, who stands on a dais in a white robe. A woman in a white dress stands beside him."

Lori saw the man and woman in white, and found herself transfixed by the woman's dusky eyes, which seemed frozen in her skull.

"Salome," Martha said, her voice trembling. "Wife of Judas Iscariot and younger sister of the High Priest. He demands to know if Judas and I are lovers. We deny it, but Salome shouts that we are adulterers and liars. From a fold of her dress she produces a knife, and takes a step toward Judas, until her brother grabs her arm, holding her back."

As if viewing a narrated film, Lori saw all of this. A cold draft seemed to run down her spine as she continued to listen, and she trembled.

"Terrified of his own wife, Judas continues to deny the charges. Then, to deflect the attention from himself, he makes even more false statements, asserting that Jesus has been engaging in sexual relations with all of the she-apostles, including me. Judas Iscariot charges that all twelve of us are, in effect, the harem of a would-be king."

Martha shuddered with anger. "None of it is true, of course. Jesus is celibate, and has always treated us with the utmost respect and courtesy. I am outraged at the lies, so I scream at Judas. I know I have made a big mistake in trusting him, and I tell him I want out of the terrible bargain I have entered into with him, that I only went along with it out of my love for him, my belief in him. Judas tells me to shut up, that he and I have never been anything to each other. He strikes me in the face and knocks me down."

Lori continued to look through Martha's eyes as Martha hit the hard tile floor, and blackness enveloped her. When her eyes flickered open, Lori saw the sandaled feet of the priest and his sister, and the bottoms of their robes. As she looked higher, she saw something that chilled her to the bone: Dixie Lou's eyes peering down at her from Salome's skull.

Abruptly, Lori no longer heard Martha's words, and actually seemed to experience the long-ago events. The High Priest told guards to take hold of Martha and Judas, then released his hold on his sister.

"I sentence all of the she-apostles to death," the High Priest said, "as abominations before God."

Martha fell to her knees and prayed, while Judas whimpered and pleaded for his own life. Salome stood before them with the knife.

"Spare Judas," the Priest commanded. "He still needs to earn the thirty pieces of silver we are paying him."

As Martha knelt, Salome plunged the knife into her back, then fell upon the she-apostle in a murderous frenzy, stabbing her repeatedly. Lori did not feel the physical pain of this, but was horrified. As moments passed, and Martha bled to death on the floor, Lori felt a disconnection and all went dark. But it was only temporary, and again Lori was sitting on the bench in the garden beside Martha of Galilee, with a warm breeze washing over them.

"That is how I will die," Martha said, in a voice from the vault of time.

Martha went on to say that God was not a bearded old man in the sky, as portrayed in Christian literature and art, and was not male or female, either, but was instead *both*, a multidimensional deity. The She-God referred to by the she-apostles was not really a separate entity, she said, but was instead a reference to the *feminine side of God*, to the counterbalance needed to keep the male side under control.

Martha spoke excitedly, lovingly. "God is both physical and non-physical, both matter and antimatter. God is a loving entity, but a thunderous one as well . . . a complex force of peace and war. God is omnipotent and omnipresent, heavenly light and eternal darkness."

More information followed, of a nature that was even more damaging to Dixie Lou Jackson, and as she listened Lori felt foreboding and mounting fear. Hypnotized, she had to hear the entire story anyway, every fascinating word of it. . . .

* * *

In her dreamlike state Lori reached out, and was about to touch the blessed, bearded face of Jesus. Suddenly his serene brown eyes became troubled, and his expressive mouth formed words. But someone else spoke, not him.

"Watch out!" a woman shouted. It was the voice of Martha of Galilee, one of the apostles of Jesus.

In a fraction of a second Lori felt herself break free, and she was transported across centuries, back to the third floor of the Vatican Palace, where she sat with the baby. Her senses accelerated. Compressed into a fragment of time, she felt the warmth of the child in her arms, smelled talcum powder and baby's milk.

Lori opened her eyes. Something bright and metallic glinted, a sword blade, and Dixie Lou was thrusting it toward her!

Quickly, Lori rolled off the couch with the baby, onto the floor, using a method of falling that she had learned in *t'ai chi* class.

The Grand Messenger, her eyes burning with primal fury, had emerged from a hidden wall panel, having reached the room via the honeycomb of secret passageways inside the walls. She lunged with the Sword of She-God, but fell across the settee, narrowly missing her target. Curses flew from her mouth.

Rushing up behind Dixie Lou, unconcerned for her own personal safety, Martha's mother chattered excitedly in Spanish and pulled at the assailant's sword arm. Dixie Lou kicked her away, and the woman crashed against a side table, knocking it over and hitting her head hard. She groaned and fell to the floor, stopped moving.

The first priority for Lori was to protect the child, so she placed her on the floor behind herself. Lori went into a defensive *karate* posture, with her hands stiff and arms cocked. But she was only a beginner in that discipline, and didn't feel confident in her skills yet. Darting to her left, she grabbed a fireplace poker and used it to ward off the attacker's sword.

Lori heard pounding on the hall door, and the anxious voice of Alex, calling her name. The door was thick, and had been fortified with electronics. On the floor, Martha's mother was not moving. Lori tried to dash around Dixie Lou to reach the door and open it, but the stocky black woman drove her back by brandishing the sword.

"No one can save you," Dixie Lou said. "I am the supreme law, and I sentence you to death!" The Grand Messenger's dark eyes peered through narrow slits; her lips were tight as she spoke.

Taking a deep breath to calm herself, Lori remembered one of her martial arts instructors telling her about the flow of *chi* energy in her body and throughout nature, and the need for balance. She felt the weight and balance of the poker, used it to deflect the sword and drive her opponent back, but only for a few steps before she rushed at Lori again.

"It will look like you murdered Martha and then took your own life," Dixie Lou said. "Why did you do it, Lori?"

The blade slashed the sleeve of the teenager's blouse near her wrist, cutting through to the skin. She felt raw, burning pain. Blood seeped onto the sleeve.

She heard more men outside the room, rattling the door handle and shouting. They were having trouble getting through.

Lori's injured arm ached, but with it she still swung the fireplace poker. It struck Dixie Lou on the side of the head, and with a cry the woman fell back. Now Lori rushed at Dixie Lou with the heavy iron, striking her on the top of the head and on her arms, which she put up to ward off the blows. The Sword of She-God clattered onto the hardwood floor.

Blood ran in Dixie Lou's eyes, inhibiting her vision. Nonetheless, she was able to grab one of Lori's ankles and topple her. The girl thudded to the floor, lost hold of the poker.

Lori tried to roll away and grab the sword. But Dixie Lou moved with the quickness of a black cat, and before Lori could escape, the powerfully built woman was on top of her, using demonic strength to tighten her fingers around Lori's throat. Blood dripped from Dixie Lou's face onto Lori's.

With a surge of strength, Lori curled her legs and kicked her attacker. Grunting in pain and surprise, Dixie Lou fell back, but saw the sword. It lay within her reach.

Just as she was about to grab hold of it, however, the sword lifted high into the air and floated toward Lori. Little Martha was on her feet looking upward, her eyes focused like laser beams as she struggled to keep the weapon in the air. But it was a mighty effort of telekinesis for the developing child, and the mental muscles began to falter. The sword drifted down, halfway between Lori and Dixie Lou.

Leaping for the sword, Lori got hold of the hilt and rolled, then sprang to her feet with the legendary weapon, both hands gripping it. She wanted to kill this evil woman more than anything, most of all for what she had done to her mother, not getting her the medical attention she needed.

Dixie Lou held up her hands. "Please," she whimpered. "Don't!"

For an instant, Lori tasted the terror on the face of the Grand Messenger, and she savored it. The sword blade was razor sharp, and with a strong swing she might decapitate her hated adversary, or maim her. But the teenager wondered if she could go through with it. A moment's doubt was erased when she told herself she *had* to.

But still she hesitated. . . .

As Dixie Lou looked at the young woman in front of her, holding the weapon so uncertainly, she realized who Lori had been a long time ago, and much more. She knew who she had been herself, under a different name.

I was Salome, sister of High Priest Caiaphas.

An overwhelming feeling of guilt overtook the Grand Messenger of the Holy She, and she knew that no matter what she did in this lifetime, no matter the lies she told or the steps she took to conceal her past identity, the horrible truth would still come out, over and over again. She could not escape the eyes of the Supreme Being, or the judgment of history.

"I confess my sins and ask for forgiveness," she murmured. "I was the sister of Joseph Caiaphas and the wife of Judas Iscariot, the man whose mistress was Martha of Galilee, a female apostle of Jesus. I did terrible things."

"The Savior forgives you," Lori said.

Tears streamed down Dixie Lou's face. "Blinded by jealousy, I stabbed Martha to death, in front of my brother and Judas. The following evening, after the Passover meal, I brought Roman soldiers to the Garden of Gethsemane, where they arrested Jesus and nine she-apostles who were with him. Only the hand of God prevented all of the male apostles from being arrested as well, and two she-apostles—Mary Magdalene and Veronica. But they were not there."

Lori had never beheld such anguish as she saw now on the face of this woman whom she loathed for causing so much grief, not only to her personally, but to the entire world.

"From my brother I obtained the key to the women's cell, and with the blood of Martha still on my blade I stabbed nine she-apostles as they slept. It was *katilta*—slaughter. Afterward, I saw Jesus in the courtyard of the prison. Somehow he'd gotten out of his own cell. Unarmed and completely unafraid of the knife I waved at him, he approached me. In shame, I dropped it and ran away."

Lori didn't know what to say. The immensity of the story seemed to weigh Dixie Lou down, causing her entire body to sag. "After everything I've done, it's too late for me," she said. "I am eternally damned."

"It's never too late to seek forgiveness," Lori said. She wanted to reach out and comfort the pathetic woman, but held the sword steady, remaining wary of this mortal enemy.

Two she-apostles survived the slaughter, Lori thought. *Mary Magdalene and Veronica.*

Thoughts rushed upon her. Lori's mind sped up, and puzzle pieces snicked into place, based upon what she had learned from Martha of Galilee, Dixie Lou Jackson, and other sources: Two days after his crucifixion, Jesus rose from the dead, and was first seen by the only surviving she-apostles Mary Magdalene and Veronica, along with other women. Some of the others were undoubtedly disciples of Jesus, among a large group of his followers. It struck Lori how important women must have been to Jesus, if he appeared to them first. Perhaps it was a signal of what was to come. . . .

Her cheeks wet with tears, Dixie Lou raised her face to the heavens. "Forgive me, Lord," she wailed, in the most pitiful of tones.

The door burst open, and NATO soldiers rushed in.

With a sudden movement, Dixie Lou lunged forward into the sharp tip of the sword. It pierced her chest.

Startled and horrified, Lori pulled the weapon back, but the hilt had slammed against her shoulder, giving support to the blade when Dixie Lou rammed into it. She slumped to the floor, bleeding.

She looked dead, but Lori didn't take any chances. Dropping the weapon, she gathered up the baby and ran with her into the corridor, then sent a soldier back to check on the mother, who was groaning and beginning to move.

* * *

As blood flowed from her body, Dixie Lou thought back, questioning the poor decisions she had made in this lifetime. If the Pope had been where he was supposed to be, she could have taken control of him and used him as a bargaining chip, to gain an advantage over her enemies. But she had placed Deborah Marvel in charge of him, even after suspecting Deborah's motivations and loyalties.

I set a trap for myself, and walked right into it. I did it on purpose.

Deep in her soul, Dixie Lou knew she had to atone for the misdeeds of a prior life, and for the misdeeds of this one. Her Judgment Day could not be avoided; the time of reckoning had arrived.

The guilt of two thousand years. I need to be free of it!

With her last bit of strength, she realized that she was not Dixie Lou Jackson or even Salome, the sister of an ancient High Priest. Instead, she was a wandering, tormented soul, longing to be free of her accursed existence.

These were her final thoughts . . . in this incarnation.

* * *

Peering through peepholes from concealed passageways and rooms, Deborah Marvel looked out on every floor and corridor of the palace, and finally satisfied herself that the fighting was over. On the third floor, she saw NATO soldiers carry the bleeding, lifeless body of Dixie Lou Jackson on a stretcher. She heard them say how she had died. Female fighters either lay dead or were surrendering.

A tear ran down Deborah's cheek. Not so much for Dixie Lou Jackson, but more for what had happened to United Women of the World. The sisterhood had begun with such promise, and it seemed a terrible tragedy for it to fall into complete disgrace, on an immense, global scale with billions of eyes watching.

Under Dixie Lou's command, the UWW had committed suicide with her.

Sadly, Deborah returned to the room where Pope Rodrigo waited. "You're free," she told him. "The Vatican is liberated."

As he rose to his feet, stooping under the low ceiling, he looked straight at her and vowed, "I will not forget this."

At first, Deborah thought he intended to avenge himself on her and on the tattered remnants of her organization, but soon she would come to realize that he had something entirely different in mind.

Chapter 43

Some people claim that Dixie Lou Jackson made one of the greatest blunders of military history in not learning enough about the Castel Sant'Angelo tunnel system. But they are wrong. She could not have held out in the Vatican forever anyway, and eventually she would have been dispatched from her roost—either through force of arms or attrition.
—Paolo Jacobi, *Crisis Revisited*

Four days passed. . . .

With the blessing of Pope Rodrigo, Deborah Marvel called a meeting of the Council of Cardinals, which consisted of eight women, all former UWW councilwomen who were now in charge of the Holy She. They held the session in the ancient fortress of Castel Sant'Angelo. At the urging of the pontiff, the owner had permitted them to lease part of the ancient fortress on favorable terms—turning former art galleries and apartments over to them. Fulfilling his promise, the Pope had not forgotten Deborah Marvel's good deed in rescuing him.

As part of the agreement, the commandeered jewels in the hilt of the Sword of She God had been returned to the Vatican, and the legendary UWW weapon—fitted with only its original jewels now—had been locked away, to be brought out one day and restored as a museum piece.

On a wide, hardwood floor stage, the female cardinals sat in black leather chairs arranged in a half circle, facing an unoccupied red leather chair. Separate from them, but on the stage, sat Fujiko Harui, wearing a green-and-orange robe like the others. An audience of around fifty, mostly women, looked on, including Fujiko's daughter Siana, Liz Torrence, and Rea Janeg.

Lori sat in a spectator chair at the front, and as she waited for the proceedings to begin, her father and Alex were brought in and given seats on either side of her. Alex's curly black hair stuck out at the sides. Uncertain of why the three of them had been invited here, she exchanged troubled glances with her father, who wore his customary officer's uniform. It occurred to her that she had never seen him wearing anything else, not in photos or in person. But she had not really known him very long.

From the center of the stage, Deborah Marvel called for a resolution. Rising to her feet, Nancy Winters said, "I call for the disbanding of the Holy She, and restoration of United Women of the World. I also call for reformation of the council, to consist of nine members, including Fujiko Harui—and for the council to eventually grow to the sixteen specified in the original charter, when qualified candidates can be located."

The proposal passed unanimously, after which Deborah Marvel was selected by vote of the council to take Dixie Lou Jackson's place.

Newly installed as Chairwoman, Deborah peered down to the front row of the audience, and spoke in a throaty voice. "Please rise, Lori Vale, Alex Jackson, and Zack Markwether."

The three of them stood.

"We wish to commend all of you for your bravery in the liberation of the Vatican, and especially for saving the life of the last she-apostle."

Deborah paused, tapping a pen on the armrest of her chair. "Is it true that you are with child?" she asked, looking at Lori.

"Yes," Lori said, without shame.

"And the father is present?"

"I don't want to say," Lori answered. She glanced sidelong at Alex, then at her own father, smiling at both of them. She had explained everything to them, and they believed her. Or at least, they *said* they did. The truth seemed unbelievable, and she wasn't sure when—or if—she would ever make it public. Maybe, despite what Mary Magdalene had told her, it hadn't happened the way she thought. Maybe Dixie Lou Jackson did something to Lori when she was her prisoner, under some sort of sedation that the teenager didn't realize had been administered.

"That's understandable," Deborah said. "Forgive us for prying, but you're a very special person to us, and we just want to know you."

Lori nodded.

"Tell us about Dixie Lou's death," Deborah said.

After taking a deep breath and gathering her composure, Lori summoned a memory of Martha of Galilee's eerie words—and the confession of Dixie Lou Jackson—in which Lori learned things that no other apostles, male or female, had ever revealed before. Lori described the startling vision she had experienced upon touching the child Martha, and how Judas Iscariot had lied to Martha about Jesus, calling him a false prophet and tricking her into joining the betrayal plot.

Then Lori related the stunning additional information that Dixie Lou had told her, the terrible crimes she—as Salome—had committed against the female apostles.

"She *murdered* ten of them?" Deborah exclaimed.

"In a prior life," Lori said. "Mary Magdalene and Veronica later died natural deaths, after escaping persecution and journeying to distant lands. Now all of the she-apostles have returned to deliver an astounding message to the world, and after Martha appeared, Dixie Lou could no longer hide her ghastly secrets. I don't think Dixie Lou had all the details until just before she took her own life. They were such frightful memories that her subconscious buried them in the deepest part of her soul."

"That might explain her increasingly erratic behavior," Tamara Himmel suggested, "since she was at war with herself."

Lori went on to say that Martha of Galilee had been present when the Lord Jesus spoke to all twenty-four apostles in the Garden of Gethsemane a week before his arrest in that very place. Closing her eyes, she brought forth the exact words of Jesus, as related to her by Martha: "'The cosmic pendulum will swing, and a time will come when destructive male energy is replaced by nurturing female energy. For five thousand years thereafter, women will rule the earth, but they must do so without acrimony or retribution against men. Women must forgive, and rule with the abundant love in their hearts. They must be compassionate, nurturing, and non-violent—distinctly feminine attributes. During the new reign, a holy book will be compiled with all the teachings of our cherished God, a book that honors women and men equally, since both genders are in God's image.'"

Lori paused and said, "Shortly after I heard that, Martha shouted a warning and I saw Dixie Lou coming at me with the sword. I told you the rest."

Looking at her fellow councilwomen, Deborah said to them, "Think about what Lori said: God is *both* male and female!"

It was indeed an awe-inspiring thought.

"But what about the She-God spoken of by some of the she-apostles?" Tamara wanted to know.

Lori spoke with clarity, and absolute certainty. "That's the feminine side of God, the cosmic change that's bringing in more passionate female energy, balancing the overly aggressive male side, keeping it under control."

"'The She-God is coming,'" one of the women in the audience intoned. And others around Lori picked up the mantra, repeating it over and over. "'The She-God is coming' . . . 'The She-God is coming. . . .'" Finally, the voices died down.

With her blue eyes misting over with sadness, Deborah gazed at Lori, and said, "Some of us are afraid Dixie Lou may have been an instrument of Satan, and—" She looked down at Lori's stomach. "There have been rumors."

"Something about my baby?" Lori asked.

"Of course the theory is preposterous and unworthy of consideration," Deborah said. "I shouldn't even bring it up."

For the briefest of instants, a thought flashed in Lori's mind of the paired entities that had swooped down on her as she lay in bed—the brilliant light and its dark companion. But the thought barely touched her consciousness.

326

And Lori asked, in a tremulous voice, "You're thinking my child may be an instrument of Satan? Impossible! If that were true, Dixie Lou wouldn't have tried to kill me!"

The councilwomen concurred with this assessment, and went on to say many things about Lori's great virtue and courage—attributes that could not possibly have anything to do with Satan. Presently, they gathered around the pretty, lavender-eyed girl to congratulate her for putting a stop to the insanity of Dixie Lou Jackson.

The women also invited Lori to work with them, and promised her she would not be mistreated in the future. "We need your assistance with a big project," Deborah said. "Now that all of the she-apostles are together, and we have the blessing of their families and the authorities to work with them, you're needed more than ever. You have a special bond with the children, an ability to bring out their incredible stories."

Pursing her lips, Lori said, "Martha won't talk to you without me, will she?"

"No," Deborah admitted.

Lori glanced at her father, and he nodded. Before coming here, they had discussed the possibility that the UWW might want to negotiate something with her. "I'll work with you," Lori said to the council, "but it has to be on my terms."

"Agreed," Deborah said.

In her left hand, Lori squeezed Alex's hand, and in her right, her father's.

* * *

To the UWW staff it was announced that Lori was to be accorded special status. Under her father's supervision, bodyguards were assigned to her. And, in order to further the new project involving her, modifications would be undertaken to the Sala Paolina, an exhibition hall on the third floor of the huge castle fortress, setting up a new Scriptorium there.

Chapter 44

Previously, United Women of the World had powerful armed forces, on the scale of some nations. Now, under a treaty arranged by Pope Rodrigo, the UWW will never again be permitted to have such capability, only guard forces to protect Castel Sant'Angelo and other sensitive installations.

−Global News Network

On Easter Sunday, Pope Rodrigo stood tall and elegant in a white and gold robe, as he broadcast messages of prayer and thanksgiving to his followers all over the world. In every Roman Catholic congregation there was new hope, and talk of the miraculous rescue of the Vatican. Throughout Christendom, churches were decorated with bright flowers and ribbons, in joyous celebration.

From the holy shrine of St. Peter's Basilica, packed with his followers, the eminent religious leader granted forgiveness to United Women of the World, and said that only one person−Dixie Lou Jackson−had been responsible for the terrible deeds. But he fell short of fully endorsing the women, saying that their religious beliefs diverged widely from his own, and that Jesus Christ only had twelve apostles, and they were all male . . . a number Jesus may have selected because it was the number of tribes in ancient Israel.

"I respect and admire women," the Pope went on to say. "And to prove it, we are undertaking a new study to investigate and improve the condition of women all over the world. For calling my attention to this problem, I am deeply grateful to my friend, Deborah Marvel."

He then prayed for the guidance of God in this new endeavor, and for deliverance from all forms of evil.

* * *

That morning, Deborah opened a heavy wooden door, and stepped out of the way, so that Lori could enter first. "This is your personal suite," the Chairwoman said.

Stepping inside, Lori saw a modestly appointed, though spacious, apartment. To her delight, it featured a private terrace, up a short flight of stairs. On a higher terrace, atop the fortress, stood a large bronze angel, sheathing a sword.

Lori led the way up there, and marveled at the breathtaking views of the Villa Borghese park, the Tiber River, and Vatican City. The holy city seemed to have a fresh brilliance in the sun, like the aura of a person who was close to God. Yellow-and-white Vatican flags fluttered on the buildings once more, imparting a sense of peace and tranquility to the scene.

"Do you like it?" Deborah asked. "The furnishings can be replaced if you wish, and we could bring an interior decorator in."

"I love it just like it is," Lori said. "Don't change a thing."

"Good," Deborah said. "We'll get along just fine."

* * *

In the castle Scriptorium the following week, the UWW set to work on a new holy book that would incorporate elements of the King James Version of the *Bible* and the *Testament of the She-Apostles*, with an emphasis on equality between men and women. Some sacred texts from other religions would be included as well, insofar as they could be linked to the glorious life and teachings of Jesus.

An amended introduction to the new holy book would contain an admission that the first Martha had been a "mistake," but that the authentic Martha of Galilee had been rescued with the Vatican. The tome would undergo many edits by scholars, and the complete story of Dixie Lou's violent earlier life as Salome would be revealed, as described by Martha of Galilee . . . how both Judas and Martha betrayed Jesus, and how Salome subsequently murdered ten of the she-apostles.

Inexplicably, the she-apostles began to treat Lori quite differently, now that all twelve of them were together. They became even more strangely quiet and withdrawn than before. Other than Martha, who dictated her new gospel to translators and sometimes to Lori, the children stopped communicating with Lori, in contrast with their past behavior. Before that Lori had assumed, quite wrongly, that the inroads she had made into their shrouded world would continue, and enlarge. But now that Martha was with them, that had all changed, and she did not understand why.

None of the new Scriptorium scholars—who had become known as "handlers" of the she-apostles—offered a plausible explanation, and none of the gospels revealed any answers, or even clues.

The children had always been insular, very much tied into their own mysterious realm. From the beginning, they had only rarely answered queries put to them by the scholars—inhibited, perhaps, by the handlers' awkward Aramaic accents and mispronunciations that presented additional communication difficulties. Whenever the children spoke, it was usually in a sudden, rapid flow of ancient phrases, as if a switch had been flipped on. And, as before, they used one spoken language for outsiders and another when they communicated among themselves, along with their wordless means of relating to one another.

On the summer solstice that year, the Apostle Veronica finally said something to Lori privately, in the secret language of the she-apostles. With a very serious expression on her angelic little face, Veronica said: "When all is in readiness, Lori Vale, more will be revealed to you. The time must be right, the heavens must be in alignment, and you must be in complete synchronization with them."

Following this curious, cryptic statement, the she-apostles stopped communicating with Lori again.

Nonetheless, in ensuing months the UWW council and staff proceeded to organize and edit what they had. Bits and pieces of the in-progress revisions appeared on the Internet, and around the world a great clamor arose for more information about the new holy book. The approval rating of United Women of the World, which at its peak had reached thirty-two percent, slipped to twenty-four percent and held. It was agreed by most of the public that the radical women—no matter the righteousness of their cause and no matter the forgiveness of the Pope—should never have overthrown the Vatican.

Initially, both Alex Jackson and Zack Markwether remained in Rome with Lori, and she spent as much time with both of them as she could. In July, they celebrated her sixteenth birthday together, and that night her father said how proud he was of her, and how her mother must be looking down on them at that moment, feeling the same way.

As Lori thought of her mother, she felt good about giving up smoking for her. Each time the teenager felt like using a cigarette, she remembered how her mother had been so opposed to the habit, so she renewed her personal vow to never touch one again. Some people might think it was a small gesture, perhaps, but Lori saw it as a sign of her own strength, and of her love for a woman she missed so much.

If she weren't so busy, so focused on the important work at hand, Lori might be interested in dating Alex. Gallantly, he still claimed to be too old for her, but she didn't feel that way at all. She just didn't have time for him.

Her father, who had only been in her life for a few months, seemed deeply remorseful for the past blunders in his life, and vowed to make up for them. One afternoon, as he and Lori stood out on the terrace of the castle, gazing at Vatican City, he told her he would need to return to his work in Washington, DC, and that he would be leaving the following week. They made plans for her to visit him one day at his home in America, and for a trip together to Seattle for Camilla Vale's private memorial service.

It struck Lori as curious how fate worked, the way she'd lost her mother so tragically and then found her father. She wondered if a higher power had something to do with it, if God had somehow countered the destruction that evil forces had wreaked on her little family.

In August, Deborah Marvel delivered a revelatory speech carried by satellite around the world. In it she said a cosmic shift was required, a sharp break with the male-dominated past. Fresh pathways needed to be cut, so that new facets of human behavior could be explored and discovered. "God is both male and *female*," she proclaimed, to an astonished audience of billions.

In another speech the following week, she described the important contributions of Lori Vale in the restoration of the ancient gospels. "Lori is a most unique individual," Deborah exclaimed. "The finest young woman any of us have ever met."

Soon it was rumored that Lori was being groomed for a high position in the organization when she was of age, perhaps even the number one job. She didn't know how she felt about that.

Chapter 45

The masculine and feminine elements, exactly equal and balancing each other, are as essential to the maintenance of the equilibrium of the universe as positive and negative electricity....

–Elizabeth Cady Stanton, *The Woman's Bible* (1898–Essays about women in the *Bible*)

It was a Tuesday in mid-December, shortly after Lori's daily tutoring session, conducted by Raffaela Inez. The Mexican professor—now on the UWW staff—had remained in Rome with her husband, Arsinio, and with Consuela Santos, the birthmother of the reincarnated Martha of Galilee. Lori liked Raffaela very much, and was excelling in all of her studies.

Just before flying back to Washington, DC several months ago, Zack had arranged for the tutor. He told Lori about it at the airport, when she saw him off. "As your father, I couldn't just let you drop out of high school," he had said, with a twinkle in his eye. "No matter how important your job is."

She liked having a parent care about her again, someone to watch over her in a different way than the Lord Almighty did, a person who could help her with seemingly small details of her life. Lori and her father spoke often by videophone, several times a week. . . .

Now she and Alex stood just inside the large nursery of the she-apostles, looking on as women cared for the children. The attentive matrons had hung handmade Christmas decorations on the walls, and had decorated a fir tree, placing gifts beneath it. A new emblem of the UWW was emblazoned on one wall: interlocked female and male icons superimposed over a Christian cross. Beside that hung a memorial plaque for the she-apostles' birthparents and siblings who had been killed . . . both at the hands of the UWW and of the now-defunct BOI.

Toys and games were strewn in one corner, but were of little interest to the children, who seemed content to interact with one another in different ways, perhaps even engaging in veiled forms of mental amusement. Thus far, Lori had seen no sign of the telekinetic powers the she-apostles had displayed previously, moving objects around. She wondered if they practiced by themselves, or if her own presence—as she had earlier thought—might have something to do with their abilities. The powers had certainly been limited, but in the case of Martha of Galilee had been just enough to help Lori in a time of desperate need.

In the eight months since Dixie Lou's death the special children had grown, and so had the fetus in Lori's womb. The teenager's stomach was quite protuberant now, as she was due to deliver any day.

"Maybe I should have my baby in Seattle," Lori said. Pressing both palms against her stomach, she felt the life within her shift a little. For months Lori had been troubled by the continued silence of the she-apostles, which gave her a feeling of unease. Perhaps if she returned to the city of her own childhood to give birth, the place in which she had grown up, she would feel better, more centered.

"It's a little late to think of that," Alex said, looking at her profile.

"You're right."

Glancing at his watch, Alex said, "I'd better get going. Deborah has a busy travel schedule, and I need to make the reservations."

"She says you're a great personal secretary."

"Maybe so, but don't ever call me a stud knight or a *him*bo," he quipped. Then he gave her a light kiss on the forehead—as an older brother might do—and left.

Alex was proving to be a fine asset for United Women of the World, and Deborah often said he was much more than a secretary, and did more work than two or three women. He was an exception in that regard, she always liked to quip, because it was usually the other way around.

Lori smiled as Veronica, now two years old, went to the younger Martha of Galilee, and hugged her. The brown-skinned Martha could walk well, but often preferred to sit on the floor. She was subject to apparent bouts of depression, perhaps a carryover of guilt because of her part in the betrayal of Jesus. But whenever this feeling came over her, the other she-apostles were quick to come to her aid, showing that they forgave her, just as Jesus would have wanted.

Veronica was doing exactly that now, kneeling by Martha, stroking her head and communicating with her in the wordless way that the she-apostles seemed to prefer at times. Lori was beginning to recognize a variety of facial expressions that the children exchanged . . . slight variations around the mouth, or in the wrinkling of the forehead, or in the brightness of the eyes. But she still had a long way to go before she understood, and so far the children were not giving her any additional assistance.

Nonetheless, Lori was pleased at the way the she-apostles were getting along together, and she felt a special affinity for them. Each day she came in the nursery and watched them, while maintaining a polite distance, so as not to disturb them. The children seemed to take scant notice of her, which occasionally brought tears to her eyes. She didn't understand, but desperately wanted to.

Suddenly, she became aware of a change in the little girls. All were gazing at her at once, a mixture of races focused on her. When she moved nervously to one side, twenty-four eyes followed, seemingly linked as one organism.

In concert, the she-apostles began to walk toward her with remarkable proficiency for their ages, almost striding in their little bodies. The matrons remained behind, as if they had been given a signal.

Lori's heart raced.

The she-apostles formed a circle around the American teenager, and linked hands with one another. Then Veronica and Martha, who were side-by-side, released their grips and reached for Lori.

Taking this as an invitation, Lori slipped into the circle, where she knelt and took hold of the little hands. They were warm.

Brightly colored lights filled Lori Vale's vision, and in *panakh* . . . an ancient form of epiphany . . . she beheld a glowing galactic keyhole, a heavenly pathway to the next threshold for humanity. With words that made no sound, the she-apostles told her what lay ahead, a remarkable, unprecedented journey led by women but dependent upon the harmony of both sexes. The twelve male apostles would return, and when combined with their female counterparts would reveal the full, glorious story of Jesus Christ and the Kingdom of God . . . a tale that would be collected and organized by Scriptorium scholars, but in different ways from the biblical editing of centuries past.

As Lori learned these things, she experienced a warmth within her soul, a heavenly radiance, and she fully understood her place in the remarkable events that were to come. In the shelter of her womb the messiah, Yeshua, grew.

Yeshua . . . Hebrew for Jesus, a name that was not male or female.

With all that had occurred, Lori wondered if she could possibly be carrying a girl child. How appropriate that would be, and exquisitely balanced . . . a female Jesus for the millennia to come.

But the young mother had already decided not to ask a doctor to determine the gender. She smiled gently to herself. After all, that would be like opening a present too early, spoiling the wonderful surprise.

* * *

For ye are all the children of God by faith in Christ Jesus. For as many of you as have been baptized into Christ have put on Christ. There is neither Jew nor Greek, there is neither bond nor free, there is neither male nor female: for ye are all one in Christ Jesus.

–The Epistle of Paul, in Galatians 3:26–28, *The New Testament*

* * *

About the Author

Brian Herbert, the son of Frank Herbert, is the author of numerous *New York Times* bestsellers. He has won many literary honors and has been nominated for the highest awards in science fiction. In 2003, he published *Dreamer of Dune*, a moving biography of his father that was nominated for the Hugo Award. After writing ten DUNE-universe novels with Kevin J. Anderson, the coauthors created their own epic series, HELLHOLE. Brian began his own galaxy-spanning science fiction series in 2006, TIMEWEB. His other acclaimed solo novels include *Sidney's Comet; Sudanna, Sudanna; The Race for God;* and *Man of Two Worlds* (written with Frank Herbert).